D0821301

JONATHAN JANZ

THE RAVEN

This is a **FLAME TREE PRESS** book

Text copyright © 2020 Jonathan Janz

All rights reserved. No part of this publication may be reproduced, stored in
a retrieval system, or transmitted in any form or by any means, electronic,
mechanical, photocopying, recording or otherwise, without the prior written
permission of the publisher.

FLAME TREE PRESS
6 Melbray Mews, London, SW6 3NS, UK
flametreepress.com

US sales, distribution and warehouse:
Simon & Schuster
simonandschuster.biz

UK distribution and warehouse:
Marston Book Services Ltd
marston.co.uk

Publisher's Note: This is a work of fiction. Names, characters, places, and
incidents are a product of the author's imagination. Locales and public names
are sometimes used for atmospheric purposes. Any resemblance to actual
people, living or dead, or to businesses, companies, events, institutions, or
locales is completely coincidental.

Thanks to the Flame Tree Press team, including:
Taylor Bentley, Frances Bodiam, Federica Ciaravella, Don D'Auria,
Chris Herbert, Josie Karani, Molly Rosevear, Will Rough, Mike Spender,
Cat Taylor, Maria Tissot, Nick Wells, Gillian Whitaker.

The cover is created by Flame Tree Studio with
thanks to Nik Keevil and Shutterstock.com.
The font families used are Avenir and Bembo.

Flame Tree Press is an imprint of Flame Tree Publishing Ltd
flametreepublishing.com

A copy of the CIP data for this book is available from the British Library
and the Library of Congress.

HB ISBN: 978-1-78758-530-0
US PB ISBN: 978-1-78758-528-7
UK PB ISBN: 978-1-78758-529-4
ebook ISBN: 978-1-78758-532-4
Also available in FLAME TREE AUDIO

Printed and bound in Great Britain by Clays Ltd, Elcograf S.p.A.

JONATHAN JANZ

THE RAVEN

FLAME TREE PRESS
London & New York

"'Ain't many guys travel around together," he mused. "I don't know why. Maybe ever'body in the whole damn world is scared of each other.'"

John Steinbeck
Of Mice and Men

'How quickly one accepts the incredible if only one sees it enough.'

Richard Matheson
I Am Legend

'Was there ever a trap to match the trap of love?'

Stephen King
The Gunslinger

This one is for Joe R. Lansdale. In addition to being one of the best writers ever, you're generous, kind, and endlessly inspiring. Thank you, Joe, for your friendship and support.

PART ONE
PREY
CHAPTER ONE
Ambush

The night he met the cannibals, Dez made the mistake of leaving his hiding place too early. Later on, he'd attribute it to his eagerness, his maddening desire to rectify his mistake, to for once save someone he loved rather than failing them. But as he crept through the shadow-laden forest, he knew it was all wrong, knew his rashness would cost him.

But Dez kept moving. The clearing lay ahead, though from his vantage point the only suggestion of a clearing was a darkness less oppressive than the one through which he stepped. He hadn't glimpsed another soul in three days, which was a blessing. Seeing *anyone* was invariably bad. Particularly in a benighted stretch of forest like this.

The fine hair on his forearms prickled. Dez halted on the trail, one bootheel tilted askew by a jutting root.

He looked down, discovered it wasn't a root at all, was rather the arm of a corpse.

Dez frowned.

Finding a dead body wasn't uncommon – the creatures who ruled the world now didn't scruple about leaving their victims exposed to the elements. But it was still a nasty jolt to find himself standing on a dead man's forearm. The semidarkness and the advanced state of decomposition made it impossible to discern the man's age, but the flies had mostly abandoned the corpse, and the putrid odor Dez detected was a faint one. The black eye sockets gaped up at him in accusation.

Dez swallowed, his senses groping outward through the shadowy glade. The only sounds he discerned, other than his ragged breathing, were the chitter of a small animal, and from somewhere above, an infuriating strain of birdsong, one so repetitive he suspected the bird was tormenting him.

Dez tightened, every muscle of his frame thrumming. Although cannibals were among the fiercest predators in this twisted new world, they were also, paradoxically, among the quietest. Only vampires moved with more stealth, the bloodthirsty beasts as noiseless as puffs of smoke.

No, he told himself. *Don't think of them. You've survived this long by remaining in the moment, not by imagining a gruesome death.*

His ankle ached. To relieve the pain, he lifted his foot off the corpse's arm and planted it on level ground. As he did, the pebbles underfoot let loose with an audible crunch.

He froze, teeth bared. As happened so often, the voice in his head sounded like his father's: *Get moving*, Dad's voice urged. *If they are hunting you, you won't do a damned bit of good playing freeze tag in the wilderness.*

Yeah? Dez shot back. *You're as dead as the guy I just stepped on, Dad, so forgive me if I ignore your advice.*

Dez's throat tingled; he'd have to cough soon. Careful not to let the stiff fabric of his shirtsleeve rasp over the handle of the holstered Ruger, he pressed a fist to his lips and coughed as soundlessly as he could.

But rather than assuaging the tingle in his throat, the act of coughing only inflamed the tissue there, and for perhaps the millionth time Dez marveled at how many things he'd taken for granted before the Four Winds. Two years ago, you got sick, you popped a few pills, slurped some chicken soup, and cozied up with a good novel.

Now a cough could kill you. Not by the infirmity that caused it – though he'd seen people die of ailments that would have, before the world devolved, been easily treated – but because it revealed your whereabouts to predators.

Behind him, perhaps thirty yards back, there came the whooshing of a branch being thrust aside.

They've found you wherever you've tried to hide, Dez. They've smoked you out of every hole.

Footsteps, crunching without stealth on the trail behind him.

Dez bolted.

As his legs strode out, his muscles pumping, he scoured the forest for a hiding place. Dez veered around a bend in the trail, the saplings that framed the path crowding nearer. He thought he'd been shrewd starting the day's trek before dawn, but now he realized his error, leaving his place of concealment too soon. Exposing himself to peril.

He hoped it wouldn't get him killed.

Dez hurdled a downed sycamore. As he ran he tuned his ears to what stalked him, but no matter how he tried to filter out the noise of his own flight, he still found it impossible to detect anything other than the slap of his boots on the soil and the steamshovel chuff of his own breath.

Dez pounded down a decline, the machete handle banging against his hip. He cast a glance behind him, noticed the woods were devoid of movement. Had his pursuer given up?

He couldn't risk it. Ahead, the trail opened wider. He could enter the clearing, turn and face his pursuer. Either that or dart into the woods, where a sinkhole or a root could snap his ankle and effectively end his life.

Dez emerged into the clearing and slowed.

The forest floor was a mélange of moist leaves, humus, and darkly glistening stones. The clearing was oblong, maybe a thousand square feet. But despite the openness of the space, very little predawn light shone through the overarching boughs.

He turned slowly as he scanned the forest's edge. He could no longer hear anything pursuing him, but that didn't mean he was safe. Pausing here could be suicide.

But he didn't think so. He'd learned long ago to trust his gut, and his gut told him there was something else watching him now.

But not what had been chasing him moments earlier.

Dez's breathing slowed. There was someone watching him. Someone....

He whirled and spotted a man huddled against a yew tree.

Like the green tangle of the tree itself, the man looked unkempt. His pale hair hung in greasy ribbons, curtaining a face mad with fear, the eyes staring moons, the whiskered jowls aquiver. As Dez's eyes adjusted to the distance, which was perhaps thirty feet, he discerned the deep creases in the man's forehead, the spray of crow's feet bracketing the light eyes. A tick over fifty, Dez judged, but the past two years of hardship had added a decade to the grizzled countenance.

The man wore a denim jacket and what looked like breeches for pants, the dark fabric supported by a frayed hemp rope. He looked dangerous, not because of what he could do to Dez, but what his terror could draw to this clearing. Whatever had been hunting Dez seemed to have lost interest, at least for the moment, and Dez didn't care to invite it back.

Dez took a step forward, and immediately the man began shaking his head so vigorously that his greasy hair whipped the bark of the yew trunk. Dez brought an index finger to his lips to shut the frightened bastard up, but the gesture appeared not to register. The man now raised his palms in a warding-off gesture, as if Dez were anything but a Latent, one of the few nonthreatening creatures left in this godforsaken world.

Dez inched closer and the gaunt man suddenly spoke. "Keep away! I've got a gun!"

Dez grimaced at the man's reedy voice, which was teeth-chatteringly loud. "Easy," Dez said, a palm out. "There's no need to—"

"Another step and I'll fire!" the man yelled.

It was a bluff, and a transparent one at that. If the man were about to shoot him, he'd at the very least have dropped a hand to the butt of a gun, or more likely, drawn his weapon and leveled it at Dez. But this man no more carried a gun than Dez owned a posh mansion with a harem of supermodels.

Dez halted, knowing the fool wouldn't curb his shrill threats until every creature within a two-mile radius had converged on the clearing.

"I won't come any closer," Dez said. "But you need to tell me something."

"Don't need to tell you *shit*," the man shouted. "You need to move on before you mess up everything!"

Another voice spoke from the shadows. "You one of them?"

The gaunt man jerked his head toward the speaker and growled, "Let me handle it. We don't need this cocksucker drawing attention, do we? Ain't I taken care of you so far?"

"Except for food, you have," another voice said, this one younger-sounding.

The gaunt man's face scrunched in irritation. "I told you we'd have it soon. Just a mile from here's a peach grove with a few that ain't fallen."

"You said that three miles ago," the older speaker said.

The gaunt man massaged his stubbly jaw. "Okay, I miscounted. But we gotta have solidarity. We can't be no group if you guys are gonna question every little thing."

One of the speakers moved into the bluish light and stood a couple feet from the gaunt man. He was of Asian descent, roughly the same height, and though he was thin, he looked a good deal healthier and ten years younger. Fortyish, right about Dez's age.

"We haven't questioned anything," the new man said. "That's the problem. How can we keep trusting you when you—"

"*Trustin' me?*" the gaunt man demanded. "Ain't we been together every waking hour? Ain't I saved you from those maneaters?"

"So you claim," the younger voice said. Dez made out a third form in the shade of the yew tree. The younger man looked like the son of the Asian man and just about college age, if colleges still existed.

The gaunt man agitated a hand at the boy. "Don't you go pipin' up. You been bellyachin' the better part of the night."

"Because his belly *is* aching," the father said. "He's not had a bite to eat since leaving the shelter."

"Hole in the ground, you mean," the gaunt man said. "And I bet he hadn't eaten more than a rotten ear of corn in the days before I found you."

The father puffed out his chest a little in a combination of pride and guilt that was difficult to behold. It reminded Dez too much of his own dad.

"We were doing okay," the father said. "We certainly weren't exposed like we are now."

Dez cleared his throat audibly.

All three turned and regarded him.

"Have any of you heard of the Four Winds Bar?" Dez asked.

Something cunning crept into the gaunt man's face. "Maybe I've heard of such a place. But I can't for the life of me imagine why anyone with half a brain would want to go there."

The father emerged from the thicket. "We know of it."

"The Four Winds is a death trap," the boy said.

The father hesitated, then explained, "I'm Rikichi. My students at Purdue called me Professor Rik. This is my son, Kenta."

Dez remembered the face of his own son, and though he attempted to bury the image before the anguish could take hold, Will's features clarified. His blue eyes. His dark blond hair. His subtle chin dimple, not as pronounced as Dez's, but there nevertheless. Dez remembered Will's guileless expression, and Dez's heart ached. The boy was only four when the bombs flew; he would be six today if he were still alive.

If he were still alive.

The gaunt man squinted at Dez. "No reason to talk to this asshole. If he ain't a maneater, he could be somethin' worse."

"We don't know that," Rikichi said.

"Don't know *anything*," the gaunt man countered, "which is why I say we keep moving."

"How far is it?" Dez asked Rikichi.

An infinitesimal shrug. "Forty, fifty miles."

Something deep in Dez's gut began to flutter, but he kept the excitement out of his face. Before the missiles flew, he had no poker face at all, couldn't even pull off a harmless prank without giving it away. But after the world ended, out here in this hellish new reality, you learned.

You learned or you died.

The gaunt man glanced from face to face, and then, realizing he was outvoted, heaved a resigned sigh. "I suppose I've been too rough on the newcomer." A curt nod at Dez. "There's no reason to think you're a monster. Least...not yet."

Dez glanced at the young man. "How old are you, Kenta? Twenty?"

"He's eighteen this December," Rikichi answered, with more than a touch of pride.

Dez felt a moment's affection for Rikichi, then brushed it away. Emotions like that had no use anymore, especially for people he'd just met. For all Dez knew these three were conspiring to kill him.

Perhaps the suspicion showed on his face because Rikichi said, "We aren't dangerous." A gesture toward the boy. "We're not that way. But..." He cleared his throat, the words obviously costing him an effort. "...we *are* hungry. Do you know how to use that?"

It took Dez a moment to realize that Rikichi was eyeing the crossbow strapped to Dez's back. But rather than answering, Dez surveyed Rikichi's face, then Kenta's.

Rikichi frowned, an alertness dawning. "What's wrong?"

"Watch him, Dad," Kenta said.

The gaunt man nodded vigorously, wiped his mouth. "Told you two. Told you we couldn't trust him." He jabbed a finger at Dez. "Them black eyebrows, I seen 'em on werewolves before. One time before we got overrun, a guy in our group was shitbrained enough to let one in." His face twisted bitterly. "Goddamned beast tore up a dozen people. Shouldn't a ever let him in, but someone did. Just cuz he was pretty like this one."

Dez laughed softly. It had been a long time since anyone had called him handsome, much less pretty.

"Can you tell us about yourself?" Rikichi asked.

Dez said, "Your face is unmarred. Your son's too. And you're paler than most survivors."

The gaunt man leveled a finger at Dez. "That's why I say we can't trust 'im! Look at how dark that skin is. He's been in the sun all that time. The only way he could survive is if he's a monster."

Dez repressed a smile. "You're tanner than I am."

The gaunt man jolted, an astonished look widening his eyes. "I ain't tan. I'm...." A glance at Rikichi, a lick of his cracked lips. "My mom was part Native American."

"Which tribe?" Kenta asked.

The gaunt man's mouth opened, shut. "How the fuck should I know? It's not like we lived on a reservation."

"Your name is French," Rikichi said to the gaunt man.

"My father's side," the gaunt man explained. "Gentry was one of the most respected names in the county before...."

There was no need for him to finish. In the dour silence that followed, Dez became aware of a new stirring in the forest, one that made the skin on the nape of his neck tighten.

But Rikichi seemed not to notice. He approached Dez. "We need food. We—" He made a pained face. "The reason we're so pale is that we've been belowground. Until recently."

Dez said, "Overrun?"

Kenta grunted mirthlessly. "Burned out's more like it."

"Someone dropped a Molotov cocktail into our shelter," Rikichi said. "How long they knew we were there, I have no idea. It was the perfect place of concealment."

"It must've been," Dez said, "to last so long."

"Not good enough," Rikichi said. "Since then we've been hiding in abandoned houses, barns. We even slept in a cave one night."

"Have you considered going back to your shelter?"

Rikichi's face grew troubled. "If we'd gotten the guys who did it, sure. I think they were Latents, like us. I—"

"Dad killed one of them," Kenta interrupted. "The other three ran away."

Rikichi glanced at his son, some new tension arising between them. "They would've returned though. Maybe in greater numbers."

"You don't know that," Kenta said.

"No," the father agreed. "I don't. So I made the best decision I could make." He turned to Dez. "And we're alive. That's what matters."

The gaunt man – Gentry, Dez remembered – said, "You didn't have no life, hidin' in the ground like worms."

Rikichi broke into a wan smile. "We had plenty of time to hone our conversation skills."

Kenta smiled too – the spitting image of his dad. "And I got to kick your butt at cards."

"Not every time," Rikichi said, his grin widening.

"Sitting ducks," Gentry said. "That's all you were."

"Dad, why are we trusting Gentry?" Kenta asked. "I'm telling you, the only way to stay alive is to hide—"

"We've hidden enough," Rikichi overrode him. "We can't spend our lives cowering in holes. If there's any chance of rebuilding the world, it's got to start with people like us—"

"Dad—"

"—doing more than hiding."

"But this old bastard is—"

"Enough, Kenta."

"He's not—"

"*Enough*," Rikichi snapped.

Kenta compressed his lips, his nostrils flaring, but he didn't fire back.

Gentry shambled toward Dez. "We've wasted enough time jawing with you. It'll be daylight soon, and we need to find that peach grove. It's time for—"

It all happened in an instant. Gentry whirled, Kenta let out a cry of pain, Rikichi screamed, and Dez felt a hard-boned arm cinch around his throat. Something cold was shoved against his left temple.

"You fight," a voice said into Dez's ear, "and I pull the trigger."

CHAPTER TWO

Stomper

Dez's body had turned to stone the moment the man had seized him, but now his mind unlocked and his thoughts became a swarm of panicked rats scurrying inside a burning house.

The ambush had been coordinated. That much was obvious, even before the one who'd fired the arrow at Kenta – the arrow now buried in the boy's right thigh – appeared on the path.

You've failed again, the cutting voice in his head declared. *You weren't alert enough, and now, because of your weakness, more will die.*

Dez could scarcely breathe, so powerfully did the forearm compress his windpipe, and what air he could draw was tinged with the sickening raw-meat odor puffing out of his captor's mouth. Yet he could still see too well the hellish scene unspooling before him:

The massive, heavily muscled archer striding out of the forest.

The shorter but somehow more imposing figure who followed him, a man with militaristically short hair, a neck festooned with crudely drawn tattoos, and a garish gold chain dangling over the chest of his tight black tank top.

Rikichi hurried toward Kenta, the boy howling with pain and grasping his leg wound, the arrow wagging like some dreadful joke as Kenta thrashed.

"Nice one, Paul," the man with the neck tattoos said. He had a raspy voice like a habitual smoker's and a thick Irish accent. He moved with a fluidity that reminded Dez of an accomplished athlete, a fleet running back or a champion wrestler. "Was afraid you'd nail the kid in the guts. Unleash all those nasty fluids into his bloodstream."

Dez had forgotten Gentry for a moment, but when the gaunt man spoke, Dez could see the abject terror on his face. "You guys are maneaters, ain't you?" He licked his lips. "You're…you're cannibals."

No one answered him. Even if one of the new arrivals had said anything, Dez wouldn't have been able to hear it over the horrible caterwauling of the wounded boy. Rikichi was cradling his son and reassuring him, though his voice kept breaking.

The sight made Dez sick. It seemed he felt that way every day now, but this…this was an especially harrowing tableau.

Dez couldn't help remembering his own son. God, if Dez were half the man he should be, he would have saved Will. He would still have his little boy.

"It's gonna be okay," Rikichi said, his voice trembling. He slid a shaking hand over Kenta's forehead, slicking his son's sweaty hair back. "Just breathe for me, okay? I'll fix it in a second."

Dammit, Dez thought as his eyes shifted to the massive archer and the scrappy-looking man who appeared to be the leader. *Goddamn these sons of bitches to hell.*

As if sensing his thought, the one holding Dez captive pressed harder on his voicebox. Dez began to cough, his eyes watering. He lifted his hands, but the muzzle burrowed into his temple, the cozening voice laced with warning: "Hands down, friend. Unless you want a hole in your head big enough for my cock."

Kenta wailed.

"Quiet your boy," the leader of the group said, the Irish accent lending his words a singsong quality.

Kenta didn't hear, or was in too much pain to notice the command, but Rikichi turned, shot a fierce glance at the leader. "You ruthless bastard."

The leader's mild expression didn't slip. "Attend to the boy, Paul."

The archer's eyes were riveted on Rikichi and Kenta. "Want me to finish him, Stomper?"

Stomper nodded.

Paul, the mountainous archer, whose bulging arms were bare despite the chill of the night, strode over to where Rikichi clutched his son. Paul tossed his bow aside, bent, and tapped Rikichi on the shoulder.

Rikichi didn't turn.

"Hey," Paul said and tapped Rikichi on the shoulder again.

"Get away from us," Rikichi muttered without turning.

With almost loving care, Paul reached around to position one huge hand on the father's throat. "Come here *now*," he said, and swung Rikichi away from his son. Kenta's head, unsupported, thumped down on the forest floor, and Kenta let out a strident wail. Rikichi's arms were flailing about as though he were being electrocuted, but the size disparity between Rikichi and the archer made it impossible for Rikichi to connect with anything but the archer's immense shoulders.

Holding Rikichi at arm's length, Paul straddled Kenta's midsection. Rikichi was frantic, smacking and raking at Paul's arm. Bloody contrails bloomed on the archer's biceps, but Paul betrayed no sign of pain, only reached toward his ankle.

Retrieved a wicked-looking buck knife.

Involuntarily, Dez's hand twitched toward the Ruger.

The muzzle dug into his temple, setting off a vicious throb. "Last warning, friend," the voice said, the gagging stench of his breath making Dez's eyes water.

"Don't—" Dez managed in a strangled voice, but Paul's buck knife was out, and though Dez was more than a dozen paces from the ghastly drama being played out on the ground, he could see Kenta's frightened eyes, and infinitely worse, Rikichi's crazed expression as he fought wildly to save his son. Rikichi tore at Paul's forearm, his shoulder. Rikichi kicked at the huge archer, but the blows deflected fruitlessly off Paul's hip.

"Shhhh..." Paul said, and as Rikichi looked on, the giant archer placed the buck knife against Kenta's throat, just under the left ear. Kenta thrashed his head against the blade, but that only made the damage more acute. The blade opened a yawning slit in Kenta's throat, a slit that bubbled and spumed as the boy thrashed berserkly against his murderer. Through it all, Rikichi's vast, staring eyes remained fixed on his son, the sounds tumbling from Rikichi's lips a mixture of horror and sorrow.

Dez felt tears sting his eyes. He'd often believed himself beyond tears, but each time he was proven wrong. Before the end of the world, he'd heard the human psyche possessed a mechanism that closed the floodgates of negative emotion once a certain threshold was reached. The mechanism, he seemed to recall, was designed to prevent a mind from going insane. But if such a threshold did exist, Dez's mind wasn't equipped with it. God knew he'd witnessed enough atrocities to trigger that safety valve a thousand times.

Tears streaming down his cheeks, Dez watched the giant archer complete the indelicate incision, place the buck knife on the ground beside the dying boy, and reach into Kenta's ragged, jetting throat.

Rikichi was still fighting madly, but when he saw the giant pull a stringy mass of pulp and cartilage from his son's throat, he let loose with a blaring howl of heartbreak.

Unconcerned with Rikichi's reaction, Paul brought the handful of viscera to his open maw and began to chew. The blood, black and oily in the early dawn light, painted the archer's chin a glistening obsidian.

Rikichi continued to wail. Stomper appeared beside Paul, and without speaking, took hold of Rikichi's shoulders and laid him on the ground beside the motionless Kenta. To Dez, the gesture was hideously reminiscent of a parent laying his child down in bed for the night.

Dez had a memory of Will, of his little boy. The bedtime routines they used to share. His son's insistence that Dez lie beside him until he fell asleep. The warm, soft feel of his son's forehead. The sweet smell of his hair.

Dez choked back a sob.

"Your boy is dead," Stomper murmured to Rikichi. "See? He's at peace."

The words apparently broke through because Rikichi turned his head to look at his son, and that's when Stomper raised a boot and stomped on the side of Rikichi's face. One eye plopped out of the socket, the cheek and nasal cavity giving a horrid crunch as the face crumpled. Rikichi's body jittered and spasmed, and Stomper brought his boot up, slammed it down again. This time Rikichi's forehead folded in on itself, the sound similar to an egg dropped on a tile floor. Rikichi's quivering face was a mask of wine-colored blood. Before Dez knew it, Stomper was on his knees beside Paul and scooping up the dangling eyeball. With a graceless tug, Stomper plucked it loose from the ocular cord and popped it into his mouth.

"Save the other eye for me!" the man holding Dez called.

The words jerked Dez back to his own plight, but it was the yearning, insatiable quality in his captor's voice that galvanized him. Dez was going to die, and this man was going to dine on him as emotionlessly as the other two cannibals were dining on Rikichi and Kenta. Dez realized the man's pelvis was jammed against him. Unbelievably, the man was erect.

"I want the boy's tongue too," his captor called. "Don't get it dirty before—"

Dez swung his head back as hard as he could and felt the man's nose implode. The forearm slipped away from his throat, and Dez sucked in his first unobstructed breath since the nightmare had begun. Peripherally, he saw his captor stumble, the man's hands slapped over his spewing nose. Dez bolted toward the southern edge of the clearing, where Gentry stood watching him with an amazed look. Dez spotted movement from his left and discovered Paul the Cannibal Archer already nocking an arrow into his bow.

"*Down,*" Dez shouted at Gentry, and in one motion draped an arm around Gentry's shoulders and dove forward. They skidded on the dirt as an arrow whistled over their heads.

"Up," Dez commanded, hauling Gentry to his feet and breaking toward the treeline.

"Don't have a chance," Gentry moaned.

"*Move,*" Dez answered.

As they punctured the vale of forest, Dez heard a snatch of shouted conversation:

"Get them!" Stomper commanded.

"*...my nose....*"

"Fuck your nose. It's your own goddamned fault!"

Dez was dragging Gentry as they raced past elms and aspens, thorn bushes and pines.

"No way we'll escape," Gentry groaned. "They'll eat us too."

Dez gritted his teeth. "If they only send one, we've got a chance."

They veered around a broad oak tree, found what might have been a disused trail. Gentry was moving on his own now, but his gait was a staggering, inefficient one. If Dez set off by himself, his chances would improve considerably.

Sure, his conscience spoke up. *Abandon this man the way you did Kenta and Rikichi.*

Dez said, "I didn't abandon them, dammit. I had a gun to my head."

From the corner of his eye he sensed Gentry's wondering stare. "Who you talking to?"

"Nobody," Dez snarled. "Get your ass moving."

CHAPTER THREE
Whiplash

It didn't take long for the cannibal with the broken nose to find them. What amazed Dez was the rapidity with which the injured cannibal tore through the forest. It shouldn't have surprised him, not after all he'd seen. But it did. It was as though the last vestiges of the old world refused to relinquish their hold on him, and as a result, his reason still recoiled when confronted with another testimonial to this new, nightmarish existence.

He knew Gentry's strength would give out before long. And he could hear the cannibal stealing through the forest behind them. Before, the son of a bitch had moved with the stealth of a timberwolf. And while the cannibal still ran with a surprising lack of noise, the rage and the broken nose were making him careless.

Dez slowed to a trot, fingered the handle of the Ruger. He didn't want to use it, but he would if he had to. The noise would give away their whereabouts, and he doubted the other two cannibals would allow the murder of one of their own to pass unavenged.

Even worse, they'd be newly fed.

Newly empowered.

Dez wouldn't have believed it had he not once witnessed it. For a time he'd been a member of a struggling colony based in a network of caves along the Tippecanoe River. He'd been asleep – fitfully, as always – when a barrage of screams had assaulted him and the others slumbering in a moist tunnel just uphill of the water. By the time Dez had disengaged himself from the woman he'd slept with that evening and who'd insisted on slinging an arm over him as though to moor him to the slimy rock floor, the slaughter was already in full bloom. He'd stumbled out of the cave to find a middle-aged woman with curly brown hair – one of the leaders of the colony – spread-eagle on the ground with a cannibal's face buried in her split stomach. Three other colonists were similarly laid out, each with cannibals grafted to them like skulking hyenas. Dez and another man had drawn their guns to blast away at the killers, but before they could fire, the cannibals had darted away into the night or, in one case, leapt up to grasp an oak bough that hung fifteen feet off the ground. The cannibal, surcharged by the flesh he'd just devoured, swung from the bough, landed nimbly on the grassy riverbank, and bounded into the forest with the agility of a jungle cat.

The sound of Gentry stumbling brought Dez back to the present. Dez threw a look over his shoulder. Had the cannibal pursuing them eaten from Kenta or Rikichi before setting off after Dez? It was a vital question.

One he had no time to ponder.

"Can't run anymore," Gentry panted. "Can't—"

"You have a weapon?" Dez demanded. His lungs were burning, but that was more from fear than fatigue. The only favors this ghastly lifestyle had done for him were hardening his muscles and expanding his endurance.

"Just my knife," Gentry answered. "I use it to clean squirrels—"

"Get it out," Dez told him.

A flash of movement from their right, and then pain seared through Dez's shoulder. Somehow he was on his knees, and the cannibal was laughing, and some instinct made Dez flop down on his stomach, and it was a good thing because he heard a whistling sound, and the air he'd just vacated was rent by some fast-moving object.

Dez pushed to his hands and knees and thought, *Holy Christ. The bastard has a leather whip. And where the hell had he hidden it?*

Save Indiana Jones, Dez had never seen a whip used as a weapon, but as he scrambled to his feet now and backed away from the grinning cannibal, who was smaller than the other two but who appeared completely unhinged, Dez decided the whip was uniquely suited to this new world. Lethal enough to inflict serious damage, yet relatively silent. A man skillful enough to wield it would have better reach than a man using a knife or a machete. Sure, a bow had better range, but as Dez could attest, a lot could go wrong with a bow and arrow because you needed space to shoot.

The whip was whistling at him again.

Dez lunged sideways and only partially evaded the leather's sting. Cold fire scalded his hip, but he didn't think the denim of his jeans had been parted.

Dez unsheathed the machete.

The grinning cannibal had shaggy black hair and a scraggly beard smeared with what could only be human viscera. So the bastard *had* eaten from Rikichi or Kenta before setting off after Dez. Bad news.

Dez didn't comprehend the biology of it, but the experience by the river had taught him the effects of cannibalism were almost instantaneous, not unlike those old *Popeye* cartoons. Only instead of spinach creating bulging muscles, the ingestion of human tissue induced a maniacal power that was as extraordinary as it was revolting.

"Come now, kitty," the cannibal said, twirling the whip handle at his side. Dez tried not to be hypnotized by the way the long slender lash swirled and danced in the predawn air.

"Watch him," Gentry said.

Dez nodded, hoping Gentry had exercised the good sense to draw his knife. Two against one, they still didn't stand much of a chance, but if they were lucky, they might catch the cannibal off balance.

"Tell you what," the cannibal said, the whip writhing at his side like a restless serpent. "I'll give you a head start, old man. Fifteen, twenty minutes even." The grin broadened. "I'll want to enjoy this meal."

Dez took in the man's overwhite teeth, the too-pink gums. Tell-tale signs of cannibalism. No regular person was that healthy anymore. Only cannibals looked virile enough to star in toothpaste commercials.

Of course, the starey, darting eyes and the expression of lunatic glee would probably disqualify this man from most ad campaigns.

"Not goin' anywhere," Gentry said.

Dez glanced at the older man and beheld a mettle that hadn't been there before. Maybe they would live yet.

"Fine then," the cannibal said, nodding at Dez. "I'll give you a chance to save your hide. You come back to the clearing and tell us where other survivors are, we'll let you live."

"Maybe you should run that by Paul and Stomper," Dez said, "since you're obviously their little errand boy."

With a snarling growl, the cannibal swung the whip in a wild looping strike, and Dez dove for his knees. Dez slammed into the cannibal in a barrel roll violent enough to upend him, and before the son of a bitch could untangle his whip, Dez swung the machete and buried it two inches deep in the man's calf muscle.

The cannibal squealed, pawed at the blade, which Dez abandoned. Dez somersaulted forward and reached back for the crossbow. Pivoting, he drew back the bow and took aim even as the cannibal fidgeted with a revolver. Dez strode forward, leveled the crossbow at his breastbone, and knowing he'd get no better opportunity, fired.

The bolt split the man's sternum, the sound reminding Dez of an axe striking a cord of ironwood.

The cannibal let out a breathless grunt and grasped the impacted bolt.

Dez knew he couldn't wait. Cannibals possessed uncanny recuperative powers. He reached down and snagged one of the cannibal's scissoring feet. The cannibal didn't seem to notice, only emitted a series of pitiful mewling sounds and fondled the fletching of the embedded bolt as though he couldn't decide whether to risk yanking it out or not.

While he was thus engaged, Dez crouched and got hold of the machete handle, but it was slimed with blood. He wiped his hand on the ass of his jeans, ventured to grip the handle again, but it was still slippery.

Dez eyed the cannibal, whose lips were peeled back in agony. How long would the man lie there grimacing? Further, who was to say that Paul and Stomper weren't tromping their way toward them right now? Cannibals were voracious; they might not be content with Rikichi and Kenta.

Time was short.

Dez slid his hand up his shirtsleeve, gripped the machete handle with his leather coat, and tugged on it. At first he worried it wouldn't come free – the edge of the blade seemed to be lodged in bone. Worse, he had realized what Dez was up to and had begun to kick at him, albeit weakly. The cannibal's blood spurted over Dez's forearms. Dez ground his teeth, pulled on the handle. The leg from which he was attempting to wrest the machete suddenly jerked down, and for a moment Dez lost his grip.

He covered his palms with his sleeves, grasped the handle with both hands, and yanked up.

The machete slurped loose from the calf meat, and Dez nearly overbalanced. It occurred to him that if the cannibal abandoned the arrow that was lodged in his chest and instead removed the gun from his pocket, he could simply shoot Dez, and then all of this would be over.

The image of the gun firing into his guts was enough to motivate Dez. He gained his balance, took a couple unsteady strides, and stood over the cannibal. The man was peering up at him, teeth bared, a dull glaze of hatred in his narrowed eyes. He wanted with all his soul to murder Dez and would do so in an instant if given the chance.

Dez raised the machete, and the cannibal's eyes widened.

With a cry, Dez slammed the machete into the cannibal's throat. The blade had apparently not been damaged when it lodged in his leg because it cleaved through the man's larynx like a prow through placid waters. He was nearly decapitated by the blow, the arterial spray shocking even to Dez, who had slain more than one creature this way. He turned his head, but not before being enameled in blood.

After a moment, Dez eyed the man's crimson-stained chest, the fractured bolt poking out of it. He hated to waste a good arrow, but he would accept this trade-off, all things considered.

Dez finished the decapitation, then stood panting. He became aware of Gentry, gaping at him in the bluish light.

"You killed him," Gentry said, his tone hushed.

Dez wiped the machete on the fabric of the cannibal's arm. "Thanks for the help."

CHAPTER FOUR

By the Fire

Luck was with them. For once.

After Dez was convinced they'd reached a safe distance from Paul and Stomper, they slowed to an enervated walk. While the dawn wasn't warm enough to take the edge off the constant breeze, the dishwater sky made it possible to build a small fire at the summit of a tree-lined hill. In short order, Dez shot a squirrel with his crossbow.

Dez and Gentry sat eating before the fire.

Watching him there, shoulders slumped and chest heaving with labored breath, Dez wondered how the hell Gentry had managed to stay alive this long, when so many better men had been slain by predators.

Dez shook his head, marveling. The heap of branches they'd scrounged seethed orange and black like some pagan Halloween ritual. Dez scarcely noticed. Because a thought had snagged in his brain, and as always happened when a thought took hold, he was utterly incapable of dismissing it until his overactive mind was satisfied.

He peered at Gentry from the corners of his eyes and wondered how such a scrawny creature could have lasted two years.

Two years. Dez had flirted with death on too many occasions to number, one of them less than a month ago. And though Dez wasn't as powerful as, say, a cannibal or a werewolf, for a Latent he knew he was respectable. He could shoot, he could run, he could defend himself when the situation called.

But this man…this *scarecrow* could barely thread a sharpened stick through a hunk of squirrel meat.

How could Gentry have survived in this sick, violent world?

Then it hit him.

He couldn't have.

Keeping his tone measured, Dez said, "'Before you mess up everything'."

"What's that?" Gentry asked in a faraway voice. He was gazing hungrily at the frying squirrel meat as though it were the last morsel of food on the planet.

"When I first saw you in the clearing," Dez went on. "You said to move on before I messed up everything."

Had a fearful expression flitted across Gentry's face? "Those maneating sons of bitches were what I was referring to." He shook his head soberly. "They'd been after us for the better part of two days."

"How'd you manage to keep ahead of them? That big one moved like a storm cloud."

Gentry grinned, his teeth yellow and specked with brown. "Fast fucker, wasn't he? For such a big guy?" He studied his hunk of squirrel. "Shit, man. I still can't believe we got away."

"Because I saved you."

Gentry's eyes flicked to Dez. "You did at that. Mighty impressive." His expression darkened, the pale eyes unseeing. "Hope it doesn't bring the wrath of God down on our heads." Gentry grunted humorlessly. "'Course, most would say He's already shown us His wrath."

Dez frowned, slowly rotated his stick, the aroma of cooked meat wafting over him, making his saliva glands squirt.

Hunger, he thought. Always the hunger.

Gentry turned his stick over, the squirrel meat charred on one side. "Before," Dez said.

Gentry appeared not to have heard.

"Before the cannibals showed up," Dez persisted.

Gentry looked at him. "Come again?"

But Dez had grown very still, his own length of squirrel meat hissing and bubbling fat and dripping into the fire.

Gentry shook his head. "I thought we was goners, for sure. That Stomper, he don't leave many folks behind. What's the saying? Dead men don't—"

"—tell tales. Why did he kill the boy and his father first?"

Something new came into Gentry's eyes. "Just lucky, I guess. You'd rather he offed one of us?"

"You were closer."

Now Gentry did turn his full attention on him, and the smile became flinty. "At first I was, sure. Look, would you rather I stayed there front and center like a...." He trailed off, seeing Dez's expression. "What're you tryin' to say? I'd soon enough hear it."

"They never went for you."

"Hell they didn't." He brought up an elbow and tapped it with a quaking finger. "Threw me down's what they did. Woulda killed me if I hadn't—"

"Out of the way," Dez muttered to himself.

"How's that?"

Dez stared into the fire, his skin taut. "Paul. The archer. He threw you out of the way."

Gentry was on his feet, moving faster than Dez had seen him move, and gestured down the length of his body. "Oh yeah? And who can blame that big bastard for casting me aside? Would you want a bag of bones like this or a boy in the prime of his—"

"They weren't following me."

Gentry's eyes narrowed. "What the fuck are you talkin' about?"

"They were following the trail, but they weren't following *me*." Dez looked up at Gentry. "They were meeting someone."

Gentry's mouth worked. His eyes flitted to the left, as though he considered fleeing. "I don't know what you got against an old man, but I got enough on my plate without you—"

"That's how you've stayed alive."

"Goddamn you, boy, you've had your brains scrambled to shit."

"How many?"

Gentry's scowl deepened. "How many *what*?"

"How many people have you gotten killed?"

"To hell with this," Gentry said, lifting his stick, which glowed a brilliant red.

"They say they're protecting you, but the only reason the cannibals let you live is because you lure food for them."

"Goddamn you, I'll tell you something—"

Gentry swung the blazing branch at Dez's face. Dez just had time to throw up an arm before the fiery tip smacked his leather sleeve and sparks exploded over Dez's face like an errant firework. Angry wasps stung his temple, but he couldn't worry about that because the seething red tip was flicking back at him, at the side of his face. This time Dez had no time to protect himself, so he thrust himself backward off the log, the fiery tip tracing an icy line from his underjaw to his earlobe.

"*Stomper!*" Gentry bellowed. "*Paul!*"

Dez completed the backward roll, came up with his machete, but Gentry wasn't coming for him. He was scurrying toward the edge of the summit, hands cupped around his mouth, his voice lusty and more resonant than it had been all morning.

"*Stomper!*" he shouted. "You gotta get up here!"

Gentry's head swiveled around, but by that time Dez was halfway to him and closing, the machete gripped in his right hand.

"Now don't you even think about—" Gentry's mouth snapped shut, apparently realizing he was beyond keeping the fiction alive. Without another word he darted down the slope, and as Dez gave chase he saw how nimble Gentry was, how well he navigated the hillocks and washouts. Earlier, Dez had been too fearful of the cannibals to notice, but now that he saw Gentry moving, he couldn't believe how dullwitted he'd been not to see it before.

How'd you stay alive this long, a hectoring voice demanded, *behaving this stupidly?*

But Dez's mind, for the first time since awakening in the small hours of the night, was calming, his thoughts lucid now, purposeful.

I am alive, Dez thought. *And I'll still be alive when night falls.*

He was gaining on Gentry. Despite the man's terror-fueled agility, Dez was faster and more athletic by far. Dez descended the hillside in vast, swooping leaps, his boots grabbing the sparse grass with ruthless efficiency.

"*Stomper!*" Gentry yelled, but his voice was stitched with panic. "Help me, goddammit! This maniac's gonna—"

Dez leaped at him. Had Gentry the clarity of mind to turn at that moment and defend himself, he would have found Dez vulnerable: his legs splayed, his belly and chest unprotected, both arms spread wide as if skydiving.

At the very last instant, Gentry did glance back. And in that moment Dez imagined what Gentry saw. A powerful body clad in black leather and faded denim, a lunatic grin splitting his face, the uneven hair forming vengeful spikes against the heather-colored sky.

And, of course, the machete.

Gentry flung up a forearm and Dez hacked it clean through at the elbow. They landed in a heap on the grassy decline, Gentry's severed stump jetting like a scarlet flamethrower. Gentry was trying to scream, but the words were indecipherable and no more than a choking gurgle. Dez pinned the spraying arm with a knee, seized the man's remaining wrist with his left hand, and with the machete, tore down at Gentry's head. The greasy gray-blond hair parted down the middle, then gushed burgundy. Beneath Dez, Gentry's body convulsed. A buzzing rip sounded as the man voided his bowels.

Gentry gaped sightlessly as a single rivulet of blood wended its way from the wounded cleft of his forehead to collect in the cup of his left eye. But the dying man never blinked, only stared up at Dez.

Careful to keep the hemorrhaging stump away from him, Dez pushed to his feet, braced a bootheel on Gentry's foam-covered chin, and yanked loose the machete.

He wiped it on Gentry's quivering breeches, checked the man's pockets, and found a silver lighter. He raised it to better illuminate the engraving he spied there.

An ornate letter *E*. A closer look revealed thorny vines twined around the letter.

Dez had never seen the symbol before, but if he ever made it to the Four Winds Bar, he'd ask the patrons if they recognized it.

Without a glance at Gentry, whose convulsions had ceased, Dez pocketed the lighter, turned, and made his way up the hill, where he devoured both portions of squirrel, his and Gentry's.

PART TWO
THE END OF THE WORLD

CHAPTER FIVE

The Bastards from Baltimore

October 21st

I wish this were a work of fiction.

Would that the past two years had never happened, that the world, as imperfect as it was then, could be restored.

But it can't. Nothing can be the way it used to be.

Two years ago, on October 17th, the world ended.

As I write this today, my story is yet to be completed. Granted, it could end with a slit throat as it almost did last night with those cannibals, but as of this writing, I'm still alive. I'm still surviving.

Gloria Gaynor would be proud.

The irony is that by the time you, my reader, find this, I could be long dead. As I'm stupid and sentimental enough to tote these notebooks around with me – eight of them filled so far, each one a hundred and fifty pages – if you're reading this account, it either means I had to jettison the backpack or you're discovering it on a corpse. Or I guess it could mean you captured me and plan on killing me.

If that's the case, fuck you.

If not, let's go with the notion that you found my backpack because I had to abandon it. And let's imagine I'm still alive because I hate to imagine otherwise.

The will to live is uncanny. So many times over the past two years I've been close to death. But because I'm a bullheaded pain in the ass, I didn't give in to despair, didn't acquiesce to my fate.

Acquiescence isn't my strong suit.

Neither, apparently, is staying focused.

Isn't it funny how we as a species seem to excel at not talking about the most important things? We'll discuss the weather, our favorite sports teams – I'm talking past tense here, of course, since for two years no one has played any sport except killing each other – or perhaps our favorite foods. We were shallow before the world ended; I'd like to say we're better adjusted now, but I can't.

So let's talk about the end of the world.

Of all the countries I would have bet on to destroy humanity, I never would have guessed the one that actually did. If you're finding this record, you're presumably a survivor and know about how everything went down, but just in case you're from some distant future discovering these notebooks the way paleontologists used to unearth brontosaurus bones, let's see if you can pick which one of these countries ruined everything:

North Korea.

Russia.

China.

Iraq.

Have you guessed yet? Okay, that wasn't exactly fair, as the answer is None of the Above.

It was the United States.

Of course, that's not really fair, is it? It wasn't our government that orchestrated the launch of the six bombs but rather a cadre of extremists working in conjunction with some rogue scientists at the Applied Physics Lab at Johns Hopkins University. Heard of the Applied Physics Lab? I hadn't either, not before the bombs were launched.

When we finally did learn who was responsible, we realized the extremists had been planning the end of the world for years. That they were able to keep their plot a secret speaks to their devotion. Or to the obliviousness of the American government.

I mean, Johns Hopkins wasn't exactly in the middle of nowhere. It was in Baltimore, for God's sakes, and the plot involved more than a dozen leading professors and scientists, as well as a hundred or so individuals employed by Four Winds Aerospace.

Four Winds, of course, is where the apocalyptic event got its name. I'll talk about that later.

Again, I'm going on the assumption that whoever is reading this is reading it in the distant future, which means it's important you know as much as possible about how the world ended. With that in mind, let's dispel one notion right now:

The missiles were not nuclear.

A group of Johns Hopkins professors, it turns out, was on the cutting edge of biological warfare. And genetics, particularly the study of human DNA.

Yet 'the cutting edge' doesn't do their research justice. Wherever the edge was, they were about fifty steps beyond it, and light years ahead of the rest of the world. Had they used their insight for positive ends, who knows what they might have accomplished? A cure for cancer. An end to world hunger. No more infant mortality.

Instead, they devoted it to eradicating the human race.

Let me provide a little context.

In the year prior to the apocalypse, nuclear tensions had escalated. Rogue nations had acquired the wherewithal to blow up the world, and the supposedly civilized nations had amassed arsenals that could blow up the world a thousand times over.

I won't lie. It was scary.

The professors at Johns Hopkins found it even scarier than the rest of us. And the extremists at Four Winds Aerospace found it intolerable.

Let's face it. Deep down, the human race is – or was – pretty goddamned selfish. Oh, we talked about empathy, but when it came down to it, we wanted *our* lives to be better, wanted *our* children to be safe. If you asked a man whose life meant more, his or his neighbor's, he'd don a Zen-like mask and claim that all life was sacred.

But if he had to, he'd cut his neighbor's throat to survive.

The group at Four Winds Aerospace – and believe me, I'm loath to give them any credit – they understood man's hypocrisy. They recognized the threat of nuclear annihilation, and they knew it would only take one itchy finger, and the world would be plunged into another dark age.

Because if *we* can't survive, we don't want anyone else to either.

It was probably this sort of selfishness that motivated the Bastards from Baltimore – that's what many called them, and I suppose it's as good a name as any for the people responsible for the transformation or the slaughter of all but a handful of the world's population.

Uh-huh. I know you caught those words in the above paragraph: '... responsible for the *transformation* or slaughter of all but a handful of the world's population'. *Slaughter* you understand. Everyone understands that.

But what, you ask, do I mean by *transformation*?

Four Winds Aerospace prided itself on research. In fact, shortly after the bombs flew but before the Internet was knocked out for good, Jason Oates – the leader of the colony – looked up Four Winds Aerospace and printed out all the information he could. One particular paragraph from FWA's front page struck me so powerfully that I recall it verbatim, despite the fact that I read the article years ago:

'Progress remains liberated from governmental shackles and must, as a matter of course, embrace experiments and risks.'

To your eyes, that passage might seem innocuous. Admirable even. But to my eyes, eyes that have witnessed horrors no one would have dreamed possible, the words are absolutely chilling.

Experiments and risks. What images do those words conjure? Laboratories and test tubes? Petrie dishes and beakers?

How about the manipulation of human genetics?

No one saw their plot coming, which meant the human race was uniquely unequipped to deal with the fallout once it began.

Here's something no one else knew: The reason why the same legends show up in all cultures is that the legends aren't really legends.

Vampires.

Werewolves.

The Wendigo.

Satyrs.

Psychic powers.

Even the myth about a cannibal's superhuman powers.

They were all based in fact.

You're probably laughing. Or, at the very least, cocking an eyebrow in disbelief. Which is what the rest of the scientific community would have done had the Bastards shared their research with anyone.

But they didn't. All they did was unravel the mysteries of human DNA.

And human nature. You see, it all makes sense in retrospect. We've been around for quite a while, we humans. And for as long as we've been walking upright, we've been discriminating against those who are different than us.

In unlocking the mysteries of genetics, the Bastards learned that, long ago, the creatures you hear about in horror novels were all pretty much real. But because of these creatures' defects – the vampires' lust for blood, for instance, or the satyrs' overwhelming desire for sex – the creatures were either hunted down, forced into hiding, or had their tendencies suppressed.

Do you take my meaning?

All of these creatures were *human beings*.

All species are hardwired for survival, and humans are no different. But what separates us from other animals are our sophisticated methods of justification, our ability to commit evil acts in the name of virtuous pursuits.

Long ago, there were humans with vampiric tendencies, others with the ability to transform into werewolves. Some possessed the talent to manipulate objects with their minds, others the power to plague their enemies with curses.

Yes, I'm talking about witchcraft.

But as mankind grew and its population doubled and quadrupled, procreation and persecution either bred the aberrant tendencies out of people or diluted them to the point that no one sprouted horns or fangs anymore. No one feasted on the flesh of other men in an attempt to acquire power. Or at least they didn't do so where their cannibalism might be discovered.

Over hundreds of thousands of years, monsters disappeared entirely, though some – like the Wendigo-like Children and what we now call the Night Flyers – simply went underground, where they dwelt for eons.

Until the Four Winds.

By the time the monsters disappeared from the Earth, their genetic codes were so altered that anyone experiencing an unnatural desire would, if he were smart and civilized enough, overcome that desire and keep his ignoble urges to himself. By the time the twenty-first century rolled around, every unwholesome whim could be explained away by psychology.

Not that I can relate.

I'm what's called a Latent. This means I have no extraordinary powers. The term itself is rather ridiculous, of course, because it implies there are powers within me that haven't yet been expressed. When the truth is that if I had any powers they would have revealed themselves by now.

So 'Latent' means 'Powerless'. Which is why, when a Latent utters the word, it's always in a tone of shame. When a monster uses the word, it's spoken with a sneer.

I need to get moving. The shadows are elongating, and dusk is approaching. I need to find a safe place to hole up for the night. Shelter is what you miss most when you go on the move. Well, that and food. As you'd imagine, food is a constant source of anxiety.

Even so, when you have a reliable place to sleep, one where the creatures can't scent you and the elements can't batter you, the constant hunger isn't quite as soul-sucking. What meager sustenance you scrounge goes further and tastes better when you have a place to hide for more than a night. You also figure out where the fruit trees are, where the animals like to water.

I haven't settled in one place for going on seven months now. Yet I know I'll have to locate a safe haven soon. When our bunker was discovered, it was March. Yes, it was cold then – March is almost always cold and miserable in Indiana – but it wasn't full winter.

But it's late October now, and that means winter is coming. There's no way I can keep wandering through the end of the year, much less the brutal months of January and February.

I've always despised the cold.

Now I fear it.

Enough. I have to go. When I sat down to write a couple hours ago, I was certain that Stomper and Paul were far away, that they'd decided not to pursue me.

Now?

I'm not so sure.

Time to move.

CHAPTER SIX

The Peach Grove

Dez shouldered his backpack, shimmied his other arm through the strap, and inhaled deeply when he felt the crossbow compressed between his leather jacket and the pack. He could feel the weight of the books and journals in there, but he'd be damned if he'd get rid of them. Better to be slightly encumbered than bored. Depression could be as lethal a killer as the monsters, and the first step toward depression was boredom. Idle time.

Dez made it a habit to keep his mind occupied. Like now. Yes, he was leaving the thicket of spruce trees in which he'd eaten his pitiful supper of overripe apples and what was left of the squirrel, but he was also scanning the forest for signs of life, be it food or foe. He rummaged through his memories of this area, which were admittedly few. The country between the tiny burgs named Brookston and Battle Ground had been sparsely populated before the bombs. Now the land seemed entirely desolate. If not for his encounter with Gentry and the others, he would have assumed no one was alive in this stretch of countryside.

Descending a hill, Dez furrowed his brow.

The cannibals' attack had been troubling on a number of levels. Witnessing the brutal slaughter of Rikichi and Kenta had been horrific. Even though he'd seen it happen on numerous occasions, he never got used to seeing people eaten.

Yet nearly as troubling as this were the ramifications of the attack.

Cannibals rarely lived alone. Like some monsters, they favored communities. This was likely because they were lesser monsters and prone to becoming prey themselves. Though fearsome, a cannibal was no match for a vampire, a werewolf, or one of the Children.

Dez smiled ruefully as he reached the bottom of the hill and made his way across a stretch of lowlands. So many horror authors in the old world had written about battles between werewolves and vampires. How would those same writers feel now that their fiction had been vindicated?

Not too wonderful, Dez judged.

He began the slog up the long incline. The October leaves were changing colors rapidly now, the forest a riot of red and yellow and tangerine, with only occasional smatterings of green. From overhead came the fretful twitter of a finch.

Movement to Dez's right made him whirl and grasp the handle of the Ruger.

A rabbit.

He compressed his lips and cursed his skittishness. Granted, wildlife was plentiful now that most of the humans were gone – the Bastards from Baltimore would have been delighted – but rabbits were still rabbits and never easy to catch. The one that'd just escaped was a plump specimen, worth three or four meals.

Dez paused, unshouldered his pack, and extricated the crossbow. Climbing hills would be awkward with the bow in hand, but he couldn't afford to let more meals elude him. The squirrel scraps and cidery apples sat uneasily in his stomach, and the prospect of his belly growling all night didn't do much to cheer him.

Dez repositioned the backpack and continued up the slope.

One thing he hated about being alone was the lack of another opinion. When Susan had been with him, she'd been his voice of reason. He tended to be more capricious than she did, to make decisions on impulse. She'd enjoyed pointing that out, the fact that their roles were inverted, that stereotypically, it was the woman who'd choose a campsite based on a whim, and the man who'd have to point out the flaws in her logic.

But that was his nature. Passionate. Irrational at times.

He often joked to her, not really joking, that he wished the world had ended ten years later, after all the immaturity had been knocked out of him, that he'd gladly trade a slower body for a sounder, more reliable mind.

Of course, that had been seven months ago, and in that seven months he supposed he'd aged the equivalent of ten years.

Being alone in a hostile world tended to do that.

At least the urge to cough he'd experienced the night before had disappeared. Maybe, he mused, his experience with the cannibals had scared the sickness out of him.

Dez's Achilles tendons began to ache, a product of last night's terrified flight, but at least he could rest when he wanted to. One of the positive aspects of being companionless.

Dez experienced a rush of guilt, as he always did when such thoughts invaded. But the truth was, there were several advantages to solitary travel. The most profound, of course, was that he was considerably less nervous most of the time. Oh, he still spent moments in mortal terror, but because it was his own skin he was worried about, the constant fear was more manageable.

When Susan had been with him, he'd been perpetually certain he'd fail her. This led to a torturous cycle of doubt, paranoia, and guilt. He knew she deserved a better protector, yet she viewed him as capable of not only providing for their needs, but of fending off the numberless threats to their safety.

Dez hadn't felt capable. He'd felt hapless and small, uniquely unsuited to the role of protector.

A fear borne out by later events.

Teeth clenched, he continued up the hill. He'd been a reader his whole life, as well as a movie lover, and one thing that had always driven him crazy was the lovelorn hero, the brooding figure unable to let go of his true love, the woman dead or married to someone else.

Now, to his dismay, Dez had become that figure.

But there were advantages. God help him, there were.

Gone was the insecurity over his inability to protect Susan. Gone was the need to scrounge up enough food and fresh water for two people.

Gone was the belief that his story would have a happy ending.

Oh yeah? a voice asked. *If that's the case, if you're so fucking resigned, what are you doing now? Why are you trying to make it to the Four Winds Bar?*

Dez sighed, scanned the approaching ridge. He had no answer to these questions, at least none he wanted to admit. His Achilles throbbing, his chest burning from the exertion of scaling the precipitous rise, he crested the incline, gazed down the other side, and beheld what had to be the peach grove that Gentry had mentioned.

This both pleased and alarmed him.

On one hand, he was excited to eat fruit other than apples, which he'd been devouring for several weeks. On the other, it meant that

Gentry knew this area better than Dez had believed, which meant the cannibals' base was close enough that Dez was in danger.

Images of Stomper and Paul strobed through his head. Rikichi's wails. Kenta's futile attempts to stave off the archer's killing knife stroke.

Ghastly.

So block them out, he told himself.

The advice was about as effective as it always was. Dez had been wary of doctors since childhood – considering what his mom had gone through, he figured his mistrust could be forgiven – so he'd never undergone an examination for what his ex-wife claimed were rampant obsessive thoughts.

Deep down, he knew it was a problem.

Frustratingly, it had grown worse in the past few months. It seemed to Dez that spending so much time alone would have decreased the self-flagellation and the suffocating guilt. If he wasn't in contact with anyone, how could he wrong someone and wallow in guilt over it?

Apparently he needed no new issues; the old ones simply grew more corrosive in his isolation. The bad decisions he'd made with Susan. His wife and son. The manner in which he'd spoken to his father. His failure with his little brother. Most of all, the things he hadn't said and done.

Dez ground his molars and trudged down the leaf-strewn hill. He knew he shouldn't mistreat his teeth the way he was. He often woke with a headache from grinding them so incessantly. If and when they wore down to nubs, there'd be no dentist around to fit him with crowns. He supposed he could rustle up a set of dentures from somewhere, but the prospect of wearing a dead man's teeth didn't particularly excite him.

Remember the look of Joey's teeth?

Dez moaned. He shook his head, trying to rid his mind of Joey's bloated corpse, his little brother having succumbed to drug abuse and depression, and Dez discovering him, realizing he might have prevented it had he only paid more attention, had he not been so wrapped up in his career, trying to start a family.

Joey was your family. Joey and your dad.

I know that.

And you abandoned them.

I didn't—

Not in any dramatic way. There was no falling out. But you saw them less and less as you went through your twenties. Barely saw them at all by the time you reached your thirties.

I'm sorry!

But the slithery, sadistic voice broke in: *Sorry doesn't cut it, Dez. They're both dead, and maybe they didn't have to be.*

Dez turned and spat, his whole body shaking.

He reached the bottom of the hill and moved into the peach grove. He eyed the shriveled twists dangling from the yellow-leafed trees, the desiccated brown peach corpses dotting the grass.

Fuck.

If he knew more about botany he'd be able to identify the type of peaches growing here, but whatever they were, they were decidedly not edible anymore. He thought of Gentry and wondered if this were some sort of final insult from beyond the grave.

He should have known there'd be nothing here to eat. Other than corn, what grew in October? Before the world ended, Dez hadn't exactly been the agricultural sort. Now, it seemed, he was paying for that ignorance.

His stomach rumbled.

Dez winced, pressed a hand to his belly. Maybe there'd be rabbits or squirrels nearby. Deer that used the overripe fruit for foraging. Maybe...

...maybe there was an old man watching him from the far end of the row.

Dez froze and stared at the old man.

In contrast to Gentry, this wasn't a guy who looked old because he didn't take care of himself. No, this was a senior citizen, certainly over seventy.

Instinctively, Dez moved his fingers toward the Ruger.

"No need for that," the old man said. The voice was scratchy but friendly enough. The man stood thirty yards away, his plaid shirt a combination of mustard yellow and navy blue. The man wore blue jeans, quite faded, and had a longish white growth of beard. Though the man's general appearance was a bit ragged, in this terrible new world he was an exemplar of good grooming.

This should have reassured Dez, but its effect was the opposite. True, if the man were wild and unkempt like Gentry had been, it meant he was desperate to survive. Desperation made people do hideous things.

But the ones who didn't look desperate were almost certainly monsters.

Monsters didn't need to worry about surviving.

The old man regarded him in silence. No weapon that Dez could see. No sign of confederates, but that didn't mean anything. If you weren't deft at sneaking around, you were either at the top of the food chain or you were dead.

The old man asked, "You a maneater?"

Dez hesitated. "Are you?"

"I own this grove," the old man said. "A hundred-and-sixty acres in all."

When Dez didn't speak, the old man added, "Was over a thousand before I had to sell some off."

"Am I supposed to feel bad for you? Want me to organize a benefit concert on your behalf?"

Unexpectedly, the old man broke into a grin. "It'd be you and me sitting on my front lawn drinking moonshine and munching on popcorn."

Though it made him feel pitiful, Dez's saliva glands responded to the thought of popcorn. He imagined his old life, a movie theater tub, yellow and glistening and wet as hell with all the greasy shit they pumped over it. Half a tub invariably gave him a gut ache, and invariably, he ate it down another couple inches before stopping. Then he'd smuggle the dregs home with him and devour those before bed and wake up at three a.m., dehydrated, the sodium count in his blood approaching toxic levels and his mouth as dry as a blighted cornhusk.

Man, he missed movie theater popcorn.

The old man asked, "You gonna take me up on my offer or aren't you?"

"I didn't think you were serious."

"Hell's bells, boy. If you want, I can get down on a knee and propose, though it might take a while to get back up again."

The ease of the man's voice seemed a bit practiced. Though older, he didn't look the slightest bit feeble.

Dez chewed the inside of his mouth.

The old man shrugged. "Suit yourself."

Dez watched him turn and disappear into the grove. He supposed that was how the man had appeared so suddenly. One minute cowled by the trees, the next staring at Dez from down the row. So yes, the man was sneaky. But was there anyone alive who wasn't?

Dez stared at the cleft in the peach row.

Moonshine, the old man had said.

Dez had never tried moonshine, couldn't recall a time when it had been offered to him. He had little interest in drinking alcohol now, even less in hard liquor. Alcohol dehydrated you, gave you headaches. Made your mind foggy and your body listless. No, moonshine didn't much appeal to him.

But popcorn did. Was it possible the man had some? How long did popcorn stay good? Two years seemed an impossible amount of time, yet Dez had been surprised before. Only a month ago he'd discovered a cache of condensed soups – celery, broccoli, chicken noodle. He'd feared botulism, but he feared starvation even more. He'd boiled all five cans over a glorious three-day stretch, and he hadn't been poisoned. If canned soup could keep for two years, maybe popcorn could too.

Or so he told himself.

Regardless, it wasn't really about popcorn, was it? It was about trusting the man. Though he told himself it was unwise to do so, particularly less than twenty-four hours after he'd nearly been killed, he found himself approaching the shadowy cleft in the trees, ducking beneath a leafless branch, and scanning the grove for signs of the old man. Dez moved through the row, realizing as he did that the grass here was matted, that even though he was crosscutting the rows of peach trees, this was a path of sorts.

After cutting across several rows, Dez caught sight of him. There was a country road about eighty yards distant. The rough path the man was treading took him toward the road, but it kept him safely concealed by the forest. Dez couldn't tell whether the man was aware he was following. Then again, the man's very nonchalance could be a ruse.

Huh. Dez had no idea if he could trust him yet, but here he still was, trailing along after him, both of them moving with a casual gait, both of them potentially fatal to the other. Granted, Dez didn't think of himself as dangerous, but how many people had he killed?

Too goddamned many.

Which meant the man was in as much peril as Dez was.

Still not looking back, the man angled toward the road, and after pausing only perfunctorily, he crossed, the acceleration in his steps subtle but unmistakable.

It gave Dez courage. If the man were afraid of being spotted, that meant he—

The man paused and glanced back at Dez. "If you hurry up we can talk on the way. It's just up the hill here."

Scowling, Dez glanced right and left, but the road appeared empty. Which meant exactly nothing. Just because the road was devoid of life didn't mean the area was.

Echoes of Stomper's laughter sounded in his brain.

Dez hesitated. "Why are you so keen on getting me back to your house?"

The old man eyed him. "Maybe you're not as smart as I thought." He turned toward the woods.

Just as he was about to disappear, Dez called, "Do you really have popcorn?"

"More than I can eat in a lifetime."

"How is that possible?"

Instead of answering, the old man waded into the forest across the road, and the underbrush swallowed him.

Dez imagined the salty taste, the spongy texture. Yes, he'd risk death for popcorn.

CHAPTER SEVEN

Popcorn

The first surprise was the chickens.

Dez was used to possums, raccoons, loads of deer now that there were no cars to mow them down. But chickens?

Like cows and pigs, chickens had all but disappeared, save rumors about them existing in cannibal compounds. The meat was not as appealing to the flesh-eaters, but palatable enough to stock and use whenever human prey couldn't be found.

Dez suspected that was frequently the case these days. Why else the need for Judases like Gentry?

Only a few chickens were pecking about the fenced-in area next to the barn, but there were enough of them to make Dez believe the adjacent coop housed even more. Just beyond the coop and the weathered barn stood a yellow outbuilding, the corners and siding showing rust. Since the house didn't have a garage, Dez figured the pole barn had served that purpose.

The old man's house was a two-story with yellow aluminum siding and navy-blue shutters. Dez expected the color scheme to continue inside, but the kitchen looked like every farmhouse kitchen he'd ever seen. Oak table, oak cabinets, oak flooring. Hunter-green trim along the ceiling featuring red apples. Beige wallpaper beginning to brown, also featuring red apples.

They stood in silence, the old man in the center of the room grasping the back of a chair, Dez in the doorway between the mudroom and the kitchen. To Dez's left, there were a couple iron hooks affixed to a board that read KEYS. On one hook there was a big key ring he figured went with the house and the outbuildings. On the other hung one with the Dodge insignia.

"Come in if you want," the man said.

Despite his wariness, Dez felt a bit overprepared in the old-fashioned kitchen. The crossbow spread behind him like dragon's wings, the Ruger and machete and everything else weighing him down, making him feel like some kind of astronaut come to inspect an inferior alien species.

The man nodded at the crossbow. "You travel heavy."

"You know of the Four Winds Bar?" Dez asked.

The man's eyebrows gathered inward. "Best stay away from there."

"You know the one who owns it?"

The old man gave a shudder, nearly imperceptible, but definitely there. "Steer clear of him. They say he's something…unnatural."

"He took someone from me."

The man regarded him in silence. At length, he reached up, touched his wizened chin. "How do you keep your beard looking so nice?"

"I trim it."

The man nodded. He leaned toward Dez. "You wanna see the popcorn?"

Dez suppressed a grin at the other man's eagerness. It was as if he was showing off a '68 Corvette rather than a food that until a couple years ago was no more exotic than wheat bread.

The old man gestured. "It's just here in the pantry."

Dez started across the kitchen. "You're not going to smack me in the head are you? I'd just as soon not wake up roasting on a spit."

A corner of the man's mouth lifted. "I look like a maneater to you?"

"Why does everyone call them that? What's wrong with 'cannibal'?"

The man thumbed on a flashlight and stepped aside so Dez could enter the pantry.

"Holy God," Dez breathed.

"Told you," the man said, and though Dez wasn't looking at him, he could sense the breadth of the man's grin.

Dez counted five cedar shelves in the pantry. A section about four feet wide, from floor to ceiling, was stockpiled with boxes of popcorn.

Dez read the label on the box. "'Bacon Popcorn. The Purest Corn in the Midwest'." He glanced back at the man. "Bacon-flavored?"

The man was already shaking his head. "It's not bacon-flavored, and we all tried to tell Gary it was stupid to call it Bacon Popcorn, but you think he listened? 'People will think it's bacon-flavored,' we said.

'But my name is Gary Bacon,' he argued, 'so the name has to be Bacon Popcorn. Same as Orville Redenbacher.'"

Dez started to smile.

The old man shook his head. "'It's *not* the same,' we told him. 'Orville and Redenbacher aren't flavors, now are they?' Gary would fold his arms and look like a kid sitting in time-out. 'There's nothing wrong with my name. It goes back generations.' 'We're not saying there's anything wrong with your name,' we pointed out. 'But at least add an apostrophe – *Bacon's Popcorn* – to show that the Bacon is possessive.'"

"No go?" Dez asked.

"'Not catchy enough,' Gary said." The man grunted. "As though Bacon Popcorn is catchy." He shook his head. "Hell."

"Plus," Dez added, "you could see it as false advertising. If people buy the popcorn thinking it's bacon-flavored—"

"I know!" the man said, swatting Dez on the arm. "But do you think he listened to me?" He fetched a sigh. "Well, Gary died in the first month anyway, so it didn't end up mattering."

Dez reached out, trailed a finger across one of the pale blue boxes, which featured a man's red-mustached face in the center. "That Gary Bacon?"

"Nice enough guy. Stubborn though."

"You get all these from the store?"

"From the factory."

Dez tilted his head. "You're telling me there's a popcorn factory around here?"

The man nodded. "Less than a mile away. It's burned to the ground now, but I got these beforehand."

"Lucky you," Dez said, but his salivary glands were working harder than ever, despite his state of semi-dehydration.

"You want some?" the man asked.

Dez turned all the way around this time. If this old bastard was attempting to lure him to his death like the 'Hansel and Gretel' witch, he'd put a bullet in his forehead.

The old man's good-natured expression disappeared. "Can we just pretend we're not in hell for a moment? Can we pretend we both haven't done things we wished to God we didn't have to do?"

Dez inspected the man's features but found no signs of guile. "You can't cook these in a microwave."

"I could," the man said, "but that would take the generator, and I'm not using that till winter."

"Generators are loud," Dez said. "Aren't you afraid of attracting—"

"Not this one. It's a whole-house generator."

"Really."

"Yep. But not for popcorn."

"Then how—"

"Come on," the man said. They started across the kitchen, but the old man paused, nodded at the pantry. "Well, bring a box. I don't think we'll satisfy our hunger by gnawing on that crossbow of yours."

Dez retrieved a box of popcorn and followed him into the living room. "That's twice you've commented on my weapon."

"It's a useful piece of equipment," the man said. He knelt before a brick-lined hearth and set to work crumpling sheets of ruled paper.

"I found it in someone's house," Dez explained.

"Of course you did. Grab a couple logs from over there, would you?"

Dez followed the man's gaze and saw, piled waist-high between an olive green couch and the wall, a stack of logs, each about two feet long. He selected a pair and returned to the fireplace, where the man accepted them with a muttered thanks.

"My name's Dez McClane," he said as he hunkered next to the old man.

"If you say so."

"Something wrong?"

The old man said nothing.

Dez watched him position the pair of logs in the sooty iron holder. Staring at the old man's hands, which were heavily veined and not a bit arthritic-looking, Dez said, "Ordinarily, this is where you tell me your name."

The man crammed the balled paper into the gaps where the logs bowed slightly. "Jim," he said. "You were explaining about the crossbow."

"We were in this rich neighborhood, some guy—"

"We?" Jim had frozen, listening.

"This was a while ago," Dez explained, "after the first community I was in got…raided, I guess." His throat constricted at the memory. "It was before I joined this place called the colony."

Jim had set to work crumpling more paper.

"The neighborhood was affluent. We expected some of the houses to be inhabited, but they weren't. The entire neighborhood…I don't know, thirty houses? All of them wiped out. No one there at all."

"That's about the size of things," Jim commented. "Could you hand me the lighter? It's on the piano."

Dez looked around and was surprised to discover an upright piano in the corner. He hadn't noticed it because the lighting in here was so dim – just the single window in the center of the southern wall – and because there was a burgundy dropcloth running the length of the keyboard.

Dez headed over and spotted a Zippo lighter on top of the piano. Glancing at the burgundy dropcloth, Dez saw the words ALL WE NEED IS LOVE embroidered in gold.

Without turning, Jim raised his hand for the lighter. Dez placed it in his palm, and as Jim activated the flame and held it first to one and then to several of the crumpled balls of paper, he said, "Mary was a big one for The Beatles."

Dez watched the white balls of paper darken and send little tongues of orange flame to lick at the coarse bark. "My mom was too."

"Never cared for them myself," Jim said. "More of a Doors fan. And Hendrix."

The fire whorled around the logs, the bark scorching and throwing up slate-colored smoke.

Dez considered asking the man about Mary but decided against it. His stomach felt shoveled out and achy, the prospect of popcorn nearly too tantalizing to entertain. He couldn't jeopardize this opportunity. How long had it been since he'd eaten popcorn? He remembered seeing a movie a week or so after the bombs flew, before anyone had clued in to how the virus was spreading or what it was actually doing to them. The film had been a remake of *Jaws*. Godawful. But the popcorn had been otherworldly.

Jim stood with a groan, ambled over to a built-in bookcase, and produced a cast-iron pot, which he placed on the mantel, next to the box of Bacon Popcorn. "You were saying about the fancy neighborhood."

Dez watched Jim rip open the popcorn box with strong, sure fingers.

Dez said, "Most of what was worth finding was picked through. We found an indoor court where we could shoot baskets, but the sound of the ball echoing in that cavernous space…we couldn't get any enjoyment from it. Plus, when you scrounge for every morsel…when you're just subsisting and trying to stay alive and everyone out there is a threat…it makes you angry, you know?"

Jim produced a pocketknife, folded out the blade, and slit first the cellophane wrapper and then the brown paper bag within. He shook the kernels into the cast-iron pot with a clatter.

Dez grunted. "Indoor basketball court. What an extravagance, right? When some people – I'm talking about before the Four Winds – couldn't even afford food."

Jim set to work on another bag. "Some might say those folks should have gotten jobs."

Dez's mouth watered at the tapping of kernels in the pot. "Would you be one of those folks?"

"Depends," Jim said, placing the empty bag on the mantel. "Some people, sure. Laziness is bred deep inside us. We have to fight against it. Who wouldn't rather take it easy than bust his rear?"

"So, what…the people who owned the basketball court were just harder workers?"

Jim slit open another bag, regarded Dez in the big rectangular mirror over the mantel. "Likely he was a rich prick who inherited everything and acted like he earned it." He returned to his work. "Tell the rest of the story."

"We got sick of shooting around and were ready to leave. Truth be told, I was scared shitless. Something about that basement-level airplane hangar of a basketball court…the windows like glowing boxes near the ceiling…I imagined there were ravenous faces lined up along those windows staring down, ready to dine on us the minute we walked out of that house." Dez didn't much like appearing weak, especially in front of a man he'd just met and didn't wholly trust, but he asked the question anyway. "You ever feel like that? Like someone's watching you?"

The rattling of kernels. A small smile. "I know the feeling."

"Anyway, Wagner – nobody ever knew his first name, and he never offered it – he rears back and kicks open this side door at half-court. Scared the hell out of us. 'What are you doing?' we ask him."

"How many guys?" Jim asked, glancing at Dez in the mirror.

"Four." Dez shrugged. "That day it was four. Sometimes it was five, sometimes three. The biggest it ever got was seven, but that was a mistake."

Jim picked up the cast-iron pot and knelt before the fire. "What was inside the door?"

"Nothing much. Just one of those wide brooms they sweep gym floors with. A couple of empty pop cans. Five-gallon buckets of some cleaning chemical. More basketballs." Jim placed the faded black pot atop a pair of iron crossbars Dez hadn't noticed before. They looked like they were constructed for just this purpose. "There was also something in the back of the closet that caught my eye."

Without turning, Jim said, "Hidden compartment?"

Dez nodded. He couldn't decide if the man's shrewdness was endearing or alarming.

"There was a cedar panel behind the five-gallon buckets. You could barely see it, and even if you did, you wouldn't think twice about it. Just an entry into the crawlspace."

Jim turned. "Weapons cache?"

"It was that," Dez agreed. "But it was more too. A hidden bunker."

Jim stood, dusted off his hands. "Anyone inside?"

Despite his hunger, Dez's appetite shriveled. "No one alive. There'd been...there'd been a family. Man, woman, three kids. The woman and the kids were barely recognizable. They'd been devoured. Even the marrow in their bones...." Dez paused. He realized his breath was coming in shallow heaves. "There were two compartments in the bunker. One right behind the small cedar door. That's where we found the remains. And one down a long tunnel. We had to crawl to get there. I told the others I didn't want to, but they told me they wouldn't share any of the stuff we'd found if I didn't go. The crossbow was the piece I wanted the most, though the others were more attracted to the heavy artillery. The M-16s...the AK 47s. The owner of the house, he must've been a real gun enthusiast." Dez frowned. "Back when he was still human."

Jim walked by him, scooted an old walnut chair closer to the fire. "He a vampire?"

Dez nodded. "The tunnel led to his room. It was...." He licked his lips. God, he needed water. "The room was equipped with weights. I realized the weight room and the bunker weren't really supposed to be connected...not in any practical way. But—"

Dez jolted as the first popcorn kernel exploded. He gripped his chest, heart thundering.

Jim grinned. "Pull up a chair. The pot will really start thumping in a minute."

Dez retrieved the chair Jim had indicated and sat facing the fire. Dez couldn't help wondering if anyone outside would see the gray rising from Jim's chimney, or perhaps scent the woodsmoke in the air. Vampires, especially, had sensitive noses.

Of course, it wasn't dark yet.

"You were saying about the weight room?" Jim prompted.

Dez leaned against the chairback. "You know the apparatus called the Pec Deck?"

Jim folded his arms. "The fly machine. Believe it or not, I used to lift quite a bit."

"The machine had been fitted with handcuffs. Soldered to the bars. The dad must've regressed into the vampiric form at some point, and this was their solution. Imprison Daddy in the weight room at night so he wouldn't kill his wife and kids in a blood frenzy."

More kernels pinged within the pot. Jim sighed. "That never works."

"It didn't. The place where the chains had been soldered to the machine, they were sheared off. You know how strong vampires are."

Jim didn't comment. A fusillade of popping kernels went off like machine gun fire.

"When we saw the torn chains, we were sure we were goners. You know, like in a horror movie? We'd turn and the vampire would be grinning at us, preparing to rip our throats out in a flurry."

The popping was well nigh unceasing now, but rather than amplifying Dez's hunger, the staccato bursts jangled his nerves. Jesus, if anyone walked past the house, they'd surely hear it, wouldn't they?

"Thirty more seconds," Jim said, perhaps sensing Dez's disquiet.

Dez took a breath. "Wagner saw it first. He was an obnoxious bastard, but he was good at sensing trouble. Of course, he caused most of it, but still...."

Jim rose, crossed to the built-in bookcase, from which he fetched a pair of heavy umber work gloves. The popping was still frequent, but it had decelerated appreciably.

To the old man's back, Dez said, "The dad, vampire, whatever you want to call him, he'd shot himself in the roof of the mouth. The wall behind him was painted in a vertical streak, like shit smeared on a public restroom stall."

"Regretted killing his family," Jim said, hefting the pot out of the fire. The popping had grown sporadic. Dez inhaled the aroma of fresh popcorn, and some of his hunger rekindled.

Jim disappeared into the kitchen. Dez heard him clattering around in there. But though the logs were burning steadily now and the heat emanating from the fireplace was pleasant, the image of the fanged creature slouched in that shadowy corner wouldn't be displaced from his mind's eye. In movies, when a vampire died, he transformed back to his human form. Dez couldn't imagine any vampire, clutched by the blood thirst, sticking a gun in his mouth and blowing his brains out. Which meant the man had killed himself in his human form and then transformed into a vampire. For reasons he couldn't articulate, this fact unsettled Dez more than anything else about the gruesome affair.

He twitched a little when Jim reentered. The old man clutched a pair of big silver bowls, each overflowing with white, fluffy popcorn. "Can't provide butter, but there's salt if you want it." He handed Dez a bowl and sat in his chair. "I always like mine better without."

Dez inhaled the scent, which was unaccountably buttery, as though his memory were filling in the gaps for him so this experience could be as satisfying as possible.

Jim began to munch popcorn, but he paused, smacked his forehead. "You'll need water."

Dez rose. "So will you. Where is it?"

"There're jugs in the back of the pantry. It's from the well, so you don't need to worry about my poisoning you."

Dez set the bowl aside and went into the kitchen. The pantry was dark, but he could distinguish the large water containers lined up on the floor, the kind of ribbed jugs once used in churches and office buildings. It occurred to Dez as he waded into the murk and bent to retrieve a jug that now would be the perfect time for the old man to strike him with a blunt object. He didn't think Jim was a cannibal, but you could never know something like that for sure.

Dez spun, hand on the butt of his Ruger.

The doorway was empty.

He exhaled, turned back to the jug, which was two-thirds full, and lifted it one-handed. Before the world ended, he would never have been capable of handling such a weight, but now, with nothing better to do than to improve his body and his mind, he was able to tote it with little problem. He brought the jug to the kitchen table, went over and fetched a pair of tall yellow cups from a cabinet. He was about to return to the table when he spotted a small brass-framed photograph on the counter. It was a couple sitting in a folding lawn chair, the woman in the man's lap. Both were grinning widely.

It was Jim as a younger man. The woman, he assumed, was Mary. She was a frizzy-haired brunette with big teeth and plenty of curves. Jim looked even wirier than he was now. Hard, but lean.

Dez hoisted the bulky bottle, tilted it, and carefully filled both cups. "Leave the jug out," Jim called. "Popcorn gives me an awful thirst."

Dez carried the cups into the living room, supplied Jim with one. Dez drained half of his at a gulp. The liquid was tepid, but it was pure and delicious and set his flesh to tingle.

Through a mouthful of popcorn, Jim said, "That was a roundabout way of explaining the crossbow."

Dez paused in mid-chew, thinking about it. He chewed a little more, swallowed. Delicious. "I guess I've been alone too long. Makes you want to talk when you get the chance."

"Some do," Jim allowed.

Dez shoveled popcorn into his mouth. "I thought microwavable popcorn wouldn't work in a kettle. Aren't they two different kinds?"

"I worried about that too," Jim said. "The first time I raided Gary's factory, I only smuggled home a couple boxes. No use filling the pantry with stuff you couldn't eat."

"Bet that was a happy discovery."

Jim grinned, popped a large white kernel into his mouth. "When this stuff started popping, I damn near danced a jig. A half-hour later I returned with the wagon bungied to the back of my bike." He shrugged. "Could've taken the truck, but I like to leave that in the pole barn. Never know when I might need it. Anyway, with the bike and the wagon, I probably made twenty trips to the factory over the next couple days."

When Dez frowned, Jim explained, "There are more boxes in the basement. The pantry only holds so much."

Dez sipped his water, set it on the floor. "When did you know you were a werewolf?"

Jim's reaction was so subtle Dez would have missed it had he not been watching for one. The man's strong jaw muscles kept flexing, the steady chewing unbroken. Only in the eyes could Dez see the words had affected him. Where before they'd been sedate, perhaps a bit unfocused, now they were laser sharp, wary. And though Dez didn't reach for the Ruger, he visualized himself doing so, a tactic he'd found useful in the past. You went through it in your head beforehand, when it came to doing it, it was easier, more fluid.

Of course, with a werewolf, it probably wouldn't make a difference.

Jim took a slow gulp of water, ran a forearm over his lips. "How did you know?"

"I wasn't sure. Just a suspicion."

"But something gave me away."

Dez guzzled the last of his water, made sure his hand didn't shake as he placed the cup on the floor next to the chair. "I ran afoul of a group of cannibals last night."

Jim was silent a long moment. At length, he said, "How many?"

"Three. And the guy they had enticing victims for them."

Jim's mouth curled in a sneer that Dez suspected was entirely unconscious. "Some people will do anything."

Dez asked, "What's your catalyst?"

Jim didn't answer, instead finished off his water in a great swallow. Swiveling his legs toward Dez, he said, "Give me your cup. I'll fill us up."

With an effort, Dez took his eyes off the man long enough to reach down and retrieve his cup. When he faced Jim, who stood above him now, looking down at him with an expression Dez couldn't interpret, Dez said, "Thanks. It's good water."

"Yes," Jim said. "It is."

The werewolf stared at him a moment longer. Then he went to refill their cups.

CHAPTER EIGHT

B.F.R.C.

October 22nd

It might still be October 21st, but without a clock it's difficult to tell. It sure seems late though, with the old man's house so silent I can hear the nightbirds calling outside and the bugs scuttling around the walls.

That's one thing I can't get used to, the difference two years have made in the animal and insect populations, not to mention the surge in plant life. If not for how lawless the new world is, it would be a veritable Eden. Though I'm not a skilled hunter, I'm surviving pretty well on what I kill or forage.

But the fact is, life is extraordinarily dangerous.

Take the old man who owns this house.

How did I know Jim was a werewolf?

Most regular humans – or Latents, if you want to be fancy – are dead. After the virus began to do its work, people started changing, but at first it was unnoticeable. Or barely noticeable. Vampires beginning to crave blood but dismissing their urges as anomalies. Werewolves, only slightly changed, going crazy in fits of road rage or battering their spouses because of petty disagreements.

But at some point folks began to grasp the truth.

The slow realization that we were surrounded by monsters.

Yet even now, you can't tell for sure, and that's the worst part.

Everyone looks human. No one looks like a monster, not all the time.

I take that back. Satyrs, they say, are communal creatures whose horns are permanent fixtures. Supposedly, they've congregated into miniature societies and utilize their telepathic powers to keep their borders impregnable.

So the satyrs are satyrs full time, or at least that's what we were told in the colony. Ditto for the Children and the Night Fliers, who have always been beneath us, lurking in caverns and remaining dormant for decades at a time. That was a particularly shocking truth we all learned.

But werewolves? Vampires?

They look like we do.

The really big shock was cannibalism.

Oh, not the fact of it – in a way, I'm surprised it didn't happen sooner. Whenever human beings become desperate for food, they turn to each other for sustenance, occasionally by the casting of lots but more often by brute power, the strong overtaking the frail and chowing on them until the next kill is needed.

No, what surprised everyone was what eating flesh did for the cannibals.

If you wanted to predict the end of the world, all you had to do was go back to the beginning of recorded history, examine the folklore of each society, and notice the patterns that emerged.

For example, no matter how remote the region, every society – from the Native Americans to Australian Aborigines – possessed a vampire legend. All these societies spoke of shapeshifters.

And all of them contended that by eating the flesh of another man, you could absorb his power.

Why were we so surprised when it proved to be true?

But only for some.

If being a cannibal – an honest-to-goodness superhuman cannibal – were as simple as dining on someone else, everyone would do it. Well, not *everyone*. I certainly have never felt the desire to eat a person, and I'd like to think I never would, even in the direst of circumstances. That's not just because it's morally reprehensible to me, but also because the prospect is repugnant. Maybe I'm just too civilized.

Or maybe there really has to be a desire there, a bloodlust not unlike the urge a vampire experiences before exsanguinating someone. I don't know.

All I know is that the revelation about cannibalism marked the final turning point for humankind. It's when humans stopped being humans. Or at least when the majority of us did.

Only about a tenth of the remaining population developed a taste for flesh. Of course, that figure is based solely on my limited experience. But in my small town of Shadeland, Indiana, the day the man tore a policeman's arm from his body and proceeded to rip the flesh off it in gobbets, was the day it all started to come undone.

The same day my father died. Died because I didn't act quickly enough, bravely enough, or decisively enough.

But I don't want to talk about that now. What I want to do is sleep, though for some reason I can't do it.

Maybe it's the werewolf in the house with me.

Since I can't sleep, and since I can't bring myself to talk about the day my town fell, I'll tell you why I knew Jim was a lycanthrope.

For one, he's alive. That's a massive accomplishment. So massive that I'm deeply skeptical every time I encounter another supposed Latent. To have remained alive over the past two years, regardless of what manner of creature you are, would have taken a great deal of skill, though I tend to attribute it mostly to luck.

Another factor to consider, as cruel as this sounds, is Jim's age. The guy is simply too old to have survived this long, not without some special power.

Remember Gentry? I was wary of him, despite his tattered appearance, because he appeared to be on the wrong side of fifty. Oh, I've seen Latents older than Gentry, but not many.

Gentry was in his fifties. A man in his *seventies* would have to be an amazing individual indeed to have survived this long. I'm not saying it's not possible – of course it's possible. But a person that age would have had to fortify his home, amass a considerable arsenal, and remain constantly vigilant in order to scratch out any kind of life.

This man's home is not fortified.

This man doesn't appear to have much in the way of weaponry.

Jim doesn't seem worried about anything.

But why, you wonder, did I assume he's a werewolf?

Cannibals travel in packs. They're basically cowards who know they're more powerful than normal humans but nowhere near as ferocious as the rest of the monsters now populating the world. To keep themselves safe, they seldom live alone. Like Jim.

And he's not a vampire, that much is certain. Contrary to legend, vampires can endure the sunlight, though they much prefer the dark. Seeing a creature during the daytime isn't a guarantee he isn't a vampire, but it's a strong indication.

When a vampire spends time with a human, the bloodlust becomes overwhelming.

A cannibal eats because of what he will gain.

A vampire feeds because he cannot avoid it.

A werewolf only transforms when something pushes him toward the change. Jim seems like a good guy with a curse.

In a way, Stomper and Paul are far worse than any vampire. They could subsist on smaller game, like I do. The fact is, they *like* killing and eating people. They relish the power their diet provides.

When I think of cannibals like Stomper and Paul and Judases like Gentry who'll lead an innocent father and son to slaughter, deep down, a hideous refrain sounds in my brain: *Maybe the scientists were right. Maybe humankind did need eradicating.*

I'd never say those words aloud, and if you find this record, you'll think me a lunatic, or worse, a misanthropic sadist. Yet I don't believe my heart has fully hardened. I don't believe I'm some sinister, depraved creature.

It's just....

The evidence is all around me.

Humans have always been monsters. We just needed a push to embrace our shadow side.

Which reminds me....

We might as well get to this now. If you're reading these journals, and I'm long gone, and if you weren't around when everything went to hell in the world, you likely have some burning questions.

Paramount among these, I'm guessing, is how the hell did it all happen?

See, this is where it gets dicey because I'm certainly no scientist, and though I like to think I have a curious mind, I've never been outstanding at research. But I can tell you what I know, which admittedly isn't much, because I'm sure you're curious.

You ever heard of 'junk DNA'?

I hadn't, at least not before the Four Winds.

DNA is coded and helps to create proteins in cells. This, remember, is the DNA we know about, the kind that's mapped and responsible for our unique makeup.

Junk DNA is non-coded. It remains a mystery, hence its throwaway name.

Here's the kicker:

Junk DNA accounts for ninety-eight percent of all DNA. Stop and think about that for a second. *Ninety-eight percent.* That means that the vast majority of human DNA is a total mystery to modern science.

This is where the Bastards from Baltimore come in. Evidently, they were able to identify the function of at least some of this junk DNA. Furthermore, these geneticists realized that the roots of mythology were intimately connected with DNA previously thought to be useless.

Turns out, it has a use.

Destroying the world.

The virus in the Four Winds bombs created a catalytic reaction with people's junk DNA, and the monstrous impulses and characteristics that had lain dormant for eons were awakened. Don't ask me how the awakening worked, but the proof is everywhere. When you came into contact with the virus, your junk DNA was activated.

Or, if you were like me, you remained the same while everyone around you transformed.

Now might be a good time to explain how they did it. The unbelievable part is how straightforward it was.

Once Four Winds Aerospace cultivated the virus and recruited some radicals from the Applied Physics Lab, it became a simple matter of dissemination. Utilizing the same technology our government employed for THAAD, its truck-based missile interception system, Four Winds Aerospace developed six Nano Satellite Launch vehicles designed to carry the payload of suborbital ballistic missiles.

Confusing? Because the first time I heard all that, it confused the shit out of me.

I'll take a step back and explain it the way Susan explained it to me. Thank God she's smart; otherwise, I'd have never understood how it all went down. She wasn't a rocket scientist in the old world or anything. She was a grad student at Purdue University. She was just getting started on her dissertation – about drones – when the missiles flew.

It seems much of the same technology we'd developed to save us from nuclear annihilation ended up bringing about the end of the world.

According to Susan, THAAD, or Terminal High Altitude Area Defense, was pioneered as a last resort to intercept missiles fired toward the continental US. Uniquely portable, the launching apparatus could be outfitted on specialized trucks. Or, in this case, on the backs of tractor trailers that were parked approximately a hundred miles away from our nation's six busiest airports.

Atlanta.

L.A.

Dallas.

Chicago.

New York.

Denver.

The semis looked like any other big rig, only they had whopping huge trailers draped with massive tarps. Twelve-person crews accompanied the six tractor trailers to sparsely populated areas, parked, and typed in their coordinates. Obviously, being in six different locations around the country, the weather varied, but unfortunately for the rest of us, the Bastards from Baltimore chose an ideal day for their launch. Only Denver experienced a breeze, enough to scatter the virus, but not enough to ameliorate its effects on the hosts who were infected.

The missiles were launched. Eight minutes later, they reached their targets.

Four Winds Aerospace detonated their bombs approximately four hundred feet over the targeted cities. Fired during daylight – for maximum infection – the bombs exploded at approximately three o'clock Eastern Standard Time. There was no fire – that would have incinerated the virus. Instead, onlookers witnessed what's known as a BFRC: Big Fucking Red Cloud.

It must have been disconcerting. Local and state governments were utterly bewildered. We'd always speculated about how to deal with a foreign attack. But a ballistic missile launched on American soil by its own citizens? Not so much.

The point is, the virus found its hosts. From that point on, it was simply a matter of travel.

Highly communicable, the virus showed no outward signs, which meant no one knew they were infected. The virus was not only airborne; it could be spread by touch. And the genius of it was, you never knew you were infected. There was no coughing, no lethargy, not even a sniffle. You went about your day infecting everyone around you, your wife, your parents.

Your children.

You boarded your airplane to Tokyo, unaware you were about to deliver the virus to one of the most densely populated nations in the world. You left JFK Airport excited for your French honeymoon; you didn't intend to doom Paris. The wealthy businessman heading to Kuwait, the entrepreneur traveling to South Africa, the Australian college students returning home after a month abroad. None of them knew about the virus. None of them knew what was happening to them, deep in their DNA. None of them suspected that, within a few weeks, they'd be ripping their loved ones to shreds. None of them knew they were turning their friends and coworkers into monsters.

Dammit. Just thinking about it makes me crazy. The question I can't get over is this: Why would a group of seemingly reasonable people – men and women of learning and, one would have hoped, empathy – take such drastic steps to avert a nuclear war? Yes, a nuclear holocaust would have obliterated much or all of the human race. At least it might have. And yes, the other forms of earthly life matter too.

But launching the Four Winds missiles ensured the annihilation of mankind and doomed a great many species as well. Large mammals, like cows, horses, and pigs, only exist now in cannibal compounds. So there you go, you heartless sons of bitches: You killed Bessie, Seabiscuit, and Babe too. Happy now?

God, I'm cracking up.

I gotta get some sleep.

If Jim the Werewolf eats me before I wake, and if you find this journal sometime in the future, please send it to the assholes from Four Winds Aerospace. Or their children.

They need to know how Mommy and Daddy murdered the world.

CHAPTER NINE

The Matter of Catherine

Dez sensed a change in the house even before he went downstairs. Moments like these, when his body thrummed with unreasoning tension and his intestines roiled and slithered as though packed with live snakes, he wondered if he really was a Latent, an individual whose powers only needed the right moment to rise to the surface. Psychic abilities were not terribly common, but they were one of the powers unleashed by the Four Winds. It was why some bands of survivors were destroyed after everything went to hell, and why others managed to cling to hope.

It helped to have a psychic in your camp.

It was one of the primary reasons why the riverside colony had lasted as long as it had. Lori, a curly brunette in her early forties, hadn't told anyone about her second sight, perhaps in the fear that her gift would be exploited, or worse, that it would give someone reason to expel her from the group. It was one of the many things that amazed Dez most about the destruction of civilization. In the third decade of the twentieth century, humankind believed itself enlightened and far removed from the abominations of its past, wholesale genocides like the Holocaust, or small-scale lunacies like the Salem Witch Trials.

If the Four Winds proved anything, they proved mankind hadn't changed at all.

So Lori kept her secret hidden, and to her credit, no one had any idea she could see the future. Until one evening around moonrise, she stood, her face going fishbelly white, and clapped a hand over her mouth.

"What is it?" one of the colonists asked, half-smiling.

"They're coming," Lori said.

Exchanged glances. Uneasy laughter.

"Who's coming?" This was the leader. Jason.

"The maneaters."

That word sobered everyone quickly.

No idiot – he was many things, but he was not an idiot – Jason Oates had ordered everyone inside the cave.

Less than a minute later, they'd heard the haughty voices echo over the river. Had the colonists left any trace of food or clothing outside, the cannibals would have spotted it and descended on the camp. But due to Lori's early warning, the killers passed them by.

Within the murk of the cave, Dez had been present when Jason clicked on his flashlight and regarded Lori first with awe, then with hunger. Not for her flesh of course – Jason was no cannibal – but for her gift.

One of Lori's fears did come to pass. Her gift was exploited. Again and again. The colonists only felt safe when she was awake, which meant they gave her little rest.

It drove her insane.

Compressing his lips, Dez crammed his things in his backpack, snatched up his bow, and toted it all down the creaky farmhouse stairs.

He told himself the tension he was feeling had nothing to do with psychic powers. It was just...tension. Who wouldn't be tense under a werewolf's roof?

Dez entered the living room, where the aroma of popcorn still perfumed the air. His stomach growled in response, but he was eager to get going. He could probably snag another meal from Jim, but he'd tested fate too long. Dez abided by the theory that werewolves were largely like regular people. Many didn't want the change, had no desire to rend and kill. Of course, others felt no compunction about eviscerating people, and Dez had heard of werewolves like that. Thankfully, he'd never been around one.

He had, however, witnessed the change twice.

Twice was more than enough. On both occasions, he'd been lucky to escape with his life.

Best not to push his luck.

He came around the corner into the kitchen and discovered the old man cracking open eggs, the stovetop clock magically illuminated.

Seeing Dez's frown, Jim said, "The generator." He cracked another egg, his fingers long and carved with tendons. "Only use it during the winter months, and then only when a deep freeze is on. But this morning I just felt like eggs on the stove, you know?" A smile.

Dez relaxed infinitesimally.

It apparently wasn't enough because a hint of frost crept into Jim's eyes. "Now come on. If I was gonna eat you, don't you think I'd have done it last night? You snoozing down the hall from me, helpless as a lamb?"

Dez fought off a surge of annoyance.

"Mistrust," Jim muttered, waving a hand over the black skillet to test for heat. "A minute or so longer," he said.

"Sorry," Dez said, placing the crossbow on the floor beside a small round table. "It's just conditioning, you know?"

Jim opened a drawer, came out with a metal whisk. "How do you like yours?"

Dez sat. "I'm not picky."

"I favor sunny-side up." Jim returned the whisk to the drawer, poured the eggs into the skillet, where they immediately began to crackle.

Dez noticed the old man wore a different plaid shirt today, this one navy blue, carmine, and a dingy white. His shoulder blades bulged like harrows.

Dez said, "My mom always claimed a hot pan was the key to good eggs."

Jim reached out and retrieved a metal spatula that looked a couple years older than Abraham Lincoln. "Can't be suspicious of everybody all the time," he remarked. He scooped the eggs, flipped them over. "That way leads to prejudice, and prejudice leads to hysteria."

Dez propped his elbows on his knees, chastened. "I'm sorry for doubting your motives. You don't encounter much kindness these days."

But Jim went on as though he hadn't heard him. "One minute we're a community, and the next we're raving at each other in the streets and barricading ourselves in our homes." Jim's right arm, the spatula arm, moved jerkily, punctuating his angst. "Looting businesses. Stealing all the goddamn gasoline. Turning into petty thieves and forgetting basic human decency."

Dez decided against reminding him of his popcorn looting. He sought for the right words, if only to break the old man's gloomy mood. "Would you like me to help with anything?"

"Like what?" Jim snapped.

Dez looked around. "I don't know, maybe I could get some plates? The silverware?"

"You really want to do me a favor?" Jim asked, glowering at him over his shoulder.

Dez shrugged. "Anything."

"Stop looking at me like I'm a goddamned monster."

Dez opened his mouth, but the old man half-turned, jabbed the spatula at him. "Don't tell me you're not doing it, because I *see* you doing it. Could barely enjoy my popcorn last night because you acted like I was gonna go all Lon Chaney on you and fillet you like a smallmouth bass."

"Hey, I—"

"It's *bullshit*, Dez. I open my home to you and you act like it's a trap. You ever think a guy might just want some company? Some fucking *conversation*?"

Dez put his hands up. "Okay. Okay. No need to get worked up."

Jim made a face, flapped the spatula at him. "Don't give me that stuff. I'm not gonna start howling at you." He shook his head. "For Christ's *sakes*."

Dez saw no sign of lycanthropic change, so rage wasn't Jim's trigger. He had no idea what was, but he was reasonably sure anger wasn't it. It had been the catalyst for one of the werewolves he'd encountered. For the other, it had been lust. The theory – one that Dez ascribed to – was that werewolves' triggers were powerful negative emotions, but for every werewolf it was different. For Jim, it appeared rage had no effect. And Dez doubted very seriously the old man would be experiencing lust any time between now and the end of breakfast.

Yet for some reason, the fear sweat still trickled down his back.

Psychic?

Dez brushed away the thought. He stood up because he'd go crazy if he continued to sit at the table. He hated being idle while others worked, and the fact that the one working was a werewolf only intensified his unrest.

He moved to the cabinets at the opposite end of the L-shaped counter. "You keep the plates in here?"

Jim eyed him for a long moment. Then, apparently deciding he was done being irate, nodded at the cabinets to his immediate right. "In there. Use the paper ones. I don't want to waste good water washing dishes."

Glad to have something to do besides worry, Dez went to the cabinet, opened it, and spotted a thin stack of paper plates. Not the cheap kind, the ones you had to double up on in order for them not to get soggy and rupture. He separated two plates from the stack, closed the cabinet. He eyed the eggs and noticed the skillet was scummed with a substance that resembled chocolate cake. A miasma of burnt eggs reached his nostrils.

Jim shook his head. "Got me going. Too distracted...." He noticed the paper plates, jerked his head. "Over here on the counter, so I can shovel the eggs onto 'em."

Dez moved around behind the old man, set the plates on the counter to the left of the stove.

Jim worked the spatula under the eggs. "The yolks broke. Guess we're having scrambled after all."

"Scrambled's fine with me."

Jim had transferred half the eggs to one paper plate when his gaze flicked to something at the rear of the counter. Dez followed his eyes and discovered the picture of Jim and his wife, the one where Mary was in his lap, both of them smiling broadly, their life together still ahead of them.

Something small and furtive scurried down Dez's spine.

Jim's eyes took on a glaze, the skillet and spatula still held before him. Like a troll at dawn, he looked like he'd been turned to stone.

Dez glanced from Jim to the picture, knew there was no avoiding it. "How long were you two married?"

In a croaky voice, Jim answered, "Forty-seven years."

Dez chewed the corner of his mouth. "You look happy together."

"Most of the time," Jim said, but his voice was distant. Was he imagining them as they were back then? The feel of his wife in his lap, the taste of a cold beer in his mouth? Making love to her that night, both of them tipsy from the cookout?

Or was he remembering the way she died? Had she been changed by the Four Winds? Or victimized by them?

"She saw everything," Jim said, his eyes on the picture but unseeing. "She saw it before I did."

There was no need for Dez to ask him what he meant. Dez glanced at the stovetop coil, which glowed a seething, satanic red.

"Our daughter didn't call after things went haywire. We knew that was a bad sign. We were worried sick, her halfway across the country in Boulder, married to a nitwit who happened to invest in the right technology...some app...acted like he was a genius or something...."

The heat from the stove shimmered the air. Dez longed to sidle around the old man and twist off the burner, but something kept him rooted in place. Pants-shitting terror, probably.

"We didn't hear word one from Catherine for more than a week. By that time I was frantic with worry. Mary was too. We'd loaded up the Dodge, had the topper on so we could sleep in it if we got stuck. You know, all the highways were snarled up by then."

Dez remembered it well. Just like in the movies. Things go to hell, people flee the cities for the country. Then again, after the Four Winds, the country was just as precarious as the cities.

Monsters everywhere.

Including right next to you, a voice warned. *Get him off the topic or get the fuck out of the house. Now!*

"Hey, Jim, maybe we should—"

"We'd fired up the Dodge," Jim went on, "actually had it idling in the driveway. Mary was on the way to the passenger's side when my cell phone rang. We both stopped and gaped at each other…service had been so spotty, we were surprised anybody was able to get through. Less than a week later, they went silent forever, but that evening, they worked."

Dez watched him, heartbeat thumping. Had a cloud passed over the already muted sun? Or had Jim's face gone a half-shade darker?

Jim said, "My trance broke, and I fumbled the phone out of my pocket. Damn near dropped it, my hands were shaking so badly. When I picked it up, I knew who it would be even before I heard Fabian's voice." A hollow chuckle. "You know, I should've known what kind of guy my daughter was in love with when I heard that name. Fabian. That's a weasel name if I ever heard one."

The eggs in the skillet stank now, the majority of them burned beyond edibility. Dez's feet itched to cross to the table, to heft his backpack and his crossbow and get the hell out.

But Jim was going on. "It was Fabian all right, but his voice was different, and I knew already. But I also knew I had to hear it. Like the gavel strike after the death sentence. Mary was watching me all along and my face must've shown something and the next thing I know she's on her knees, wailing, her fingernails clawing at her cheeks."

Jim's voice had taken on a raw, gravelly quality. Dez saw with a sinking gut that the old man's hands *were* darker. Hairier. "'You're wrong,' I said to Fabian. 'She can't be dead.'"

Jim favored him with a horrid, heartbroken grin. "'But she is,' Fabian said. 'She is, Jim. They came for her in the night. They had…horns.'"

Satyrs, Dez thought distantly. *Get out of this house now.*

Were Jim's eyes flecked with yellow? "'Where the hell were you?' I shouted into the phone. 'Where were you when my baby was being snatched?' Fabian answered, 'They didn't take her, Jim. They…they held me down…made me watch while they…they ripped her clothes off….'"

Jim shook the spatula and skillet, the eggs too grafted onto the black surface to go flying. But it was at Jim's fingers that Dez stared. They were elongating.

"'I'd never seen anything like it,' Fabian said. 'I didn't know what they were there to do.'"

Dez watched Jim's hands with paralyzed horror. Wiry black hairs threaded out of the skin, made the cuffs of Jim's flannel shirt undulate. Dez heard a strained, groaning sound, knew the plaid fabric was stretching.

Jim flung the spatula away and slammed the skillet down on the glowing scarlet coil. "'Well, you should've saved her when you saw what they were doing!' I screamed. 'You should've had the courage to protect my little girl!'"

"'I didn't think they'd rape her, Jim!' my worthless piece of shit son-in-law wailed. 'And even if they did, I didn't think they'd kill her!'"

Jim rounded on Dez, fists balled at his sides. "'What are you telling me?' I screamed at Fabian. 'Just what in the hell are you trying to say?'"

Dez took a backwards step. "Look, Jim, I know you're—"

"'The third one killed her!'" Jim shrieked. His shoulders were expanding, pulsing under the old flannel. "'She gave out while the third one was raping her!' I asked that coward son-in-law, 'Why didn't you save her? Why didn't you do something before it got that far?'" Jim's eyes flashed, the irises a lambent gold. "You know what he said to me?"

Dez bent down, grasped the strap of his pack.

Jim bared his teeth, teeth that were longer than they'd been. "He says, 'I was afraid they'd kill me too!'" Jim reached up, seized handfuls of white hair, and ripped out two big clumps of scalp. "That stupid…fucking… *weasel!*"

Jim let loose with a soul-shattered wail and dropped to his knees. His face contorted in pain. "*And all the time,*" Jim said through curving scimitar teeth, his voice a hoarse rumble, "*my Mary was sobbing on the driveway gravel. How was I to know I was changing too? How was I to know what I was becoming?"*

Jim flopped down on all fours. His shirt split up the spine, the knobby backbone cracking, undulating.

Shoot him, a voice in his head demanded.

Dez shook his head. *But it's not his fault!*

Dez shouldered his backpack. His fingers were numb, drenched with perspiration. His heart was hammering so thunderously he thought he might faint. Jim was doubled-over, roaring in agony, his head jittering, his feet splitting through his workboots and drumming on the floor. The stench of animal hair and feces overtook the sulfuric odor of burnt eggs.

Head swimming, Dez got hold of the crossbow, pivoted toward the mudroom. He'd reached the threshold when he glanced back at the werewolf, whose transformation was nearly complete.

The beast shot a look at him, the eyes leonine, enraged. *"WHY?"* he roared. *"Why my Mary? I didn't mean to—"* He twitched his head, the neck muscles hopping. *"—to kill her! My poor Mary! She didn't even recognize me when I – oh GOD!"*

Dez bolted for the door, but it was locked. Behind him, the werewolf's words devolved into an ear-splitting bellow. Dez fumbled with the lock, the kind you twisted, but his fingers were too sweaty. He'd seen what a werewolf could do. It wasn't *if* they killed you, it was how brutally. He seized the lock again, turned it the correct way this time. His body turned to ice at the sounds echoing from the kitchen. Growling, snarling. Was Jim done transforming? Was he even now stalking forward to rend Dez to shreds? Jesus Christ, he had to get out. He ripped open the door, flung the storm door outward, and was halfway onto the porch when he froze, remembering the key hooks in the mudroom.

For a millisecond he stood there, agonized, knowing the end was upon him. Then he lunged back inside, made a grab for the Dodge keys. They came off smoothly, and he turned to go, but then he remembered the pole barn would be locked. He'd need the larger key ring. Moaning, he seized the ring, yanked, but it was tangled on the hook – goddammit! – and his eyes darted to the kitchen, where a shape was writhing on the floor. It was Jim, of course, but it wasn't Jim. It was a pulsing humanoid abomination, a rippling, twitching figure with muscles so huge it seemed they'd burst, the face so diabolical Dez felt his bladder let go at the sight of it. The beast's eyes were closed in agony.

Dez backed away, felt for the storm door handle, and that was when the eyes flipped open, the irises a glowing amber, the pupils black slits that bore no trace of compassion, no semblance of humanity.

Dez fled. His hands were trembling so wildly he could scarcely focus on the right set of keys, much less select the proper key from the ring. The pole barn was only a short distance away, yet there were seven, eight, nine keys to choose from. And goddammit, he didn't have time to *try* nine keys. The werewolf was coming, might already be gathering for a barreling rush through the kitchen.

Dez neared the pole barn. Twenty feet, ten. He reached down, fumbled for a key, a bronze-colored one, tried it.

Not even close.

He riffled through the keys, found another bronze one. Nope.

Teeth bared, Dez shot a look over his shoulder at the back of the house. No sign of the werewolf, but he'd be coming. Any moment....

Find the fucking key!

Right. He tried another one, this one silver. No luck. Another, the same color. No.

Almost halfway through his options.

A howl split the morning air. Dez whimpered, dropped the truck key.

Ignoring that, he tried another one from the ring. If he couldn't get inside the pole barn, he'd have no need of the Dodge key, would he? He'd be dead where he stood, torn into a million—

The key turned.

Sucking in air, Dez flung open the door, scooped up the Dodge key, and plunged inside.

For a ghastly moment, Dez was sure he'd somehow erred, that the truck was in the gray, weathered barn. Or maybe there'd never been a truck, and this was all an elaborate ruse. He peered into the gloom – no windows in here, no nothing except dust motes, sparse tufts of straw scattered about, a junker El Camino that appeared not to have run since Reagan was president.

Then he spied it, a faint glint in the far recesses of the pole barn.

It had to be the truck.

Mouth twisting into a relieved grin, Dez set off across the dim, dusty expanse, and was halfway to the truck when a plangent thud, followed by a tinkling of glass, made his legs liquefy.

The werewolf was coming.

Dez gained the Dodge in a few seconds, tried the handle on the hope it would be unlocked, but of course it wasn't. Jim might allow his chickens to roam free, but he wasn't trusting enough to leave his primary means of transportation vulnerable to thieves.

Dez fumbled for the truck key, but his hands were too full. With a frustrated grunt, he dropped the big key ring, realizing he no longer needed it. He got hold of the Dodge key, stabbed at the lock, gouged an ugly groove in the silver paint.

Did he hear the huff of the approaching werewolf?

His hand was shaking so violently, he was forced to grab it with his other hand just to steady it. The pole barn was so murky he could barely make out the silver circle of the key assembly, much less the slit where the teeth were housed.

The key sank in. He turned it, heard the locks of the quad cab release. He grasped the handle, yanked back, and from the front of the pole barn the daylight flickered, a tenebrous shape filling the doorway.

Dez didn't need to look up to know the werewolf was coming. He lunged into the driver's seat, slammed the door shut, not even bothering with locks. Werewolves wouldn't bother with handles. They'd just—

A huge shape thundered onto the hood.

Dez screamed, pushed involuntarily away from the enormous black mass. The werewolf's momentum pounded its snarling face into the windshield, the taloned hands instantly scrabbling for purchase. His vision swirling with a sick vertigo, Dez aimed the key toward the ignition and could hardly believe it when it slid in smoothly. At the sound of the engine's rumble, the werewolf's face froze in a wide-eyed stare, the eyes of the monster so vast and profound that Dez could scarcely summon the strength to reach up, shift the truck into Drive.

The werewolf's eyes narrowed, the lips curving in a snarl. The teeth were long and hooked, the lips black and speckled with pink. Dez depressed the accelerator, only dimly aware of the new problem he faced. Not only was there a bloodthirsty monster preparing to spring through the windshield at him, there was no way out of the pole barn. Had he more time or composure, he might have raised one of the rolling barn doors so he could simply drive out. Now, however, he was left with no choice but to motor straight at the wall opposite and hope the Dodge could punch through the sheet metal without shredding the tires or detonating the airbags. As the Dodge veered around the El Camino and picked up steam, he imagined himself pinioned behind an airbag, unable to reach the steering wheel, the werewolf simply stalking around to the side of the truck to feast on him as Dez thrashed in terror.

The werewolf grinned through the windshield.

No!

Dez floored the gas. The werewolf thudded against the windshield. Roaring, the creature clambered higher, but the sheet metal wall was fast approaching, the truck doing at least twenty miles an hour. Dez reached up, clutched at the seatbelt, but it was too late.

At the last moment, the werewolf swiveled its head toward the wall racing toward it, and when they crashed through, the impact wasn't nearly as bone-jarring as Dez had imagined it would be. The werewolf was mashed against the windshield, but he was up immediately, climbing onto the roof.

Then Dez could see between the creature's knees.

And the house racing toward them.

Hissing, Dez pumped the brakes and cut the wheel to the left. He hoped the skidding action would fling the werewolf off, but the creature's talons were too keen. The truck slid over the frost-kissed lawn, rose up on two wheels, then jounced down with an outraged squeal of shocks. Dez depressed the accelerator, ground his teeth at the strident cries of the spinning tires, then let off the gas. A harsh chunking sound from directly above him, a spine-tingling roar. Dez shot a look at the ceiling, saw the clawed hand that had punched holes through the roof and dug furrows through the thick metal.

What would the talons do to human flesh?

Dez toed the gas. His instinct clamored for him to floor it, but then he'd be spinning futilely in the yard, and in moments the beast above him would peel the truck roof off like a kid's decal.

He banished the thought and focused on navigating the yard. The ground appeared level, but like most lawns, the terrain here was lumpy, the Dodge bouncing like some unserviced carnival ride.

The metal split directly above his lap and a swarthy forearm pistoned down a foot from his face. Dez pressed backward into his seat, his foot standing on the accelerator. The Dodge leapt forward, its back end fishtailing. He surged toward the primitive country lane as the huge talons snatched at him, the lethal claws slicing the air inches from his face. Dez slid downward in his seat to evade the whickering claws, but one slashed his cheek anyway, the gash an instant dousing of ice water. Dez leaned hard to his right, thinking to elude the talons, but the Dodge swerved with him, directly in the path of the mailbox. He slammed into it, worried it would damage the truck's chassis as they bounced into the road, but the engine merely coughed once before catching again.

The talons snagged his shoulder.

A yellow-black claw punctured the leather of his jacket, curled upward until he was levered off his seat. For the love of God, it could lift him with one damned *finger*?

Dez swatted at the talon and managed to detach it. He plopped down. The truck was angling toward a ditch. It wasn't a deep ditch, but it might be steep enough to trap the Dodge, and once the werewolf had the truck stopped....

The other fist punctured the ceiling, this one directly over Dez. They were revving along now at forty miles per hour, but that didn't matter. The beast showed no signs of relenting, would at any moment have the roof split wide open and Dez plucked from his seat. Both clawed hands darted down at him. Dez moved as low as he could without losing sight of the road.

Both hands grabbed hold of him, and then he was rising rapidly toward the roof of the Dodge. His head rammed the roof fabric, the talons rupturing his leather jacket in several places. The werewolf lowered him and jerked up again, this time smacking his head on the roof with such force that Dez worried about a fractured skull.

There was a ringing in his ears. They had traveled perhaps a hundred yards down the country road, but that didn't mean a damned thing. The beast had him now, didn't give two shits whether they veered off the road or not. Up ahead, the road plunged into a steep valley, both sides wooded and dark. The werewolf jerked him toward the roof, cracked his head on the thinly padded steel. Dez's vision blurred.

Desperately, he reached down and seized the Ruger. The Dodge drifted toward the left shoulder, beyond which was a drop-off into a gully.

Dez gritted his teeth, righted the wheel, and thrust the Ruger toward the roof.

As the werewolf lifted him again, Dez fired. Judging from the way the hairy legs slung over the windshield went ramrod straight, the slug had found its target. Dez heard a guttural roar that he at first mistook for the truck's descent down the steep gravel decline.

Then blood pattered on his arm, and he realized the roar was coming from the werewolf.

"Sorry, Jim," he said and aimed the Ruger.

Then the whole roof disappeared.

Dez looked up in time to see the werewolf heaving up the huge flap of steel and casting it aside like a ragged sheet of cardboard. The wound in the werewolf's sternum sluiced blood that was whipped away by the rushing wind, and for a moment the beast perched on its knees, roaring and glowering down at Dez, its arms spread in challenge.

Dez swung the Ruger up and blasted the creature in the throat.

The werewolf slapped its hands over the wound a split second before it started to gush, and then, horribly, the monster tilted forward as though he would tumble into the cab beside Dez.

Dez slammed on the brakes.

The werewolf somersaulted over the hood, and Dez lost sight of it as the Dodge was plunged into a nauseating spin. There were no guardrails here, and though he was nearing the bottom of the valley, the drop-off on either side of the road was ten feet or more. As the back end skidded around, Dez gripping the wheel for dear life, he imagined what would happen if the Dodge crashed. He doubted the werewolf's wounds were fatal. He'd heard that werewolves, like vampires and other creatures, could heal rapidly, could even regenerate missing limbs. If the truck did plunge into the gully—

The spin ended, the front tires perched on the soft shoulder. The engine stalled. Distantly, Dez was aware of a notification dinging from the dashboard.

Dez's breathing was shallow, his heart triphammering so hard that he feared he'd faint after all. He was lathered in sweat, still terrified the Dodge would nose down the hill, flip, end up in a bed of fallen leaves upside down, the creature still strong enough to finish him in a flurry of claws.

Fingers numb, Dez keyed the engine, certain it wouldn't start. It would be flooded, wrecked, screwed up in some way. He never did know much about cars.

The engine turned over.

Adrenaline surged through him as he reached for the gearshift. He listened for the werewolf, but couldn't hear anything above the ragged growl of the Dodge and the continual dinging from the dash.

He slid the Dodge into Reverse and backed away from the edge. He thought he might roll over the werewolf's prostrate form, but there was no jarring thud, no sensation at all save the sparse gravel under the tires. He cut the wheel, shifted into Drive, and nosed the Dodge toward the road again. He yearned to floor it and rumble up the hill, but he was terrified he'd spin out. He knew he should be searching for the werewolf, but terror had sapped him of the strength. It was all he could do to drive straight. When the Dodge began to climb the long incline, he risked a look in the rearview mirror, which was miraculously intact despite the fact that most of the roof had been removed.

The werewolf was pushing shakily to its feet, a hand clamped over its throat. Though the beast glistened with blood, its eyes remained fixed on the receding truck.

Slitted in rage.

A chill gripping him with icy fingers, Dez guided the Dodge up the hill.

He didn't look back again.

PART THREE
THE FOUR WINDS BAR

CHAPTER TEN
Missing Obi-Wan

October 22nd

I can't see the Four Winds Bar yet, but I know it's there. First off, there's the sign I passed a minute ago. If it was any indication, this is going to be more unpleasant than I assumed.

I guess that's why I'm sitting here in this copse of forest rather than striding my way down the crumbling macadam toward Bill Keaton's headquarters. Oh, I'm not going to drive there. No way. If the patrons – or worse, one of Keaton's goons – see this truck, they'll seize it before I set foot in the door. The only chance I have of keeping it is stashing it here and hoping no one discovers it. That way, if I get the chance, I can return here and drive away afterward.

Something tells me I might need to leave in a hurry.

I know I should tell you about Bill Keaton now, but the thought of that son of a bitch makes me grip this pen so tightly I fear I might snap it. So first I'll tell you about the sign I passed.

It's impossible to know what the sign used to advertise. It's broad and tall and arched at the top. The whole thing has been spraypainted black, with the letters done in red. It would have been more logical – more legible – for the sign's creator to have used white since that would have shown up better than red, but I suspect that red's similarity to blood had something to do with this decision, even if you can't read the damn thing unless you slow to a crawl and squint at it.

THE FOUR WINDS BAR, it says in dripping crimson letters.

And beneath that: HOME OF BILL KEATON BARTER AND TRADE.

That might sound innocuous to you, but when you consider what Keaton barters and trades, any trace of harmlessness vanishes like a filigree of smoke from one of Keaton's smelly cigars.

Keaton deals in human flesh.

His chief clientele are vampires and cannibals, though I hear the satyrs have begun to creep northward in search of new victims.

Bill Keaton is more than happy to accommodate them.

Back in March, I first became aware of Keaton from a whiff of his foul-smelling smoke. I was out scrounging for food when I smelled it. My first reaction upon detecting that withering odor – a combination of flatulence and wet, rotten grass, the kind caked on the bottom of a lawnmower after mowing a yard you've put off for too long – was slow-witted confusion. I stood there frowning and wondering who in the vicinity was smoking. Not even worrying about the threat they might pose.

It was early morning at the time, so maybe that was part of my sluggishness. But most of it, I'm sorry to say, was complacency. Susan and I had survived far longer than just about anyone. A slatternly, stupid compartment of my brain had come to view our new existence as permanent, that the universe had somehow been put right again, that the worst was behind us.

My God, was I a fool?

You might think I bolted in the direction of the camp then, but you'd be wrong. What followed was a sort of agitated incredulity. Who, I remember thinking, still smoked cigars in this bleak new age? How did one even *find* cigars when it was difficult to go anywhere without becoming someone's dinner?

The answer, of course, was if you were powerful – say, powerful enough to build a depraved empire using fear, intimidation, and animal cunning – you could locate all the cigars you desired. Or have them found for you by your army of emissaries.

It was the voices of Keaton's thugs I heard next.

That and Susan's screaming.

What happened next…I can't think about.

I still might have tracked them down had I not run into another Latent that same night. It was a man with a nasty scar on the underside of his nose. The guy claimed to have seen Keaton's men transporting a woman fitting Susan's description north on Highway 421. He claimed there was a cannibal compound in Kalamazoo, Michigan, where Keaton's most generous buyer resided.

I spent the better part of three months making my way to Kalamazoo, only to learn the whole city had been burned to the ground long ago. Then I spent the next three months getting back to where I am now.

For the false information, I had paid the man with my best gun – a nearly-new Smith & Wesson .38 – and all the food I'd scrounged.

I failed. Miserably. And the problem with failure, at least where I'm concerned, is that I can't let it go. In fact, I've never been able to let anything go, but failure most of all.

I was a teacher in my former life. English, Creative Writing, Short Stories, whatever else my department head needed me to do. My strength as a teacher was the fact that I gave a shit about my students.

This is also a reason why my students still haunt me.

And not just the ones who died or became monsters when the world changed. I'm talking about the ones from before the Four Winds, the ones I tried to help but couldn't.

Dammit. I can't think about that now. I have work to do tonight. I didn't survive a werewolf attack and drive all this way down hazardous, bottlenecked roads in order to camp out in this thicket, as pretty and peaceful as it might be.

I came to find Bill Keaton.

I'm close. Less than a mile away. The sunlight is fading, and in another hour it'll be full dark. It's no good to be out at night. Exposed.

Not that the Four Winds Bar will be any safer, if the rumors I've heard are true. If what Jim the Werewolf told me before he transformed is right. If the behavior of Keaton and his henchmen were any indication.

Crazily, I'm reminded of a line from *Star Wars*, Obi-Wan telling Luke, "You will never find a more wretched hive of scum and villainy."

God, I miss *Star Wars*. I miss movies.

I remember the first time Dad showed me the original trilogy. We watched the VHS cassettes when I was ten years old, and it was magic. I remember believing my dad was a lot like Obi-Wan, even if he wasn't much like him at all. At least, not physically. While Obi-Wan was white-haired and sort of slender, my dad was full-bellied and his hair was a gentle brown until the day he died.

The day he died, we were watching the news – everyone watched the news when the outbreak happened – but what we should have been doing was hunkering down inside some safe place. Before the bombs flew, people made fun of preppers. I suppose I was one who mocked them. But I'll tell you, a stocked bunker sure as hell would have come in handy that awful autumn afternoon.

CNN was running a story about the apparent transformation of a prominent politician into a vampire. The politician, a high-ranking Democrat whose views on immigration and global warming I respected, began to lose it in the middle of a press conference. Her eyes, brown before, glowed a lambent orange. She lunged at an unfortunate aide standing beside her podium. The camera had cut off at that point – or CNN had ended the tape – and while my dad and I sat there flabbergasted at what we'd just witnessed, a crash sounded from the front of my dad's house.

We'd told ourselves that the house was fortified, but looking back, the measures we'd taken had been a joke. I barely had time to push out of my chair before the pair of cannibals appeared in the hallway. My dad was still attempting to climb out of his recliner – as I've mentioned, my dad was not a small man – when the pair fell on him. Like I wasn't even there.

And that was the worst part. Being ignored. Being discounted.

I lunged for the recliner, where they'd begun to rip and tear at him. They must have recently fed because their strength and ferocity were nothing short of ghastly. I grabbed one of the cannibals by the shoulder, who I'd first assumed was a long-haired man, the kind who'd been into heavy metal before the Four Winds shifted his interests to devouring human flesh. But the cannibal was a woman; she snarled at me. I aimed a punch at her, and she backhanded me such a blow that I flew across the room and cracked my head on the carpetless wood floor. I thought for sure she'd come for me then, but as I crawled away, I saw she'd returned to feasting on my father. One of the best men I've ever known.

Could I have saved him had I acted faster, or more heroically? I don't know. But I *do* know I didn't try hard enough.

I should have done more.

And Future Reader, whoever you are, I suppose I've just admitted something to you. My darkest secret. It's a simple one, sure, but it's still a difficult truth for me to accept.

I'm a coward. I've proved it again and again. Any steel I've shown has been feigned or dumb luck. I'm scared pretty much all the time, even if I don't admit it to myself. Hell, I was scared before the missiles flew.

Now? My nerves are stretched taut all the time. My sleep – what meager sleep I manage – is a carousel of nightmares. I see the faces of my loved ones every time I close my eyes.

Will. Joey. Susan.

And my father.

I'm sorry, Dad. I'm sorry I failed you the way I've failed everyone.

I wish I'd been a better son.

And now, as I sit here in the savaged pickup truck, I find myself wishing I had a companion, someone like my dad. Or someone as sage and formidable as Obi-Wan Kenobi. Maybe I should have tried to persuade Jim to travel to the Four Winds with me. Werewolves are dangerous company, I realize, but at least Jim craved normalcy. He didn't wish me harm.

I heave a rueful sigh and peer at the early evening horizon, the sunset-washed trees. If Jim ever sees me again, he'll kill me. Hell, he might be pursuing me now, just as Stomper and Paul might be pursuing me. It seems everyone wants to kill me these days.

Might as well add a few more adversaries to the list.

CHAPTER ELEVEN
The Doorman

The first sign Dez glimpsed of the Four Winds Bar was a brazen cloud of smoke rising from what appeared to be a broad, shallow valley. One of the most persistent problems of this new age was how to conceal smoke. It could be seen from great distances, scented by all manner of hostile beasts. Yet you needed it for warmth, for cooking meat. So you prayed for a windy day and did your best to shelter it so it wouldn't be snuffed out. If the wind scattered the smoke ribbon, no one could fix your location visually. Sure, it was possible for the keen, evolved noses to pick up the acrid tang in the air, but if you didn't linger where you'd built the fire, you'd be safely on your way before predators arrived.

Bill Keaton evidently didn't worry about predators. Maybe because he was one.

Dez emerged from the copse of trees, but kept to the far edge of the lane. Maybe sixty yards and he'd reach the valley, and from the looks of it, he'd be woefully exposed once he was there. Would Keaton have his henchmen standing sentry over the valley? Or would he, as his cigar smoking suggested, be too arrogant to brood about such precautions?

Dez suspected the latter, but it didn't make him feel any safer.

Nor did Jim the Werewolf's suggestion that Keaton was something unnatural. Of course, the notion had occurred to Dez. To reach the top of any hierarchy, particularly one as depraved as the one over which Keaton presided, you had to be ruthless, spiteful, capable of intimidating others who craved power. Though Dez hated to give him credit, it was apparent that Keaton possessed a well-honed species of jungle intelligence.

Did he possess fearsome physical abilities too? Jim had certainly believed so. Dez crunched along the sparse gravel lane and thought of the shudder that had run through Jim's body when the subject of Keaton had been broached.

Best steer clear of that place, Jim had said.

Ironic advice, Dez thought, considering how Jim had nearly ripped him apart.

He reached the end of the woods and beheld the shallow bowl of valley. On the far side of a vast, grassy meadow lay the Four Winds Bar.

It was nestled against a backdrop of forest, its mammoth chimney broadcasting an unhealthy plume of yellow-brown smoke into the otherwise gorgeous evening sky, which painted the gray shingled roof in hues of pink and orange and indigo. The structure itself was nearly all brick, quite large, with a towering A-framed center flanked in back by a pair of single-story outcroppings. Dez had to laugh as he realized what the Four Winds once was, before the world went to hell.

A church.

Someone had removed the crossbar from the steeple protruding from the building's roof. The sleek spire now rose to the level of the treetops like a tribute to a pagan god.

Dez realized there was a figure leaning in the alcove of the front porch. A tiny vermilion eye glowed in the shadows of the covered porch, died down, the figure smoking a cigarette, or perhaps a cigar like Keaton.

Whether he'd spotted Dez or not, there was no going back now. And anyway, Dez didn't plan on storming in and taking Keaton by force. There'd be too much security for that. Besides, who knew if Keaton was here? In his business, a man needed a constant flow of bodies to satisfy his buyers. Chances were good Keaton was out on a collection run, and all of this would come to nothing.

That's untrue and you know it.

Yes, Dez thought. He did know it. When someone recognized him, they'd know he'd come for Susan or revenge or both, and then they'd kill him. Or try.

Dez's fingers curled into fists. *Let them try.*

But the words felt forced, empty. Just what the hell was his plan? To stride into the bar and holler, Old West-style, for Keaton to come on out and settle this man to man? That it was time for a reckoning? That you took my woman, and I aim to get her back?

Hell.

The lurid eye from the porch glowed, dwindled. The figure had surely marked him by now. Dez became aware of a muffled thrum, the steady burr of a generator.

He made the mistake of taking his eyes off the figure on the porch.

To Dez's immediate right was a flyblown corpse. It had no head. Its midsection was a gory ruin.

Dez shivered. Thank God the grass in the surrounding meadow was so high. He could make out numerous cadavers littering the valley, but they were only shapeless humps on the dismal green landscape. Just objects. Not humans who'd been savaged by monsters.

Dez forced his legs to move. The evening was crisp but not unpleasant. High forties maybe, with little breeze. The gravel lane wasn't pristine, but someone had evidently been performing minimal upkeep. Unlike many gravel roads he'd encountered, this one featured very few weeds. Which meant Keaton and his men drove it with reasonable frequency.

Dez realized he'd been keeping to the edge of the lane despite being completely exposed out here in the center of the meadow. Annoyed with himself, he angled toward the middle, did his best to ignore the unmoving shadow on the porch and the eerie red eye's sluggish throb. If he needed to make an escape from here in a hurry, the only option was the southern woods. Approaching as he was from the north, he'd be utterly defenseless if he attempted a straight flight to the truck.

Which was damned inconvenient. He'd need to duck into the sheltering forest, evade capture as he threaded his way through the dense trees, and, if providence was on his side, reach the truck and peel ass out of here. A million things could go wrong. The chances of him living through the night seemed smaller and smaller. Dez felt tiny out here on the lane by himself, incapable of doing what he planned on doing.

What is your plan? a wry voice demanded.

Fifty yards from the bar, Dez shivered as a chill plaited down his back.

The plan is simple, he answered. If Susan is here—

She's not.

—if Susan is *here*, I'll find her, smuggle her out, and if we both live, if that improbable miracle occurs, I'll keep her safe and apologize to her for the rest of our lives for screwing up and allowing them to take her in the first place.

She's not here.

Then I'll find her, goddammit! I'll ask the patrons or the bartender or—

They won't know. Or won't care. You think Susan matters to them? She's just another body, a piece of livestock they sold off months ago to the highest bidder.

No!

She's dead and eaten by now, Dez. Digested and shat out and fertilizing the lawn of some cannibal compound. Or her desiccated corpse is lying on some refuse heap outside a vampire's lair, exsanguinated, then mummified by the sun.

She's alive.

Uh-huh. Just like Joey's still alive. Just like your dad and your son and—

Dez stopped, grasped handfuls of hair, and shook his head until the voice ceased taunting him.

He thought he'd outrun it. Then, the words came as clearly as if someone had spoken to him from three feet away: *You failed them. You'll fail everyone in the end.*

Heart pounding, he got moving again.

Thirty yards from the bar, Dez spied another sign. At least this one hadn't been painted black. Half-obscured by a cheerful red X, he made out the words FIRST ASSEMBLY BAPTIST CHURCH. Beneath that, unmarred text read PASTOR BRYCE WEEKS PRESIDING.

But that wasn't what stopped Dez. What stopped him was the reef of withered mushrooms that formed a ragged border around the sign. Each mushroom had been nailed to the wooden surface, and though some were nothing more than shriveled brown twists an inch long at best, others were longer, and not as dark as the shriveled ones were.

The realization smacked Dez like a brutal cuff to the head. The mushrooms weren't mushrooms. Their stalks had been pulled not from the ground, but from nests of pubic hair.

Bill Keaton was collecting severed penises. Dez counted thirty-five before he lost track and felt his gorge clench. A few of them were fresh, or relatively so. Their ragged bases indicated they hadn't been severed cleanly, but either sawed off like pesky willow branches or ripped off by savage hands.

"Think yours would look good up there?" a voice asked.

The smoker on the porch. Dez resisted an urge to look at the man, did his best to form his features into a mask of hardness, as though the severed penises didn't unnerve him, as if he were confronted with sights this grotesque every day.

The smoker chuckled. "Or maybe you don't have one. In that case, the nutsack will do. That is, if you've got a pair."

Dez deliberately waited another few seconds before turning and staring at the man. Maybe it was the fact that Dez was down here on the lane, and the smoker stood eight or nine feet higher at the apex of the steps, but from this perspective, the man looked rangy. Six-four at least, but slim. Delicate almost.

The way the man watched him was disconcerting, but Dez couldn't let it show. He approached the man leisurely, noting as he did how motionless the figure was.

"Looking for a girl," the man said.

Dez faltered mid-step. He couldn't help it. Was the man just guessing, or was there, as Dez now feared, something more to the man's accurate diagnosis?

"You don't have to talk," the man said, the cigarette pinched a few inches from his face like a marijuana joint. "I can read you like a billboard." A pause, the man's scrutiny a palpable thing. "Sarah," the man said. Within the shadows, Dez saw the man's eyes widen. He stabbed the luminous red tip of the cigarette at Dez. "Susan! That's her name."

Dez felt his guts curdle.

The man cocked his head, took a slow drag on his cigarette. "Don't recall a Susan. But then again—" A chuckle. "—there're so many. You know how it is."

Dez paused at the base of the steps.

"'Nevermore'," the man said.

Dez squinted at him.

The man continued to stare at him. Dez experienced the weirdest sensation...like the man was rummaging around in his head.

"'The Raven'," the man said.

"What about it?"

"You...you used to teach it."

Dez didn't answer.

"That would make you...." The man's eyes bored into him. "You taught freshman English."

"Among other things."

The man nodded, pleased with himself. "Think I'll call you the Raven."

Dez ignored that. "Keaton," he said.

"This is his place all right," the man answered. "But I'm not Keaton."

"I know that."

"Boss takes the others on his runs, but not me. A couple of us guys have got the touch." A pull on the cigarette, the white cylinder little more than a stub now. "He doesn't take me out scouting." A sly wink. "I'm too valuable. You believe that, Raven?"

Dez became aware of music within the building. It might be loud in there, but the sturdy brick façade dampened it enough that out here it was only a formless murmur. The song was familiar, but Dez couldn't place it. The thrum of the generator was louder now. Dez wondered what the electricity was being used for. It wasn't heat, or there wouldn't be smoke rising from the building. Lights, maybe.

"You don't belong here," the man said. "Latent like you."

"Why do you think that?"

"You're forty-two years old," the man went on. "Forty-two and scared."

"Only fools aren't scared," Dez said.

The man nodded. "Name's Lefebvre," he said. "And your name is really…McClane?"

Dez couldn't stifle a grin. "How do you do that?"

"Don't know," Lefebvre said. "The ability came on fairly abruptly. At first I thought I was just really perceptive. Or a good guesser. Then I started to see things I knew others would never want me to see." He sucked the cigarette, exhaled slowly. "That's when I knew."

"Bet you found out stuff you didn't want to."

"Like my wife was cheating? You bet." He took a last drag of his cigarette, dropped it, and mashed it with the toe of a black loafer. "Found out who was transforming into what. Neighbors, predators converging on my house at night. It kept me alive. Still keeps me alive. You need to leave."

"If you're really so perceptive, you know I can't do that."

"Drinking seawater," Lefebvre remarked. "That's how revenge is. You think you've slaked the thirst, but no matter what you do, no matter who you hurt…or kill, you can't get back what was taken." He crossed his arms, leaned against the alcove wall. "Susan's dead."

Gastric juices elevatored up Dez's throat, clogged his airway. He knew how naked and frail his voice sounded, but all he could manage was, "Are you sure?"

For a moment, Lefebvre's gaze remained oblique. The Stetson hat shadowed his eyes, but to Dez, the man's expression didn't seem bereft of feeling.

At length, Lefebvre said, "I don't know if she's alive or dead. But if she was taken in March—"

"Late March."

"—the odds of her still living are—"

"But you don't know," Dez said.

A pause, Lefebvre studying him. "No," he finally admitted. "I don't know."

From inside the bar, the music faded to silence. Dez could make out the murmur of voices, but nothing more.

Dez mounted the steps, never taking his eyes off Lefebvre. When he reached the top, he realized he was correct about the man's tall, slight build. In his Stetson hat, his denim jacket, the red-and-black flannel shirt and dark blue jeans, Lefebvre resembled some ineffectual dandy sheriff from a Hollywood western, the sort of man who's in league with the outlaws and is usurped by a grittier lawman halfway through the film.

"You're letting me go in?" Dez said.

"I screen," Lefebvre said simply. "You're not a threat to my employer." The ghost of a smile. "No offense, Raven."

Dez ignored that. He studied the man's sardonic face, placed him in his early forties. "You aren't one of Keaton's thugs. Why do you work for him?"

"I was a teacher too."

Dez made sure not to show his surprise. "Yeah?"

"Journalism mostly. It was a small high school, so I also ran the yearbook and the theater program. I work for Keaton to stay alive."

"By sanctioning murder."

Lefebvre stiffened. "Go inside."

Dez grinned. "By allowing them to rip apart the few good lives that are left. By letting them eat decent people."

Lefebvre's mouth twitched. His hand moved to a holstered gun.

Dez didn't go for one of his own weapons. "You won't kill me."

Lefebvre licked his lips. "The hell I won't."

Dez glanced at the gun on Lefebvre's hip, the polished walnut handle, another nod to cinematic Westerns. His eyes returned to

Lefebvre's. "I don't have to be a clairvoyant to know a coward when I see one." Dez winked. "No offense."

Lefebvre flinched. "I'm a telepath, not a clairvoyant. Now get the fuck inside, or get out of here."

Dez stared at the man a moment longer before dismissing him and striding the final few feet to the sturdy wooden double doors. He reached out, grasped a copper handle, and pushed down the thumb lock, which was sticky to the touch.

With one final thought of the severed dicks nailed to the First Assembly Baptist Church sign, Dez opened the door and stepped inside.

CHAPTER TWELVE

Erica

It wasn't like the movies where everyone turned and gawked at the hero when he walked inside. In a way, that would have been better. Rather than having every gaze swoop toward him and stare him down until he spoke, not one thing in the room changed when he entered.

But *room* wasn't the right word. This was obviously the place where the parishioners of the First Baptist Church had congregated to worship, an A-framed sanctuary capacious enough to seat perhaps five hundred people. Not a gigantic church like some of the ones he'd seen in big cities, but not a quaint country church either. Before the bombs flew, the First Baptist Church might have been thriving.

There was nothing holy about the place anymore. There were a few pews scattered here and there in the far reaches of the space, but most of them, he suspected, had been chopped up for firewood. In their stead had been arranged an assortment of wooden tables and chairs, so that the church now resembled an Old West saloon. Most of the tables were round, but a few were square, and though there were empty seats here and there, the majority of them were occupied.

It was the largest gathering Dez had beheld in years.

The stench was revolting. Unaired flatulence and unwashed bodies, spiced with a whiff of putrefying corpses.

Dez breathed through his mouth.

Opposite him, forty yards ahead, lay what had been the primary worship area of the Baptist church. He half-expected the enormous wooden cross on the wall to be desecrated in some way – perhaps festooned with one of Bill Keaton's crucified enemies – but curiously, the cross appeared unscathed by human hands.

Rather than housing an altar, the head of the church was now a lengthy bar, and not of the makeshift variety. Dez supposed it wasn't all that difficult to fathom. After all, now that society was destroyed, it would be relatively simple to find an abandoned bar and, if one possessed the manpower, have it transported here in sections. Nevertheless, seeing the length of polished wood and the patrons ranged on stools was a shock. Above the shoulders and heads of the figures seated at the bar, Dez made out an assortment of bottles, a swath of mirrors about four feet high spanning the length of the bar.

Evidently, Keaton was a fan of cowboy movies. Though he was loath to admit it, this meant that Dez and the ruthless son of a bitch who owned this house of horrors had something in common.

Furthering the impression of a Western barroom were the long balconies enshadowing the flanks of the main sanctuary. From where he stood he couldn't see much of these balconies, but there were quite a few figures up there, just elbows resting on handrails or faces limned by wall sconces.

He'd been right about the generator. The light in here wasn't dazzling – some of it was provided by old-fashioned kerosene lamps or squat candles within ruby-glassed globes – but the illumination spilling out of the overhead lights and wall sconces was enough that he could make out the architecture and the patrons.

He could also, he realized now, discern some of the Four Winds Bar's décor.

Dez's guts gave a sideways lurch. And he'd thought the penises on the sign outside had been bad.

Before the world ended, the word *terrorist* meant one thing: enemies of peace, foreign or domestic, who blew up buildings or hijacked airplanes or fired automatic weapons at defenseless people. Since the bombs flew, however, terrorism had come to mean something very different, at least in Dez's mind. The invocation of terror was now as common as a word of greeting. What remained of the human race had adopted the belief that frightening fellow survivors was preferable to befriending them.

Bill Keaton clearly understood the benefits of terrorism. Keaton could now count Dez among the individuals who'd been suitably terrified by his handiwork.

The strips of wood running beneath the balconies on both sides of the sanctuary were adorned with human heads. Their eyes had been opened, their mouths arranged in permanent screams.

Dez knew it would mark him as weak-stomached, but he couldn't help it. He closed his eyes and braced himself on the back of an empty chair, yet the afterimages still pursued him.

Fuck me, he thought.

Reluctantly, he opened his eyes. It was useless to pretend the severed heads weren't there, so he allowed his gaze to rove over them, thinking vaguely that meeting the horror head-on – *Christ* – might, like some macabre species of immersion therapy, inure him to its effects.

Nope, he thought after a few moments. *It's not working at all.*

The gory flaps of throat were horrid enough. Worse still were the words carved into the foreheads of the deceased. MUTINEER, read the head immediately over Dez's left shoulder. The face beneath the mauve inscription was shriveled and dark, like a prune into which some amateur sculptor had etched human features. Next to that was a female face, not as decayed, with the word SLUT sliced raggedly across her brow. LIAR, COWARD, and SODOMITE came next, and though these were ghastly, the inscription that stopped him was the sixth.

WEREWOLF, the forehead said.

The face was half-human, half-beast, the werewolf apparently having been beheaded mid-transformation. Dez was reminded forcibly of Jim, who'd murdered his wife against his will, who was forced to live out the rest of his days in a purgatory of guilt and excruciating metamorphoses. Pity wasn't the right word for what he felt for Jim, but it came close. Dez gazed upon the face of the werewolf and wondered if the man had been similarly tormented by what he'd become.

"Like them, do you?" a voice asked.

Dez glanced at the speaker and saw a bald man with a tangled growth of beard and sunken eyes watching him from a table full of patrons. The man looked familiar. Dez stared at him until he realized who the guy reminded him of. Evan Gattis, a former Houston Astros slugger.

Gattis was grinning. So were the others. All but one, Dez realized. Of the six ranged around the circular table, one man kept his back to Dez, the figure small, a bit hunched.

"He asked you if you liked the heads," another voice said. This speaker was a younger man, full of piercings, his dun-colored hair messily cut, like he'd done the job while inebriated. All the men gripped heavy pewter steins. Not the sort of receptacles Dez would have expected.

Of course, he wouldn't have expected a Baptist church to be decorated in severed heads either. He supposed it could be an allusion to the fate of John the Baptist, but that would be giving Keaton too much credit.

"You a mute?" a third member of the table asked. This one had shoulder-length red hair, pale blue eyes, and a nose so pockmarked it appeared he'd been mauled by wild dogs.

At least the men's hostility took Dez's mind off the heads. He didn't feel good – he figured he'd be queasy for several more minutes – but he no longer worried he'd faint.

Ignoring the jeering patrons, he navigated his way between a pair of tables. He drew even with them as the ginger man with the dog-chewed nose pushed up from his chair and barred his way.

Okay, Dez thought. *You knew you'd have to prove yourself one way or the other. It might as well be with this asshole.*

But only if you have to, a voice cautioned. At the sound of the voice, Dez suppressed a smile. His dad. A smartass, but a smartass with a heart. Man, Dez missed him.

"Something funny?" Gattis snapped.

"Just thinking of someone," Dez answered without heat.

"Is that right?" the red-haired man asked, his breath puffing over Dez's face. It smelled of bourbon and death. The man apparently didn't spend much time on dental hygiene. "Well, we always enjoy a good story."

"It passes the time," Gattis explained.

"Pull up a chair," the one with the piercings said and stifled a burp.

Dez inspected their faces. The problem was you never knew. The red-haired man could be a werewolf. Gattis could be a cannibal. He certainly appeared burly enough to be a flesh-eater. Even the young man with the piercings and the butchered hair might be a monster.

You could never be sure. Not until it was too late.

"Thanks for the offer," Dez said, "but I'm heading to the bar."

Gattis shrugged, leaned back on two chair legs. "No need for that. Iris's servers will be by any minute. They know I like my beer full."

Dez tried not to show his surprise. He hadn't tasted beer in two years, had assumed it was as extinct as Major League Baseball and the Internet.

Gattis seemed to catch his train of thought. "Keaton brews his own. Or rather Hernandez does."

"Hernandez?"

"One of Keaton's guys," the red-haired man said. "Hernandez grows his own hops. Was a real aficionado before the Shift."

Dez grunted. It was the first time he'd heard the extinction of mankind referred to as the Shift. He supposed it was as apt a description as any. If, that was, you considered the deaths of nearly seven billion people a shift.

"Sit," the red-haired man said, gesturing toward an open chair. It wasn't a request.

Dez made to sidestep the man, but he stepped along with Dez, his pale blue eyes widening. "Hey now, we've been nice. No reason to make enemies when we can be friends."

A corner of Dez's mouth rose. "You want to be my friend?"

The man's face split in an icy grin. "Why else would we invite you into our crew?"

"Simple camaraderie," Gattis said.

The red-haired man spread his arms. "See?"

"I get the crossbow," the one with the piercings said.

The red-haired man grinned and Gattis chuckled softly.

"Let him pass," a voice said.

Dez looked askance at the speaker. It was the man with his back to Dez, the hunched, scrawny figure seated opposite Gattis. This man's hair was trimmed in a style Dez associated with medieval monks, minus the bald tonsure. Furthering the monastic appearance was the black cloak draped over the man's shoulders.

Gattis frowned at the man in the cloak. The red-haired man did too, something uncertain, even fearful creeping into his pockmarked face.

When no one spoke, the figure in the cloak half-turned in his chair, looked up at the red-haired man, and said, "Let him pass."

It was a woman, Dez realized. His first reaction was surprise. You didn't encounter nearly the same ratio of women now as you did before. The Bastards from Baltimore had seen to that. Just one of many flaws in their hideous plan. You didn't have to be a genius to see that men had been at the root of most of humankind's problems before the Four Winds. Now men had even more power, and look at how fucked up the world was.

However, Dez mused as he studied the woman now, there *were* still women, but if they were free and respected, it meant they possessed some special power. The majority of vampires were women. Some of the most ferocious cannibals Dez had encountered had been women.

So what could this woman do? Plenty, Dez guessed, judging from the aura of solemnity the men around her exuded.

Dez studied her upturned face, was surprised by the unblemished youthfulness there. The woman was likely thirty, but she looked like she'd never suffered hardship of any kind, had spent the past two years of hell cloistered away in study and prayer. The woman's eyes were intelligent, a coffee-hued brown. There was a vitality there that Dez found unsettling.

Evidently, the red-haired man found staring at the cloaked woman difficult too. The red-haired man smiled in the way of all lackeys. "Come on, Erica. This fella's armed to the gills. You think Keaton's gonna like him strutting around here like some prince?"

"Lefebvre let him through," Erica answered.

A look of disdain rippled through the red-haired man's features. "Lefebvre is just the doorman. He's—"

Unaccountably, the red-haired man stopped speaking and took a backward step, his pale eyes flitting downward. Dez followed his wide-eyed gaze but saw only the chair he'd been occupying before confronting Dez. Now, however, the red-haired man was gaping at it like it was a viper poised to strike.

What's this? Dez wondered.

"Hey," Gattis said, his tone conciliatory. "Let's just drink, all right?"

The red-haired man looked like he might bolt in the other direction. But his shoulders twitched in what might have been a shrug. "Sure. Hell, I was only being helpful."

With that, he moved out of Dez's way. He retreated a couple paces from the table rather than returning to his chair, a decision Dez judged strange. Whoever or whatever the woman in the cloak was, the others at the table were scared silly by her.

As were, he now realized, the rest of the patrons in the vicinity of the table. A score of men had taken notice of the scene, and their expressions ranged from sleepy curiosity to a rabid, glitter-eyed hunger.

Dez passed the red-haired man. He sensed the eyes of the patrons marking his passage. Dez kept his gaze fixed on the bar at the far end of the room as he moved.

Something hard thumped him painfully on the back. Cold liquid splashed his neck and soaked his collar.

Dez kept the pain out of his face by gritting his teeth. Someone had nailed him with a beer stein.

He spun around and scanned the faces for the perpetrator, but the dozens of eyes only watched him sleepily. For a wild moment, Dez found himself on the verge of shouting, *Who did it? I want the culprit to reveal himself now!*

But that would be worse than foolish. It would be suicide. If he showed how rattled he was, they'd rend him to pieces. Who knew what manner of creatures lurked behind those impassive faces?

Dez was turning back toward the bar when a voice called, "Did you enjoy your drink?"

Dez paused. The voice had been bland, uninflected.

Don't show anything, he reminded himself. *You show your anger, whoever pelted you with that stein wins.*

At the thought of the object that had knocked him in the ribs, Dez looked down and discovered it lying on its side. There was a moose featured in bas relief, its antlers raised to a full moon, as if it had turned feral like so many of its human counterparts. Dez's eyes crawled up to the nearest table, where he discovered a man with a thick, brushy mustache staring at him. The guy's features were arranged in gloating defiance.

Dez was sure the man was the guilty party, but how could he prove it? Ask him, he supposed, but then what? If the man said yes, he'd done it, Dez would be cornered. Either fight the man or turn the other cheek and be branded a coward.

Fleetingly, Dez was reminded of what he'd heard about prisons: You either proved your toughness by killing another man, or you became a victim. Several times, Dez had found this stark axiom to be true in the new world.

But what if the mustachioed man had hidden powers? Would a Latent frequent a place like this? Dez doubted it. If there still existed Latents like himself, they were almost certainly in hiding the way he and Susan had been before Keaton had shown up.

Dez's lips thinned.

Keaton. The memory of the man's soulless face reminded him why he was here. He needed to locate Keaton; he was the key to finding Susan. If Dez were killed now, he'd never learn what happened to her. He couldn't save her. If she were still alive.

She is, he thought. *She is alive.*

He forced himself to move toward the bar.

"I did it," someone called, and this time Dez knew who was speaking.

Knew it even before he turned and saw the woman in the cloak rising from her chair and facing him across an expanse of thirty feet.

Erica folded her hands before her, smiled charmingly. "It's a pleasure to know there are still Latents in the world."

Now everyone in the bar was watching.

There was no use protesting. Nor of speaking at all. If Dez claimed to have powers, Erica would demand he display them. If he confessed to having none, the others would slaughter him for sport. He could see the violence in their eyes, sensed it baking out of their stinking clothes.

Erica lowered her head and pressed the tip of a forefinger to her bottom lip. "You're probably wondering how my aim is so accurate. After all, you were a good distance from me." She looked up at Dez with mock inquisitiveness.

"I know how you did it," Dez said.

Good, he thought. His voice had been tight, low, but it had been steady. Not a scared voice. Not a plea.

"Care to educate the denizens of the Four Winds?" Erica said, smile broadening. She flourished a hand to encompass the vast room. "Perhaps you, like Lefebvre, are gifted with the ability to penetrate the psyche?"

"It's nice of you to take an interest in my gifts," Dez said.

Erica's smile wavered a little. Rustles of movement stirred here and there, all eyes shifting to Erica.

Erica's eyes narrowed, then her self-possession returned. "Perhaps you'd like to see the trick repeated." The finger touched her lips again as she observed her surroundings. She tapped her lips. "Ah, yes. That will do."

A heavy square table halfway between Erica and Dez began to vibrate, then to rattle. The men seated there shoved away, their faces blank with surprise. Several snatched up their drinks, but a couple opted to forsake them.

The table came to rest. A febrile energy charged the air.

Then, as Dez watched in horrorstruck silence, the large wooden table, which must have weighed two hundred pounds, began to rise from the floor.

CHAPTER THIRTEEN

The Wurlitzer and the Brawl

Despite the fact that they had no doubt seen tricks like this before, a kind of awed sigh breathed through the room. Dez was keyed up, frightened, yet there was a childlike part of him that found this feat amazing.

The heavy table floated six feet off the ground.

Dez dared not take his eyes off the huge object, but he sensed Erica beyond it, hands raised, fingers splayed like some storybook conjuror. Was that necessary? he wondered. Would the table levitate without the sorcerer's pose, or was this merely for effect?

The table scarcely tremored as it floated toward the center of the room, where it hung suspended fifteen feet off the ground. Every eye in the bar remained riveted on it, the men in the main seating area peering up at it like it was some wooden god. The patrons from the upper galleries watched with expressions as fixed as the severed heads on the wall.

In the silence, Dez fancied he could hear the beat of his heart. He glanced at Erica, who watched him with satisfaction.

"Yes," Erica said. "It is rather quiet in here, isn't it?"

What did you used to be? Dez had time to wonder. *You talk like a pretentious literature professor. Or were you manager of a video game store who treated your customers with disdain?*

"Wainwright," Erica called. "Please grace us with a song."

An older man in overalls and a green John Deere cap scuttered over to a Wurlitzer jukebox Dez hadn't noticed. As the table levitated, its legs only wobbling slightly, Wainwright fumbled coins out of his pocket. Several of them clattered on the hardwood floor. He finally managed to feed a quarter into the Wurlitzer, which glowed an infernal red. His palsied finger hovered over the buttons as he scanned the selections. Then, evidently finding what he was after, he punched buttons, stood back from the jukebox, and waited.

The honkytonk strains of Hank Williams Jr. filled the barroom. Dez knew the number well. Hank Jr. sang, "*All my rowdy friends have settled down....*"

The table hung in the air between him and Erica.

Erica grinned and exhaled. "Ahh...that's nicer. I sometimes find it difficult to think in the silence. When I write, I must have music playing."

Dez sensed the men to his left scooting away. The patrons to his right didn't move.

Erica studied his face, seemingly untaxed by the effort of levitating the table. "Decorum suggests you ask me what I write. After all, you're the invader here, not us."

Dez watched the floating table. "I just came for a drink."

The response elicited a smattering of laughter from the crowd. Erica's expression tightened. She strafed the room with her eyes, and while some patrons quieted on the instant, others showed no apprehension. That made sense, Dez reflected. Some would regard a telekinetic with fear; others would be unimpressed by such displays. Maybe they possessed greater powers. Maybe they had simply witnessed too many horrors to be frightened any longer.

Dez almost didn't move swiftly enough.

The only warning he had was a curl of Erica's lip. The next moment the table was hurtling toward him. Erica's control of the ponderous object was so thorough that the table flipped as it accelerated, making escape more difficult. Dez surged dove sideways, flattening his limbs and head as well as he could. The edge of the table still dealt him a glancing blow in the middle of the back, knocking out his wind and planting him on the grimy carpeted floor.

He shot a look over his shoulder to watch the table's progress. As the soaring table rocketed along, several of the men at another table displayed the sense to leap out of the way. One man, however, did not. In the split second before the tables collided, Dez saw the man's brushy mustache, his slack expression. Poor bastard, he'd been observing the confrontation as though taking in a particularly engrossing movie, but as the flying table crashed into the one at which Brushy Mustache was sitting, his expression morphed from starey-eyed surprise to extreme pain. The flying table struck Brushy Mustache in the torso. Then the whole lot – tables, beer steins, and the too-slow man – went toppling over in an unruly heap.

Patrons scattered, chairs were overturned, but very few voices sounded. What was there to say? Another man was knocked down by the tumbling tables, but he made out better than Brushy Mustache, who lay groaning several feet from where he'd started. Though the flying table – now at rest on its side – obscured Dez's view, he could see well enough the way the man's boots twitched. He knew Brushy Mustache wouldn't be getting up again.

Dez pushed onto his elbows and regarded Erica.

Who beamed at him. "My friends would like you to relinquish your belongings," she said. She gestured toward the red-haired man who'd confronted Dez earlier. "If you give Crosby your weapons, I might consider mitigating your sentence."

Sure you will, Dez thought. He imagined cowering before Erica and begging her for mercy.

Never.

Nor could he run. A fleeting vision of himself scurrying from one hiding place to the next strobed through his mind, Erica making sport of him, roaring laughter and toying with him as objects careened at Dez from every corner of the bar.

Only one option, and not much of one at that.

The red-haired man, Crosby, reclined in his chair and propped his shitkickers on the table. "I've always wanted a crossbow like that. Yours is slicker than the one the nappy dude had in that old TV show."

Erica tilted her head at Dez. "You see? My friend has a need, and you can satisfy it. Now unless you want to—"

Dez was already on his feet and sprinting at Erica. Surprise registered on the telekinetic's face – clearly she didn't possess Lefebvre's ability to read minds – and then, with Dez fifteen feet away and closing fast, Erica backpedaled and swept a hand at Dez.

An object blurred toward him. He assumed it was another beer stein, but what did it matter? The object nailed him in the elbow. Torrid heat blasted up his arm, the impact point like a core of ice. He was almost upon Erica when the woman finally moved, bolting to Dez's left and leaping upon a table. Dez had groped clumsily for her as she passed, but he'd missed Erica by a good two feet. Dez was skidding to a halt and preparing to go after Erica when something hard slammed him in the lower back. He grunted, half-spun, and saw that Gattis had driven a chairback into him, the grinning man paying no mind to the concept of a fair fight. Crosby, too, was coming around the table after him.

Three against one, at the least. Maybe the others at Erica's table would fly at Dez too. Maybe the whole bar would converge on him.

But Dez didn't think so. Erica's posse didn't play fair, but they seemed an isolated unit. Solidarity didn't exist in the Four Winds. The menagerie of severed heads attested to that, as did the emotionless response to Brushy Mustache's likely fatal collision with the table. These men cared no more about Erica and her clan than they cared about Dez, so long as they stayed alive. And, perhaps, were provided with diverting entertainment.

A sharp intake of breath behind Dez made him whirl. The sound had emanated from the men sitting at the table upon which Erica stood. Their surprise stemmed from a pair of heavy beer glasses shooting from their table straight at Dez. He sidestepped in time for one heavy glass to rocket by his head, but the second crashed into his already-smarting elbow, which he'd flung up to ward off the blow. The glass didn't shatter in a million pieces, which might have saved Dez's eyesight, but because it was so thick, it hardly gave upon impact and fractured instead into jagged shards that twirled like piñata candy. Damn, it hurt.

Gritting his teeth, Dez surged toward Erica.

And was promptly tripped. He landed hard, heard cackling laughter, and saw the man with two-dozen piercings pointing down at him. Dez had forgotten all about the pierced man, but now he made a mental note to deal with him after Erica.

Dez realized he'd taken his eyes off Erica. He flopped onto his back as another glass exploded where, a moment before, his head had been.

In the next instant a knife darted at him. Dez was crowded against a man's legs, so he rolled in the only direction he could, into the shattered glass that had nearly brained him. It crunched under his shoulders, but his leather coat kept it from puncturing his flesh. The knife skittered harmlessly away.

A flash of movement from the table of assholes drew his attention. He craned his head toward them in time to be doused with lukewarm beer. Dez coughed, blinked, and discovered Gattis was the one who'd flung the liquid into his face. The red-haired Crosby was coming around the table toward him, and Dez knew this was it. Erica would be unleashing another assault, Gattis and Crosby looked demented enough to commit murder, and the guffawing moron with the piercings was too unhinged to predict.

Four against one.

Dez pushed to his feet, was pelted in the back with another blunt object. Dez reached for his Ruger, but Crosby, his pale blue eyes agleam, was upon him. The man carried a drooping, leathery object Dez recognized as an old-fashioned policeman's blackjack, the kind of thing meant to knock a man out. But the glitter in Crosby's eyes told him it wasn't subduing Dez he had in mind. No, if Crosby nailed him with the business end of that blackjack, Dez's head would soon be added to the wall of sightless trophies, some messy epitaph – LATENT or TRUCK STEALER – carved into his forehead.

Dez brought up a boot and slammed it into Crosby's chest. Crosby, who'd evidently expected Dez to offer no resistance, didn't even swing the blackjack, but just went flying backward and disappeared between a pair of seated patrons.

Dez ducked, not because he had eyes in the back of his head, but because Erica's onslaughts occurred with metronomic regularity. He suspected Erica had never been forced into varying her methods, her victims so awed by her telekinesis that deception hadn't been necessary.

The chair Erica had sent at Dez went skidding over the table and plowed into a sullen-faced man with a salt-and-pepper crew cut. The man's expression never changed. He merely let out a soft grunt and toppled over backward.

Gattis stalked around the table, his long, tangled beard dripping. What had drenched Gattis, Dez had no idea. What *was* clear, though, was the weapon Gattis carried.

A medieval mace was the first thing Dez thought of, though that wasn't quite right. Clearly an object of Gattis's own fashioning, the implement was two feet long, the arm red, the handle black. At its terminus was what Dez first mistook for a Styrofoam ball, one of those crafty things you'd find near the pipe cleaners and fabric. Then he saw the stitching and realized it was a softball with shards of colored glass embedded in it.

Dez had been so transfixed by the bizarre instrument that he forgot about Erica. Something crashed into his temple, knocking him sideways. Molten liquid poured down the side of his face.

Aw hell, he thought. *This isn't good.*

He slithered to the floor, and he didn't even see the next object before it thudded into his shoulder. He was on all fours, blood dripping down his cheek. He watched the crimson droplets patter the carpet between his fingers. A shadow spread over him, and he knew it was Gattis, the son of a bitch no doubt preparing to finish him with his lethal mace. In desperation, Dez clambered forward and took refuge beneath the table. Behind him the mace whistled down and bashed the floor. Dez saw, beyond Gattis's legs, Erica's hand flick in his direction, a glittering object arrowing at Dez. The butter knife chunked into the side of Dez's calf. The dull blade penetrated no more than a half-inch, but the pain was more than enough to rouse him from his stupor.

Gattis swung the mace under the table at him, and this time a shard of glass sliced Dez's bottom lip. Dez scrambled back, and without thinking, he unsheathed the machete. Gattis crouched like a baseball catcher, reared back for another strike, and Dez whipped out with the machete. The bottom of Gattis's beard sheared off, the blade scything through his black t-shirt and the flesh of his upper chest.

The cut was not deep, but it was enough to startle the man, to make him glance down uncomprehendingly at his torso, the blood seeping through the slit in his shirt.

Someone pawed at Dez's shoulder. He shot a look that way and saw the idiot with the piercings trying to get at him. Dez kicked out at the young man, his boot striking him in the throat. With a phlegmy cry, the young man twisted sideways and clutched at his neck.

Erica was hollering at Gattis to move, but Gattis remained squatting where he was and gazing with disbelief at the blood he'd palmed off his black t-shirt. Dez could see Erica sidestepping into position, no longer eclipsed by Gattis, and then a flickering kerosene lamp was spinning at Dez. It was projected with such force that Dez hardly had time to react before it struck him in the rotator cuff and exploded against the base of the table.

Heat puffed around him, and knowing the shoulder of his coat was drenched with kerosene, Dez dove forward, away from the spreading fire. Gattis was pushing to his feet, retreating. Dez slammed into him, channeling his days of youth football, driving Gattis backward, straight at Erica, who rolled onto the tabletop, perched on her knees, and projected another beer stein at Dez.

Dez wrenched Gattis sideways and the stein pounded him in the back. Gattis groaned. With his free hand, Dez thrust Gattis aside. With the machete clutched in his right hand, Dez bent, got his shoulder beneath the table on which Erica stood, and before Erica could fire another missile at him, Dez lifted the tabletop, upended it, and heard Erica thump to the floor on the other side.

The men who'd been sitting there had scooted away from the table, which now lay on its side at a seventy-degree angle. Erica was behind it, and Dez knew the next decision he made would determine life or death. It was right or left, attack Erica from one flank or the other. If he guessed wrong, he'd run straight into a knife or another hurtling kerosene lamp. If he guessed correctly….

Shouting voices from behind him, the hungry crackle of flames. Dez blocked all that out – it didn't matter – when a figure lurched toward him from the direction of the fire.

Dez half-turned and saw the sullen-faced man with the salt-and-pepper hair staggering toward him. The man's eyes were slitted, his cheeks a livid purple. He looped a wild haymaker at Dez, who ducked, pumped a left-handed jab into the man's belly. The guy jackknifed, and Dez shoved him toward the overturned table. Dez damned near lost hold of the machete, but he regained his grip, was about to dart around the table, when he saw the sullen-faced man explode in flames.

Erica had mistaken the man for Dez.

The man was wrapped in fire before the fragments of kerosene lamp had settled on the carpet. The man squealed, windmilled his arms, and Erica made a frantic supplicating sound. The kerosene ignited as it spread, the man staggering toward Erica. Dez heard Erica gasp, no doubt alarmed at the fiery man's approach.

Dez grasped the table's edge and leaped. As he sprang over the tabletop, he swung his feet around at Erica's face. Erica saw him at the last moment but wasn't quick enough. Dez's right boot smashed Erica in the mouth. She was knocked backward into a mountainous patron in a black jacket. The man shoved Erica away and roared, "*Watch it, motherfucker!*"

Erica landed on her back and stared wild-eyed at Black Jacket. The guy seated with Black Jacket said something placating, but Black Jacket, his face wide and scarred and malicious, strode forward, reared back, and punted Erica in the side. The kick was so bestial it lifted Erica six inches off the floor.

From Dez's left, Crosby reappeared and shouted something at Black Jacket, and it was exactly as Dez had suspected: There was no loyalty in the Four Winds. A man might have a conditional ally or two, but the notion of solidarity here was laughable.

Black Jacket hollered in pain, and Dez glanced at him in time to see fragments of white shrapnel – a broken dinner plate – clattering over tables and chairs behind the massive man. So Erica hadn't been in as much pain as she'd let on. In fact....

Dez saw Erica grin, extend her arm toward the kerosene lamp on the neighboring table.

Dez reached back, flipped the crossbow into position, and loaded a bolt.

Fired.

Erica jerked her hand at the bolt, which veered off course just enough to miss her by a couple inches.

Dammit! Dez thought.

Behind him the flames seethed like demons.

Erica grinned. The kerosene lamp leapt from the table.

It zoomed toward Dez's face. Dez lunged forward, corkscrewed sideways to elude the lamp. Its base caught him in the cheek, but it didn't ignite like a firebomb, instead went into an ungainly twirl, and Dez continued his spin and landed on Erica. The two of them ended face-to-face on the floor. One of Erica's arms was wedged against her body, Dez's knee trapping it. Distantly, Dez heard the lamp crash and a chorus of voices shouting. Shadows and light danced all around them, the patrons scrambling to put out the fires. Dez ignored it all, focused on his adversary.

Erica raised her free hand to summon another object, but Dez seized her wrist, wrenched it with all his strength. Erica whimpered. Dez raised the machete. Shock registered in the telekinetic's face.

"Tell me you won't come after me," Dez said in a low voice.

Erica's face clouded. "Huh?"

Dez squeezed Erica's wrist harder. Erica's trapped arm squirmed under Dez's knee, but Dez had the woman firmly contained.

Dez spoke in an undertone so Erica might preserve a vestige of dignity. "If you let me alone, I'll let you live."

Erica stared at Dez as if seeing him for the first time. Then her mouth twisted. "Liar."

"Goddamn you, I'm trying to—"

Dez nearly didn't realize it in time. Erica's eyes flitted to the machete in Dez's right hand. The machete vibrated, and before Dez could register what was happening, the wicked blade was at his own throat, pressing the skin.

"*Stop…it*," Dez growled.

But Erica was positively leering now, all her considerable mental energy bent on severing Dez's jugular. Another inch or so…Dez could feel the blade beginning to part his flesh…he struggled against it.…

With a sick moan, Dez hammered down with the machete. The blade buried itself in the soft cup of the telekinetic's throat, burrowing deep enough to unleash a torrent of blood.

The din in the bar immediately died, the only sounds the hustling of men trying to put out the fires and the honkytonk strains of Hank Williams Jr.

Beneath him Erica gagged, shuddered, her eyes fluttering white. Blood bubbled in the corners of her mouth and slopped over her lips. Dez pushed away from the dying woman and closed his eyes, all the energy draining from him. Erica coughed a syrupy gout of blood, then went boneless, the only movement the rush of blood from her throat wound.

Unable to bear the sight of it, Dez unseated the machete, stood and wiped it on his pant leg. The jukebox lapsed into silence, the shouting voices of the men now subdued murmurs.

Dez was aware of every eye in the Four Winds upon him. He stood panting and staring down at Erica's lifeless form. He listed a little on his feet, not from his injuries, but from the surfeit of adrenaline. He heard a voice.

He turned and discovered a pretty woman with an emotionless face. His eyes lowered to what hung at her side.

His crossbow.

CHAPTER FOURTEEN
Iris

Dez eyed the woman gripping his crossbow. "I need that back," he said.

She didn't respond, didn't even blink. Behind her were a dozen or so patrons rushing around, beating the flames with burlap blankets, chucking handfuls of sand from gallon buckets. Evidently, this sort of fire happened regularly.

Motion from the woman's left, Crosby striding toward Dez with a nasty-looking Bowie knife clutched at his side.

The waitress didn't look at Crosby, but said in a level voice, "You touch him, Keaton will decorate the wall with you."

Crosby froze in mid-step, his pale eyes widening. He opened his mouth, shut it again.

Black Jacket made a move toward Crosby. Dez noted the messy spiderweb of blood crisscrossing the huge man's forehead. "Your dead friend smashed a plate over my face." Black Jacket jabbed a finger at Crosby. "I'm gonna take it out on you motherfuckers."

"You're going to sit down," the woman said in the same even tone. She nodded toward Crosby. "So are you."

Gattis rounded on the woman, the glass-speckled mace clutched dangling from one big hand. "This sonofabitch started it." He poked the mace at Dez. "He's the one should be punished."

Dez eyed the woman. Her royal-blue shirt was sleeveless and tight with a zipper at the throat, her eyes a notch bluer than her shirt. Her black hair was cut fairly short, but unlike most people's hair these days, hers actually appeared to have been washed in the past month. It was glossy, parted in the middle so that it framed her face, which was fixed in a grim stare. Her pants were khaki and form-fitting, her boots faded leather. She was likely no more than five-five, but in the boots she was as tall as many of the men.

Gattis moved into her sightline and tugged on his mangy beard, which looked even worse now that it had been lopped off at a diagonal. "Look what he did to me, Iris. I guarantee you Keaton will have his head for this."

"Or his dick," Crosby said, his bullying grin reappearing.

"Hernandez," Iris said. "Badler. Get these men to their seats."

A pair of hulking figures left off the firefighting – the flames had been contained, but several spots in the carpet were still smoldering and breathing sour wisps of smoke – and approached Gattis and Crosby. Dez felt his pulse quicken. He had met one of the hulking figures before, but there was no time to linger on that now.

Gattis, who was no dwarf himself, looked childlike next to the pair of gorillas. The one named Hernandez crowded into Crosby, who looked like all the fight had gone out of him. Hernandez was maybe six-and-a-half feet tall and possessed a leonine mane of curly black hair. Though he wore a long-sleeve gray shirt and blue jeans, his muscles bulged visibly.

Gattis made a face. "Goddammit, Iris, I tell you it's not fair. No way Keaton would put up with this."

"He'll be back soon enough," the one named Badler said. He was slightly shorter than Hernandez but appeared even beefier, his shoulders broader than a doorway. "You behave now, you might live through the night."

That was enough to persuade Gattis. He ambled toward his table and paused, his face expressionless. "It's still smoking. So's my chair."

"Then find another chair," Iris said.

Crosby joined Gattis and the young man with the piercings at their scorched table.

Hernandez jerked a thumb at Black Jacket. "You sit too. You've caused enough shit for one night."

Black Jacket didn't move. He gave up an inch or so to Hernandez, but he was nearly as wide. "I could do your job, you know."

Hernandez squared up to Black Jacket, but it was Iris who spoke. "Drop it, both of you."

The two behemoths watched each other a moment longer. Then, Black Jacket turned, grinning, and went back to his table.

Most of the patrons seemed to relax, but some in the general vicinity continued to watch Iris uneasily.

Dez said, "I'll take the crossbow."

Iris's expression didn't change. "Your guns."

Dez smiled. "I'm attached to them."

Hernandez took a step toward him, and Dez rested a hand on the butt of the Ruger.

From his right, Badler said, "You don't wanna do that, friend."

Dez stared at Badler, the noxious memories of their first encounter bubbling to the surface. Badler's face broke into a grin. "*Hey...I remember you.*"

Dez's grip tightened on the Ruger's grip.

"Look around," Iris said. "You see any guns?"

"You mean ones that are visible, or the ones they're concealing?"

Iris stared back at him. He had the impression she was communicating something subtle, but that might have been imagination.

Hernandez and Badler drew nearer.

"When do I get them back?" Dez asked.

"You won't if you're dead," Badler said.

Dez noticed the gleam in the muscular man's eyes, wondered what manner of creature he was. There were several possibilities, but his size and robust health suggested Badler was a cannibal.

Hernandez loomed over him and snapped his fingers. "Gun."

Dez gazed up into the man's stygian eyes. Was Hernandez a cannibal too? It made sense. Keaton peddled human beings to the highest bidder. The two most obvious consumers were vampires and cannibals. Wouldn't it be natural for Keaton to employ those sorts of creatures, the kind who wouldn't scruple about his flesh trade?

No point fighting it, he decided. Besting a telekinetic was one thing; defeating a pair of brawny cannibals was another. Besides, it might have been dumb luck that had allowed Dez to thwart Erica.

As Dez unholstered the Ruger, he kept his eyes on Hernandez. He noticed Hernandez didn't even look at the gun when Dez handed it over. Instead he stared straight into Dez's eyes with a gaze that exhibited not a trace of human emotion. If Dez didn't know better, he'd guess the giant man was from outer space.

"Any others?" Hernandez asked.

Dez thought of the Smith & Wesson on his ankle. His jeans weren't especially loose. Did the gun show?

"That's all," he said.

"I don't frisk people," Hernandez said. "If I find out you've got another one hidden, I'll gut you."

"Then let's hope you don't find one."

Hernandez's indifferent expression slipped, but only for a moment. With a smirk, he turned and lumbered toward the bar. Badler watched Dez a bit longer, radiating a disquieting mixture of hostility and lunacy. He brought to mind someone who in the old world would have gotten his kicks by torturing cats.

Or humiliating people.

Eyes glittering, Badler followed Hernandez.

Iris was still watching him.

Dez nodded at the crossbow. "That's not a gun."

Did he detect the merest hint of a smile? "You're not getting it back."

"Where's Keaton?" he asked.

She scowled, her eyes darting to the table where Crosby and the rest sat watching. "You need to learn caution."

"I guess I don't have a choice, with you stealing all my weapons."

Her eyes flicked to his ankle, back to his face. Did she know?

"I'll fix you a drink," she said. "Then you have to go."

He followed her toward the bar. "What if I like it here?"

She glanced at him over her shoulder. "Then you're dumber than I thought."

CHAPTER FIFTEEN

Joe, Smile, and the Boy

"What kind of monster are you?" he asked.

She looked up from the whiskey bottle she'd just replaced. "Are you remotely familiar with the concept of subtlety?"

"Don't see the point of it," he said. "Not anymore."

She sighed and moved down the bar to a pair of black men, both of whom wore the sort of leather hats he associated with the Australian outback. As Iris walked away Dez couldn't help notice how perfectly the khaki pants adhered to her buttocks. The flare-up of lust took him aback. What libido he'd experienced lately had been spurred by fantasies of Susan. To have a beautiful woman before him was an unexpected novelty.

Iris spoke to the men, and Dez studied her silhouette. Her small nose was slightly upturned at the tip, her cheekbones curved with good humor. An endearing overbite. And her hair....

What did it say about her that she took so much pride in her appearance? Was it vanity or something else? A desire to cling to what dignity remained? A refusal to acquiesce to this barbaric world?

Who the hell knew? Dez knocked back a slug of whiskey.

Nearly choked. He covered his face and coughed until the fire in his throat subsided.

One of the black men, his face smiling and his hat tipped roguishly to one side, remarked, "Should have made his a virgin, Iris."

"Still would've been too strong for him," the other black man said.

Dez shivered, wiped his mouth. Without looking up, he said, "You two find that a man's alcohol tolerance is an accurate measure of his virility?"

They were silent a moment, perhaps reassessing him. He noticed how still Iris had become.

The second man, the one who wore his hat like a normal person, said, "Did you feel manly when you gigged that mover in the throat?"

It took Dez a half-second to connect the word 'mover' with Erica's telekinesis. "Do I look like I enjoyed it?"

The smiling man said, "You don't seem remorseful."

Dez stared down at his drink. "What I felt is none of your business."

The smiling man let loose with a delighted laugh. "You hear him, Joe? He's channeling Clint Eastwood."

"The Man With No Name," Joe said and nodded. "Love that guy."

The other man lowered his voice to a cartoonish growl. "'When you hang a man, you better look at him.'"

Joe scowled. "'Dyin' ain't much of a livin' boy.'"

Dez looked up, saw Iris suppressing a grin. He regarded the men. "You two wear those hats before the bombs?"

The other one shrugged, unabashed. "Wasn't socially acceptable back then."

Joe sipped his drink. "One of the benefits of an apocalypse."

The smiling one nodded. "You wear what you want to wear."

Iris held a glass of some clear liquid but didn't drink it. She said, "Did you go around in that leather jacket before the bombs?"

Dez shrugged. "I was more of a cargo shorts and t-shirt kind of guy."

"See?" the smiling one said. "Now you can let your leather freak fly."

Joe nodded. "Getting in touch with his inner Village People."

"To hell with you both," Dez said, but he grinned as he took another sip of whiskey, this one much less ambitious. He only shivered a little as the fire trickled down his esophagus.

Joe and his friend thanked Iris and moved toward the stairs. Watching them go, Dez said, "What's their story?"

Iris turned her back to him, began filling beer steins from a tap. "You mean, what kind of powers do they have?"

"Don't tell me if you don't feel like it."

"It's nice to know I have your blessing."

He studied her back, her shoulders. Good muscle tone. That sort of vitality suggested she was one of the most dangerous types of monsters. Or, like Dez, she worked like crazy to keep in shape.

But to survive in a hellhole like this…to remain in Keaton's employ rather than becoming one of his human trading chips….

"How long have you worked for him?" Dez asked.

Iris paused in mid-pour. "Are you asking if I'm his concubine?"

"You're awfully cynical."

She commenced filling the steins. "You wondered though."

"What your story is, sure."

Iris arranged four steins on a tray and placed them on the bar. She repeated the process, this time with three steins. "Wainwright," she called. "Terhune."

On the instant a pair of figures hustled to the bar. Wainwright's John Deere cap was slightly askew, maybe from fighting the fire. Like Wainwright, Terhune was an emaciated man of advancing years.

"Where to?" Terhune asked, choosing the tray with three steins.

She pointed toward a table under the balcony to Dez's right. Wainwright asked where his tray was going, and she motioned to the balcony on the other side of the bar. Both men bore their loads away wordlessly.

"Keaton put you in charge?" Dez asked.

"He trusts me."

"Should he?"

"A year," she said. She retrieved her drink, which looked like water.

"You've been in charge for a year or you've been working for him for a year?"

She took a swig of the clear liquid. "Who are you looking for?"

A tingle of electricity began at the base of his spine. Might she know what happened to Susan?

He tilted his head noncommittally. "Maybe I just wanted in from the cold."

She eyed him over her glass. "You've never been here before. You're a Latent—"

"You don't know that."

"You're a Latent," she repeated. "You come here and risk death at the hands of that mover."

"You guys have cute names for every monster?"

Her eyes did a quick scan of the bar. "Nothing cute about any of these guys."

"About that," Dez said. "Why are there so many men and only a few women?" He hesitated. "I know…after the world changed, the women who didn't change were—"

"Some of them changed."

"Then where are they?"

"Look around," she said. "If you were a woman, would you spend your time in this shithole?"

It was a fair point, he decided. Even up here, away from the congregated patrons, the odor of unwashed bodies was overpowering.

She tilted her head. "I think you are looking for someone."

Dez didn't answer. Drank his whiskey.

Into the silence, Iris said, "What was her name?"

Dez cleared his throat. "Why do you say 'was'?"

She favored him with a grim smile. "Is Keaton the type to keep people safe?"

"Why do you work for him? You enjoy being part of the process?"

Iris's smile vanished. She set about wiping the bar, but Dez could see her mind wasn't on it.

Good, he thought. It was heartening to see someone else distraught for once.

He sipped his whiskey, which didn't go down any easier. He imagined there were cleaning products less potent. He sensed someone staring at him. He took his time about it, sipped again, fought off the fit of shivering that threatened to overtake him. He swiveled his head slightly and there they were, the two black men, Joe and the smiling one, whoever he was. They occupied the corner table of the balcony, Joe reclining on two chair legs, the smiling one's chair flat but his boots propped on the table. Joe was watching Dez, but the other one's hat brim was pulled low over his eyes, as if he'd decided to sleep at the table, all that grinning having worn him out.

"They're okay," Iris said.

"What does that mean?" Dez answered, not breaking eye contact with Joe. "They kill you but don't eat you?"

"No need to make enemies."

"You're right. Especially when you've got my weapons under your bar."

She seemed barely to have heard. She polished the smooth, cherry-dark wood.

He sat forward. "What does Keaton do with them?"

Her arm slowed, the colorless dishrag in her hand an inch or two from his fingers. She wasn't looking at him, but he realized her breath was coming in heaves, as though she'd just hiked through the hilly forest outside and come in for a rest.

Something clicked in his mind. "He took someone from you."

"*Keep your voice down,*" she hissed.

It took all his will not to recoil from those widened cobalt eyes, those bared animal teeth.

Iris stared him down a long moment; then she braced her hands on the bar for support, the dishrag lying between them like an accusation.

Dez shook his head. "I didn't mean to—"

"Shut up a second," she muttered.

He shut up.

She tipped her glass, drained what was left. Dez watched her. He noted the line of her inner arm, the bicep slim but defined. She wiped her mouth and watched him steadily. "What do you know about Keaton?"

"Just what I've heard."

She waited.

"He kidnaps people, sells them," Dez said.

"Sells them to who?"

His throat went dry. "Cannibals."

An infinitesimal nod. "Who else?"

"Vampires?" he guessed.

"Yes."

He tried not to show how sick he felt. He'd heard Keaton bartered with the vampires, but held out hope it wasn't true. Cannibals were grueling to fight, but they were easy to find. They set up farms, barbed-wire compounds where they created a twisted parody of agriculture. Only instead of raising cattle and crops, they farmed people.

Depraved. Insidious.

But predictable.

Vampires on the other hand....

"There are others," she said.

He came back from where he'd been, licked his sandpaper lips. "Others?"

She gave him a pained smile. "The highest bidders are the satyrs."

His stomach did a hard lurch. "I thought they were too far away."

"Sixty miles. But once or twice Keaton sent men that way with a specialized load."

God, he thought, *that's a hideous phrase.*

He looked up at Iris. "You think Susan was part of the..." He couldn't say the words, swallowed. "...group?"

"I have no clue who that is," Iris said.

He sensed a softening in her expression. Or maybe he was just feeling sorry for himself and wanted a friend.

Dez scooted the drink aside. "Keaton's going to tell me where Susan is."

Iris crossed her arms. "You're going to make him, are you?"

"That or kill him."

"Have another drink," she said.

"I don't need another—"

"Hell's bells, are you that stupid?"

"Huh?"

She rolled her eyes, spoke through her teeth. "If you think Joe Kidd and Smile Summers are the only two watching you, you're simpler than I thought. Just look in the mirror, would you?"

When Dez did, something funny happened. If Iris hadn't just said it, he would have dismissed it as paranoia. But the moment his gaze fixed on the long strip of reflective glass, half the eyes in the bar flicked away from him. Several patrons seemed overly interested in the walls, and truly, how many people stared at walls when there were so many other fascinating sights to behold? Like severed heads. Like Iris.

"She's right, you know," a voice said.

Dez jerked his head around and discovered a boy who couldn't be over twenty staring at him with wide eyes.

"I don't remember inviting you to join me," Dez said.

"You're the first one to beat a mover," the boy said. He had light brown hair and eyes so bright and trusting you'd never guess he lived in a world where nearly the entire population had been murdered.

Dez eyed him warily. "What are you?"

The boy shrugged guilelessly. "I'm me."

"How many 'movers' have you seen?"

"Three since it started," the boy said. He nodded toward where the showdown had taken place. "Erica was the best, though. She could do anything."

"Except live," Dez said.

The boy smiled at Iris. "I still can't believe he did it. I never thought anyone would stand up to Erica."

"I've got orders to fill," she said and set about retrieving glasses from under the bar.

"I say something wrong?" Dez asked.

"If I stop, everyone's gonna wonder why." Her mouth twisted bitterly as she poured amber liquid into the glasses. "'Iris has a thing for the newcomer. Iris wants to share her bed with him.'" She shook her head. "Assholes."

Dez couldn't help imagining what she'd look like in bed. Her hair on the pillow like raven cornsilk.

He cleared his throat, tried to sound like a regular customer. "I'll have another whiskey."

She snorted. "You do and I'll have to carry you out of here. You'll have water."

"I can't handle my liquor either," the boy remarked.

Dez lifted an eyebrow at him. He'd forgotten the boy was there. He noticed something about him he hadn't before. There was an unsightly scar on the back of his right hand – a brand, Dez realized with a pang of unease. The mark was a capital letter *E* done in an old-fashioned, ornate script. It spanned nearly his whole hand.

If the boy noticed Dez's scrutiny, he didn't let on. "Before the bombs, I never drank," he explained. "Afterward, I tried, but—"

"You better go back to your table before somebody takes it," Dez said.

The boy blanched. Got up. "Don't have a table. I usually sort of stand around."

With that, he moved away. Iris placed the glass of water before Dez.

"Thanks," he said. He took a sip, and though it was slightly eggy, it was a hell of a lot better than the liquid fire he'd just choked down.

"Keaton lives a few miles away," she murmured. "You go around back and find the southern trail. Follow it all the way to the house."

For a time he didn't know what to say, so he drank his water. Too quickly. He hadn't realized how parched he was, but now that he'd drunk of the well water, he grasped just how dehydrated he'd grown after driving all day in the werewolf's truck. He wanted to ask for a refill, but figured he'd better be polite. She'd been nicer to him than anyone since Susan. Of course, nearly everyone he'd met since Susan had tried to murder him, so his standards weren't very high.

"You going?" she asked after she'd sent Wainwright and Terhune away with more loaded trays.

"You want me to kill Keaton," Dez said.

Her eyes did a quick loop around the bar.

"Why?" he asked.

She polished the bar some more, her movements jerky. "You know why."

"Who was it he took from you?"

"You've got no chance if you try to do it here," she muttered. A small shrug. "You've got no chance of getting him at home either, but it's a hair less hopeless. There you've got the possibility of surprising him, however small the possibility is."

Dez remembered Keaton's jocular laugh, his massive shoulders. His thugs, most of them as enormous as Hernandez and Badler.

"Is he there?" Dez asked. "At the house?"

"Not at the moment," she said. "He's doing business."

"And after?"

She flung the rag onto a shelf. "He'll come here, or he'll go home. Or they'll be gone for a couple more nights."

"But you don't think so."

"You better get moving."

He stood. His legs felt pierced with a hundred sewing needles, his back creaky. His bruises and cuts began a chorus of howling heat, remnants of his encounter with Erica the Psychotic Telekinetic.

He rubbed his bruised jaw. He was in no condition to fight.

He said, "I'm going to need my things."

She bent, came up with the crossbow, which she placed on the counter. She knelt again, and this time she clutched his Ruger. Rather than handing it over, she inspected it. There was something sensuous about the way her fingers glided over its lusterless gray surface. Dez felt another stirring of desire.

She said, "You should find looser jeans."

He couldn't prevent his mouth falling open. My God, could she actually see—

"The gun on your ankle," she said, eyes teasing. "It shows when you walk. Looser pants will cover it better."

Cheeks burning, Dez collected his weapons and left the bar.

CHAPTER SIXTEEN
A Word with Smile

Outside, he inhaled deeply, permitted himself a moment to savor the clean air. Uncanny, really, how much difference two years had made. Without man's constant pollution, without his incessantly dirty factories and his glut of ozone-killing vehicles, the air tasted better, soothing your nostrils rather than irritating them. The water was cleaner, as well. Dez despised the Bastards from Baltimore, but there was no question they'd accomplished several of their goals. Another decade or so of this unindustrialized world, and the world would become a paradise.

Too bad he'd likely be dead by then.

Stop, he told himself. *It's time to find Keaton.*

Time to find Susan.

He was about to mount the southern path when a voice called out, "Clint Eastwood!"

Dez froze, halfway between the converted church and the forest, and thought, Crosby. Or the bald one. Or the pierced imbecile with the butchered hair.

Dez turned and saw a shadow drifting toward him along the backside of the Four Winds Bar. It wasn't Lefebvre, the figure was too muscled. It wasn't Hernandez or Badler either, way too short. It wasn't quite pitch black out here, but what light there was didn't aid him.

Dez laid a hand on the Ruger.

"Gonna draw on me, gunslinger?"

This time Dez recognized the voice.

The figure sauntered nearer, the hat tipped sideways, the head held high.

The black man, the one Iris called Smile, stopped twenty feet from where Dez stood, only one eye and part of his mouth showing in the moonlight.

"What kind of a name is Smile anyway?" Dez asked.

"Could ask you the same thing," Smile answered. "Sorta reminds me of *I Love Lucy*." He spoke in a mock announcer's voice. "'Desi Arnez as Ricky Ricardo'."

Dez permitted himself a grin. "That's not where it's from."

Smile nodded over his shoulder. "Joe told me not to bother. That you could live or die and it wasn't any of our business."

"Sentimental guy."

Smile nodded. "Real teddy bear." He tilted his head, the hat going level for once. "Aren't you gonna ask?"

"Ask what?"

Smile chuckled, but there was a hardness to it. "You know, the same asshole question Joe and I get everywhere we go."

Dez said, "Not everyone's like that."

"No? You'd be surprised." Smile began walking in a slow, tight circle, as though working out some issue on a moonlit stroll. "First time we entered the Four Winds, that group with the mover and Dildine—"

"Dildine?"

Smile gestured toward his hat. "The bald one? One whose beard you chopped in half?"

"Ah."

"Erica and Dildine and Crosby and Wyzinski – he's the one with all that metal in his face – they start in on us, calling us butt pirates and dirt farmers."

"Dirt farmers?" Dez said. "Never heard that one."

"Me either. Joe wanted to kill them, but I talked him down."

"Must've been difficult."

"Sure it was. But not for the reason you think."

Dez was quiet.

Smile paused his circular stroll. "See, Joe has this theory. He believes that prejudices never went away at all. In the last century, I mean. He thinks people just got better at hiding it. Racism, homophobia, the rest. Now the prejudices are free to reign, like the monsters."

The word made Dez tighten. He glanced left and right, fought an urge to look over his shoulder. But what if Smile was just distracting him while Joe stole around behind to knock him down, steal his crossbow and his guns? Maybe even sell him to the cannibals. No reason to believe the pair didn't work for Keaton. They hung out at his bar, after all. Maybe everyone was part of the operation.

"Chill, Dez," Smile said. "I'm not out here to trick you. Truth is, I hate the fucking cold. My balls are shrunk to the size of BBs."

"Why you here then? To give me a sermon on bigotry?"

Smile chuckled louder this time, more genuinely. "I'm not preaching. That's Weeks's job. No, I'm just telling you to make sure he kills you."

"You with Keaton?"

Smile favored him with a look that was at once incredulous and world-weary. "Shit. Maybe Joe was right."

Dez nodded toward the path. "I'm going."

"To Keaton's house?"

Dez nodded.

"Once it starts," Smile said, "you can't accept anything other than death."

Dez lifted his chin. "I can beat him."

Smile hooked his thumbs in his pockets, shook his head. "In a movie maybe. Not in this world. Unless you get out now, he's gonna kill you. Him or one of his men." He sobered. "You need to make sure that's all he does."

"You think he'll sell me like he sold my…."

Smile's eyebrows rose. "Your what? Your girlfriend? Wife? Your pet rabbit?"

"He won't get close enough to do that."

"He'll get what he wants. It's what I'm trying to tell you."

"I need to go."

"Uh-huh," Smile said. "You gotta go, get the drop on Keaton. Surprise him at his house."

"You have a better idea, share it."

Smile took his hat off, brushed the brim. His hair was very short, like he'd just trimmed it. "There's a basement under the church."

"Thanks. I'll know where to hide in case of a tornado."

Smile went on inspecting his hat. "There's something under there."

"Keaton's man cave? Big screen TV?"

"You don't want to have it happen to you."

Dez thought of the penises on the sign, the heads on the wall. "Keaton keeps bodies down there?"

"One body," Smile answered. "A live one. The Hound."

"Keaton has a dog?"

Smile ceased his ministrations and fingered the brim of his hat. "That's not...." He sighed, refitted his hat, the angle not so jaunty this time. "What I'm telling you is don't let him take you alive."

Dez saw Smile was about to turn away. He said, "You care about that."

Smile looked at him. "What, you?"

Dez waited.

Smile's doleful expression made him look older, his skin slightly bluish in the glow of the sickle moon. "There was a time when I cared about everything and everybody."

"Not anymore, huh?"

Smile was a long time in answering. At length, he said, "Some things stay with you. Even if you wish they'd go away."

With that he turned and strolled toward the Four Winds.

His chest hollow, Dez moved in the opposite direction.

Dez was a couple paces from the woods when he stopped, called back, "What the hell kind of a name is Smile?"

"Real name's Michael."

Dez paused. "We friends now?"

"Friends, hell," Michael Summers said. "I'm only telling you because you'll be dead soon anyway."

"Thanks a lot."

"Bye-bye, Desi," Michael said, walking away. "Say hey to Lucy for me."

CHAPTER SEVENTEEN
Family

Iris said a few miles, and while that was probably true, to Dez it seemed much farther than that. Maybe it was because he'd driven all day. Maybe it was because he was bone-tired. Maybe it was due to the fact that Michael Summers had scared the bejesus out of him, and he no longer felt so compelled to have it out with Keaton tonight.

Whatever the case, when he finally reached the house, he reckoned it was going on ten o'clock. There was no light at all in the sky now save the fingernail-clipping moon and a smattering of puny stars whose glow brought to mind the old world's technology, those miniscule TV and DVD lights that remained on no matter the hour. The thought depressed him, but he preferred the emptiness to the crawling fear that had dogged him through the forest.

Cannibals were everywhere, and if rumors were true, vampire country was uncomfortably close to here. But this, he realized, was more than *risking* trouble – this was courting it. He was venturing onto Keaton's property, the man

(*What is he?*)

everyone within hundreds of miles feared.

(*A vampire?*)

Dez didn't have a choice though. What else was there? Scraping out an existence alone, scurrying from one hiding place to another in the post-dawn hours. Praying it was too early for the day prowlers to spot him but too light for the vampires to be roving.

(*Or a cannibal?*)

No, he thought, hunkering on the verge of the yard, the forest ringing the property so dense it strangled all but the starlight directly over the house.

(*Maybe Keaton's something else, something you haven't seen yet*)

Dez pushed to his feet. There was no point in speculating about Bill Keaton's DNA. Whatever he was, he was a sadistic bastard who'd taken an innocent woman and sold her to monsters.

Keaton was also bold and clever, Dez had to admit as he shook out his arms, attempting to invigorate his body for whatever it was about to endure. Keaton's trade would make him the most hated man in the region. How many families had been torn asunder by Keaton's incursions? How many wives given to the satyrs? How many babies had the cannibals purchased? And what of his vampire clients? Did they select Keaton's largest victims? Did people who weighed more contain more blood?

No matter. All that mattered was this chance. The house was dark, which meant Keaton was either sleeping or away. The house was big enough, he supposed, but prosaic. Just a single-story ranch with brick and wood siding.

Go in, he told himself. *No reason to wait.*

But he waited. He couldn't shake the familiarity of Keaton's house. There was one very much like it in Eastern Indiana, where his son would be attending school if he were still alive.

Maybe he is *alive.*

The gush of images overtook him. To ride it out he directed his unseeing gaze upward, waited for the choking wet throb in his throat to subside. As usually occurred, images of Will were accompanied by ones of Carly, his ex-wife, and though it awoke a pulsing red knot in his chest, it at least took his mind off Will, off his boy, and the ruinous undertow of sorrow. Hatred, he'd found, was an effective substitute for guilt. He often wondered, even if he lived to be a hundred, if he would ever forgive Carly for what she'd done to him. Somehow, he doubted it.

His hands had knotted into fists.

But the guilt had risen around him like floodwater, submerging him in its merciless embrace. *You should have fought harder for him.*

I did, dammit! I did. I spent damned near everything I had—

You should have spent it all.

She lied about me! She paid people off because her family could afford it. They never liked me, but they owned half the town. What was I supposed to do?

Anything to stop them from taking your boy away.

Dez was moaning, shaking his head, but the voices would not be silenced.

You might have saved him.

No.

You might have kept him safe from whatever monster that got to him.

No no no no.

Instead you left that fuckwad of a stepfather in charge. Oh, and Carly too. Let's not forget the raging bitch who ruined your life.

I can't think about this.

You have to think about this. Because it's happening to Susan, or has already happened.

Please.

You started east too late, and by the time you met up with that sad sack of a stepfather, the only thing left was the news that Will and Carly were dead.

No!

You failed again, Dez. You'll always fail the ones you love.

Dez choked back a sob. To outrun the voices, he got moving. If he could go back and change everything, he would. It just so happened that he couldn't. He'd fucked up at every turn, and as a result, everything he loved got taken from him. His son, his father. And now Susan.

Dez fought off the thickness in his throat, turned and spat into Keaton's grass. He looked up and saw how the house was overrun with junipers and yews, its entire bottom half a bloated green snarl.

As Dez approached, his calf began to throb. He remembered being skewered by the butter knife, the delirious battle with Erica and her cronies. On one hand, it was good to have gotten the brawl out of the way. At least the denizens of the Four Winds Bar knew he wouldn't shy away from a confrontation. But it had taken something out of him. As had his flight from Jim the Werewolf. As had his run-in with Gentry and the cannibals.

Dez stopped, hands on his hips. God, he longed for a little peace.

Is Susan at peace?

He set his jaw, strode forward, drew out the Ruger. He was almost positive Keaton wasn't home. The house was as dark as a tomb.

Wait for him to show up?

Maybe, though it was too damned cold to wait for him outside. Dez could see his breath, the temperature dipping below forty.

Inside then. He shuffled forward, gun drawn, and tested the screen door. Locked, but it rattled. He took his backpack off and fished out a flashlight. He kept two, but he chose the larger one, the black Maglite of an impractical weight but a brilliant beam.

He clicked on the light, shone it on the crack between the door and the jamb. A sliver of steel was all that kept the door closed, likely a hooked bar that housed in an eyelet. One kick would rip it out of the jamb.

You better hope Keaton's not home.

"Fuck it," Dez muttered. He raised a foot, kicked.

The door banged open, the noise like a thunderclap in the October night. Dez listened, sweating despite the cold, but there was no answering sound within.

He moved inside, hoping the next lock would be as flimsy. He reached a sliding glass door, tried it.

It slid easily.

Dez shook his head in disbelief. Keaton wasn't bold. He was *brazen.* He was so secure in his superiority that he didn't even bother to lock his doors, not beyond that silly hook Dez had kicked through.

Dez stiffened. A hook like that, it would have to have been engaged from the *inside.*

He swallowed, his arms gathering into gooseflesh.

Dez raised the Ruger, edged through the open sliding door. His fingers trembled.

Take it easy, he told himself. *Keaton just left through the front door, not the back.*

Or he's booby-trapped this place and welcomes intruders.

This seemed likely, and in keeping with the kind of man Keaton was. Lure someone in, let him think he was getting the drop on him.

Then incapacitate the man, let him wail until Keaton arrived to finish him off. Or torture him.

Shut up, Dez told himself.

He was standing in a kitchen. Nice, but not ritzy. Maybe Keaton had a modest streak after all. Or maybe he had several houses, and this was a lesser one.

Dez quickened his steps, made his way through a short hallway into a family room.

Empty.

He'd crammed the heavy Maglite in a hip pocket, and now he longed to pull it out, strafe the floor for tripwires.

Dez moved into the living room. Beyond that, he could see the foyer and the front door. Dez had enjoyed real estate back in the old world, and crazily, he found himself calculating how much this house would fetch. If Keaton owned the acreage around it, and if the basement were finished, it wouldn't be a stretch to price it at four hundred grand.

Would you focus?

Dez shook his head, clearing it. He supposed it was a bad time to play real estate appraiser.

He strode toward the hallway, where he assumed the bedrooms would be.

He came to a closed door. The sight of it kindled in him a crawling dread. Why would Keaton close doors?

Because he's inside, sleeping?

Shit. Dez gripped the Ruger, the handle sweaty and slick. He'd have made a horrible prowler.

He pushed out a tremulous breath, regarded the polished nickel doorknob. He turned it and thrust it open.

Empty.

But tidy. A guest bedroom? The bed was made, the furnishings orderly, but the room had a disused, unaired quality that filled him with desolation. How many people were left in the world now? How many millions of rooms that would never be slept in again?

No time to be philosophical, his practical side reminded. *Move your ass.*

Dez did and closed the door behind him. He came to a door cattycornered from the closed one, only this door was open. If appearances were accurate, it was inhabited by a young woman.

Dez clicked on the flashlight and swept it around the room. Posters of pop stars, strings of jewelry, a shelf of gymnastics trophies.

The bed unmade.

Did someone still live here?

Jesus Christ, did Keaton have a daughter?

The notion that Bill Keaton, baron of the Northern Indiana flesh trade, might have a family had never occurred to Dez. And though this room proved nothing – Keaton could have left it this way after his daughter was killed or turned – he couldn't shake the feeling it was currently lived in.

Well, not *currently*, he amended. No one was in here now.

So get out before someone returns!

Don't be stupid, he told himself. The whole damned point was to find Keaton, force him to give up Susan's whereabouts. To kill Keaton if possible.

What about Keaton's family?

You don't know he has a family!

Dez passed a hand through his hair, struggled to regain his equilibrium. He'd come here, he realized, with the goal of burning down Keaton's house if he couldn't find the man, but if Keaton had a family, that would make Dez no better than Keaton.

Dez plunged on and encountered another open door at the end of the hallway. He went inside, saw this was the master suite, and just as Dez suspected, it was nice.

More importantly, it didn't look like the home of a bachelor. Though the bedclothes were a trifle rumpled, the bed was made, and the rest of the room was nicely decorated. His flashlight beam picked out ivory curtains, framed silhouettes of children.

Two children.

Dez continued his scan of the room. He shone the light through a doorway across the room, made out a vanity mirror. The master bath. The Maglite picked out another door on the right side of the room, probably a walk-in closet.

You're wasting your time, Dez thought. *He isn't here. You need to come up with another plan.*

He'd turned and was about to make his way back down the hallway when he stopped and regarded a door across the hall from the master suite.

The door was closed. A second guest room?

Dumbass, he thought. *No one has two guest rooms.*

But there *were* two children.

A chill breeze misting over him, Dez opened the door.

The room had been destroyed.

The mattress had been gored, its chalky innards spilled on the floor. A small desk had been reduced to splinters, the chair legless and chucked in a corner. The wallpaper hung in torn skeins, the sheetrock beneath harrowed by what could only have been giant fingernails.

Dread clutching him by the throat, the thought came to Dez again:

What is Keaton?

He wanted to move on, wanted to leave this disaster zone behind, but his eyes, unheeding, lit on several objects. A Chicago Cubs lamp. An overturned RC car. An Xbox trailing a severed cord.

Dez had been so absorbed by the sight of destruction that he hadn't, until now, noticed the footsteps approaching.

He pivoted, swung the Ruger and the Maglite beam, and pointed both into the faces of a woman and a teenaged girl.

CHAPTER EIGHTEEN

Remembering Emma Russell

The woman, who was maybe forty, squinted into the light and drew her daughter closer. "Don't shoot!"

Dez shifted the beam to the girl. She was blond, willowy, and appeared to be fifteen or sixteen.

"Don't look at her," the mother said, squeezing her daughter tighter.

Dez aimed the beam at the mother's midsection so as not to blind her.

"Who are you?" the mother demanded.

Dez had no idea how to respond. *The guy who came to kill your husband?*

The woman screwed up her eyes, no doubt attempting to make out Dez's face above the glare, and when she spoke again, her voice was threatening. "You know whose house this is?"

Dez swallowed. "Where is he?"

"He'll have you killed."

That's more like it, he thought. Now he could imagine this woman being married to Keaton. She'd be attractive if not for the haughty callousness in her face.

Dez felt a wintry smile forming. "He out abducting more children?"

Her lips drew a hard line. "Get out of my house."

"Doesn't matter at all, does it?" Dez asked. "As long as it's someone else's daughter."

Keaton's wife glowered at him. "You're *filthy*. Get out of here."

Dez ignored her, glanced at the daughter. Smooth cheeks, blond hair framing her face. Eyes wide with fear. None of the haughtiness of her mother. None of the suspicion.

It was uncanny, he realized now, how much the young woman resembled one of his former students. Emma Russell, her name had been. A gifted writer. But more importantly, a genuinely good-hearted kid.

Had she been murdered when the monsters took over? Or had she become one of them?

Keaton's daughter was staring at him. Yes, she looked very much like Emma Russell.

"Keep away from the Four Winds," Dez said and started forward.

Keaton's wife sucked in a breath, huddled with her daughter against the wall to give Dez room to pass.

"Don't touch us!" Keaton's wife hissed when Dez drew even with them.

But he kept going, said, "Keep your daughter away from that bar."

To Dez's back, Keaton's wife demanded, "Why would I take her there? It's a disgusting place."

Dez clicked off the Maglite and regarded her over his shoulder. "At least we agree on something."

"Get the hell out of my house!" she screamed.

Dez holstered his Ruger. "If you see your husband—"

"He'll have you *disemboweled* for breaking in."

"—tell him there's someone waiting for him at the bar."

Her face broke into a hateful smile. "No one tells Bill anything. Bill does the deciding."

Dez appraised her. "Sometimes I think the surviving Latents are worse than the rest."

She grinned viciously. "Your head will be on the wall."

"I ran into one yesterday a lot like you," Dez said. "He was a Judas cow, led innocent people to their deaths."

"I'll laugh while he tortures you," she said, spittle flying from her lips.

The daughter only stared at Dez, wide-eyed.

"I suspect you're not as hands-on," Dez said to the mother. "You don't go out and endanger yourself. Maybe you handle the finances…."

She raised her chin primly. "I'm not part of the business."

"Sure as hell benefit from it, though, don't you? You can move about freely, everyone so scared of Keaton they leave you alone."

Mania glinted in her eyes. "They're right to be scared."

"But what kind of message are you sending your daughter?"

"What are you—"

"That it's okay to profit from murder?"

Her mouth fell open. "How...*dare* you...."

"There've always been people like you," Dez said, teeth bared. "The tyrants, they're depraved, of course. But there are also the hangers-on who sit around and enjoy the fruits of the depravity."

The daughter had begun to cry. No callous veneer there. Maybe there was still hope for her.

"You're a monster!" Keaton's wife shrieked.

Dez looked at the daughter. "Monster. You hear your mom?"

"Get out!" Keaton's wife screamed, fists shaking. "Get out of my house!"

But Dez was already making his way through the living room. He stepped a little faster once he turned the corner – Keaton's wife was just the type to shoot someone in the back, and he had no doubt she had a firearm close by – and soon he was stepping through the screen door and hurrying across the yard toward the forest.

CHAPTER NINETEEN
The Owner of the Establishment

When Dez returned to the Four Winds, he sensed an alteration as soon as he stepped through the back door.

The entryway branched off in three directions. To the left was the main barroom, which only two years earlier had been used for church services. Straight ahead was a long corridor that appeared to lead to a series of smaller rooms, likely of the kind that were used for Bible studies and church potlucks in the old world.

To the right were stairs descending into darkness.

Peering into the murk, Dez recalled what Michael Summers had said:

There's something under there. The Hound.

Dez shivered. Just what the hell was Michael talking about? Did Keaton keep a rabid dog in the basement? Cujo on steroids?

Before he could freak himself out, Dez entered the Four Winds.

The sensation of furtive gazes tracking his movements was stronger this time, but Dez shrugged it off, glanced behind the bar and discovered Iris, her back to the main room, her hands pouring drinks.

He resumed his place at the bar, said to Iris's back, "He wasn't home."

"That's because he's coming here."

Dez tightened. "How do you know that?"

"His men are here. The ones who do his scouting."

Scouting. Jesus.

Dez scanned the crowd. "Which ones are they?"

"Does it matter?" she asked, and to Dez she sounded tired.

"If I know who they are, I can—"

"Badler and Hernandez are Keaton's men, too. Did you forget that?"

Though her back was to him, Dez realized she was staring at him in the long strip of mirror.

Iris went on. "Don't you know that everyone in here is either employed by Keaton or so scared of him they'll do whatever he says?"

"Keaton's the only one I need to see."

Iris turned, grinned at him incredulously. "Why do you act like you're in control here? You don't even have powers."

Dez regarded her levelly. "I've stayed alive so far."

"Please tell me you didn't do anything to his house."

It seemed an inopportune time to mention his encounter with Mrs. Keaton. "The house is fine," he said.

Iris blew out a relieved breath.

Dez asked, "Who did Keaton take from you?"

Iris glanced down the length of the bar, as if considering fleeing. Then, in a voice that was almost inaudible, she said, "My daughter."

Dez felt like he'd been slugged in the gut. He thought of Will, his dead son.

His voice a croak, he asked, "How old is she?"

"She'd be five by now. If she's still…." Iris stared down at the burnished wood. "I didn't think Keaton recognized me when I showed up to ask for a job. I thought I could insinuate myself into his business, find out where he'd taken Cassidy. But within a few hours…he knew…."

"Lefebvre," Dez guessed.

She nodded. She wiped her nose roughly, scowled, obviously grappling with her emotions. She was good at it, Dez reflected. Had plenty of practice.

"Once Keaton found out who I was, it was easy for him to keep me in line. Tease me now and then about rewarding my loyalty. Or punishing me for screwing up."

"Using your daughter?"

"He never makes it clear whether she's alive or dead, and he never says what direction they took her."

"You've been here a year?" he asked.

"A year of my daughter's life."

Dez frowned. "That means she was—"

"Only two when the bombs came. And my husband was still alive."

Dez tried not to let his surprise show. It shouldn't have shocked him; Iris was a beautiful woman. But somehow he couldn't imagine her with a husband.

He knew the question was potentially devastating, but he asked it anyway. "Was Cassidy your only child?"

Iris laughed mirthlessly. "Patrick and I'd only been married a few months when I got pregnant. We didn't have much time to have another kid."

Dez kept his eyes averted. "Do you believe she's still alive?"

"I have to."

"And Patrick?" he asked.

She turned away, began lifting steins off a drying rack and hanging them on hooks.

He toyed with the idea of bringing up his son

(*Will. His name was Will.*)

but decided against it. What good would it do? Iris would feel no better, and Dez would feel worse.

Too late, he thought. He already felt worse.

Why did you have to marry so badly? a voice demanded. *Why couldn't you have chosen better? That way, you might have been with Will when everything went to hell. You could have protected him.*

Dez clenched his fists, leaned forward on the bar. *If I'd have married someone else, there would never have been a Will. Now stop torturing me and let me enjoy a goddamned drink.*

Shivering a little, Dez made himself as comfortable as he could on the barstool. He considered retrieving a book from his backpack, distracting himself that way, but opted to sit in silence, to risk glances at Iris when he thought it was safe.

Terhune materialized at the bar and relayed a sizeable drink order. Dez was watching Iris fill the glasses and steins when a gust of frigid air from his right told him someone had just entered the building the same way Dez had.

Keaton barged through the doorway.

So unprepared for the man's entrance was Dez that he merely gaped as the powerfully-built boss strode into the Four Winds.

"Where the hell is he?" Keaton growled. "Where's the son of a bitch who broke into my house?"

Dez's barstool was only thirty feet from where Keaton stood. There was no point in drawing it out.

Dez swiveled on the stool and stared at Keaton.

When the broad-shouldered man's gaze fixed on him, Dez remembered everything: Susan's screams, the laughter of Keaton's thugs as they effortlessly knocked Dez aside, Dez's consciousness dimming as the men dragged Susan away. Dez awakening to find himself broken and alone.

"Where is she?" Dez asked, then silently cursed himself. He'd planned on letting Keaton speak first. But now, with every eye in the Four Winds on him, Dez no longer trusted himself to play it cool.

Keaton eyeballed him. Sizing him up. The larger man appeared amused. "'She'?" Keaton asked. He took a couple slow steps toward Dez. "Who is 'she'?"

Dez glanced at Iris, whose face had gone as pale as the ivory dishrag she clutched.

Keaton continued his slow advance, his whiskered mouth split in a malicious grin.

"Your face is familiar," Keaton said. "I remember it because it's sort of pretty." Keaton beamed at the patrons of the Four Winds. "Ain't he pretty, folks?"

A fusillade of assent from the crowd.

Keaton drew closer and Dez was afforded a better view of the man. What he saw only confirmed the assumptions he'd made about Keaton since Susan's abduction. The man lived like a king, compared to the rest of the world. The dusky beard was stitched with white, the smile lines around the man's eyes augmenting Keaton's charm rather than aging him. Keaton had used some sort of product on his hair, the sheen catching the phantasmagorical orange glow of the wall sconces and sharpening the upjutting locks of dark hair, giving them a vaguely horn-like appearance. His attire was an amalgam of conflicting eras and styles. Black jackboots swallowed his blue jean cuffs. Though Dez was sure Keaton had trekked through all sorts of terrain in them, there was nary a scuff on the dully gleaming leather. Probably had his lackeys shine them, Dez thought ruefully. Another benefit of being the boss.

"You're not quite as bewitching as the girly we found in your warren," Keaton said, his attention returning to Dez. "You really oughta be ashamed of yourself, boy. Making such a delectable creature live down there like a mole."

Dez continued to study Keaton, who'd closed the distance to twenty feet. The sports coat was old-fashioned, single-breasted with brown checks. Tweed maybe, like the kind a 1930s gangster would wear for a casual evening out. Beneath the coat was a chocolate-brown vest buttoned to the middle of Keaton's broad chest, above which peeked a beige shirt with an unbuttoned collar. Tufts of black chest hair ended just shy of his muscular throat.

Keaton fingered his checked coat. "You like it? I found it in the home of an old couple who used to live in the Leonard Mason Mansion. Know the one I mean?"

Dez did, but he didn't see the point of telling him. The house wasn't twenty miles from the Four Winds, in a city called Lafayette. Nestled in a historical district, the home was three stories tall, with a square turret protruding from its center. Dez had only driven by the home a couple times, but wasn't at all surprised Keaton had pillaged it.

And staring at the man now, Dez thought he understood him better. He wasn't just a flesh peddler; he was a collector. He'd collected these old-fashioned clothes, perhaps after butchering the elderly couple who'd lived in the Leonard Mason Mansion.

Had he collected Susan too? Was it possible she was still nearby? Stashed away as a concubine?

Dez was on his feet before he knew it.

"You want to know if she mentioned you?" Keaton asked.

Mentioned, Dez thought. *Past tense.*

No!

Keaton grinned. "Boy, you've got it bad, don't you?" He moved closer and stood only eight feet away. At some point, a trio of Keaton's thugs had slunk forward to stand behind their boss, but Dez had been too fixated on Keaton to notice.

"You *do* have it bad," Keaton said in a meditative voice. "I was the same way when I first met Barbara. Lovesick, smitten. I would've licked her toes had she asked me." A laugh. "Come to think of it, I guess I did lick her toes. Always been a foot man, I have."

Keaton's goons chuckled. The goons were not remarkable in any way, save their musculature. It appeared that Keaton had recruited the area farms for the sturdiest young men to form his abduction squad. None of them had made an impression the day they'd kidnapped Susan, but now that Dez was in their company, yes, he was pretty certain these were the same cretins who'd carried out Keaton's orders.

"Your wife is skittish," Dez said. "Your daughter too."

For a millisecond Keaton's smug mask slipped, and Dez saw the rage banked beneath. Then the man recovered.

"Well, good for you. I thought we'd need to beat the hell out of you to get you to admit you were the one who broke into my home. Yank out your fingernails with pliers maybe. But you saved us the trouble."

"You didn't find it," Dez said.

Keaton leaned forward, eyebrows raised. "You're gonna try that old gambit, huh? Gonna tell me you planted a bomb in my house and the only way you'll reveal its whereabouts is if I tell you where I sent your bitch?"

Dez's stomach plummeted, but he kept his expression neutral. It was exactly what he'd planned to tell Keaton.

Keaton chuckled, strode up close to Dez, who tightened but did his best not to betray how frightened he was. "You really that simplistic, boy?" Keaton made a fist, tapped his knuckles on the side of Dez's head. "Got shit for brains?" Keaton stepped toward the crowd, spread his big arms. "You show up to challenge me, and your only plan is to insinuate I better fess up before you blow up my house?" He turned, leveled a forefinger at Dez. "Forgive my political incorrectness, boy, but when I was a kid, we'd have called someone like you mentally retarded."

Behind Keaton, the patrons roared laughter.

"I did rig an explosive," Dez lied. More laughter from the crowd. Dez felt his composure slipping. "And there's something else too."

Keaton raised his eyebrows, nodded. "Oh, I'm sure there is."

"If anything happens to me," Dez said, raising his voice to be heard above the raucous crowd, "someone will come looking."

More laughter, but a few patrons grumbled. Paranoia was ever present in the new world, and threats such as the one Dez had just uttered tended to draw it to the surface like poison.

There was mock-seriousness on Keaton's face. "I see. And what manner of beast is this mysterious individual? Vampire? Werewolf?" His bushy eyebrows rose. "Empusa?"

Dez had no clue what an Empusa was, and the mention of a new creature caught him off-guard. If, that was, such a creature existed. It was entirely possible Keaton was making it up.

"He'll come," Dez said.

"If I don't tell you where your woman is."

"That's right."

More murmurs from the patrons. Beyond Keaton, Dez caught a glimpse of Crosby, Gattis—Dez was too nervous to recall the man's real name—and the pierced simpleton. They looked eager for retribution.

Keaton took out a cigar, lit it. Stepped closer and blew the smoke in Dez's face. He began walking in a slow revolution around Dez, whose eyes watered from the smoke. "You got no special powers, no heavy artillery that I can see. That crossbow of yours looks cool, but it won't do much against my crew." He sucked on his cigar and blew smoke at the ceiling. "You got anger, but that's about it."

Dez didn't answer.

Directly behind Dez, Keaton said, "Admit it. You had no plan. You just hoped it would work out."

Dez said nothing.

Keaton stepped around so Dez could see him. "It's been a night of surprises. You surprising my wife and daughter, you showing up here all by yourself. Hey, that reminds me," he said, glancing at someone over Dez's shoulder.

Iris, he realized.

"Hey, Iris. My spies tell me you've been sweet-talking our new friend here. That about right?"

Dez turned and took in the defiant set of Iris's jaw. She said, "I found out his story, if that's what you mean. Would you rather I not speak to my customers?"

Keaton punched Dez chummily on the chest. "You hear that? 'My customers'. Like she's the one owns the place." He spread his arms in that grand, scornful way of his. "Lady Iris, you're just a barkeep."

When Iris didn't answer, the grin drained from Keaton's face. In a toneless voice, he said, "Maybe you did forget. Maybe you need reminding."

"You're the boss," Iris allowed. "But I don't think I did anything wrong."

Keaton appraised her a long moment. "What about your lapdogs? What'll Wainwright and Terhune say about it?"

Iris shrugged. "Ask them."

Keaton's grin reappeared. "Jeez, Iris. It's too bad I'm a married man. Your feistiness makes my loins boil."

From what Dez had heard, Keaton's marriage didn't prevent him from partaking of other women, but now probably wasn't the time to mention this.

Or maybe he should. Maybe now was *precisely* the time to rankle Keaton, goad him into a mistake.

Like what? his rational side wondered. *You're out of options. You're outnumbered, outgunned, you're—*

Dez froze.

He still had his guns.

He could put a bullet in Keaton's forehead right now, and without their leader, maybe the others would reveal the truth about Susan.

Or maybe Keaton's the only one who knows.

Dez hesitated. His thoughts raced.

No, Keaton wouldn't be the only one who knew. Someone else would. Whether one of the farm boy thugs or another confidante – Lefebvre, Hernandez, Badler, Keaton's wife – it seemed likely that *someone* would know about Susan, and that meant that killing Keaton could increase his chances of saving her.

Dez reached down, drew.

Keaton's face went blank as the muzzle of the Ruger rose. Dez was taking aim and squeezing the trigger when something crashed into his side. The Ruger fired, but the slug went wild – Dez knew that even before Keaton leaped atop him, began raining blows on his face. A weight left him – Badler, he now saw. Christ, the guy tackled like a freight train – and then another set of fists joined Keaton's. The patrons roared in exultation, but the sound was going fuzzy. Dez had a fleeting glimpse of Badler's laughing face, then Keaton unloaded again and Dez's vision winked out.

CHAPTER TWENTY

Firsts

Dez is lying in their nest, spooning with Susan. He knows it's a double standard, but whenever other people engage in romantic behaviors, he gets a little nauseated. Pet names, cuddling, mooning over one another across a candlelit table. When others do it, it gives him the willies.

But secretly, he really digs doing it, at least when the woman is right.

He's always been affectionate, and though he figures his upbringing has something to do with that, he suspects it's mostly just his nature. Some like to be touched, some don't. Dez always has.

His first time, he was ten days shy of seventeen; the girl was a year older and quite a bit more experienced. Dez had no idea what to do and actually unrolled the condom before putting it on. Then, as she watched him with barely restrained laughter, he had to shimmy into the damned thing, the unfurled condom longer than he was, so that it drooped off him like a limp windsock.

He mounted the girl, and after a couple of pumps, he was done.

As mortifying as that first encounter was, he remembered the smell of the girl's hair, some fruity spray that came from a purple can.

The smell nearly made up for the embarrassment.

He'd get better at it as time went on, and that allowed him to enjoy the little pleasures more. By the time he was in college and getting laid on a semi-regular basis, he'd begun to yearn for those moments before and after sex, the nuzzling and the gazing and the caressing and the kissing. Never in a million years would he admit these things to anyone, but they were undeniably true. Sure, he loved sex, pined for it, but aside from the act, he reveled in the subtleties. The accouterments of intimacy. The poetry of that secret sharing.

And though he had plenty of girlfriends in his twenties – including Carly, whom he eventually married – few had moved him the way Susan had. Susan with her sweet closed-lipped smile, Susan with her sleepy-lidded gaze.

Dez knows, at a level deeper than dream, that this is only a memory, this lying with Susan in their nest. But at that deeper level, where he knows something nasty is awaiting him, he refuses to let the vision fade until he must.

Their nest, as Susan calls it, is a hollowed-out bunker likely excavated in the old world by enterprising adolescents. Dez never would have found it if not for the trap door that had been left open, its hinges rusty from exposure. Nestled in the forest, shielded from the elements by a screen of pines, the subterranean space was approximately twelve-by-twelve, and not deep enough for them to stand erect. Dez found that if he covered the hinged door with a thick patina of mud and humus, one could actually walk right over the door without hearing the hollow thump.

The day Dez was dreaming about, he had propped open the door just a smidge so the midafternoon sunlight could spill over their bedding. Over a period of months they'd scrounged enough pillows and blankets and sleeping bags that their nest was as cozy as any proper bed would be, and what made it even better was the knowledge they'd remain safe, even with the door slightly ajar.

You wanted to be captured or killed, you found a house. Dez had seen that scenario play out too many times, folks thinking, *Hey, free house*, and setting up shop there. It must have felt too good to be true, and it was. The problem with monsters was that they were also people, or at least retained enough of their humanity to understand how people reasoned.

People gravitated toward houses.

Many even tried to return to their own homes after fleeing for their lives.

Every time it ended in bloodshed.

So Dez and Susan had survived by living in caves, in derelict stores – not grocery stores or drug stores; the monsters monitored those places – and barns.

But none of those sites had provided the safety or comfort of the nest.

Susan rolls over and gazes into his eyes.

His love for her makes him ache.

Her brown eyes seldom blink. In another woman that would have been creepy, but with Susan it makes him feel valued. *I'm putting my trust in you*, those eyes say, *because I believe in you. You can touch me and kiss me however you like because I know you respect me.*

Susan was with another man — Jason Oates — when Dez first arrived at the colony, and though Dez knows the pair had been intimate, he also suspects they'd never shared a bond approximating the one Dez and Susan share.

Susan gazes into his eyes, and though the sight of that profound gaze makes him doubt his worthiness, today it makes him feel strong. He reaches out, traces her cheekbone with his fingertips. He brushes her bottom lip with his forefinger, feels the moisture there. She watches him, her expression eloquent.

Dez can't help it; he leans forward and kisses her cheek, her temple. He threads his fingers through her brown hair, sweeps it away from her ear. Her hair is oily — bathing is a luxury in the new world — but it retains the scent of her body, and he leans closer, buries his face in it. Inhales. He takes in the aroma of her, luxuriates in it. Kisses her hair, and though he can't see her, he senses her smiling, maybe because she's ticklish.

The March chill is in the air, but down here it's warmer, so he draws the shabby quilt off her shoulder, kisses the bare skin there. He knows his beard has gotten wiry and coarse, so he's careful not to scrape her as he kisses the supple knob of her shoulder, allows a hand to slip over her back. She's wearing a red cotton tank top, and the fabric is soft under the quilt. He massages her back, enjoying the feel of the cotton against her warm flesh. She must like the sensation too because she burrows into him, makes a contented humming sound, an encouragement that sends his languid arousal into a heightened state.

But this isn't about sex, or at least isn't *only* about sex. He's tingling down there, erect and hypersensitive to the press of her thigh, but they have all afternoon, all week, all their lives to savor these moments, and just as he thinks this, the first dissonant chord interrupts their closeness, forms his face into a fleeting scowl.

He kisses her shoulder, delves lower with his fingertips, kneading her lower back, but the shirt is in the way, so he hikes it up, finds honest-to-goodness flesh, and the heat of it enflames him, and though she molds her body into his, welcoming him, another dissonant note sounds, and he realizes what it is this time. His other hand, the one that's not touching Susan, is fixed in place. There's something hard and sharp around his wrist. He glances down at the shadowy space between them, but it's too sludgy to make out. He can feel Susan slipping away from him, can feel their nest darkening, growing colder, and his breathing thins. He longs to make love to Susan, or simply to snuggle with her, but he can't… move…his goddamned…*arm*. He jerks on it, and then the smell floods in, and it's nothing to do with Susan or the nest.

The smells are fetid, vile, the odors of disease and corruption. The shadows are all around him now, the blue-black darkness like a defective lens filter. He realizes he's cold, exposed. He thrusts a hand to his crotch and finds he's at least wearing underwear, but other than that, he's naked. His elbow is pressing down on some hard surface, and what's more, his elbow and forearm are wet. He rocks onto his rear end, stares down at his arm, but can't tell why it's so moist. Or smelly.

"Peed yourself," a voice says.

Dez shoots a look at the man and beholds a bizarre sight. Though it's too dim to see well – the basement? Yes. Now he sees the small rectangular windows near the ceiling, which allow him to discern a figure reclining against the wall, the blue-black light rendering half his face visible, the other half swaddled in darkness. The man is naked. His shoulders are the hairiest Dez has ever seen.

Which could be why the chains around him are so thick and numerous.

Dez pushes the suspicion away.

"Isn't that overkill?" Dez says and winces at the clanging in his skull. He remembers it all in a flash, the confrontation with Keaton, the blow to the back of the head, dealt by God knew whom. Badler? Hernandez? Lefebvre?

Iris?

No, he thinks. Iris would never do that. You either trusted someone or you didn't, and if you trusted no one, you were down to primitive survival.

"Got some blood in your hair but not too much," the man in chains says.

Dez fingers the back of his head gingerly, finds it's as the man says. Some blood where he was struck, the hair messy and crusted.

"What's overkill?" the man asks.

Dez looks at him then, for the first time registering the man's throaty, too-deep voice.

"What's an overkill?" the man persists, a testy note in his voice. Did he think Dez was mocking him?

"The chains," Dez answers. "They've got you shackled like Samson."

The man scowls. "Who's Samson?"

"Why did they wrap you in all those chains when I've only got—" Dez glances down at his limbs. "—one on an arm and one on an ankle?"

The man continues to stare at him, the bafflement plain in his protuberant forehead. "That's what an overkill is?"

Dez takes in the man's shaggy black hair, the matted beard, and wonders how long he's been down here.

"Why are there so many chains on you?" Dez asks.

The man only stares at him.

"Answer me," Dez demands. "Why'd they only use two chains on me?"

For the first time, the man's face registers something other than puzzlement. He grins bitterly.

"Because you're not a werewolf," the man answers.

PART FOUR
THE HOUND
CHAPTER TWENTY-ONE

The Flayer

Dez took in the man's hairy shoulders, the furry mane running in a V down his torso. "You're the Hound?"

"They call me that."

"Why?"

"'Cuz of how they keep me, I guess."

Dez surveyed the hairy frame, the thick manacles and leg cuffs, the chains crisscrossing his limbs. He counted fourteen thick chains before the throb in his skull made him shut his eyes.

"They're gonna kill you," the man said.

"You a clairvoyant too?"

"Don't know about that stuff. But I can hear real good."

That brought Dez's attention back. The man was grinning.

"Heard Keaton and Weeks talking. They don't think I can hear, but I can. Even through the floor."

"Weeks?" The name rang a bell, but Dez couldn't place it.

"The preacher," the man said. "That's what he calls himself."

"What should I call you?"

The man riveted Dez with his glittery eyes. "You don't like Hound?"

"Do you?"

"The fuck do you think?"

"Well?"

"Tom Chaney."

"That your real name?"

"No. Is Dez yours?"

Dez looked away.

"Why'd you come here?" Chaney asked.

Dez shook his head.

"A girl?" Chaney asked. He smiled, but there was something sinister in it. "For you to be so stupid, it's gotta be a girl."

Dez decided he'd underestimated the man's intellect. He supposed most people did. Or maybe Dez was a lesser person than he thought he was.

Chaney's expression changed, a hunger there. "You see Iris?"

"Of course I saw her. She runs the bar."

The black eyes glittered. "What'd she look like?"

"Why you want to know that?" Dez asked, though he already knew.

"She's pretty," Chaney said. "She's the prettiest girl I ever saw."

Dez tilted his head. "How old are you, Tom?"

Something cagey seeped into Chaney's face. "Old enough."

"You enjoy being a werewolf?"

"Don't joke about that."

So he'd killed someone he loved. That was the way with so many monsters. As if becoming one meant performing an evil act, some sinister rite of passage.

"Why'd you say that?" Chaney demanded. But he didn't look angry, looked instead like he was about to cry.

Was crying, Dez realized. Unexpectedly, Dez felt a rush of pity for the man. Tears streamed down Chaney's face, his chest shuddering.

"Hey," Dez said, "I didn't mean to...I shouldn't have brought it up."

"Damn right you shouldn't have!" Chaney bawled. A bubble of snot formed in one nostril, popped.

"Holy Christ!" a voice boomed down the stairs. A broad shadow appeared on the stairwell, followed by a pair of smaller shadows. The first was Keaton. Dez could tell from the voice. But the other two....

Iris? Dez thought hopefully.

"You make me sick sometimes, Hound. All that blubbering," Keaton said. "Haven't you been told how pathetic it is when a man cries? Especially an ugly bastard like yourself?"

Keaton flipped on the lights, which proved to be overhead hanging fluorescents. And though there were only a few of them in the lengthy unfinished space, their glow was brilliant enough to drive dual icepicks into Dez's brain. He shielded his closed eyes with a forearm, but the afterimage still taunted him. The two attending Keaton were Lefebvre and a woman he hadn't seen before. Lefebvre appeared to be studying the wall, but the woman, who was short and freckled and unkempt, was glowering at Dez.

"Can't help it," Chaney moaned. "He was talking about...."

"What you did to your little sister?" Keaton supplied.

Chaney's eyes widened, then he let loose with a wail of soul-shattering anguish.

"Ate her right up," the freckled woman said. Her auburn hair was thick and tufted, and the more Dez looked at her, the younger he judged the woman to be. Little more than a teenager, though there was no innocence there. The freckled woman exuded nothing at all, save meanness.

"I didn't wanna hurt her!" Chaney wailed.

"*Hurt* her?" Keaton asked. He bent at the waist and spoke into Chaney's tear-streaked face. "You ripped her *apart*, Hound. Wasn't a thing left of her but red mush."

"How do you *know* that?" Chaney asked in his croupy voice. He stared at Keaton with superstitious terror.

"You know how I know," Keaton said. He jerked a thumb at the freckled woman. "Bernadette here watched you do it."

Chaney's eyes went wide. "We was alone. Wasn't nobody home with us."

Keaton flapped a hand dismissively. "Never mind, Hound. I've given up trying to explain it to you."

Dez looked questioningly at Lefebvre, who said, "Bernadette has retrocognition. She can tell you anything anyone's ever done, just by staring at him long enough."

Dez glanced at Bernadette, who was still grinning pitilessly down at Chaney. He had heard of such powers before, but he'd never met someone who possessed them. As devolutionary abilities went, retrocognition seemed far down the pecking order. However...

...Dez could imagine how such a skill might come in handy for a man like Keaton. With retrocognition, Keaton could learn about the people he encountered, what sort of things they'd done.

Or, in the case of Tom Chaney, what sins they'd committed.

Bernadette's gaze fell on Dez.

The sensation was not unlike the one he'd experienced with Lefebvre, only it wasn't identical either. Yes, there was a sense of exposure, a feeling of violation, but along with that he felt something deeper and even more troubling. It felt as though powerful hands were reaching through the top of his head, slithering through his neck, into his torso, and then spreading his entire core to rummage through his entrails. Images began to flicker in Dez's brain, some of them pleasing, most of them not.

He saw himself stealing a G.I. Joe figure – the black one named Snake Eyes – from a peer at his childhood daycare center. He watched himself catching a toad with friends, lighting fireworks near the toad, then *under* the toad. Watching the toad blasting into the air, pirouetting, and somehow landing on its feet. But not dying. Watched his younger self stuff a cylindrical firework into the toad's mouth so that the wick poked out like a droopy gray cigarette. Watched his younger self light the wick. Watched him and his friends gasp and laugh as the firework blew the toad's head off.

Jesus Christ. Dez was thrashing his head, the smell of his own piss a fitting reminder of the monstrousness of his sins. He pictured the obliterated toad and thought, *Monster. I was a monster that day.*

Bernadette grinned as she flayed open Dez's secret memories, laid them bare, absorbed them like some especially engrossing movie.

"Ah, boss," Bernadette said delightedly, "you're not gonna believe all the good shit I'm seeing."

"Take your time," Keaton said.

Bernadette did. When Dez did venture to open his eyes, his vision was filled with that nasty freckled face, that malignant gaze. The invisible hands plunged into his guts, mashed them and churned them until another vignette squirmed to the surface, a twelve-year-old Dez plotting to peep a friend's sister after a lake swim, the girl Dez's age, but still, Christ, only twelve. Dez directing her, a tremor in his voice, to change out of her swimsuit in a specific bathroom, one at ground level, one that afforded Dez a glimpse through the window, and he'd only spied her shoulder blades before she spotted Dez's horny, slack face in the mirror, and she shrieked and Dez blundered away, knowing what trouble he was in, knowing what a bad thing he had done.

Bernadette continued to chuckle.

The probing stretched on. Dez had no idea how long, but it seemed interminable. Dez betraying a friend in early high school, making out with the friend's girlfriend. Dez claiming he hadn't touched her and getting away with it, his friend believing Dez a better person than he was.

Dez cheating on his algebra homework then bombing a test, the teacher knowing what he'd done and not needing to say a word, just staring at Dez in silent judgment.

Sophomore year, Dez embellishing the details of his night with Kathleen Levy, offhandedly announcing they'd done far more than they had, which was nothing, not even a kiss. Kathleen finding out, Dez sick and ashamed of himself, as he should have been. As Bernadette kneaded his guts and coaxed his sins to the surface, Dez fancied himself shrinking in the presence of these people. He'd judged Keaton, Lefebvre, and Bernadette, pronounced them monsters, and so they were. But where he'd erred was his perception of himself. Thinking himself superior when he was merely a skulking, duplicitous creature too. Maybe not a monster – that designation implied too much power – but not a human either. At least, not a worthy one.

And now the vicious mental fingers delved deeper, and there was Joey, Dez's little brother, wasting away because of drugs, and here was their father, their lonely, caring father, wasting away from a lack of love and attention. Abandoned by their mother and never seeming to find another who could take her place, his father had ghosted about their house after his boys had grown, a combination of television and tortured rumination his only companions.

Dez had not visited him enough, had not done what he could to fill that emotional void. No, a son was not the same as a wife, but a son could spend time with his father, couldn't he? Could call or text his dad to let him know he wasn't forgotten?

But he had been with his dad the day the world went to hell. Oh yes, he'd been with him then.

The same way he'd been with Joey, with his little brother, at the end. Always at the end. He hadn't been with Joey when Joey was veering off course, back when Joey was a sophomore at Shadeland High and Dez had been a senior. He'd heard his little brother was getting into drugs, but he'd been too busy or too apathetic to say anything about it. Later, when Dez was in college and Joey was a senior at Shadeland High, their father had prevailed upon Dez to intervene, to talk some sense into Joey. Dez had spoken to him all right, but there'd been no love in his tone, no real investment. As if sensing this, Joey had nodded and gone through the motions – *You're right, Dez. I'm sorry. I've really been making stupid choices. I'll do better, I promise* – but both of them had known it was only for show, the two of them playing their parts so they could continue on their chosen paths.

The years flickering by. Dez seeing Joey on holidays and sometimes not even on those. Joey showing up for the baptism of Dez's son, the purpled eye sockets and the shaky hands enough to make Dez wish Joey had stayed away. Dez praying Joey wouldn't ask to hold baby Will. Dez relieved when Joey didn't ask. Joey showing up at Will's third birthday party. Joey looking like a perambulating corpse.

And at the end, Joey in an Indianapolis hospital, the doctors telling Dez and his dad that Joey had suffered a stroke, a motherfucking *stroke*, and Joey only thirty-six years old. *What thirty-six-year-old dies from a stroke?* Dez had wondered then.

The immediate answer: *A thirty-six-year-old who's been doing hard drugs for over two decades. A thirty-six-year-old whose big brother was always too fucking busy to help him.*

In some deep-down region of his brain, Dez knew he was sobbing and he hated himself for doing it in front of these people, but the knowledge was blotted out by a sudden sideways lurch, as though Bernadette had located a new and infinitely more tender clutch of memories, a pulsing scarlet knot of images featuring Dez's son, the boy who'd never see his fifth birthday, the child who meant everything to Dez.

The memories tore through him:

The afternoon Carly, his ex-wife, entered the living room with the Wal-Mart pregnancy stick in her hand. Tears in her eyes, tears in Dez's.

The night her water broke, Dez half-asleep, coming awake when he realized this was it; this was what they'd planned for, a situation for which he now realized he was woefully unprepared.

In the hospital, six in the morning, Carly resting after a grueling thirty-hour labor that ultimately resulted in a C-section. Dez holding Will in his arms, the vinyl recliner sticking to Dez's bare back and Dez not caring. The baby books had told them to go skin-to-skin with the baby as much as possible, and of all the advice he'd absorbed, Dez decided this to be the best, the feel of his newborn son's tiny body against his chest the most fulfilling sensation Dez had ever known.

Months later, Will colicky, Dez and Carly short with each other because neither one was sleeping. Endless hours dancing his son around, singing to him, uttering soothing words that had no effect, the colic as unstoppable as the tides.

But they were together.

They were together.

In the basement of the Four Winds Bar, Dez heard a voice wailing and knew it was his own. Bernadette had located the most painful memories now, Will's first few years, which were Dez's best years, and they ended because his wife cheated on him, and then Will too was gone.

The sorrow and rage and horror and guilt gushed through him, enveloped him, and Dez was sure his mind would shatter under the onslaught. Dez screamed, screamed, and then he was released, Bernadette stumbling back. Dez slouched sideways on the dank concrete, desiring nothing more than to escape himself.

As Bernadette recounted what she'd witnessed in Dez's rancid soul, Keaton nodded appreciatively, his delight over the recitation almost pornographic. Chaney listened too, but seemed neither pleased nor appalled by what he heard. Dez supposed the Hound was too jaded by human behavior to be scandalized any longer. Or was it possible he was merely caged by his own thoughts and damned to repeat his little sister's murder on an endless loop?

Lefebvre looked neither happy nor horrified. The tall man peered at nothing in particular and waited for Bernadette to stop inventorying the sable treasures she'd uncovered in Dez's past.

"I like that Peeping Tom story," Keaton said, grinning down at Dez. "Should have figured you for a perv. No wonder you want that fine piece of ass back."

Dez's pulse quickened. *Susan.*

"Hold on," Bernadette said, a hand up. "I'm getting something else."

Don't, he thought. *Don't unearth that.*

But she did, and he could see himself stumbling into their paltry camp, not *after* Susan was taken, but *while* Susan was being taken, and Keaton's men told him to lay down his weapons, and he had because there seemed no other choice. Susan had a gun to her head, and there were four of Keaton's henchman and only one of Dez.

When Dez discarded his weapons, Badler stepped forward, the biggest by far of the four henchman.

"Tell you what," Badler said to Dez that terrible day, "you take me in a fight, we'll let your girl go. How'd that be?"

Dez had done his best, but it was over in less than a minute; Badler was too huge and too experienced for Dez. The muscular man had mauled him, had sat on his chest, taunting him like a sadistic older brother, laughing in his face as they dragged Susan away.

Badler's knockout punch had been a blessing.

"My God," Bernadette was saying now. "Badler really did a number on you, didn't he? No wonder you buried the memory that deep. A real man would've put up a better fight."

At Keaton's questioning look, Bernadette told him what she knew of Dez's humiliation.

Dez had no response. He gritted his teeth and waited for them to leave.

"You've outdone yourself, Bernadette," Keaton said, nodding. "I'll have Pastor Weeks work that into his sermon."

Bernadette stared up at Keaton like a child sensing an impending gift. "It gonna be one of those?" she asked. "One of the good ones?"

"Sure enough," Keaton answered.

Bernadette clapped her hands and performed a little hop. "Hot damn. It's been ages."

"Less than a month," Lefebvre corrected. "There was that double-execution three weeks ago."

Bernadette glowered at Lefebvre, but Keaton kept on grinning at Dez. "Lefebvre's conscience is tender," Keaton said. "He's got that poet's soul you hear about. Suppose it's from teaching all those novels. Some of it was bound to rub off."

Dez found himself longing for a reaction from the tall man, but Lefebvre remained impassive.

"Bet he used to mess with his students," Bernadette said. She whapped Lefebvre on the chest. "Bet he got on with the girls *and* the boys."

Lefebvre turned his face toward Bernadette, and in it there was a feverish new light, challenge and contempt and self-loathing all mixed together. "Why don't you find out?" Lefebvre said.

Bernadette's sleazy grin disappeared, her eyes darting to Keaton.

"I'm waiting," Lefebvre said. "Go ahead. Show Keaton what a skilled servant you are. Show him how cunning."

"Be gentle," Keaton said, eyeing Bernadette. "Bernadette's powers are useful, but they only reach so far."

Bernadette glanced askance at Lefebvre. "I'll get it from you one of these days. You wait."

"Get it now," Tom Chaney said, and they all turned in his direction. Dez had forgotten about the werewolf reclining in his bundle of chains. Chaney smirked at Bernadette. "Show us what a tough woman you are, you ugly bitch."

Bernadette looked ready to pounce on Chaney, but Keaton only laughed. "Such coarse language, Hound!"

"That ain't my name."

"Your name is what I say it is," Keaton said, ice water in his gaze.

To Dez's dismay, Chaney fell silent.

Why do they fear him so much? Dez wondered. True, Keaton was imposing. His personality was even bigger. Yet Dez could find nothing in the figure looming over them to evoke such superstitious dread. *What are you?* he wondered again.

Keaton clapped his hands so loudly Dez jumped. "I feel like shaking things up," Keaton said. "Lefebvre, you make sure Iris is in the back when Weeks starts his show."

Lefebvre gave Keaton a look Dez couldn't interpret. Something passed between the men, and Dez wondered what the command meant. Was Keaton testing Lefebvre's loyalty?

Bernadette frowned. "Why can't Iris watch? After all, it's her boyfriend gonna get executed."

The words raised goosebumps on Dez's flesh. So he *was* to be executed. His head nailed to the wall like the others. Would they decorate the sign out front with his severed penis?

Dez suppressed a groan.

"It would be good for her to see," Keaton agreed. "But I've already got something over her. She'll stay in line." He turned toward Chaney. "But the Hound here. He's getting restless, I can tell."

"This is a mistake," Lefebvre said softly.

Keaton ignored him. "Hound, you need to be reminded of your place. That miniscule brain of yours tends to forget what happens to those who're disloyal."

Though the fear was still in Chaney's face, Dez saw challenge there too. "I ain't never been loyal to you, Keaton. I'd shit on your grave."

"Only place you're gonna shit is that there bucket," Bernadette said.

Chaney and Keaton continued to stare at one another.

Lefebvre asked, "Why do you keep him alive?"

Keaton's voice was faraway. "You know why."

A dreadful smile appeared on Chaney's face. "I'd do it again."

Lefebvre shot a look at Chaney. "Don't you know when to shut up?"

Keaton drifted toward Chaney, crouched beside him, close enough for Chaney to touch if he desired.

Keaton nodded. "You know, Lefebvre, I believe you've got a point. Go up and tell Weeks it's gonna be a double."

Lefebvre closed his eyes, whether in sadness or relief, Dez couldn't tell.

Bernadette's face grew animated. "You mean it, boss?"

"Uh-huh," Keaton said, his eyes never leaving Chaney's.

"Hot damn!" Bernadette said. "Can I tell the others?"

Keaton's lips formed an indulgent smile. "Sure, Bernadette. You can tell the others."

Bernadette hustled toward the stairs, her enmity toward Lefebvre evidently forgotten.

Keaton searched Chaney's face. "You at peace with your past, Hound?"

"You're damn right I'm at peace."

Keaton's smile was unperturbed. "Except for your sister."

Chaney cringed.

"You know, I'll miss you, Hound," Keaton said. He reached out, mussed Chaney's black hair. Chaney pulled away, but of course he couldn't go far. "Whenever I get sad, coming down here always cheers me up."

Chaney wouldn't look at Keaton now. Dez could see Chaney's bottom lip quivering.

"What's your reading level, Hound? Second grade? Third?" Keaton glanced at Dez. "In old-time literature, they would've called Hound here a manchild."

Lefebvre started for the stairs.

"Where're you going?" Keaton asked.

Lefebvre stopped, stared down at his boots. "I thought I'd return to my post."

"It's after midnight," Keaton said. "The only trade we'll get now is vampires."

Cold air misted over Dez's skin. He couldn't imagine vampires mingling with the other patrons of the Four Winds. When their bloodlust was roused – which was often – there was no reasoning with them.

Keaton was watching Dez. "You've seen vampires," he said.

Dez swallowed. "Yes."

A grin. "You're wondering if maybe I sold your piece of ass to them."

Dez didn't trust himself to answer.

Keaton stood and moved toward the stairs.

But he stopped with a hand on the banister. "Tell you what, McClane. I think I will tell you what I did with her. Right before the end." He smiled, his white teeth sharkish in the dismal fluorescent glow. "I like that. It's fitting. The last thing you'll hear is what became of your sweet little girl."

With that, Keaton mounted the stairs. He flipped off the lights, leaving them in near-darkness.

Chaney's eyes glinted. Dez wondered if the yellowish glint stemmed from the man's lycanthropic nature. Or maybe it was only Dez's imagination.

Lefebvre stirred. Dez had forgotten all about the tall man. "I better tend to Iris," Lefebvre muttered.

"You could stand up to him, you know," Dez said.

Lefebvre grunted. "I'm sorry, Raven, but you clearly don't get it."

"He's not like you," Dez persisted. "You could play it so he wouldn't see it coming."

"Someone would," Lefebvre said. "Someone always does."

Still, Lefebvre didn't make a move for the stairs.

Dez's heart pounded. "Help us," he said.

"There's no help for you two," Lefebvre said. "For any of us. Goodbye, Raven."

Head down, he made for the stairs.

CHAPTER TWENTY-TWO

Condemned

Badler and Hernandez came down to collect them not long after. Badler went straight for Dez, but Hernandez called out to him in the murk.

"What?" Badler snapped.

"The Hound first," Hernandez explained.

"What's the difference?"

Hernandez sighed, strode over and flicked on the lights. Dez blinked in the comparatively blinding glow. "I really need to explain it?"

Badler grunted. "That hairy bastard too much for you? Put your gun to his temple, he'll do whatever you want."

"We follow directions," Hernandez said. To Dez it sounded as if Hernandez had stated this fact a thousand times.

Badler ignored Hernandez, squatted before Dez. If Dez wanted, he could kick the muscular son of a bitch in the balls. The chains would certainly stretch far enough.

Then again, maybe that's exactly what Badler was inviting him to do. Maybe Badler was goading Dez to attack so he'd have a reason to retaliate. If Badler did unload on Dez, there'd be little hope of survival. The man's muscles were ludicrously corded, and what was more, Dez was nearly certain both of these goons were cannibals. They weren't Latents. That much was obvious. Keaton seemed to have little use for Latents. And the virile bodies and gleaming white teeth bespoke of the preternatural good health that marked eaters of human flesh.

To Badler's back, Hernandez said, "We do the Hound first. Then you can be as rough with the other as you want."

Badler continued to appraise Dez. Something calculating permeated his face. "You won't tell Keaton?"

"Long as you cooperate with this one," was Hernandez's answer.

At once Badler joined Hernandez, who began to unlock Chaney's shackles.

Though barred from Chaney's face by the goons' broad backs, Dez heard real trepidation in the hairy man's voice. "What are you two doin'?"

"Now come on, Hound," Badler said, working open one of the leg cuffs. "Don't pretend you don't know what's going on. You're dumb, but you're not that dumb."

"Don't rile him up," Hernandez muttered.

Badler chuckled. "Sometimes I wish the boss would find me a tougher partner, you know that, Hernandez? You look the part, and you can lift a goddamned car, but under all that muscle you're a bowl of Jell-O."

"*Hey*," Hernandez growled, his hand squeezing the back of Badler's neck. "Watch your mouth."

Badler winced but returned Hernandez's stare with equal animosity. "You better think about touching me. We start something, we're sure as hell gonna finish it."

Hernandez didn't let go. "You better learn when to shut up."

They'd shifted enough that Dez could see Chaney's face. The hairy man glanced from one goon to the other, then finally said, "You guys wanna solve this, you should go outside."

Badler shot him a look. "You'd like that, wouldn't you, Hound? Spare your smelly ass, and have us killed by the goddamned vampires?"

Chaney's eyes went wide. "They're not out there, are they?"

"Maybe they are," Badler said, grinning. "Maybe they're sniffing around for wolf meat. We should string you up out there, let them follow the stench."

"You done with that cuff yet?" Hernandez asked.

"Keep your panties on," Badler answered. He unlocked the leg cuff, moved the key toward the cuff on Chaney's right wrist.

"I don't wanna go outside," Chaney whined.

Hernandez tapped his fingers impatiently. "You're not goin' outside."

"What Hernandez says is too true," Badler said as he unlocked the handcuff. He seized Chaney under the arm and hauled him to his feet. "Though outside would be a hell of a lot better. Least out there you'd have a chance."

Hernandez gripped Chaney's other arm, and though Chaney's muscles were well-defined, his nakedness and weakened state rendered him a pitiful sight. The hairy man swayed on his feet, causing Dez to wonder how long it had been since Chaney had been permitted to stand.

"We ain't goin' outside?" Chaney asked.

Hernandez shepherded him toward the stairs. "Uh-uh."

"Where then?"

"Why, the service," Badler said brightly. "You're a guest of honor."

"Upstairs?" Chaney asked. Dez noted the dried nuggets of shit caught in Chaney's furry butt crack. How long since the man had been bathed?

"Come on," Hernandez said, towing Chaney with a bit more force.

"But...." Chaney stumbled, almost went down. "Can't I...can you give me underpants? If Iris is up there—"

"Jesus H. Christ, Hound!" Badler shouted. "Everything's coming to an end, and all you can worry about is some barmaid seeing your winky?"

"Up," Hernandez instructed. Chaney began the long climb up the staircase.

"A pair of drawers?" Chaney asked. "Please, Hernandez?"

"We'll see," Hernandez said.

"Mother*fucker*, this bastard stinks," Badler said.

"Please gimme some drawers," Chaney pleaded, this time stopping halfway up the stairs.

Badler spun Chaney around and slammed him against the cinder block wall. "You get what we goddamned give you, you hear that, Hound?"

When Chaney continued to beg, Badler seized him by the shoulders, smashed him against the wall so hard that Chaney's head bounced. "Never met someone so feebleminded," Badler said. "I explain it clearly, and you still don't have a clue." He rammed Chaney against the wall again to accentuate his point.

"Let's move," Hernandez said, taking hold of Chaney's arm and dragging him up the steps.

Badler cuffed Chaney on the back of the head. "Dumb mutt. Never smelled anything so godawful in my life."

Hernandez sounded bored. "You wanna bathe him before the service?"

"Rip his head off is what I'll do," Badler answered. "Can't believe all the fuss we've made over this bastard. He's done nothing but blubber and shit all over the floors since we brought him here."

Chaney moaned, "I don't want Iris to see—"

"She's gonna see your little pecker," Badler teased, "and she's gonna laugh like hell."

As they passed out of sight and the lights were extinguished, Chaney began to sob.

In the ensuing silence, Dez strained to listen for a commotion upstairs. He wondered what Chaney's trigger was. Clearly it wasn't rage or sorrow. He might never again transform, at least if tonight were to be his execution, as Dez assumed it would be.

And reclining in the dark, Dez wondered what it would be like to die. True, he'd pondered the question hundreds of times since the world changed — he assumed all survivors had pondered that question — but now he was facing execution.

He'd witnessed a couple of them. The most recent, he supposed, had been the reason why he'd ended up with Susan, although it wasn't until a few weeks after the execution that they'd even kissed.

The man who'd been killed had been caught stealing food.

It was near the end of the colony — looking back, it might have been the reason the colony disbanded — and it had been Jason Oates who'd decided on the death sentence for the condemned. Whenever there was violence, Jason Oates was invariably behind it.

Jason had caught a colonist — a middle-aged man named Suresh Sharma — stealing beef jerky from the storage area. What complicated matters was the fact that Sharma had supplied most of the food they still had from the grocery store he'd run in the pre-bomb world. Sharma had only joined their group a few months prior and had been enthusiastically received due to the supplies he'd ferreted away under his store.

When Sharma's thieving was discovered — and there was no doubt he'd been taking food on the sly — many colonists had pointed out that it wasn't really stealing since Sharma had brought the food in the first place. But Jason claimed it was a matter of principle and if they ignored this transgression, it would embolden others.

Jason and those who supported his draconian methods had dragged Sharma to the mouth of the cave, and Jason had drawn the Smith & Wesson with which he claimed to keep peace.

It was Susan who'd nearly saved Sharma's life.

"You're turning us into a police state, Jason," she'd said.

"It needs policing," had been his answer.

Dez and several others had joined Susan in a semicircle at the mouth of the cave, where Jason and a trio of his followers held Sharma captive.

The grocery store owner had looked pathetic standing there by the younger, stouter men. Sharma's bronze head was nearly bald on top, with a disheveled thatch of black strands hanging loose off to one side, like a graduation tassel. Sharma's belly was round beneath his faded maroon shirt. On his face were several welts and contusions, a cut lip where Jason had struck him. To Dez, Sharma looked like he wanted to curl up in a ball and go to sleep.

"You've made your point, Jason," one of the colonists said.

"You're *missing* the point," one of Jason's loyalists shot back. "If Suresh isn't punished, this will happen again."

"Let him go," Dez said.

Something new permeated Jason's face, like he'd been yearning for Dez's protest. Later, Dez realized this was the case. The tension between the two had been growing over many months, and at the center of it was Susan. Not only was she the prettiest woman in the colony, she was likely the smartest. When he'd shown up at the colony, Susan had already been with Jason, but increasingly, Dez had come to believe her decision to take up with their leader had as much to do with lack of options as it did any genuine emotion.

Later, after the colony had come to its brutal end, Susan had confirmed this. Though she hated to admit it, she'd chosen Jason by default.

But that chilly October afternoon, just about a year ago, Dez realized, she'd still been with the sadistic son of a bitch.

"Punishing him is one thing," Susan said. "Killing him would be shameful."

Jason's eyebrows had risen at this, giving him a slightly mad look. The expression had surfaced with greater frequency lately and had grown at a rate equal to Susan's interest in Dez. Somehow, Dez realized as he gazed at Sharma, this had become about Dez and Susan and Jason, and that chilled him to the bone. Because if punishing Sharma became a matter of besting Dez....

"Send him away," Dez said.

Susan had turned to stare at him in amazement. "That's a death sentence too."

Jason spoke with finality, gesticulating with the .38 in a way that made Dez's guts clench. "We've survived this long because we have order. This..." He nodded at Sharma. "...this *shit* has threatened the order by putting himself ahead of the group."

"I'm sure he won't do it again," Susan said. "Will you, Suresh?"

"I'm very sorry," the man said quietly.

Dez admired the man's dignity, but he'd hoped Sharma might utter something a hell of a lot more eloquent. Jason's loyalists looked like they wanted blood.

"Words," Jason said. "They're just words. Don't you know they don't mean anything? He gets away with this, he'll do it again, only worse next time."

"What about the kids?" one of the loyalists asked. It was a common rallying cry used to justify Jason's decisions. The truth was that there were only three children left, and one was twelve years old. The other two were infants and only drank breast milk. Neither infant had exhibited signs of changing into a monster.

"Suresh brought the food," Susan said.

"Not all of it," one of Jason's men answered.

"And we gave him protection," another loyalist said. "He wouldn't be alive without us."

"He survived on his own for a year," Dez pointed out.

"Because he had a fucking treasure trove of food under his store!" a loyalist exclaimed.

"Which he shared with us," Susan said, stepping forward.

The sight of Susan approaching Jason and his men made Dez's heart hammer. "Let him go," Dez heard himself say, and as soon as he'd said it, he knew he'd doomed Sharma.

Jason's eyes flitted from Susan to Dez and back to Susan.

"Ah, well fuck it," Jason said, placing the muzzle against Sharma's temple and squeezing the trigger.

The side of Sharma's face sprayed in soupy rills; the man teetered away from Jason and slumped on the ground at a loyalist's feet. Susan screamed, not in fear or sorrow, but in rage. Dez identified with that scream. Jason had killed Sharma because he'd wanted to, not because he was maintaining order. Worse, he'd done it because Dez and Susan had sided against Jason, and this was his method of retaliating.

Susan had turned away from Sharma's twitching body, and when her eyes had fastened on Dez's, he'd known she'd made her decision. She was done with Jason. All that was left was for Susan and Dez to figure out how to overthrow Jason and his men.

But Dez's memories stopped then.

Because Badler and Hernandez were coming down the steps for him. It was time for his execution.

CHAPTER TWENTY-THREE

The Sermon

"Where's Iris?" Tom Chaney was shouting. "Where'd you put her?"

Badler and Hernandez escorted Dez toward the front of the seating area, where the tables had been cleared; in the center of the clearing dangled two sets of chains, which had been threaded through eyehooks hanging from the ceiling and threaded through pulleys, after which the chains had been tethered to the thick wooden balcony supports. One set of chains was obviously meant for Dez.

Tom Chaney was already shackled in the other set. His feet had been imprisoned in leg cuffs and chains that arose from eyehooks bolted to the floor. Dez hadn't noticed any of the eyehooks earlier, but he supposed that's because there hadn't been chains attached to them. Nor a hairy, whimpering man.

"Where is she?" Chaney asked.

"She's being guarded, you ignoramus," Badler answered.

"Don't hurt Iris," Chaney was pleading. "You gotta tell me what you did with her."

"Why the hell do you care?" demanded Bernadette.

"No kidding, Chaney," Badler agreed as he muscled Dez closer to the chains. "I thought you were afraid of her seeing you bare-assed naked."

Several patrons guffawed. The tables had been arranged in concentric semicircles that emanated outward all the way to the walls beneath the balconies. Like the main level, the balconies were crammed with faces, their expressions ranging from avid interest to blank, incurious stares. Only on a handful of faces did Dez read any semblance of sympathy, but even if there were denizens of the Four Winds who disagreed with Keaton's macabre ceremony, they were a scant minority, and would no doubt keep silent while Dez and Tom Chaney were slaughtered. His scan of the balcony paused on Michael Summers and Joe Kidd. The pair looked neither pleased nor disturbed by the ceremony, merely inured to it. No help there, Dez decided.

No help from anywhere.

When Badler took hold of a chain dangling from the ceiling, Dez began to struggle. Only when Hernandez and Badler had wrestled Dez to the ground and gotten one handcuff around his wrist did he understand how hideous this would be. He glanced at Chaney, who'd been strung up until the chains snubbed taut, the tips of his toes ten feet off the ground. Chaney scarcely had room to squirm, much less kick or struggle. He was pleading to know where Iris was, and though Dez wondered the same thing himself, he was too overcome with fright to ask. The Four Winds was a kaleidoscope of taunts, blurred scowls, and gesticulating arms.

The other handcuff was cinched around Dez's wrist, and though he fought it, his ankles were imprisoned in the leg cuffs with the assistance of Crosby and Gattis, who were all too eager to join in the festivities.

Without pause, Dez heard a metallic cranking from his right and discovered a pair of patrons feeding the chains through the pulleys. The slack in the chains began to diminish. Dez shot a wild glance behind him at the bar.

No sign of Keaton.

Or Iris, for that matter. The people present – there were women, Dez realized, though only a smattering here and there – continued to jeer. Dez felt the tug of the chains on his wrists. His throat tightened. Someone whacked him on the back of the head, but he scarcely felt it. Liquid spattered his side, someone having thrown a drink in his direction.

"Cut off their peckers!" a gleeful voice called, and when Dez turned, he saw it was the man with all the piercings. What had been the man's name?

Wyzinski, Dez remembered. Beyond Wyzinski, Crosby, and Gattis, Dez caught a glimpse of a woman of perhaps forty with a hardened, wind-burnt face and remorseless ebony marbles for eyes. Absurdly, the sight of the woman reminded Dez he wore only boxer briefs, and he made to cover himself before remembering he was in the process of being strung up.

The chains lifted him.

"Shouldn't've come back," a rough voice said.

Dez shot a look at the speaker, discovered the giant in the black jacket, the one who'd nearly come to blows with Hernandez and Badler earlier in the evening.

"He's too stupid to stay away," an answering voice said.

"I ain't complaining," Black Jacket said. "It'll liven things up watchin' him die."

Dez's toes broke contact with the floor. The pain in his wrists was severe, the steel cuffs already biting into his skin. He rose higher, the cranking noise a funeral dirge. A new pain assailed him, this time in his armpits and his shoulders. He'd read about the crucifixion of Christ, knew that although this wasn't the same thing as being crucified, there were a couple parallels. For one, victims of crucifixion often expired from suffocation rather than blood loss. They were left to hang on crosses, unable to support their own weight, until their lungs were, in essence, crushed. As his body rose higher, higher, he already felt his lungs squeezing in his chest, and noted with alarm how difficult it was to draw a satisfying breath.

Asphyxiation. My God, what a ghastly word.

Also like a crucifixion, this was public. He looked out on the faces, judged there to be three hundred or more. He'd not have believed this many people

(*beasts*)

could congregate in the new world, but here they all were, eyes glittering with anticipation, voices raised in mob justice. Were any of them Latents? Or was he the only one without powers? He recalled the ending of one of his favorite novels, Richard Matheson's *I Am Legend*, how the tables turned on humankind, how the perception of villainy changed. At least in that story, the protagonist, Robert Neville, had spent his time striving for a cure for the vampirism that had ravaged Earth. What had Dez done? Pursued the woman he loved, forsaking the rest of mankind. Well, he thought stubbornly, was there shame in that?

No, he thought as he rose higher, higher, his head on a level with Tom Chaney's knees now. No shame. He supposed there was something poetic about dying in pursuit of Susan.

But only if one found such tragic endings poetic. For his part, he would have much rather lived.

"Take off them underwear!" a harsh voice demanded.

Dez twitched his head in that direction and saw it was the woman with the wind-burnt face. A tendril of childish dread squirmed in his belly. *At least allow me to keep my briefs on*, he thought. *Please allow that one concession to dignity.*

Tom Chaney's exposed genitalia came into view. Dez glanced at Chaney's face, then wished he hadn't. Chaney's eyes were pinched shut in sorrow, the tears oozing down his hairy cheeks. He was still blubbering about Iris.

Dez bucked against the chains, half-twisted toward the bar area, which was barren of people but newly fronted by a pulpit. He was unsurprised to note they'd removed the cross from the face of the pulpit, though the dark outline of the cross remained indelibly printed on the wood.

Dez finally reached a level more or less even with Tom Chaney, and the cranking ceased. The chains around his ankles weren't taut to the floor, but they didn't allow much movement. Dez labored to draw breath, couldn't, and had to perform a slight pull-up against the handcuffs to suck in enough air to prevent a panic attack.

Below Dez, maybe fifteen feet away, Keaton rose and lifted his hands for silence.

All heads in the Four Winds turned toward its proprietor.

"Glad you could all come out tonight," Keaton said. "It's gonna be a good show."

Shouts of approval.

"Folks, you might notice we've got two criminals up here. The Hound's a bonus. I hadn't planned on ending his miserable existence yet, but, hell, I like to be spontaneous. He took something from me I can never get back, so tonight we'll take something from him." He glanced up at Chaney. "After we have some fun."

Chaney wept.

"You know I'm not much of a speech giver," Keaton said, and Dez thought, *Bullshit. You eat this up.* "So I'm gonna turn it over to Reverend Weeks." Keaton jolted as if he'd forgotten something. "But before I do, one more word about the condemned."

Here we go, Dez thought.

"The Hound here," Keaton said, indicating Chaney with a lazy thumb, "he's been chained in the dungeon for what, fourteen months?"

Fourteen months, Dez thought. *Jesus.*

"And in fourteen months, the dumb fuck has never apologized for what he did. For the pain he caused."

And Dez thought of the ravaged bedroom, the little league trophies, the unmistakable signs of a young boy. Had Chaney murdered Keaton's son? It seemed the only possibility that made sense. If that were the case, Dez reflected, it was a wonder Keaton had permitted Chaney to live this long.

Keaton peered up at Chaney, perhaps giving him the opportunity to atone. When Chaney only continued to weep quietly, Keaton nodded. "Well, it'll all be square in a couple hours."

A couple *hours*? Dez thought, heart racing. Whatever they had in store was going to take a couple hours? At the thought of a protracted torture session, Dez's gorge rose. He didn't want to vomit in front of these fiends, but he didn't know how long he'd be able to control it.

"As for this other one," Keaton said, leveling a forefinger at Dez, "he's gonna be a reminder to all of you who might have harbored foolish thoughts at one time or another. He didn't like my business practices and had the audacity to break into my home and threaten my wife and daughter."

Ear-punishing bellows erupted at this, many in the crowd going as far as to hurl objects at Dez. He was pelted with ashtrays, one of which cracked him in the hipbone and shot freshets of pain down his leg.

"Now, don't trash my establishment!" Keaton yelled, his voice cleaving through the din. "You can scream at him all you want, but I won't have my floors reduced to waste bins."

Chastened, the crowd quieted a little.

"Anyhow," Keaton continued, "this chickenshit went after the ones I love, ones who were innocent, defenseless—"

"I didn't touch them," Dez said.

"Which is the reason I let you live this long," Keaton answered. "Had you laid a finger on my daughter's sweet head, I'd have drawn and quartered you already."

"People only matter if they're yours," Dez heard himself saying. "That about right?"

Keaton chuckled softly. "I really am gonna enjoy this." He turned, raised his arms. "Folks, I give you Reverend Bryce Weeks."

The crowd cheered. Dez struggled to turn and watch the reverend's entrance, but found it tough going. Every time he'd maneuver his body sideways, the chains attached to his legs would haul him back around to face the crowd. As it was, he caught glimpses of a short bespectacled man, slightly pudgy, bald on top with light brown hair remaining on the sides. He was garbed in black, with a traditional white collar, and clutched a book at one side. He appeared to be in his early forties.

Smiling beatifically, Weeks spread his arms and addressed the crowd. "Good evening, friends. Let us begin with a word of prayer."

To Dez's surprise, the entire assembly of vicious-looking patrons bowed its heads.

"Fellow survivors," Weeks began in a resonant voice, "we have come this far for a reason. Many of us entered the new order through tragedy and suffering, and we have all endured many a hardship."

Loud mutterings of agreement, many of the patrons nodding their bowed heads.

Dez studied them, fascinated. One pair, particularly, drew his attention. They were a couple, for one thing. Couples were rare in the new world. Sure, people hooked up for a meaningless rut sometimes, but something about the way the man and woman sat together – she as Caucasian as Dez, the man perhaps of Middle Eastern descent and sporting an elaborate neck tattoo – reminded Dez of the old world, of the good things they had lost. The man and woman appeared neither glad to see Dez and Chaney strung up nor especially impressed with Weeks's sermonizing.

"But we have survived," Weeks said. "That is the point. We have persevered. We have harnessed what gifts nature has bequeathed us. We have *adapted*."

Dez scanned the patrons, noticed only one other individual who wasn't immersed in the prayer.

Lefebvre.

The tall man leaned by the entrance door, his eyes on Pastor Weeks. Dez tried but could not identify the emotion on Lefebvre's narrow face. Interest? Contempt? Resignation?

Did it fucking matter?

Dez's shoulder blades ached.

"We have adapted, dear friends, that is the salient point," Weeks said, his voice full of warmth. "The wisdom of the cosmos is unknowable to us, yet when one stands in the deep, pellucid night and gazes at the heavens, one understands that there is indeed order. There is, unmistakably, a plan."

Dez couldn't deny his curiosity. He wriggled against the chains to better see Weeks.

"Does anyone doubt where this world was heading?"

A shaking of heads.

"Does anyone here believe we would have lasted another year, much less another decade, with the demagogues leading the world?"

"No sir," someone muttered amidst the voices.

"*Nuclear annihilation*," Weeks said, enunciating each syllable clearly, if incorrectly – he pronounced it *nucular*. "My dearest survivors, the apocalypse was at hand!"

Louder mutterings at this, patrons exchanging approving glances.

"And though the shift in the Earth's population was no doubt painful to many here tonight, can there be any doubt the new world appears more sustainable than the old?"

Solemn agreement. More than ever, Dez felt he'd gone mad.

"Which is why," Weeks said, stepping around the pulpit to a position near Chaney, "we need men like Bill Keaton to maintain order."

Shouts of *Amen*.

"What we have is worth protecting, dear friends. Never again will the beauty of this world be blighted by the unworthiness of man. Never again will the forests fall and the oceans darken with man's contamination."

More *Amens*. Several patrons, Dez noticed with dumbfounded hilarity, had tears shining on their cheeks.

Weeks moved closer to the assembly, stood before Bill Keaton. Weeks folded his hands before him and bowed his head. "Mr. Keaton named this establishment the Four Winds Bar. He did so because, in his wisdom, he understood the new opportunities this great change represented."

Keaton nodded, and Badler, who sat behind Keaton, leaned forward and gave his boss's shoulder an affectionate squeeze.

Weeks's voice crescendoed, the tone still high but the sound resonant in the large room. "The Four Winds liberated us! The Four Winds showed us what we could become!"

Loud cheers.

"Though we did not see it at the moment," Weeks declaimed, "the Four Winds tore the scales from our eyes and leeched the eons of iniquity from our genetic codes!"

Louder cheers, many patrons toasting with their steins.

"The Four Winds allowed us to become the legendary figures we were meant to be!"

The shouts were well nigh rapturous now.

"And if we look around, dear friends, we see joy and fellowship! We see a healthy respect and a proper fear! We see—"

The front doors opened and every head in the room turned.

In stalked a pair of figures in black clothes. Not only had Weeks stopped talking, but the rest of the patrons had fallen deathly silent as well. The two, a man and a woman, both with long raven-colored hair and sinuous bodies, moved to the left edge of the room, passing tables slowly, their eyes studying the patrons they passed. Dez noted with apprehension how the patrons averted their eyes as the pair drew closer, as though, Medusa-like, the newcomers would turn them to stone. The figures were very pale, but then again, paleness was common these days.

The pair passed under the left balcony and selected a table with empty chairs. There were three other men at the table, but they'd scooted their chairs to the table's fore in order to improve their view of the ceremony. The trio of men kept their gazes studiously forward, but Dez could see in their faces how terrified they were of the newcomers.

"Go on, Reverend," Keaton said quietly.

Weeks gazed upon the newcomers a moment longer, then shook himself loose of his trance and cleared his throat. "Yes, friends, it is a better world in which we now find ourselves. Although some—" A glance up at Chaney. "—still insist on staining the pristineness of the new order."

Dez peered at Chaney and noticed he'd ceased weeping. Contrary to the rest of the patrons, Chaney was staring at the newcomers with interest. So too, Dez realized, was Lefebvre, whom the two must have passed on the way in.

Weeks dabbed sweat from his brow with a white handkerchief. "The new world, if it is to make good on the promise afforded it by the architects of the Four Winds cleansing event—"

Dez felt the first spark of anger since he'd been strung up. Cleansing event? The phrase turned his stomach.

"—must have order. It must—" Weeks mopped his brow. "—appoint sentinels to…to protect its sanctity. We must embrace this chance to recapture what once must have been commonplace, the natural state of—"

Movement from the newcomers' table drew Dez's attention. He

turned that way in time to see one of the black-garbed figures – the female – batten onto the neck of one of the men. The pale woman's face was bestial, her teeth elongated and tapered, and when they sank into the side of the man's neck, they set to shredding the flesh and unleashing torrents of scarlet. The man, whose dark brown cowboy hat tumbled off his head, screamed and sank down in his chair as if to escape the bite of the vampire, but this only sent his attacker into wilder paroxysms of ferocity. Several men in the immediate area had stumbled to their feet to escape the bloodletting, and one of the trio who hadn't been bitten took a step toward the victim as though to intervene.

But Bernadette was there, a revolver extended at the would-be savior. "Stay back," she said, her voice unsteady. Not with fear of the intervener, Dez decided, but in utter terror of the vampires.

There was a horrible interval in which no one moved, the only sounds in the bar the repugnant biting and sucking of the vampire. The victim had ceased struggling, his lifeblood either inside the vampire's gullet or spent on the grungy floorboards.

Dez realized the male vampire was transforming, his orange eyes glowing at the men in the immediate area.

The feeding vampire stood up and wiped her mouth with a leather-clad forearm. The bottom half of her face was smeared with gore, the upper half flushed from the feeding. Her face having transformed into its vampiric form, she scarcely resembled a human being.

Dez's gaze shifted to the vampire who hadn't yet fed and noted he was staring unwholesomely at a muscular individual who was almost certainly a cannibal. The man was attired in a red athletic training shirt, a gray Under Armour insignia visible on the chest. Like the vampires' hair, the strong man's hair was longer, but unlike the vampires, who wore their hair tossed to one side, his was styled straight back with some product, reminding Dez of male models in the old world.

"Now, don't you think about—" the man with the stylish hair began, but the unfed vampire darted forward anyway, moving with an agility no human could muster. The man yelped as the vampire seized him by the hair and dragged him toward the front doors. The vampire who'd fed followed her companion, heedless of the patrons who shrank from her as she passed.

Lefebvre opened the door for them, his face unreadable, and when they'd hauled away their new victim, he closed the door without comment.

There was a dreadful silence in the Four Winds.

Keaton glowered at Weeks. "Go on with the goddamn sermon!"

Weeks, who had paled to the color of cream cheese, adjusted his collar and took in a shuddering breath. "Um, yes. Yes, we must... maintain order." He swallowed. "We must, you know, harvest new respect...."

"Get to the condemned," Keaton growled. Several patrons echoed this sentiment. Amazing, Dez thought, how quickly they'd turned on Weeks. As though it were his fault that a lifeless body was now being hauled along the side wall by Keaton's goons. Dez watched them pass the bar and disappear into the back hallway. Evidently, they were disinclined to use the same exit the vampires had used.

Dez wondered if the vampires had exsanguinated their second victim yet.

Weeks nodded, collecting himself. "Part of what makes Bill Keaton such a worthy leader is his unwillingness to allow brazen misdeeds to go unpunished. When Tom Chaney committed the atrocity of which we're all aware, Mr. Keaton's justice was as fair as it was decisive. He apprehended Mr. Chaney—"

"Hound," Keaton corrected.

Weeks opened his mouth, nodded hastily. "Yes, when he caught the, uh, Hound in the middle of his luciferian actions...."

Weeks continued, but Dez had tuned him out, focusing instead on Chaney. The hairy man looked tired, defeated. He hung from his chains like a horrid prize in some carnival game. *Knock over the milk bottle and win this werewolf!*

"Tom," Dez said.

Chaney didn't look up.

"Tom?" Dez said with more force. In the background, Weeks was railing about sin and punishment. There were no echoes of approbation, the vampires' incursion having robbed the patrons of their enthusiasm.

Slowly, Chaney glanced at him. Red-eyed, glazed, Chaney looked dead already.

"Was it Keaton's son you killed?"

When Chaney didn't answer, Dez added, "It's important."

"His mistress," Chaney said in his gravelly, thick-tongued voice.

Dez studied Chaney's face. "Why did you do it? Did she hurt you? Threaten you?"

Chaney ran his tongue along his lips. "I couldn't help it."

Dez was about to ask another question when his body was jostled. He looked down to discover Weeks shaking his leg chains. "*This*," Weeks said, much of his former gusto restored, "*this* is what threatens our new paradise. This *reprobate*—" another shake, "—dares trespass in Mr. Keaton's haven? This heathen *snake*, with neither physical nor mental abilities, a bottom-feeder who contributes nothing to our glorious age.... Who can doubt he needs to be expunged?"

A couple patrons murmured approval at this, though Dez doubted they knew the meaning of *expunged*.

"So let us bring this ceremony to its conclusion," Weeks said. "Hernandez? Badler?"

The two henchmen got to their feet. Badler looked eager to participate, Hernandez much less so.

Dez glanced at Chaney. "They going to cut on us?" When Chaney only hung there, glazed and unresponsive, Dez added, "Do they torture people first, or just kill them?"

Chaney sounded half-asleep. "They don't cut. Too many...too many cannibals in here for that...it'd go nuts if they started cutting."

Dez bared his teeth at the maddening sluggishness of Chaney's speech. "What then? They gonna shoot us? A firing squad? Or—"

The chains jerked taut, and Dez shot a look over his shoulder to where Hernandez stood. Until now, Dez hadn't thought much about the steel cranks that protruded from the winches housing the chains.

Oh hell, he thought as the chains began to tauten. *They're gonna tear us apart.*

Hernandez glanced at the chains above Dez, and the ceiling pulley over which the chains snicked. Hernandez looked everywhere except at Dez's face.

Badler, by contrast, was cranking his winch spasmodically, a repulsive lust in his muscle-broadened face. Chaney was already beginning to groan. Dez could see the blood madness in Badler's eyes.

"It *hurts*," Chaney moaned, eliciting braying laughter from the crowd. As if he hadn't made his point the first time, he said it louder.

"Well, of course it hurts, you goddamned idgit!" Crosby shouted. "Why else you think we're doin' it?"

Weeks had his hands folded before him. "Mr. Chaney, you murdered an innocent woman."

"And what did Dez do?" someone demanded.

Dez peered wildly about to identify the speaker, but the chains jerked at his wrists, and his body went ramrod straight. The pain intensified, not only in his shoulders, but in his wrists and ankles, the contact points where steel met flesh.

Keaton's voice was bland. "You got a problem with the sentence, Lefebvre?"

Despite the pinch of the cuffs and the strain in his shoulders, Dez shot a look at Lefebvre, who leaned against the front doorframe, his posture defeated, but his eyes twinkling with sardonic rage. "Chaney killed your mistress," Lefebvre said, "and you're killing him. Fine. We all get that."

As if in agreement, Badler cranked the winch harder, and Chaney's voice rose to a squeal. Dez could actually hear the man's limbs stretching.

"But why this other?" Lefebvre asked. "He didn't hurt anybody."

Several patrons shouted at Lefebvre, a couple of them calling him names.

Now Keaton was turned around to stare at his doorman. "He was coming after *me*," Keaton said. "Doesn't that concern you?"

"He's just trying to find his girlfriend," Lefebvre said.

The chains continued to tighten. The pain was obscene. Dez glanced at Hernandez, hoping to appeal to his better nature, if he had one, but the huge man kept his eyes trained on the winch. No help there.

"Then punish him," Lefebvre said, "instead of killing him."

Keaton exchanged glances with several patrons, his face fixed in an incredulous grin. His glance fell on Lefebvre. "Are you serious, son?"

"The Raven just wants to know where—"

"—his girlfriend is," Keaton finished. "Yeah, you said that. Why the hell do you call him Raven?" Keaton glanced at Dez. "On second thought, I don't give a shit. So let's ask the lovesick puppy. You really want to hear how the vampires bought her? How that luscious ass of hers caused a bidding war between two of my best customers?"

No, Dez thought. *It isn't true.*

"You sold her for blood," Lefebvre said. "And you're proud of it."

The entire bar seemed to hold its breath. Keaton turned and eyeballed Lefebvre. There was a slight grin on Keaton's face, but there was no humor in his eyes.

"You know what?" Keaton said, a dangerous softness in his voice. "I think we ought to expand the ceremony." A look at Bernadette. "Get this piece of shit ready."

Lefebvre smiled a terrible smile and reached for his gun.

Then several things happened at once.

Tom Chaney let loose with a heartbreaking squeal of pain. Badler had scarcely paused in his cranking, and when Dez shot a look at Chaney, he was sickened to see the stretch marks in his flesh, the skin at his wrists and ankles fishbelly-white, his hairy face livid with agony. Bernadette reached for her own gun, and Dez thought it would be a near thing between her and Lefebvre. It would come down to coolness and aim, but in the end neither of them fired.

Because a figure had burst out of the bar area doorway.

Keaton was on his feet and shouting. "*Get back in there!*"

Iris ignored him and strode closer. A figure stumbled out behind her, one of the fair-haired farm boys.

"Why'd you let her out?" Badler shouted.

"She hit me," the boy said, rubbing a cheekbone that was red and swelling. "She hit Aaron too, the dumb twat."

"Grab her," Keaton snarled at Badler, who was fifteen feet from Iris.

"Have Caleb and Aaron do it," Badler replied. "They're the ones you assigned to her."

"Goddammit!" Keaton growled. "Get her out of here before it happens."

Before what happens? Dez wondered, but in the next instant the thought was swept away by a stunning sight.

Iris was unzipping the top of her blue sleeveless shirt, revealing a tantalizing hint of cleavage. An irrational corner of his mind believed she was doing this for his benefit. Giving him one last sweet memory before Hernandez cranked his arms right off his body. But she wasn't looking at Dez.

She was staring at Tom Chaney.

Who howled at the ceiling and began to shudder.

CHAPTER TWENTY-FOUR

Shooter, Monster, Beast

"Spin that goddamned crank!" Keaton shouted.

For a moment, Badler just gaped at Tom Chaney, whose body was flailing in what looked like the worst grand mal seizure imaginable. His body was shivering and convulsing, and though there was no slack in the chains that bound him, his spasms were violent enough to make the eyehooks in the floor creak and to send the crank clicking in the opposite direction.

"*Badler!*" Keaton bellowed.

Somewhere in the back of his mind, Dez noted how Hernandez too had stopped cranking, but it was difficult to linger long on that, given the way Keaton was stalking toward Iris.

Chaney let loose with another wolf howl, this one more powerful and sustained. The hackles on Dez's neck stood up. The patrons sitting closest to where Chaney hung scrambled to their feet and backed away.

If Keaton noticed, he didn't let on. "I knew you'd pull some sort of shit," he growled, an index finger leveled at Iris. She'd ceased unzipping her shirt and now stood between Badler and Keaton looking supremely unworried. Keaton poked a forefinger in her direction. "I knew you were here to get yours."

"Isn't everyone?" Iris said, but her words were swallowed up by the noises issuing from Tom Chaney.

Dez was reminded of Jim the Popcorn-Loving Werewolf. When Jim had turned, Dez had been able to run away.

Now he was chained.

Ten feet away from a transforming werewolf.

Dez's throat burned with acid. He worried Chaney would break free and lunge at him, but Chaney didn't seem aware of anyone; he was writhing and jittering like a torn power line.

"I'll leave if you let him go," Iris said to Keaton.

Keaton laughed so hard he planted his hands on his knees. "You really think I'm gonna let this woman-murdering animal go free?"

"The other one," Iris said. "Dez."

Dez couldn't help experiencing a wave of emotion, despite the futility of her efforts. *We're surrounded*, he wanted to remind her. Keaton, Hernandez, Badler. Crosby, Gattis, Wyzinski. The farm boys. Bernadette. And too many other fear-twisted fiends who didn't care a whit whether Dez and Iris died horrible deaths.

Beneath that, the thought arose: *Susan.*

Was she really dead? Exsanguinated and left for the crows and feral dogs to squabble over?

Keaton's voice was flat. "Badler. Hernandez. Turn those goddamned cranks, or I swear to God I'll have your heads on the wall by night's end." He whirled. "And where the hell are you going?"

All heads turned toward the rear corner door, the one through which Dez had left and reentered on his trip to Keaton's house. Weeks was three feet from the threshold, shoulders hunched, a parody of a child caught sneaking away.

Keaton made a reproving click with his teeth and tongue. "Running away at the first sign of trouble, Pastor Weeks? Maybe I was wrong to protect you."

Weeks was wild-eyed, contrite. "You didn't make a mistake, Mr. Keaton! Besides, you know what I can do. You know how my abilities come in handy."

"Shit," Keaton said, grinning. "Of course I do, Pastor Weeks. Which is why I need your prissy ass over here."

Weeks drew back, his bespectacled eyes shifting to Chaney's writhing form, which was now so hairy he looked as much beast as man.

"*Now!*" Keaton bellowed.

Weeks jumped and began heel-toeing it across the bar toward Chaney. Despite the pounding of his heart, Dez watched with interest as Weeks bustled around to stand before Chaney.

"That won't help," Lefebvre called.

Dez glanced over and was surprised to find Lefebvre and Bernadette with guns still drawn and aimed at one another, the standoff a mere sideshow in this swirling maelstrom of rage.

"Go on," Keaton said to Weeks. There was something hungry, almost salacious in his gaze.

"Don't touch me!" Iris snapped.

Dez saw she'd drawn a gun as well, had it trained on the farm boy's face. Dez struggled for the name, then retrieved it. Caleb, the farm boy had been called. The other one was named Aaron. Had Iris killed Aaron in the back room? Or merely incapacitated him?

Did it fucking matter?

"Look at me, Tom," Weeks said.

Chaney's body had gone limp in the handcuffs. His head was bowed as though he were snoozing. But God was he hairy. Like an underfed bear strung up in chains.

"Crank it, Badler," Keaton said. "Wake the dumb sonofabitch up."

"Let go of it," Iris said, her gun shifting toward Badler.

"You like me too much to shoot me," Badler said and grinned at her.

"Look at me, Tom," Weeks repeated.

Dez noticed a fundamental change in Weeks's face. Gone was the prim smile that had been stamped on the doughy features throughout his misguided sermon; in its place was a shifty, half-mad leer reminiscent of an old movie Dez's dad had shown him when he was a kid, a John Barrymore film that had scared the living shit out of him.

Svengali.

A gunshot shattered the near-silence of the bar. Badler stumbled away from the crank, teeth bared and a hand pinned against his stomach. Dez hoped at first Iris had gut shot him, but as Badler swayed sideways to lean against a post, Dez spotted the wound in the middle of Badler's hand.

Iris was a hell of a shot, Dez decided.

"You fucking *bitch*," Badler muttered. He was bent over, a hand clamped over his bleeding one to staunch the blood flow.

"You're done," Keaton said to Iris. "Caleb, take over the crank. And you four – yes, the four of you...." Keaton nodded at the men at a table near the crank and the bleeding Badler. "You four disarm Iris. If she shoots Caleb, butcher the treacherous bitch."

Amazingly, Iris grinned. She trained the gun on Caleb's face.

Caleb, who'd been reaching for the crank, glanced at Keaton irresolutely.

"The change is reversing, Tom," Weeks said, his voice smooth as satin. "The tension is leaving your muscles."

Dez stared at Weeks's glittering eyes and thought, *Mesmerist.*

He understood immediately how useful it might be. You could hypnotize someone to gain useful information. You could plant a suggestion in a subject's mind, compel him to do your bidding.

Even reverse a lycanthropic transformation.

"Crank it!" Keaton demanded.

Iris's gun never wavered from Caleb's young face. From her distance, a mere ten feet, there was no chance of her missing. Maybe Keaton's plan was to sacrifice his henchmen until Iris ran out of ammunition. Dez wouldn't put it past the heartless bastard.

Caleb glanced from Iris to the crank, from Keaton to Iris.

"You know I'll do it," Iris said.

"All of you!" shouted Badler, who was still doubled over. "All of you rush the bitch!"

The quartet of men he was addressing exchanged glances, and in a few more seconds, maybe one of them would have done as Badler had bidden. But every face in the Four Winds Bar turned toward Tom Chaney then, who'd stirred enough to let everyone know he was still alive.

"Yessss, Tom," Weeks purred. "Your limbs are relaxing, your toes unclenching. Let the night breeze wash over you, let the cool air in."

To Dez, who was rimed with sweat from the sweltering heat of the bar, this sounded as absurd as anything had all evening. Still, it appeared to have an effect on Tom, who hung limply from the chains, the hair covering his body not retreating into his skin but certainly no longer sprouting in wiry tufts.

"Look at me, Caleb," Keaton said, and though Keaton's voice remained level, to Dez he'd never appeared so menacing. "I know you don't want to get shot, but look at Badler over there. Did Iris kill him?"

Caleb the Farm Boy glanced at Badler and licked his lips. Although Caleb didn't speak, his thoughts were plainly written on his face: *No, Badler's not dead, but I'd prefer having the use of both hands rather than one with a hole in it.*

"Think, Caleb," Keaton said, stepping toward the boy. "Once Badler feeds, that hand of his will heal." His grin widened at Badler. "Won't it?"

"You're goddamned right it will," Badler growled. His face was an unhealthy ashen hue, and sweat dripped off his chin. He nodded at the four men at the adjacent table. "You sons of bitches go to work on her. She can't hit all of you if you jump her at the same time."

But Dez scarcely heard this last. He'd glanced at Chaney, whose brow was furrowed and whose eyelids were twitching as though in the thrall of some grisly nightmare.

"Look at me, Tom," Weeks said. "I can take away the pain. Look... at...*me*."

Chaney opened his eyes and looked at Weeks.

Chaney's eyes glowed a lambent yellow.

Weeks's face went slack. He recoiled.

Chaney opened his fanged mouth and roared. The noise vibrated Dez's eardrums.

Chaney raised his head, arched his back, and before anyone realized what was happening, he wrenched his upper body down and his knees up, and though the chains didn't split in half, they did rip the eyehooks loose from the ceiling joists. The heavy steel pulleys and the chains plummeted toward Chaney, who hit the ground first, his feet landing with inhuman grace. A split second before the heavy pulleys would have crashed down on Chaney's head, the werewolf lunged forward. Weeks saw him coming but was too slow to move, too slow even to raise his hands before Chaney crashed down on him and buried his maw in Weeks's pasty throat.

The Four Winds Bar erupted in screaming patrons and overturned chairs. Many took cover behind tables or pillars.

"Bar the door!" Keaton shouted. "Bar the fucking door!"

Bernadette fired at Lefebvre, but Lefebvre, perhaps utilizing his psychic skills to anticipate Bernadette's move, was hustling under the balcony and taking refuge behind a table. Bernadette fired three times, but none of the slugs found their mark.

"Fuck *him*, Bernadette!" Keaton raved. "Bar the goddamned door!"

A tide of patrons had begun to swarm toward the front doors, but Bernadette was there first, a four-by-four gripped in one hand and her revolver clutched in the other.

"Back!" Bernadette shouted as she threaded the four-by-four through the handles of the double doors, and to Dez's dismay, no one took the opportunity to bum rush her while her gun was pointed distractedly in the air.

Chaney had torn through Weeks's neck, his wolf-like muzzle bathed in scarlet. Gattis, his mangled beard quivering in apprehension, had ventured toward Chaney with the obvious intention of bashing his head in with the makeshift mace. As Gattis widened his stance and raised the mace, Dez thought, *Don't draw Chaney's attention away from Weeks. He might end up attacking me.*

Although he recognized this for the cowardly thought it was, it did carry with it a modicum of logic. Werewolves, once fully transformed, were berserkers, so fraught with bloodlust that they did not – could not – discriminate. The elderly Jim had been a perfect example. Dez was convinced Jim would no more have attacked Dez than he would have attacked his wife when he was in his right mind. But once the change was on, there was no resisting its black vortex of hunger.

Gattis swung the mace, its glass shards walloping Chaney in the base of his skull.

The impact was colossal. So bone-crunching was the blow that Dez expected the werewolf to slump on top of the erstwhile preacher and bleed out on his remains. But without pause the werewolf scrambled to a crouch and regarded Gattis with a look so baleful Dez's own bladder nearly let go.

Keaton seemed oblivious of Chaney, all his attention fixated on the front doors, where Bernadette now stood, looking terrified, the revolver wavering in her grip as the crowd converged.

"All of you away from the doors now," Keaton commanded, but no one seemed to hear. They continued to swarm toward Bernadette.

"Goddammit," Keaton hollered. "I said get away from the goddamned—" He lowered his head, stretched his hands – *What the hell?* – and galloped along the side of the of the room like some weird gorilla-lion hybrid. Bystanders scattered before him. In moments, Keaton reached Bernadette and her dinky-looking revolver. The crowd took a step back from him.

Below Dez, the werewolf was stalking forward, hands and chains dragging the floor, the enlarged body bristling with rage. To Dez's horror, Gattis was backpedaling toward Dez's chains. The idiot was directly below him now.

Dez shot a look over his shoulder, discovered the crank Hernandez had been operating was unattended, and with a further craning of his neck, Dez understood why. Hernandez had positioned himself at one of the two exits flanking the bar, which was why no patrons were trying to get out there. An unarmed Hernandez was more imposing than an armed Bernadette.

Dez jerked around to see the other back doorway, the one through which Iris had emerged, and before he could identify the individual standing there holding back the crowd, something in the foreground flashed, the noise stunningly loud despite the clamor of the crowd, and he shifted his gaze in time to see one of the pale farm boys – Caleb – pitching forward at Iris's feet.

She'd shot him in the forehead.

"You'll pay for that, Iris!" Keaton thundered from his position near the front door, but though the boss's voice was as resonant as ever, the quality of it had altered, become deeper. As Dez watched, Keaton twitched, doubled over like he was about to vomit. Keaton's shoulders were broadening. The question in Dez's head recurred: *What the hell are you?*

"No!" someone beneath Dez shouted. It was Gattis, who swung the mace as the werewolf leaped. The glass-speckled instrument proved as ineffectual as a broomstick. The werewolf crashed into Gattis and both bodies hit Dez's leg chains so hard that something in Dez's left ankle cracked. Dez cried out, tried not to look, but the blood fanning up from Chaney's whirring claws splattered on the soles of Dez's bare feet and collected like dew in his leg hair. Gattis wailed like a squalling newborn, the voice going wet and devolving into garbled pleas for aid. Dez's chains continued to tug, the bloodbath taking place right up against the eyehooks. Dez gritted his teeth, steeled himself against the yanking, but he knew deep down that all Chaney would have to do was to pull once on the chains, and Dez's legs would be torn from his body.

"Let us the fuck out of here, Keaton!" someone shouted from the front entryway, and a score of voices echoed in agreement. But most of the crowd was backing away from the door.

Keaton was transforming.

The diminished throng near the doors seemed to clue into this fact, and they, too, began to back away. And despite the pockets of yelling and flurries of activity, the predominant sound in the Four Winds Bar was a collective inhalation, the bated breath of dread at what Keaton was becoming.

Dez's arms juddered. He realized he was being lowered from his stretched position. The slackening of the chains brought with it an elemental relief, his back and shoulders no longer so attenuated he feared his arms would be ripped from their sockets. Yet as the chains continued to tremble, his logical side kicked in, and he understood the consequence of this relief.

He was being lowered onto the werewolf and Gattis's eviscerated corpse.

But lowered by whom? The slack in Dez's chains allowed him greater freedom of movement, and though figures raced back and forth through the main bar area, he realized who was lowering him. Iris's toned arms flexed as she worked the crank, her face grimly intent on getting him down.

"Wait a second!" he shouted.

Though she was thirty feet away, she glanced up at him in annoyance.

"You're putting me right on top of Chaney!" he yelled.

"There's no time," was her answer.

No time? he thought. No time for what? If he continued to descend, he'd end up on the werewolf's writhing back.

"Stop cranking," he pleaded.

In answer, she compressed her lips but did not cease her efforts.

Dez shot a glance down – only four feet from the werewolf now. "Iris, I know you're trying to help, but—"

"Would you look?" she shouted, with a nod toward the front of the bar.

Dez swung his face around in time to see Keaton pitch forward onto all fours. His shoulders were swelling, his chest and back expanding. There were – and for a moment, Dez doubted his eyesight – ivory objects sprouting from the sides of his head, which was growing dark with fur.

The crowd backed away from Keaton. Bernadette was edging away from Keaton too, the gun hanging limply at her side.

Keaton's head was down, and the horns sprouting from the sides of his head began to curve inward, their length more than ten inches, fourteen, a foot-and-a-half long. The face remained downcast, but Dez realized what Keaton was even before he beheld the enormous hoofs that had replaced his feet, even before Keaton raised his face and Dez beheld the bloodred eyes, the enlarged nostrils.

The minotaur rose to its full height and roared at the crowd.

PART FIVE
THE MINOTAUR
CHAPTER TWENTY-FIVE

The Axemen

Holy fuck, Dez thought.

As one, the crowd undulated inward, the mass of people, unmindful of the werewolf, bent on eluding the new, gigantic horror that stood before the chief exit of the bar. Dez thought at first that Chaney was unaware of the new creature, but a downward glance showed him that the werewolf, also, had been roused by the minotaur's roar.

As werewolf and minotaur regarded one another, the crowd parting before them in a broad swath, Dez couldn't help scrutinizing the beast that moments before had been Bill Keaton. Like most monsters, Keaton was like, yet unlike the fictional conception to which society was accustomed. Yes, Keaton's bull-like face possessed horns. Yes, Keaton's feet had transformed into hooves. And true, the nostrils and cheekbones had shaped themselves into a vaguely bovine form.

But that was where literature ended and perverse nature began. The face was more demonic than bull-like, the eyes not glowing infernally, like the vampire's phosphorescent orange or the werewolf's lambent yellow, but rather a cheerless, unhealthy crimson, as though someone had painted the whites with ruby-red fingernail polish.

There was madness in Keaton's eyes. And rage. Whereas the face of the werewolf revealed nothing but an ungovernable bloodlust, the minotaur's gaze was appallingly intelligent. It knew Chaney was the one who'd murdered its mistress; it knew this werewolf was its enemy.

Chaney stepped toward Keaton, the distance between them fifty feet. The chains holding Dez's arms continued to shudder.

Iris was lowering him. Thank God for Iris.

Keaton stood on his great hooves, panting, and yes, actually snorting, but Dez scarcely noticed. Because even though Iris was relieving him of the massive pain, what then? He was still in manacles and leg cuffs; he was still, in essence, screwed.

A flurry of movement to Iris's right. Though it taxed his aching body to look behind him, Dez was glad he did. He found it difficult to breathe for fear that the new development was a mirage.

Joe Kidd and Michael Summers were hurrying through the crowd.

Both men carried axes.

Though the minotaur hadn't moved from his position by the front doors, Chaney had halved the distance between them. More, Chaney's voice reverberated in a trembling growl.

A member of the crowd rushed toward Chaney, a heavyset woman Dez hadn't noticed before. She raised a hatchet, apparently as a show of allegiance to Keaton. She swung the hatchet at Chaney, but so quickly that Dez barely tracked it. The werewolf's arm shot out, swiped a backhand at the woman's face. Her skin ribboned from chin to crown, the hatchet clanked on the floor, her body tumbling at the werewolf's feet. Her screams were muffled by her hands and the blood, but Chaney didn't seem to give her a second thought; he kept stalking toward the minotaur as though nothing had happened. For his part, Keaton's bloody eyes remained fixed on his adversary.

Something touched Dez's toes, and he sucked in breath, was surprised to see he'd reached the floor. Behind him, Iris continued to crank. The pressure left his arms, his shoulders, but before he could appreciate this development, the chain on his right ankle jumped. He whirled to see who had jerked on it.

Michael Summers and his axe. Before Dez could react, Joe Kidd went to work on the other chain, both men attacking the places where the chains touched the eyehooks. Joe was the more muscular of the two; his hewing was more effective, and by the third stroke, the chain was severed. Michael continued to hack at the chain attached to Dez's right ankle. Iris continued to slacken the chains.

Dez tested his left leg. Though the cuff and the twenty inches of chain still attached to it weighed him down, it felt incredible to be able to flex the knee, to move without encumbrance.

Another stroke by Michael, and the chain fettering his right ankle let go. He walked in place a little to restore sensation to his legs. The arm chains had loosed to the point that he could lower his wrists to his waist. Almost free.

Commotion from the front of the room drew his attention. The werewolf had drawn to within ten feet of the minotaur, was circling like a junkyard dog, its great mane bristling. For his part, Keaton merely revolved slowly, tracking Chaney's movements, seemingly in no hurry to adopt a defensive stance.

Everyone near the pair of monsters had paused to watch the showdown. The room wasn't silent, but the werewolf's growl, the slow pivot of the minotaur's giant hooves, were clearly audible.

"On your knees," a voice at Dez's ear hissed. He turned as someone seized his shoulder and drove him to the floor. Dez's knees hit the unyielding wood, and though a dim region inside him – the one where unreasoning pride still dwelt – took offense to being manhandled by Joe Kidd, Dez's more intelligent nature understood that the man was preparing to chop down at the chains binding Dez's wrists.

Joe took a step back, raised the axe, and fixed the chain in place with a boot. Dez scooted his wrists away from his body as far as they would go, and buried his face against his shoulder to protect his eyes from any debris that might be kicked up from the axe blows. Joe swung and one chain parted.

"Get him, Bill!" someone shouted.

"Rip his goddamned head off!" another voice joined in.

Dez glanced up in time to see a small portion of the crowd near him watching Joe Kidd's attempt to free Dez. One patron actually raised an old-fashioned blackjack as though to assault Joe with it.

Crosby.

Before Crosby could swing the blackjack at Joe, Michael Summers intervened, shoved Crosby back into the massed crowd, and pulled out a compact pocketknife, which he pointed at Crosby's face.

"Keep your ass back," Michael said.

"What're you gonna do with that?" someone asked. "Remove a splinter?"

"Hold still," Joe said, and with the next axe stroke, the last chain parted and Dez found himself free. Sure, he had cuffs and chains attached to all four limbs, and yes, he was clad in nothing but a pair of sweat-soaked boxers, but at least he wasn't strung up in the air like some twisted piece of modern art.

"Hey, Joe," someone said.

Dez turned to see who had spoken.

It was Badler, who shoved the muzzle of a .45 in Joe Kidd's stomach and fired.

CHAPTER TWENTY-SIX

Drew Barrymore

Joe Kidd went flying into the wall of crowd, but Badler unloaded three more slugs into his midsection just for spite. Michael Summers screamed, but it was too late to do anything for Joe, who slumped on the floor, his chewed-up belly gushing blood. Michael darted at Badler, the paltry little pocketknife extended before him, and Badler turned his gun on him.

A shot exploded, and like the rest of the crowd, Michael froze. But it was Badler who stumbled sideways, his gun tumbling to the ground, his shooting hand clamped over his bleeding shoulder. Dez went for the gun, but Wyzinski, the guy with the piercings, was there first, quick-moving if not quick-thinking. Wyzinski brought the gun up to shoot whoever had shot Badler, but Dez whipped a wrist at him. The foot-long chain dangling from it cracked Wyzinski in the jaw, sending him flying into the crowd and the .45 pinwheeling under a dozen sets of boots.

Dez only had a moment to glance at who'd saved Michael Summers's life and was unsurprised to find Iris aiming at Badler, who was crawling toward Joe Kidd's bleeding corpse.

"Don't do it," she said.

Dez expected her to shoot Badler again, but before she did, a thundering roar erupted from the front of the bar, the minotaur's voice unmistakable above the chaos.

Dez swiveled his head that way, saw the werewolf tensed to spring, but before Chaney could launch himself at the minotaur, a pair of figures detached from the crowd and darted at Chaney. One, Dez saw, was a muscular, middle-aged man who bore the unmistakably stout body of a cannibal. The other was the woman with the wind-burnt face. As she drew closer, Dez saw her lips wrinkling back from yellow teeth, her eyes enlarging in diabolical fury.

Witch, he thought. *Oh my God, I think she's a witch.*

Chaney's mouth hinged open in a bloodcurdling yowl, his body obviously plagued by some intolerable pain. Indeed the wind-burnt woman was muttering something under her breath as she approached, her cannibal cohort grinning in triumph as they bore down on Chaney.

Do something, Dez thought, and despite the adrenaline and terror coursing through him, he recognized his father's voice, the tone as unwavering as it was moral.

What am I supposed to do? Dez demanded. *I can't cast spells, can't transform. What can I—*

Something, the voice cut him off. *You're supposed to do* something.

Dez had taken two steps toward Badler's gun when movement drew his attention. He turned and saw Michael Summers with his right arm extended, palm forward, reminding Dez ridiculously of Iron Man. But instead of emitting a pulse of bluish light from a computerized palm, Michael stood there, seemingly in a trance, as the figures converged on Chaney, who'd dropped to his knees and was wailing in agony.

Three feet from where Chaney knelt, the witch froze, her lips no longer writhing. She was staring in horror at her cannibal companion, who in turn was gaping at Michael Summers from across the room.

Michael was sweating profusely, his face strained in concentration, his extended hand quivering. The cannibal shrieked and when Dez looked that way he saw the man's head was ablaze. The man was slapping at the flames but unable to do a thing to extinguish them. He fell forward, screaming and batting at his roasting face.

Dez turned and looked at Michael Summers, whose shoulders were slumped in exhaustion.

"Just like Drew Barrymore," Dez said.

Before Michael could respond, someone seized his arm – Iris. She said, "The weapons are behind the bar."

Dez moved to follow her, but before they entered the poleaxed crowd, he saw one more thing that made his skin ripple into gooseflesh.

Instead of dying, Badler had begun to lap at Joe Kidd's leaking belly.

As Dez watched in aghast silence, the gunshot wound in Badler's shoulder began to close.

CHAPTER TWENTY-SEVEN

Warriors

Dez didn't make it to the bar. The giant in the black jacket had evidently retrieved Badler's gun. As Dez watched in numb horror, Black Jacket aimed the .45 at Terhune, the old waiter, and though Terhune raised his hands in surrender, Black Jacket squeezed the trigger, reducing Terhune's head to a leaking, misshapen tomato.

Black Jacket never stopped leering. *It's his chance to kill for sport*, Dez thought. *My God, as if there wasn't enough to worry about already.*

Black Jacket didn't show signs of transformation, and though Dez wondered if he was another Latent, more imperative in his mind was the need to stop him or escape his homicidal gaze, which was rotating slowly Dez's way.

Another patron, this one a nondescript man in his thirties, was knocked into Black Jacket's vicinity by the melee; before the nondescript man could even throw up his hands, Black Jacket leveled the .45 and popped him in the left eye.

Black Jacket spun toward Dez.

Dez darted at Black Jacket, but he knew he'd stood there too long, his brain too gummed by terror to kickstart his body into action. Dez was still eight feet away when the muzzle of the .45 swung around and pointed at his face, and though Dez threw up an arm to prevent the slug from ending his life, he knew inaction had damned him.

The explosion came. A moment later, Dez slammed into Black Jacket, who, impossibly, had dropped the gun and was pawing at the side of his neck. Black Jacket didn't go down from the impact, but he did stumble backward into a table. Dez ended up on hands and knees, and looking up, he saw it was Lefebvre who'd saved him, the muzzle of the thin man's gun lowering.

Dez couldn't suppress a grin. "Well, you son of a bitch."

Lefebvre's return smile was subtle, but it was there.

Then a roar shook the Four Winds Bar, and all turned toward Bill Keaton. In the foreground, Dez could see Chaney fighting against the witch's mental assault, but if Keaton noticed the struggle, he didn't let on. He was striding through the center of the bar, toppling tables, whipping a chair out of the way to shatter against a wooden pillar. Had it connected with a bystander, it would have impaled him.

But it was toward a specific bystander that Keaton's great hooves were striding.

It was toward Lefebvre.

As the minotaur approached, Dez got a better look at the beast, and a childlike part of him wanted nothing more than to wake up and find this was all a nightmare. Dez had seen terrible things over the past two years, had beheld horrors untold.

Yet in its own way, the minotaur was worse than all of these. It was a ragged monster, the horns asymmetrical, the bloodred eyes gleaming with wicked intelligence. Keaton's clothes hung in tatters. The face was alien enough to banish all thoughts of humanity. This creature would not be talked out of violence or turned to the side of good.

This creature was a living Shade.

Dez dove for Badler's gun, got hold of it, but before he could aim it at the minotaur, a volley of shots erupted, Lefebvre yes, but a pair of others from atop the bar as well.

Iris and Michael had reached the weapons cache.

The barrage of bullets caused the minotaur to jolt and stumble sideways – Dez spotted six places where the slugs had torn into his ugly mud-colored pelt – but it would clearly take more to bring the creature down.

Dez rose and fired at the beast's head. He saw one horn chip, but the minotaur whirled on him, bellowed in rage. The minotaur bunched, preparatory to a lunge, and Dez fired again, as did Lefebvre and Michael and Iris, the four of them opening ragged flaps of hide. The minotaur roared in outrage but never quite went down. Dez's gun clicked empty, and with teeth gritted, he flung it aside, started toward Iris and Michael to arm himself again, but something bashed him between the shoulder blades and sent him sprawling on his chest. Dez spun and saw who'd blindsided him.

Badler.

The cannibal never looked healthier. He'd shed his shirt, revealing muscles that would have awed Samson.

Dez heard a squeal, turned in time to see something that knocked his breath out. Despite his many wounds, Keaton had sprung at Lefebvre. The psychic's weapon proved no match for the hulking beast. The minotaur seized Lefebvre by the throat and hoisted him into the air. Iris and Michael had been forced to cease their firing for fear of hitting Lefebvre's flailing body. They needn't have worried.

Leering, the minotaur brought Lefebvre's horrorstruck face close to his, reveled in Lefebvre's terror for a long moment, then bit into his face, the upper incisors shearing the man's forehead, the lower mandibles crunching under the nose. Lefebvre shrieked, then went silent as the gnarled teeth took a grapefruit-sized bite out of his head.

"Fuck me," Dez heard Michael Summers moan, and then Michael and Iris were firing again.

A shot rang out from behind Dez, and with a turn he saw Bernadette, the faithful stooge, firing at Iris and Michael, who were forced to take cover in opposite directions.

Chaney howled – whether in pain or rage, Dez couldn't tell – but the werewolf's struggle with the witch was the last thing on Dez's mind.

Badler was reaching for Dez. Keaton was stalking after Iris.

Dez cast wildly about for something with which to defend himself, but the only thing in his immediate area was a shard of broken chair. He grasped it.

"Come on, little sweetheart," Badler said, and Dez pumped the wooden dagger at the cannibal's neck. Quicker than Dez could believe, Badler shot up an arm, their forearms clashed, and the wood fragment was deflected harmlessly away.

Badler seized him by the neck, wrenched him forward. He grinned a fiendish grin, their noses almost touching. "You're gonna taste good, sweetheart."

Dez jerked a knee up and caught Badler in the groin. Badler grunted, but not nearly as loudly as Dez had expected. *What the hell?* he thought. *Does feeding on human flesh make your genitals tougher too?*

Badler cocked a fist at waist level, slammed it into Dez's gut. Dez had time to tense his abdominal muscles, but it scarcely mattered. Badler's fist was like a mechanical wood splitter, the hard knuckles punishing Dez's entrails. Dez sagged against Badler's shoulder.

"That day we stole your whore," Badler muttered, "I whupped your sorry ass." A punch in the gut. Dez grunted. "Easiest goddamned fight I've ever had." Badler punched Dez in the gut again, his fist like a cudgel. Dez grunted and sagged against Badler's shoulder. "That whore of yours…I bet she regretted taking up with you when she saw you lying there in the dirt."

In desperation, Dez bit down on Badler's flesh. Cannibal or not, Badler screeched in pain, shoved Dez backward to detach him. Dez landed on his ass, realized something was in his mouth, and it wasn't until he'd spat out the pinkish, bloody object that he realized he'd ripped off a gobbet of Badler's shoulder. The cannibal clapped a hand over his oozing wound and snarled at Dez.

Dez scrambled over and retrieved the wooden shard.

Under the balcony shadows he spotted Iris hurrying from table to table, attempting to keep something between her and Keaton. The bar had thinned of patrons, many of the bystanders having taken advantage of the unguarded doors to make their escape.

Badler charged Dez. Dez feinted with the shard. Badler hesitated for a fraction of a second, but it was enough for Dez to slash at Badler's midsection. A gash opened between rows of Badler's chiseled abs, but the injury was shallow. Fleetingly, Dez thought of the Coliseum, of gladiators forced to battle to the death while the crowd cheered lustily. And here were Dez and Badler both shirtless, both sweaty and bloody and knowing one would die and one would live.

Badler seemed to sense this because he was nodding now, his head lowered grimly, his smile deranged.

Badler charged at him. Dez raised the shard as if to strike him in the face. Badler leapt, hands outstretched for the wooden spike, but Dez dropped, tore down at Badler's exposed belly. For all his strength and agility, Badler was a shitty hand-to-hand fighter. It was hubris, no doubt, the cannibal believing he'd never need to improve his combat skills because his brute strength would keep him safe.

The wicked shard of wood dug a trough through Badler's abdominal muscles, and though Dez suspected none of Badler's major organs had been perforated, he'd certainly wounded the cannibal badly.

Hot scarlet drizzled over Dez's face as Badler's momentum carried him into a table. Glasses shattered and spangled the floor, and though he knew he'd cut his bare feet badly, Dez surged forward, stabbing down at Badler. The wooden shard sank into Badler's lower back. Five or six inches of wood speared Badler's skin, and the muscular man arched his back, uttered a keening shriek, his face upraised to the ceiling. Without thinking, Dez grabbed a broken glass by the handle, whipped it at Badler's exposed throat, grinned in triumph as the skin unzipped and released a torrent of blood. Dez cringed as glass fragments harrowed his bare feet, but he knew this was it; if he was ever to kill Badler, it had to be now, while the cannibal was weakest. Dez clutched the jagged beer glass, thrust it into Badler's already savaged throat, and this time the blood spray was uncontrollable, the haze coating Dez and momentarily blinding him. He dropped the glass, staggered away, and wiped ineffectually at his eyes.

Another gunshot. Iris? More shouting voices. Where, Dez wondered dizzily, were Hernandez and Keaton's other cronies? For that matter, where was Keaton? Had he claimed Iris already, or was she still fending him off, playing a lethal game of tag through the tables?

Dez glanced and saw the witch closing in on Chaney. But now the werewolf appeared enraged as well as anguished.

Someone grabbed Dez, and instinctively, he shoved against his attacker.

"Chill the hell out!" the person yelled, and with a twitch of recognition, Dez realized it was Michael Summers.

"Here," Michael said, cramming something into Dez's hands. A rag. In moments he'd wiped his eyes with it, not minding that the fabric smelled like the inside of a dead man's colon.

"Iris?" Dez demanded.

"Getting to her," Michael said.

Dez seized Michael's arm. "You don't know if she's alive?"

Michael glared at him. "I've been trying not to die." Michael's eyes flicked down. "You mind letting the fuck go of me?"

Dez did.

They set off across the main seating area, which had degenerated into a warzone. Chaney had seized the witch with his elongated jaws and was shaking the woman like she was an oversized chew toy. Dez couldn't tell whether she was alive or dead, but judging from the boneless way she flopped, he suspected the latter.

They'd almost reached the shadowed regions beneath the balcony when someone darted at them. Dez spun, saw Crosby, his eyes maniacally wide, the blackjack raised high. Michael swept Dez out of the way with one arm, brought his gun up with the other, and shot Crosby in the middle of the chest. Crosby pitched forward and curled into a writhing ball.

Michael cried out, toppled, and his gun went skittering away. Dez whirled and saw Wyzinski with a familiar object in his hands. He'd found Gattis's makeshift mace, had evidently bludgeoned Michael with it.

Dez went for Michael's gun, but in an instant knew he'd erred. The distance was too great.

Wyzinski had witnessed the deaths of Crosby, of Gattis, of Erica the Telekinetic Asshole. He was bent on revenge.

Dez continued toward the gun, but winced at a shrill yelp from behind him. He grabbed the gun, rose, and aimed it at Wyzinski, but discovered him trapped beneath Chaney, the werewolf's claws a scrabbling blur in Wyzinski's torso. Scraps of shirt and gristle hurtled about, a blood fountain gushing over the werewolf's face as the beast plunged its maw into the ruin of Wyzinski's chest.

Dez grabbed Michael and lifted him to sitting. "You still with me?"

Michael groaned, nodded.

"Come on," Dez muttered, hauling Michael to his feet.

As Michael emerged from his fog, Dez wondered why Michael hadn't used his pyrokinetic abilities on Wyzinski. Maybe, he mused, the effort needed to conjure fire was so great he could only do it infrequently.

Something wet smacked against Dez's bare calf muscle, and when he looked down he saw it was Wyzinski's heart. Dez glanced at the werewolf, and for a moment Chaney stared up at him, his face satanic, his bloody lips writhing over grossly elongated teeth.

Dez's heart thumped. He had no idea how much of Chaney remained in the beast. Judging from the mad gleam in the werewolf's eyes, Chaney was completely gone. Not a trace of humanity shone in that fiendish face, not the merest hint of recognition. Dez suspected the werewolf would feel no compunction at killing him.

"We should go," Dez said to Michael.

"Uh-huh," Michael replied.

They hustled toward the area under the balcony. They weaved

between tables, but though Dez glimpsed numerous bystanders who'd taken refuge here, there was no sign at all of Iris or the minotaur.

But the minotaur was the largest creature Dez had ever seen. So where the hell was it?

A loud thump sounded above Dez. Another.

He knew where the minotaur was.

It had chased Iris into the balcony.

CHAPTER TWENTY-EIGHT
Fire and Horns

Dez bolted for the staircase. Even as he mounted the first step and began to take two at a time, he heard the sounds of a scuffle up there, knew on a bone-deep level that Iris was still alive.

Dez and Michael reached the balcony and beheld a wild scene. More than a dozen patrons were cornered up there, another score of them rooting on Keaton as he tracked Iris slowly through the tables. Men and women pelted alongside Iris, scurrying like mice from the massive minotaur.

And as Dez drew nearer, he realized that Keaton's change had advanced even further. Where before his dark hide had been smooth, there were now bones poking through the coarse hair, some of them blunt and knobby, others as sharp as fillet knives. One jaundiced excrescence protruding from the minotaur's shoulder reminded Dez of a pumpkin stem, curved and ridged and tapered to a point. The weapon in Dez's hand felt like a cap gun. The minotaur's hide was too thick, the armor of bone and sinew impenetrable.

Iris and the other patrons in her vicinity had been herded to the far corner. Their only chance of escape was the window behind them, but a fall from that height – more than twenty-five feet, Dez estimated – could prove deadly.

The minotaur reached down, grasped a table edge, and flung it like a Frisbee. Its heavy base skidded over another tabletop and plowed into a pair of shrieking onlookers.

If Keaton noticed their deaths, he didn't show it.

Iris flicked a look at Dez, and he saw the terror in her eyes. He realized he'd been harboring the causeless belief that she possessed some otherworldly power, but now, with her life in jeopardy, she appeared as feeble as he was. It made his need to help her even greater. But how?

No ordinary weapon could penetrate the minotaur's bone-studded hide. Hand-to-hand combat meant a swift death. If only he had—

Dez caught his breath, turned to look at Michael.

But Michael was already concentrating, his hand out, fingers splayed, face pinched in concentration. He was sweating with the effort, and Dez wondered to what extent it leeched Michael's strength to conjure fire with his mind.

The minotaur went ramrod straight. The beast swiveled its head and scowled at Michael. Even as Dez recoiled at the venom on that face, he marked the changes in it. New horns had sprouted from its chin and cheeks. The teeth were a chaotic snarl. Goosebumps misted up Dez's arms, even as he took aim with Michael's gun at the creature's right eye.

It was an impossible shot. He had to get closer.

Iris fired upon the creature. Her aim was true enough to bloody the bridge of the minotaur's snout.

The creature roared.

Stunningly, several patrons near Iris took the opportunity to rush the minotaur. With a twinge of recognition, he saw at the head of the throng the man and woman he believed to be a couple. The man with the neck tattoo ran apace with his female companion, both of them wielding weapons, his a long kitchen knife, hers a length of chain maybe four feet long.

Dez charged the creature too.

The woman got there first, and in the moments before the minotaur swung at her, Dez was reminded of sports moms in the old world, the kind who wore their children's team colors and sipped Starbucks on lawn chairs.

The minotaur clubbed her so hard the side of her neck split open. The backhanded swat lifted her off her feet and propelled her over the balcony railing. The man with the neck tattoo cried out in sorrow and plunged the knife into the beast's stomach. The beast tore down with a fist, the blow so violent that the man's neck seemed to disappear as he was pounded downward like a driven nail.

Goddammit, Dez thought. These two, this man and this woman, died defending someone they probably barely knew, were snuffed out senselessly by a beast who treated life like it was worthless.

At this, another, more incisive thought occurred to Dez. Or an image, rather.

The back bedroom of the Keatons' home. The boy in the baseball uniform....

A growl sounding deep in his throat, Dez fired at the minotaur, the shot a good one, right in the side of the creature's mouth, but even as the beast bellowed in outrage, Dez could see how little it had done. The minotaur stomped toward him, eating the distance with alarming rapidity, and just as Dez took aim, just as the creature reached striking range and raised a great, clawed hand, the minotaur's head burst into flames. Wreathed in orange and blue, the massive horns whipsawing from side to side, the beast stumbled toward Iris, baying in pain.

"No!" someone shouted, and Dez had time to turn and see Michael enshadowed by a hulking figure.

Hernandez tackled Michael Summers. Both men crashed to the floor, and with a glance, Dez saw the flames encircling Keaton's head diminish.

For a moment, Dez debated what to do – help Michael with Hernandez, or attempt to finish off Keaton. But the sight of Hernandez seizing the back of Michael's head and bashing it on the floor decided him. Michael had saved Dez's life not once, but twice. Another blow like that and Michael would be as dead as Joe Kidd.

Dez took aim. "Hernandez!" he shouted.

Hernandez turned, his expression morphing into surprise.

Dez fired, the slug pulping the center of the man's face. Vaguely, Dez was aware of the minotaur barreling past him, moving toward the bar.

Hernandez toppled forward, his ursine body burying Michael Summers. Dez rushed over, his chewed-up feet shooting daggers of pain, and with Iris's help, he rolled Hernandez's corpse off Michael.

Iris knelt and shook Michael by the shoulder. "You still with us?"

Michael didn't answer, but he was still breathing.

A chorus of gasps brought Dez's head around. He saw the minotaur charging along the railing, and in the next moment the beast vaulted sideways, splintering the railing, the massive body arcing down and landing awkwardly on a table below. The whole thing collapsed, the minotaur scrambling through the rubble, and though the corona of fire still glimmered atop the minotaur's neck, Dez could see the flames had nearly gone out. A bystander in a purple coat froze as Keaton barreled forward, and rather than stopping or sidestepping the frozen figure, Keaton merely whipped his great head at the man. A jagged horn pierced the purple coat and flung the man like a flicked booger twenty feet from where he'd started.

Dez heard a gunshot and a roar and swiveled his head in time to see the werewolf disemboweling a man who'd apparently been foolish enough to attack Chaney from behind. Blood darkened the fur of Chaney's lower back, but he'd easily bested his attacker, whose shredded guts oozed like wine-drenched cutlets.

A voice rose above the cacophony. It was Wainwright, who'd gone to the sink behind the bar and filled up a gallon bucket. "Over here, boss!" Wainwright was shouting. "Over here!"

Keaton tracked the voice, moved in a desperate gallop toward the bar. Iris sprang to her feet, fired down at the minotaur, and though a scrap of hair twirled off its brawny shoulder, the minotaur scarcely seemed to register the wound.

Keaton reached the bar. Wainwright immediately doused Keaton's head with water, then dutifully refilled the bucket and repeated the action.

Dez moved up next to Iris, asked, "Should we go?"

She raised an eyebrow. "Go where?"

"The truck," he answered. "If we get out now, we can—"

"What about Michael?"

Dez glanced at Michael's prone body, his resolve faltering. "We can carry him."

She grasped Dez by the front of the shirt.

"It ends here, one way or the other," she said. "Keaton won't stop hunting us. Our only chance is to kill him now, while the Hound is on the loose."

Dez listened and realized that, yes, he did hear the sounds of ripping and tearing, and again the question came to him: Was Chaney aware of what he was doing? The minotaur possessed a semblance of control, but Chaney appeared to destroy indiscriminately.

He killed Wyzinski before Wyzinski killed you.

That doesn't prove—

But it suggests, doesn't it? Suggests Chaney is still in there somewhere. A werewolf doesn't know much beyond spilling blood, but it knows enough to recognize an enemy. At least, this werewolf does.

Dez took a steadying breath, looked into Iris's fierce green eyes. "How do we kill Keaton?"

She shrugged. "Fire seems to work."

He glanced at Michael. "He'll be out for a while."

Iris hurried over to one of the few tables that hadn't been overturned and lifted a kerosene lamp from its center.

"There are two dozen of these," she explained.

"But without Michael—"

"I've got a lighter behind the bar," she said impatiently. "Move your ass."

CHAPTER TWENTY-NINE
The Last Lesson

They hustled toward the stairs, guns drawn. Dez skirted a broken lamp, yearned for a pair of shoes to protect him from the glass that littered so much of the floor. He could appropriate footwear from one of the many cadavers that littered the main seating area, but that would require time, and time was something they didn't have. In fact, he realized as they trundled down the staircase, Wainwright had already doused the minotaur's head again, the cool water reducing the flames to a smolder.

Still, Dez was heartened by the sight of the huge beast draped over the bar, the back muscles heaving with pain and exertion.

Would the change reverse? Or was Keaton merely regrouping for another onslaught?

He got his answer a moment later.

Wainwright spotted them, jabbed an index finger like a shrill elementary school tattletale. "There they are, Mr. Keaton! There's the ones who caused all this badness!"

Dez almost laughed. *Right*, he thought. *We're the ones who set up a flesh trade business, the ones who orchestrated a public execution.*

But Wainwright's idiocy didn't matter. What mattered was the way the minotaur swiveled its great horned head and gazed at them.

The fire, Dez saw as he approached, had done significant damage to the minotaur's head. While the horns were merely scorched, the hide had been singed off, leaving raw, pink patches of skin to mottle the ochre-colored flesh. One eye, Dez saw with a quickening of hope, had been burned badly; rather than its former bloodred hue, it was now encrusted with a disgusting, oleaginous scrim of white. Dez was reminded of "The Tell-Tale Heart".

The minotaur was turning to face them.

Dez had no idea how many were left in the bar, but he suspected there were no more than twenty. With the exits unguarded and the massacre so extreme, only the chronically curious, the overly confident, or the utterly demented would stick around for the battle's conclusion.

Thirty feet away now, Dez cast a glance right and left to spot more hostiles. Of course, *everyone* seemed hostile, but he reminded himself of Michael Summers and Joe Kidd, of the man with the neck tattoo and his female companion. Of Lefebvre, who in the end had done the right thing and been murdered for his troubles. Yes, there was some good in the world, but you had to look hard to find it.

"Watch it!" Iris said, yanking down on Dez's shoulder. He let himself be dragged to the floor. It wasn't difficult. Iris was damned strong. But as the dark shape vaulted over them, Dez was glad he'd trusted her.

The werewolf clattered to the floor and raced toward Bill Keaton.

The minotaur leaped at the werewolf, Keaton's remaining good eye shuttered wide in rage. Chaney leapt too, but it was as Dez expected. As ferocious as the werewolf was, he was a head shorter and at least a hundred pounds lighter than the minotaur. Their bodies crashed together in midair, Keaton's overwhelming Chaney's and tilting the werewolf backward. But even as they rushed toward the floor, Chaney's jaws closed on Keaton's throat, and Keaton roared in pain.

Iris had stolen around the side of the bar, where Wainwright stood with a shotgun, barring her from where the lighter was apparently stored.

Gun extended, Iris stepped toward Wainwright. "Get out of the way, Kevin."

Wainwright leveled the shotgun at her. "You forgot who protects us, Iris. Just stop before I have to shoot you."

Iris's arm muscles tensed, the gun outstretched before her. "You know I don't want to – oh, fuck it."

She fired at Wainwright, whose shotgun exploded, and both of them went down.

Dez's guts somersaulted. *No!*

He raced toward the bar, vaulted it. He landed, slipped, caught his balance, and, disregarding the old man – Dez had seen well enough how Iris had put a hole in his heart – he fell at Iris's side. She was definitely alive, but she had her hands clutched to her hair, spitting out inarticulate sounds and drumming her feet.

"Iris," he said. "Are you—"

She jerked her head up to glare at him. "That asshole got buckshot in my scalp!"

He saw it then. There was blood where the pellets had torn her hairline. But the damage appeared to be superficial, and what was more, Iris looked angrier than ever, ready to take on Keaton by herself.

Dez tried to help her up, but she shoved him away and nodded. "The lighter's in that drawer. I—" She looked at the glass-strewn floor behind her. "Dammit! I dropped the lamp. There's another one over—"

"I got it," Dez said, already removing the lighter from the drawer. It was rectangular, silver, the refillable kind. He hopped onto the bar, started to climb down, but looked back at her and said, "Will you get my crossbow?"

"That thing's a pain in the ass," she said, but she strode over and lifted the trapdoor. Before Dez turned away, he caught a glimpse of the weapons there: his crossbow, a rifle and a trio of handguns, all black. He knew weaponry better than he had before the world changed, but he still couldn't tell a Luger from a Kahr, not without reading the name etched in steel.

"Toss me one!" he shouted. Iris tossed him a small black handgun, and after checking the safety, he got moving.

Head down, Dez made for one of the few intact lamps left in the Four Winds, one under the western balcony. As he ran he saw the werewolf and the minotaur struggling. Chaney was still locked on the minotaur's throat, while the minotaur rained barbaric blows to Chaney's ribcage.

Who the hell is left? Dez had time to wonder as he drew nearer the lamp. Nearly all of Keaton's confederates had been killed, at least the ones known to Dez. Still, it was likely the remaining patrons were sympathetic to Keaton's slave trade.

Dez grasped the lamp, ignited the cloth wick.

He gasped as a gunshot cracked behind him and he felt the sting of the slug in his right ass cheek. The lamp slipped through his hands, crashed on the table, and in moments the entire wooden surface was engulfed in flames. Dez dropped to his knees, a hand on his screaming buttock, and saw the kerosene pouring in runnels off the tabletop, the fire licking eagerly after it, starting a chair burning, the floor.

The whole place is gonna go up, Dez thought.

On the heels of that, a puff of smoke breathed over his face. His eyes instantly watered and stung like mad. Dez dragged a forearm over his eyes, but if anything, that only irritated them more. Dammit, it was like being blind. And of all the times—

The gun cracked again, and though the slug didn't hit him this time, it passed so near his head that the skin of his left ear burned. Dez whirled in time to see Aaron, the remaining farm boy henchman, taking aim again. The boy was only ten yards away and clearly a terrible shot.

But Dez's vision was so bleary he could barely keep his eyes from blinking shut. Aaron fired again, and this time the slug pinged off a curved decoration affixed to a pillar. An old-fashioned sickle, Dez realized as he turned tail and hustled toward the corner of the bar. The sickle might have come in handy were Dez attempting to harvest a fucking wheat field, but at the moment, it was no more help to him than the shattered lamp.

Another shot sounded and the wood of the bar's façade splintered in a fist-sized spray. *How many shots does the kid have left?* Dez wondered. He weaved a little as he neared the corner of the bar, partially because he was trying to avoid being shot, but mostly because the smoke had half-blinded him and thrown off his equilibrium.

Dez rounded the bar, dropped down before the homicidal farm boy blew his head off. Where was Iris? And was Michael still alive?

He had no idea about Michael, but Iris's whereabouts were clarified a moment later.

"Hold still, Chaney!" she shouted. "I'm trying to get a clear shot."

Dez could hear the werewolf snarling and thought, *Good luck. You really think Chaney's aware of your voice, or even his surroundings?* The lycanthropic change, in Dez's opinion, was utter madness, a mode of existence not unlike a tornado or tsunami. There was no thinking involved, no—

Dez froze, his back against the bar's shelf-lined interior.

Why wasn't Aaron still gunning for him?

Maybe he is, a voice suggested. *He's sneaking toward the bar to take you by surprise.*

Or maybe he's going for Iris.

The possibility galvanized him, made him stand and whirl, gun extended over the bar. Aaron was stealing around the overturned tables in an attempt to flank Iris. And Iris was so fixated on getting a clear shot at the minotaur's face, she had no idea Aaron was coming.

No!

Dez stowed the pistol in the seat of his underwear, hustled over, heaved up on the trapdoor, and snatched his crossbow from the cache. The bolts were still intact.

Dez slapped an arm on the bar, vaulted over it, and though his smoke-irritated eyes still watered, he concentrated all his focus on Aaron, on the broad-shouldered zealot who was still protecting his leader in spite of all the atrocities Keaton had committed.

Dez closed the distance. Straight ahead, the minotaur and the werewolf were locked together, the werewolf pinned to the floor, its blood streaming from the many wounds the minotaur had inflicted. Iris was drawing closer, already drawing a bead on the minotaur's face. Dez assumed she was planning on ruining Keaton's remaining good eye, but she wasn't going to do anything but die, for Aaron was closing in behind her, his gun extended. The shot was no more than eight feet, and even an inept shooter couldn't miss at that distance. Iris, her back to him, would never even know the face of her killer.

There was no time at all, goddammit. If he shouted for Iris to drop, Aaron would fire, and if Dez attempted the shot now, with the two lined up straight ahead of him, he was as likely to nail Iris with the bolt as he was Aaron.

No choice, Dez thought. He took one last diagonal stride, and skidded to a stop.

There. Iris and Aaron weren't quite in a line now, though the separation was minimal. Feeling very much like William Tell, Dez braced the crossbow on his left arm, squinted through the smoke tears at Aaron.

Squeezed the trigger.

Though the bolt was only in the air a moment, that moment seemed endless. He was sure, in attempting not to kill Iris with the shot, he'd erred too far to the left.

Aaron's head snapped back when the bolt caught him in the temple. His gun didn't go off – one of Dez's fears – but instead dropped from his big hand as the farm boy staggered and gaped stupidly at Iris, who'd finally turned, the knowledge of how close she'd come to dying dawning in her face.

But to her credit, she didn't pause to wonder how it had happened, didn't give Dez a wink or a smile of thanks.

Instead she marched over to where the minotaur had pinned the now-unconscious Tom Chaney, brought the gun as close as she could to its horned head, and aimed. The minotaur's head was swinging as it delivered its grim blows to Chaney, but Iris remained patient, kept the gun poised and ready for her opening. Dez hurried toward the trio, sure now Iris was aiming for the eye. Once she made the shot, the minotaur would be blind, and though Dez feared the creature could regenerate, he doubted the minotaur would be able to fight them both without sight in the fire consuming the Four Winds. Even now Dez could see the heads ranged along the base of the balcony catching fire, the flames licking the desiccated skin.

When Dez turned back to Iris and the minotaur he saw, in slow motion, the creature twitch its head away, parrying Iris's shot with its great horns. One of its hooved feet sideswiped her, striking her left thigh in a glancing blow and sending her into the sprawl of tables and bodies nearby. She landed near Aaron, who lay without moving.

Then, as if it had eyes in the back of its head, the minotaur turned and charged at Dez.

His skin prickling, Dez fired a bolt. It pierced the minotaur's snout, but rather than felling the great beast, the well-placed arrow sent it hurtling into the air, its face a rictus of mindless rage, and in that moment a revelation sizzled through Dez's brain like a lightning strike. He threw up an arm, but the minotaur's clawed hands clamped down on his shoulders, and with the beast atop him, Dez crashed down on his back.

A starburst of pain sent a billion pinpricks of light through his vision. When Dez could see again, he glimpsed the crossbow, which lay useless on the floor.

His brain foggy, his body numb, Dez gazed up at the minotaur. He knew the creature could slay him with a single swipe of its claws, but it was apparent that Keaton wanted to deal Dez a more satisfying end. Its milky eye oozed yellow pus, but its uninjured eye was slitted in a need that was almost sexual. The horned head drew nearer, the sinister face lowering toward him like a hideous portcullis that would separate him from this life, from Iris, from ever seeing Susan again.

Dez spoke without thinking. "You killed your son."

Nine inches away, the minotaur's face froze, the bloodred eye widening. "You wanted to scare your boy, teach him a lesson. Didn't you?"

Noxious saliva drooled out of the minotaur's mouth, slopped over

Dez's face, but he barely felt it, barely smelled the creature's gamy, scorched hide. Because the bloodred eye was watering, not in rage, not in irritation from the smoke, but in emotional anguish. Somewhere, deep inside Bill Keaton, there still lurked a trace of humanity, however meager it might be.

A shadow fell over them. Iris.

She shoved the gun into the minotaur's eye and emptied the clip.

The creature let out a roar that shook the building, and Dez saw, beyond the beast's furiously flailing arms, the flames climbing up the vaulted ceiling, the whole room becoming a conflagration. Dez tried to scoot out from under the minotaur, but it still sat astride him, its body immovable, so Dez stretched out, dragged the crossbow closer, got hold of it, raised it toward the creature's exposed underjaw, fired.

The bolt damn near disappeared in the tender flesh of the minotaur's underjaw. The creature howled in agony. Who knew what thoughts teemed within the minotaur's massive skull? Maybe its brains had been pureed to mush by Iris's bullets. As it tilted to its left, its claws scrabbling to dislodge the bolt from its gullet, Dez was finally able to extricate his legs and scuttle away from the beast.

He'd made it to what he thought was a safe distance when he noticed Iris limping away. The room was clouded with smoke, the heat from the growing flames raising the temperature at least twenty degrees. Dez winced as a shard of glass sliced his knee. Sucking in air, he reached down, removed the shard, and wondered if he'd have time to commandeer a dead man's clothes before he escaped. He was tired of fighting in his underwear.

Iris returned to the minotaur, this time bearing the sickle that had been affixed to the wall. Dez opened his mouth to ask her why she was bothering, but then he remembered stories of nearly dead creatures revivifying and slaughtering those who'd maimed them. Dez couldn't see how the minotaur, which had fallen onto its side and was barely moving, could recover from its wounds, but he supposed he saw Iris's point. If there was any chance of Keaton exacting revenge, they'd do well to remove it. Vindictiveness was the man's defining trait.

Iris began sawing into the creature's neck. One of the minotaur's arms whipped out, nailed Iris in the shoulder. Whether it was intentional or part of the creature's death throes, the impact was powerful enough to send her hurtling into Dez. He half-caught her, opened his mouth to ask her if she was okay, but she was muttering curses, shoving away from Dez, and collecting her sickle. She crouched over the minotaur and refitted the sickle into the untidy slot she'd created in the beast's throat.

Something landed on Dez's forearm – a scrap of burning ceiling wood. Hissing, he shook it off. In its place angry red skin formed, a couple of blisters rising like miniature ice caps. Then Dez heard a sound that made him forget all about his burned arm.

The rafters were creaking.

Dez gazed up at the vaulted ceiling in dread.

Two minutes, he thought. Two minutes until the whole thing caves in. Maybe less.

And Michael was lying insensate in the balcony.

CHAPTER THIRTY
Escape, Return

As he rose, Dez heard a wet coughing sound, glanced down and saw that the werewolf's change was reversing, the hair retracting into the skin, the bones crackling and reforming as he returned to human form. Despite their lack of time, despite the shouting voices and the sounds of skirmishes that still echoed in the Four Winds, Dez found the sight of the werewolf's reversal spellbinding. But Dez couldn't help but notice the damage that had been done to Chaney's body in the battle with the minotaur. His chest was a wicker weave of stringed meat, his throat flayed open like a dressed deer. Blood was seeping from his red mouth, the yellow eyes glazed with pain. The cracking arm bones were raised and spread as though Chaney were imploring the heavens for mercy, and his legs, similarly bloody, kicked feebly at the floor.

Dez forced himself to bypass Chaney, to hurry toward the staircase. Michael might be dead already, but Dez knew if he didn't at least attempt to save him, whatever time Dez had left would be haunted by his failure.

In spite of his shrieking feet, Dez took the stairs two at a time, and in moments he was weaving through the wreckage of the tables, chairs, lamps, and bodies. The smoke wasn't as severe up here, but the fire was fast eating its way in this direction. Dez kept the gun ready, told himself he'd fire on anything that moved, but he knew he wasn't at that point yet, despite all that had happened. While so many had forgotten their consciences, Dez's had always remained hyperactive.

Maybe that's why he was still so sick about Susan.

Don't forget your little brother. Your father, your son.

The thought was like a punch in the gut. He realized as he neared Michael's unconscious body that he'd done precisely what he was accusing others of doing – he'd shut off his emotions.

It was your fault, Dez, and you know it. You could have saved them. You could have saved your son!

"Stop it," Dez growled, and a cry sounded from a nearby table.

Dez looked that way in time to see a fair-haired young man, no more than twenty, rising from his hiding place, a carving knife clutched in one hand.

The same young man who'd spoken to Dez at the bar earlier that night, the one with the branded *E* on the back of his hand.

The young man smiled his naïve smile and gestured with the knife. "I wasn't going to stick you with this. I promise I wasn't."

Dez didn't respond. Instead he kept moving until he stood over Michael.

Michael didn't appear to be breathing. If he was, it was so shallow that his chest didn't move.

Go, a voice in his head demanded.

To hell with that, Dez thought, stuffing the gun back into his underwear. He detested the way the barrel snaked between his butt cheeks, but there was no time to rearrange the weapon for comfort.

He bent, hooked his hands under Michael's leather coat, and with a good deal of difficulty managed to hoist the unconscious man into a fireman's carry. He started toward the stairs but stopped when he discovered the kid with the carving knife barring his way.

The young man's eyes were large, pleading. "Take me with you," he said.

"Move," Dez said and pushed straight toward him.

The kid did move aside, but he clamped his free hand over Dez's bicep. "I saw you fight down there. I saw you kill Badler."

"Take your hand off," Dez growled, already panting with the effort of lugging Michael, as slender as the guy was. Dez's body was a horrorshow of cuts and bruises, he had a bullet in his ass cheek, and he worried he'd dislocated his left shoulder dangling from the chains. If Dez survived this, he'd sleep for a month.

"You killed Erica," the young man persisted, walking abreast with him now. "You just got Aaron with a crossbow. I've never seen anybody shoot one that accurately before."

They were almost to the stairs. The kid actually chuckled. "And don't tell me that arrow to the head was luck."

"It wasn't." Dez started down the stairs.

"*Exactly*," the young man said. "You've got real skills, abilities…."

Dez accidentally bumped Michael's head on the handrail – *shit* – so he slowed down, took the steps a bit more cautiously.

The kid wouldn't shut up. "…a teacher. Someone to help me reach my potential. Please. Without that, I know I'm gonna die."

On the bottom step Dez stopped and turned, Michael's body heavy on his shoulders. "You a Latent?" Dez asked.

The young man's face twisted in confusion. "Latent?"

Dez adjusted his mental estimate of the kid's age. He was twenty, maybe, but he acted fifteen. Dez waved a hand impatiently. "Yes, Latent. No special abilities?"

The young man's face went somber. He shook his head. "None that I'm aware of."

"You'd know by now," Dez said, turning.

The kid grabbed him. "Please. I need a teacher. I have to learn—"

"You want some advice?" Dez snapped. "Learn how to hide."

He reached the ground floor and moved through the shadows of the overhanging balcony toward the main room, which was hazed with smoke. Dez's eyes started stinging again. His throat itched, threatened a coughing fit.

"I *can* hide," the kid said. "I can hide and I can scavenge. I know how to cook almost anything." When Dez didn't answer, the kid added, "My grandma taught me. If you shoot something, I can tell you a dozen ways to prepare it."

Dez hardly heard this last. The sight before him stole his ability to think. Maybe he'd been too busy to really examine the main seating area of the Four Winds, but now that he did, his mind refused to register the carnage and destruction. And all of it overlaid with a thickening pall of smoke.

In the expansive space only two tables remained upright. One of those was decorated with a headless body, the ragged neck stump still leaking onto the floor.

Keaton was where Dez had left him, and Iris had finished sawing off his horned head. Dez saw no sign of Iris. Or Keaton's head.

Nor did he see Tom Chaney. The werewolf had either been dragged to safety by someone, or he'd risen on his own power.

Or, Dez amended, he'd been lugged outside for meat, perhaps the likeliest possibility of all. As if to confirm this supposition, Dez's attention was drawn by a quartet of cannibals who'd laid out a pair of bodies on the bar, oblivious to the deepening smoke and the flickering ceiling, which was sending down charred spurs of wood that landed like lethal snowflakes on the tables and chairs below. Some winked out before they made contact. Others, the larger scraps, ignited the surfaces with which they came into contact. In dread, Dez gazed up at the ceiling. *Any time now*, he thought, *the whole thing's gonna cave.*

"This way," the young man said, urging Dez away from the feasting cannibals, who, Dez realized, had taken note of him. Three men and a woman. All shirtless. Their fronts were slicked with gore, their eyes gleaming with unwholesome vitality. Dez didn't recognize them, but he suspected they'd been here all along, biding their time until they could sate their unholy cravings.

The kid's voice was tight. "Come on," he murmured. "The front door."

Dez turned that way, but Michael's body weighted Dez down, made him stagger right into a glittering lake of broken glass.

The boy sucked in air, made a face. "Ouch. Be careful."

"You really wanna help me?" Dez snarled. "Get me a pair of fucking boots."

The boy blinked at him. "Off one of the dead people?"

"Size fourteen."

"Fourteen?" the boy repeated.

Overhead, the ceiling creaked.

The boy glanced up in fright. Dez swatted him a backhand on the chest. "Over there," Dez said, gesturing toward the body of Black Jacket. "That big bastard. His oughta fit."

Dez started toward the front doors, which hung wide open.

He heard the boy say, "But the cannibals, they'll—"

"Then piss off," Dez said. "You say you wanna help…."

"*Okay*," the boy moaned.

Dez navigated the wreckage of the Four Winds, the corpses, the splintered chairs and the shattered glass. He glimpsed a beer stein lying on its side, the pewter painted crimson, a scrap of hair stuck to a corner of the base like glued felt. To Dez's right a chunk of burning wood the size of a Bible thunked to the floor.

Not long now, he thought. He coughed and wheezed against the growing smoke. His lungs were lined with nettles.

Almost to the door.

Dez's hand slipped instinctively into the rear of his underwear even before the cannibal sprang from his hiding place and ran screaming toward him, his mouth smeared with blood and Gattis's mace raised aloft with both hands. The man reminded Dez of that character from *Welcome Back, Kotter*, a TV show his dad used to watch, frizzy curled hair, big eyes, what was the character's name? Dez waited until the man was five feet away and fired. A hole at the top of the man's chest opened and the makeshift mace skidded on the floor past Dez's feet.

Horshack, Dez remembered. The character's name had been Horshack. Dez considered shooting the cannibal in the forehead and ending his misery, but that would be a waste of a bullet. He left Horshack gasping for breath and gurgling blood from the corners of his mouth.

Dez reached the trio of steps and with a supreme effort passed through the open doorway. Cool breeze caressed his skin. Dez decided to keep the gun at the ready in case another psycho was waiting for him. Hell, for all he knew one of Keaton's loyalists had marshaled the dead leader's remaining forces out here for a revenge mission.

But there didn't appear to be anyone outside. Dez staggered down the steps, his chains dragging behind him. He bent and laid Michael on the weedy gravel as gently as he could, which wasn't all that gently. Dez exhaled, rested there on his knees, hunched over, his lungs boiling. He coughed, and the burning sensation spiked.

He remembered, long ago, a teacher showing them how much damage one cigarette could do. The teacher had fashioned a pair of lungs out of cotton balls and had funneled smoke, via a plastic tube, into the tall glass jar housing the lungs. Within thirty seconds the cotton had been stained a dingy gray and soon, the color of gunmetal. Dez was never sure about the veracity of the teacher's conclusions, but damned if the experiment hadn't made an impression. How much worse, he wondered now, would the damage to his lungs be, inhaling woodsmoke and microscopic embers?

"You're not hit, are you?" a voice asked.

Dez looked through watery eyes at Iris, who had never appeared stronger. His crossbow hung on her back, behind which loomed a large blue backpack. Her hair had come loose, was dripping with sweat, but other than a scrape along her jawline, the buckshot in her scalp, and an abrasion on her forehead, she appeared completely healthy.

By contrast, Dez felt like utter shit.

"Can you move?" she asked.

"Gimme a couple minutes," he said. It felt like someone had implanted one of those blowfish in his chest, the kind that was covered with spikes.

"We don't have minutes," Iris said.

Dez cringed, lowered to all fours. His lungs....

"Hold still," she said. He felt a tugging on his wrist, then a relief of pressure. Iris had found the key, was unlocking the cuffs. Despite how difficult it was to breathe, being released from the hand and leg cuffs felt exquisite. He allowed himself a moment to savor the feeling.

"Hey," she said, shaking his shoulder. "We've got to leave. The vampires will be here any moment. And the cannibals."

Dez thought of the human buffet on the bar. Shivered.

Iris hunkered down beside Michael, placed fingers against his neck.

"He alive?" Dez asked.

She nodded. "He's small and wiry, but he's a tough little shit. He'll live. The question is how we're going to carry him around until he comes to. You're in no shape to do it."

Smoke wafted over them. Dez glanced back and saw the doorway of the Four Winds flickering orange and yellow, the room within seething like hellfire.

"Guess the kid didn't make it," Dez murmured.

Iris frowned. "Huh?"

"Never mind. What'd you do with Keaton's head?"

Iris smiled crookedly. Nodded to his left.

Dez turned that way and saw, perched atop the FIRST ASSEMBLY BAPTIST CHURCH sign, the minotaur's horned head. The ravaged eyes gazed sightlessly at Dez; the beast's tongue lolled over its serrated bottom teeth.

Dez nodded. "Appropriate."

Iris sucked in a breath, rose, gun extended.

Dez beheld a figure blundering down the front steps bearing an armload of black clothes. His hair sweat-plastered to his head, the kid stumbled up next to Dez and dropped the whole load – boots, black jacket, leather pants – on the gravel.

"I would've—" the boy with the E on his hand started, but doubled over in a coughing fit, "—would've gotten the t-shirt and underwear, but it was too smoky…the cannibals kept eyeing me…and the dead guy really reeked."

Dez couldn't suppress a grin. "I've got underwear."

Panting, hands on knees, the kid glanced at him uncomprehendingly. Then he smiled. "Oh yeah. I guess you do."

"Let's go," Iris said, lowering the gun.

Dez winced and began the job of sliding on Black Jacket's leather pants. He'd have to roll up the cuffs and cinch the belt extra tight – and the kid was right; the clothes smelled like scorched feces – but they were better than nothing.

Dez slid one leg through the pants. "Where's Chaney?"

"He staggered into the woods," Iris said, indicating the forest behind the Four Winds.

Dez coughed. He drew in a shuddering breath, concentrated on working his other leg into the pants. "Is he—"

"Recovering," Iris said. "He was half-healed already when I saw him last, and that was several minutes ago. Come on." She grabbed Dez under the armpit. "Let's catch up with him."

Dez shook free. "Not going that way. I've got a truck."

"With gasoline?" Iris demanded.

Dez nodded. "Some."

Still bent over and coughing, the boy said, "It's over there, about fifty yards inside the tree line."

Dez paused, one bleeding foot halfway inside a boot. "How the hell you know that?"

The kid gave him a sheepish smile. "I was hiding in the woods. I saw you come."

"You sneaky little shit."

The kid looked away, but he was grinning.

A moan drew their attention. Dez glanced down and saw Michael shaking his head slowly, as though he were trapped in the jaws of a bad dream.

Iris put a hand on Michael's chest. "You hear me, Michael? It's Iris."

Michael groaned, moved his head weakly.

"We gotta go," she said. "Hey." She tapped his cheek with an open palm.

A noisy crash sounded from inside the Four Winds; smoke billowed out at them.

"We've got to get away from the building," Dez said. "It falls now, we'll die as surely as if we were in it."

"Help me," Iris said, and within seconds she and the boy were hauling Michael toward the gravel lane. Dez clutched a boot and the jacket under an arm and hobbled after them. Judging from the roominess of the boot he'd slid on, Black Jacket had been closer to a sixteen than a fourteen, but Dez couldn't afford to be choosy. Oversized boots were better than no boots. Plus, it felt much nicer stowing the gun in a hip pocket than it did in the seat of his underwear.

"What about Chaney?" Dez asked when he'd caught up to them. They were fifty feet from the bar, but Iris didn't appear eager to stop.

"He'll be okay," she said. "He was mending rapidly. There was still blood...a few open wounds...." She bared her teeth from the effort of hauling Michael. "But he'll survive. If we can, we'll loop around to County Road 900, see if we can catch him there."

"Wait," the boy said, though he kept shuffling awkwardly along, Michael's booted feet clutched against his hips. "You're telling me we're going *into* vampire country? That's suicide."

Dez hobbled on, the tiny rocks lancing the sole of his left foot like fishhooks. "Who the hell says you're going with us?"

The boy looked stricken. "I got you clothes! I damned near died inside—"

But he never finished. With a mighty roar and a fusillade of crashes, the Four Winds Bar caved in, casting jets of flame and orange showers of sparks into the velvety night sky. Even from a distance, Dez felt the puff of superheated air roll over him. He raised an arm to shield his eyes from the brilliant firelight.

After a time, Dez turned and saw something coming down the lane toward them. He was sure at first it was a trick of his overtaxed senses. But the vision crystalized, swimming into focus.

It was a man on a bicycle. A wagon trundled behind it.

Iris placed Michael on the ground, drew her weapon.

The bicycle moved closer, its rider frontlighted by the inferno.

"Oh hell," Dez said.

Iris stiffened. "You know him?"

Dez didn't answer. He only watched the old man on the bike crunch to a stop, level a finger at him.

"You stole my truck," Jim the Werewolf said.

CHAPTER THIRTY-ONE

American Werewolf

Iris glanced at Dez and raised her eyebrows.

Dez shrugged. "I never said the truck was mine."

"You're damn right it's not," Jim said, nudging down the kickstand with a heel and bracing the bike. He grimaced as he climbed off.

"Look, Jim," Dez started. "I didn't plan on taking your truck. I'm sorry I—"

"You damned well *better* be sorry," Jim said, limping a little and massaging his lower back as he approached them. "You have any idea how hard it is for a man my age to pedal this far?"

The kid stared at Dez. "You really stole this guy's truck?"

"This *guy*," Dez said, an edge to his voice, "transformed into a werewolf and almost tore my limbs off."

"How did you think I was gonna go on supply runs without my Dodge?" Jim demanded.

"I didn't get that far in my thinking," Dez said.

"You just left him there?" Iris asked.

"He was a fucking werewolf!" Dez shouted.

"Okay," she said, palms up. "Jesus."

The boy stepped toward Jim. "You can come with us if you want."

"Us?" Dez asked.

The boy tilted his head. "Clothes? Remember?"

"I ain't going anywhere with you peckerwoods," Jim said. He held out a hand. "Give me back my keys."

"I don't have them," Dez said.

Jim's mouth worked in outrage. "What do you mean, you don't—"

"They're under some dead leaves, just inside the rear driver's side tire."

The boy snapped his fingers. "I didn't look there."

Dez looked at him wonderingly. "You little shit."

"What if I don't believe you?" Jim asked.

Dez put a hand on the gun handle. "What if I shoot you for trying to eat me yesterday?"

Jim opened his mouth, closed it. "That wasn't my fault. I was grieving over my—"

"Don't start in on that again, all right? I have no desire to watch you go all David Naughton on me."

Iris smiled. "I love that movie."

The boy frowned. "What movie—"

"You can all go to hell," Jim said, flapping a hand at them. He moved toward the bike.

"Wait," Dez said. "We need that truck."

Jim tapped himself hard on the chest with a forefinger. "*My* truck. My goddamned truck."

"Hold on," Dez said, starting forward.

Jim slung a leg over the bike and glared at Dez. "You really want to go another round with me?"

Dez stopped. "Not particularly."

"*My* truck," Jim said. He walked the bike in an ungainly loop.

"You're just gonna let him go?" a voice asked.

They all looked down, saw Michael scowling after Jim the Werewolf, who was already pedaling back up the lane.

"It *is* his truck," Dez allowed.

Michael made a disgusted sound. "You all are too damned nice."

"First time I've been accused of that today," Dez said.

"Can you stand?" Iris asked Michael.

"Probably not," he answered. Still, he leaned over, braced an arm on the ground, and painstakingly made it to his feet. The boy reached out to help him, but Michael grunted, "Hands off, Spider-Man."

Dez glanced at the boy and thought, *Son of a bitch. He does look like Spider-Man.* He sought the actor's name, thought it might be Tom something....

Iris shrugged. "I guess we're walking."

They glanced up the lane. Jim's bike and trailer were already growing tiny as they rolled toward the forest.

"He could've left us the bike," the boy said.

"Sure," Michael answered. "Iris could ride it, and the rest of us could've piled into that wagon."

"Take it easy, Smile," Iris said.

The boy frowned at Michael. "Your name is Smile?"

CHAPTER THIRTY-TWO

Parting

They gave the Four Winds Bar a wide berth. They had to, lest the inferno singe their eyebrows off. And though the gruesome sight of the cannibals transforming the bar top into a smorgasbord was still freshly emblazoned in his mind, Dez's greater fear was vampires. This wasn't vampire country, but it wasn't far from it, as was evidenced by the incursion Dez witnessed earlier.

Limping past the Four Winds, perhaps forty yards from the blaze, Dez recalled the way the male and female vampire had simply strolled into the bar, surveyed for potential victims, and then selected the patrons they wanted and either feasted on them or dragged them away thrashing and screaming.

No one, it seemed, was willing to stand up to vampires. Not even Keaton. Keaton had been one of their suppliers, hadn't he? Another cog in their sanguinary machine?

And now Dez and his companions were venturing nearer their realm. *Blood Country*, Dez had sometimes heard it called.

A moan from his left made him stop, swing his head around. It was Michael, dropped to one knee, apparently not able to walk on his own. The boy rushed over to Michael, and with a glance in Dez's direction – to make sure he wasn't about to pitch forward too, Dez supposed – Iris went to Michael and hunkered down beside him.

"Can you make it a little farther?" she asked. "We're exposed out here, we need—"

"I know we need cover," Michael said, his face scrunched in pain. "Just give me a minute. I think I'm gonna…."

Iris shuffled back just in time to avoid being vomited on.

"It's the concussion," the boy explained. "He's having waves of nausea."

Michael puked again, down on all fours now.

"I got two concussions playing soccer," the boy explained. "I wasn't very good but my parents made me. More my mom than my dad. She played in college and she wanted me—"

"Would it be possible," Michael said, "for you to shut the fuck up?"

The boy did.

Dez stood there, his vision gauzy. Part of that was because of the smoke billowing out of the Four Winds. But he was also growing lightheaded, and dammit, now was not the time to faint. He thought of vampires and shook his head briskly in an attempt to shake loose the cobwebs.

Iris seemed to be on a similar wavelength. She looked around, her expression less steely than usual. "We've got to get to the trees. There's a neighborhood a mile to the east. We can use one of the houses for the night."

"Willow Lakes," Michael said and nodded ruefully. "There aren't any willows, and the only lake is a small retention pond with turquoise scum floating on it. And the vampires have been raiding those houses for the past month, dragging out anyone dumb enough to take shelter there and bleeding them white on the lawns."

Iris bared her teeth in frustration.

"I know where we can go," the boy said. When they all looked at him, a quick, eager smile flitted over his face.

Either he's a great actor, Dez thought, *or he's the nicest person left on Earth.*

"How far?" Iris asked.

"Mile and a half. Two, tops."

"What is it, a cave?" Michael asked.

"An old garage."

At Michael's hopeful expression, the boy shook his head. "Everything's gone. At least everything useful. There are a couple tools, but not the sort you'd want to carry around. There's an engine or two, but no cars to put them in."

"A garage," Dez said, turning to face the boy, "would be situated in a town."

The boy shrugged. "The edge of it. A tiny place called Buck Creek."

"I know Buck Creek," Michael said. "The cannibals run it."

"That's why no one goes there," the boy conceded. "But it's the first building after the woods. The cannibals all use the houses. You know, the residential district. They're like, five blocks away."

Michael glanced at Dez. "Now *that's* reassuring."

Iris looked like she was about to shoot the idea down when they heard someone begin to shriek from deep in the forest.

Michael looked at Iris. "The cannibals?"

"Or the vampires," she answered. "We've gotta move."

Michael nodded. The boy and Iris helped Michael to his feet. They started toward the woods, moving southeast.

"What's your name, kid?" Michael asked.

"Hunter Martin," the boy said.

Michael shook his head. "I can't call you that."

The boy frowned. "Why not?"

"'Cuz you're not a hunter." Michael eyed him. "More like a hider."

For the first time, the boy's affable demeanor went away, in its place a sulky expression that made him look like an adolescent. "You don't exactly look like a Smile, either."

"I'm not," Michael said. "Least not to you."

"What should I call you then?" the boy asked.

They reached the edge of the forest, ambled alongside it, probing for a trail.

"Sir," Michael said. "You can call me Sir."

"Up here," Iris said, her steps quickening. Dez hastened to keep up. It was a good fifteen seconds before he spotted the trail to which she was referring. Man, his eyes ached. He wondered if the corneas had been baked by the heat, and if they had, if the damage was irreparable.

Starting up the trail, the shadows immediately swallowing them, Iris glanced over her shoulder at the boy and said, "Well, what should we call you?"

"Hunter," the boy said.

"Opie," Michael said.

The boy stopped, nearly causing Dez to slam into him. "Why Opie?"

Michael didn't turn around. "Because you look like one. Kind of remind me of the old *Andy Griffith Show*."

The boy gestured, though Dez could barely see his arms in the shadow-steeped forest. "Andy Griffith was a sheriff, right? He was a big guy, and older."

"No, dipshit. Not the sheriff," Michael said. "His son."

"But…" the boy started. "That doesn't seem very flattering. I mean, what did Opie do? He fished and got taught lessons by his dad."

"Sounds about right to me," Michael said.

"What's your middle name?" Dez asked.

The boy shrugged. "Levi."

Iris nodded. "I like that name."

"But it's not my first name."

Michael seemed to consider. "I can live with Levi."

The boy fluttered a hand in frustration. "Can't you call me—"

"Look," Michael said, stopping and facing the boy. "We're not calling you Opie, we're calling you Levi. Be grateful for that." He started moving again, the trail slowly rising. "Besides, Levi's a good name. I had an Uncle Levi, was a hell of a man. Used to own a farm down in southern Indiana. Let me sit on his lap and drive the combine."

Michael fell silent. Dez didn't ask about Michael's Uncle Levi, figuring – as did the others, he was sure – that the farmer had died along with most everyone else after the missiles flew.

Or maybe he'd been changed. Like Keaton, like Michael, like Tom Chaney….

At the thought of Tom, Dez's stomach clenched. He'd forgotten all about Chaney after escaping the bar, but now he remembered how much Chaney had been through, how he'd saved them from Keaton. Dez owed his life to Tom Chaney, and now Chaney was out there somewhere, likely naked and shivering, his wounds not fully healed from his battle with the minotaur.

You abandoned him, a voice whispered.

No, I didn't.

Like Joey…

No.

…like your dad…Susan….

No.

Like your son. Like Will.

Goddammit, NO!

Dez imagined Chaney out there in the woods, his flesh striped with unhealed wounds, his energy sapped from the fight. His body grown frail from being chained in that fucking basement, without sunlight, without decent food, branded an animal, tortured, nearly executed in public….

Dez stopped.

Levi was the first to notice. "You okay?"

"I have to find him," Dez said.

Levi and Michael only frowned, but Iris came toward him, her jaw set. A ghostly sliver of moonlight fell on her face, giving her the look of some mythological temptress. An especially voluptuous one.

"You're not going to find him," she said.

"I have to."

"So we're down to three," Michael said. "Shit."

Levi ventured a smile. "There were only two of you before."

Michael leveled a finger at Levi's face. "Don't talk about Joe. That's none of your goddamned business."

Iris was staring at Dez. "It's suicide to stay in the forest."

"Most of the countryside is forest," Dez answered without heat. "I'll meet up with you tomorrow. Just name the place."

Michael tilted his head. "You're gonna die out there."

"Beyond Buck Creek," Levi said, gesturing southward, "there's an old hog farm. A house, a barn, two long farrowing houses."

"Farrowing houses?" Iris asked.

"Where they kept pigs," Michael said.

"Is there any cover?" Iris asked.

"Not really," Levi said. "That's why it'll be easy for Dez to find."

"Easy for *everyone* to find," Michael said. He grunted. "Let's just stroll across an open field in broad daylight and wear signs saying 'Eat us.'"

"I've stayed there before," Levi said. "It's safe." At Michael's arched eyebrow, Levi added, "Okay, relatively safe."

"Relatively safe, huh?" Michael said. "Then why not go tonight?"

"You said yourself. Too many open fields around it. The vampires will see us."

Iris nodded. "The garage tonight, the hog farm tomorrow."

"Now wait," Michael said. "I'm hurting, goddammit. I'm in no condition to run the Iditarod."

"A mile and a half to the garage," Iris said.

"Or two," Michael amended.

"Then how long from the garage to the hog farm?" she asked Levi.

"Two miles," Levi said. "No more than that."

Michael glared at him.

Levi put his palms up. "I promise!"

"I'll be there by midday tomorrow," Dez said, starting away.

"Wait a second," Michael growled. "You barely have weapons." He nodded at the crossbow. "How many arrows you got left for that thing?"

Dez glanced at Iris.

She held his gaze for a long moment, then seemed to deflate. She stared down at the trail. "I hid your pack in a hollowed-out oak behind the bar. You've got a lot of stuff."

Dez looked at her. "You went through my things?"

She folded her arms. "Of course I did."

Dez wondered if she'd glanced at his journals. Then he wondered if that changed anything.

"Midday," Dez said.

With an effort, he tore his eyes away from Iris and started off through the forest.

CHAPTER THIRTY-THREE

Guys Like Us

The backpack was where she'd said it would be. The oak tree with the decayed base was a bit moldy. Yellow and black slime smeared his fingers as he reached inside for the pack, but it had been an effective hiding place. No one had poached his stuff.

Iris had augmented the pack, he realized as he rummaged through it. In addition to the items he'd collected, he found a newer, sharper knife, another canteen, and more ammunition for both his Ruger and his crossbow.

Evidently, her job as barkeeper had allowed Iris to amass valuable possessions in this new world. He thought of the voluminous pack she carried on her shoulders and wondered what treasures she'd kept for herself. Whatever they were, Dez decided, she'd earned them. She'd managed to stay alive under Keaton's tyrannical rule for nearly a year, and in the end, she'd gotten the information she needed and ultimately been the one to murder the son of a bitch.

He hoped he'd see her again.

Dez stood, made off through the woods. He didn't feel good, but the weight of the backpack, far from encumbering him, kindled in him a fresh surge of hope.

Dez trudged forward, along a trail that was narrow but distinct. For a time, he willingly followed it, but soon he feared he was heading too far west, and for reasons he couldn't explain, he felt that Chaney would have headed due south.

At least there was no more smoke, or only occasional tinges of it. He knew that most people who died in fires actually expired because of smoke inhalation, and he knew he'd inhaled a good damned bit of it. He took liberal draws from the canteens as he went, reasoning that a loud coughing fit was a greater peril than running out of water. Besides, he was terribly dehydrated, and the water was a balm for his itching, irritated throat.

After a couple minutes' debate, Dez peeled off the trail and moved south. Without a blazed path, the going was slower. The October ground was scrimmed with a layer of hoarfrost, and the piled leaves and mounded humus made the going arduous. Even more bothersome were the snarls of thorn bushes and downed trees littering the forest. Navigating the numerous pitfalls made Dez feel like he was a contestant in some rustic reality show competition. He felt like utter dogshit, but it was either curl into a ball and try to sleep or persist in his attempts to locate Tom Chaney. Dez persisted.

It was after he'd bulled through the rugged undergrowth for nearly an hour that the idea first occurred to him. His plan all along had been to move in relative silence and hope to locate Chaney by sight. Calling out to him would have been beyond foolhardy – it would have been a death sentence. Dawn was creeping closer, but it was still full dark, and that meant the predators were out, scouring the countryside for fresh prey. Wildlife was abundant, and for the most part, the vampires could sate their bloodlust on rabbits, squirrels, deer, and other smaller mammals. Yet there was no question about their preferred quarry.

Dez leaned against a hickory tree and considered the possibility that Chaney had returned to Keaton's house.

"Why would he do that?" Dez muttered aloud.

But he knew.

Knew and didn't want to think about it.

Remember Keaton's mistress?

No, he thought. You don't know the whole story.

Yes, you do. You know it better than you want to.

Dez turned and gazed toward where he thought Iris and the others had gone. How close to the Buck Creek garage were they? Or had they been taken?

No, don't think like that. Nothing took them. Nothing will attack them. And if something does, Iris will fight it off. She's too clever to be ambushed, too tough to be overwhelmed by brute force.

And, he thought, starting through the forest again, she was too shrewd to be duped by some sort of fabricated story. If Chaney really had done something awful to Keaton's mistress, Chaney had done so because he hadn't been himself. The incident with Jim the Werewolf had proven it. In human form, Jim no more wanted to hurt Dez than he wanted to die himself. Even after Dez had taken Jim's truck and compelled the old man to ride a bike over many miles of cracked asphalt, Jim had not taken it out on Dez with violence. Had merely reprimanded him and claimed what was rightfully his.

Chaney would not have gone back to Keaton's house.

Still, without a definite path before him, Dez found himself trending toward where he thought Keaton's land might be. It was difficult to tell for sure this deep in the forest, but Dez's sense of direction had sharpened considerably in the past two years, and he suspected he was getting close.

Would Keaton's wife try to shoot him?

Perhaps. The last time they'd met, Dez had been an intruder in her home. Whatever she'd said to her husband, it was enough for Keaton to condemn Dez and arrange a public execution.

For a time, Dez muscled his way through a particularly nasty stretch of forest. What would have taken him only minutes to navigate had there been a path took him nearly an hour because of the undergrowth's density. Dez was lashed by thorns, his cheeks scourged by branches. What irony there would be, he thought, if he lost an eye, not in the insane fight to the death in the Four Winds, but to an ill-timed run-in with a sapling branch.

Dez was just getting ready to pause for a rest when he heard a door clack shut. A screen door.

He had reached Keaton's house.

Dez knew it even before the trees thinned and he spotted the brick ranch ahead. He pushed through the bushes and saw how pallid the horizon had grown; dawn was encroaching swiftly now. As he was navigating the last few saplings on the forest's edge, he saw the pale figure staggering away from the Keatons' screened-in porch and shambling toward the front yard.

Tom Chaney. He could see that Tom was in the process of changing from a werewolf into a man again.

Dez swallowed hard. *No.*

Taking care not to make a sound, Dez emerged from the woods, made his way through the Keatons' back yard, and rounded the corner of their brick ranch. He had no desire to enter the house.

When he reached the front yard he spotted Chaney lying supine, naked, gazing up at the pearly dark sky. Even from a distance Dez could discern the gleam of Chaney's hairy skin. Something wet slicking his front. Something dark and wet.

No.

Chaney did not act surprised when Dez pulled up behind him. Dez studied Chaney upside down; the man's expression seemed beatific, as though old demons had finally been laid to rest.

"I knew you'd find me," Chaney said in his thick voice.

Chaney's transformation was nearly complete; the only signs he'd been anything but human were the greater proliferation of hair on his chest and the slightly protuberant cheekbones. Yet even these were altering, the wolf form receding into its uneasy slumber.

"You remind me of my big brother," Chaney said.

Dez could feel the heavy throb of his heart. Like mallet blows on his ribcage. "I didn't know you had a brother."

"I told you about my sister," Chaney said, "but not my brother. He's – was – very protective."

"Oh yeah?" Dez said, staring off at the forest. Unable to look at Tom.

"Uh-huh. He always watched out for me. Before the bombs, I mean. He kept me out of trouble. Stuck up for me when the kids picked on me."

Dez scarcely heard.

"When I'd do bad things," Chaney murmured.

Dez glanced at him sharply. "What bad things?"

"It's just nature," Chaney said, grinning in a way that made Dez want to shriek in horror. "I always liked women. Anything wrong with that?" He looked up at Dez in challenge.

"That depends," Dez said, his voice barely controlled.

"When my brother changed, he took off. He was smarter than I was. He knew what was happening to him. Or that *something* was happening to him. He went away so he wouldn't...hurt one of us."

A spate of dizziness threatened to buckle Dez's knees. He forced himself to remain standing.

Chaney's dark eyes scanned the sky overhead. "It's getting light out."

"What did you do?"

Chaney continued to watch the sky. "Need to find me some clothes. I bet Keaton has some."

"Tom," Dez said, louder this time. "What did you do?"

"Keaton deserved it," Chaney said, his tone conversational. "Him and his family."

Ah, fuck, Dez thought, closing his eyes. Already a wet heat was building in his chest. "Are they alive?" Dez asked, his throat dry. He nodded toward the brick ranch, where the windows were as black as pitch. "Are Keaton's wife and daughter alive in there?"

Chaney's grin widened. "They were."

Dez turned away. *Jesus Christ*, he thought. *Jesus Christ, no.*

Chaney was speaking, but Dez hardly made out his words. "…and she got all uppity. You know how she is. *Was.* She told me to go. But by that time I'd seen the girl standing in the hall behind her. She was wearing these pink shortie shorts." Chaney's voice thickened. "What a body."

Dez wiped a tear away. Said, "We gotta go, Tom. I told Iris and the others we'd meet them."

Chaney's voice altered, the fog of lust clearing. "Iris?"

Dez wiped his nose with the sleeve of his ill-fitting jacket. "She's going with us."

"She is?"

Dez nodded. "Let's get you dressed so we can catch up to her."

Chaney was on his feet in an instant. "Did she tell you to find me?"

Dez's breath came in weary heaves. "Uh-huh."

Something terrible played at the corners of Chaney's eyes, and for a moment Dez saw the lycanthrope in him. Then it was gone. Chaney moved past him toward Keaton's lane.

"Tom," Dez said.

Chaney turned, frowning.

"Clothes?" Dez said, tossing a nod at Keaton's house.

Chaney's face spread in a goofy grin. "I forgot." He came back, started toward the front porch.

Dez brought out the Ruger, thumbed off the safety.

Chaney heard it. His back muscles tensed.

Dez took a breath. "Tom?"

But Chaney was already turning. When he saw the gun he didn't seem surprised. "You could let me go," Chaney said.

Dez's hand trembled, despite his attempts to steady it. His eyes were blurring too, and it had nothing to do with the smoke sting from the bar. "You're obsessed with Iris."

Chaney didn't look scared at all. Maybe he didn't believe Dez would do it. Or maybe the prospect of death no longer frightened him. "I'll go the opposite way. Don't need to take up with you guys if you don't want me." There was an impudent, spoiled-kid quality in Chaney's tone. "Just let me go," Chaney said, confident now. "No one needs to know." The hint of a sneer. "You and Iris can be lovebirds."

"You'll do it again," Dez said, to himself.

"It was the change," Chaney said. He motioned toward the forest. "You saw it at the bar. I can't control it."

There was an infinitesimal moment in which Dez believed it, but it was gone so quickly it was as though it had never been there. "Why did you come to Keaton's house?"

Chaney's face went slack, all guile he'd been able to muster falling away. Chaney shrugged in a singularly unconvincing fashion. "I needed clothes. I knew Keaton would have some."

"Tom," Dez said, the gun steadying, "you didn't come here for clothes."

Chaney's expression changed completely, the anguished creature Dez had known in the basement of the Four Winds returning. "They had me down there a *year*, Dez. *More* than a year. They...they treated me worse than a hound. They pissed on me, made me eat their shit to survive." His eyes brimmed, his lips quivered. "Iris was the only reason they stopped it. Or stopped it some. She...she made them act nicer to me."

Dez twitched the gun toward the house. "Did you rape them, Tom?"

Chaney's eyes squeezed shut, tears streaming out the sides.

Dez asked, "Did you rape Keaton's wife and daughter before you killed them?"

Chaney shook his head, his mouth working soundlessly.

Dez bared his teeth. "She was a *child*, Tom. Keaton's daughter didn't do anything wrong." Dez's voice had gone raw, almost as thick as Chaney's. "Keaton's wife didn't do anything either. She didn't deserve to be—"

"*They were Keaton's!*" Chaney yelled. "They were *his*! They deserved everything they got!"

It worked on Dez like a jolt of electricity.

Chaney saw the change in Dez's face, and Chaney's eyes became huge, terrified moons. "You can't do this." Chaney shook his head. "You can't do this!"

As Dez took aim, Chaney's expression changed again, this time morphing into something bitter, something sinister. "My brother will hear about this. My brother will kill you." A deranged grin. "He always knew when I was lying to him, and if you see him, he'll know what you did." Chaney took a step toward him, nodding. "He's gonna make you pay for it. You and Iris and—"

Dez squeezed the trigger.

He barely saw Chaney's head snap back, didn't watch the man as he fell. Dez stood there for several moments, listening to the muted trickle of Chaney's blood on the sidewalk, stood there and wondered if Chaney could still change or heal.

He didn't.

Dez engaged the safety and returned the Ruger to his pocket. He squinted toward the lane, an irrational part of him imagining one of Keaton's trucks, drawn by the gunshot, rumbling up the lane to take retribution on Dez for what he'd done at the Four Winds.

The lane, and Keaton's yard, remained barren of life.

Though the light was coming faster now, the chill in the air seemed to have deepened, so that the opening at the throat of the voluminous black jacket he wore let in a constant draft, one that shivered his bones and made him long for a fire. A warm, drowsy bed.

The last place he wanted to be was inside Keaton's ranch.

But there were things that needed doing. After moving around Chaney's motionless body, Dez entered through the screen door.

When he came upon the first body, he wasn't prepared for it. It was Keaton's daughter. Her body from the neck down was a ruin. Like she'd been fed through a wood chipper. He hoped the damage had been postmortem. He hoped she hadn't suffered too much.

She suffered, he thought. *Of course she suffered.*

His throat burning with bile, he made his way to the back bedroom, where he found Keaton's wife, on the bed, similarly mutilated. He couldn't look at her for long.

Dez went to the walk-in closet, noted how crammed with clothes it was, both Keaton's and his wife's, as though they'd carried on a competition to see who could collect more. Between the bedroom closet, Keaton's dresser, and the front closet, Dez found everything he needed. He also found another gun – a .45 Smith & Wesson that could blow holes through cinder block – along with two boxes of ammunition. His backpack now full to bursting, he stripped Keaton's daughter's bed of sheets and blankets and began the job of wrapping her in them. It was ghastly work, not only because of the ravaged state of her body, but because of her open, staring eyes. He didn't feel accused by those eyes, but he did see dismay in them, perplexity. *Why did this happen to me?* the eyes asked. *Why did Chaney have to come here after it all should have ended?*

Though there were two sheets and a comforter around her, the blood still leaked onto Dez's new clothes as he carried her out of the house. After laying her body near the tree line, he went to the garage and found a shovel. Bone-weary, he set to work digging a hole, but the October ground was uncooperative, like chipping away at frozen clay. By the time he was finished, his palms were blistered and bleeding, and a sun the color of asbestos was glaring down at the back yard.

Her grave was no more than six feet long, a few feet wide, maybe three feet deep. And uneven, so that when he laid her wrapped body in the hole, her midsection was higher than her head and her feet. He didn't like that, but then again, he didn't like any of it. He knew he should go inside and do the same for Keaton's wife, but the lack of sleep – How long had it been? Twenty-eight hours? Thirty? – and the absolute exhaustion were conspiring to undo him. He felt like crawling into the hole with the wrapped body and sleeping for about a month.

Dez shook his head. *Jesus. Crazy talk.*

He buried the body as best he could, knowing it was a poor job, knowing full well the animals would be at it, the wild dogs and maybe even the human scavengers, cannibals and vampires and God knew what else. Then there was the matter of Keaton's wife, just lying there in the bedroom. Soon she would begin to rot, and then what? Just...leave her? He supposed he could burn the house down, but even that would require energy, and it would draw attention to him.

Maybe he was a bad person, but he couldn't do anything for Keaton's wife. It wasn't spite that made him shoulder his backpack and start for the lane; it was weariness.

And fear, he realized. If any of Keaton's entourage yet survived – and Dez thought it likely some had, as it was a good bet there were other parties spread out on raiding runs – they would eventually return here to piece together what happened to their leader. And when they found Keaton's wife, they'd want vengeance.

With a new pair of sneakers on – they were Keaton's, size fourteen – Dez stepped onto the concrete and made his way down the wooded lane. Not once did he look back at Tom Chaney's body.

CHAPTER THIRTY-FOUR

Nevermore

The hog farm was a hell of a lot farther than Levi had claimed. Either that or Dez had already passed it by. He supposed the fact that he was dead on his feet might have something to do with it, but feeling sorry for himself would do no good. He wished Jim the Werewolf hadn't reclaimed his truck. Dez could sure as hell use the Dodge right now.

It was midafternoon when he first spotted the graying barn. Like Levi had said, there were no woods around the hog farm, only cornfields. Thankfully, after two years of neglect, the fields had all run to riot, and though very little of the vegetation was comprised of good, healthy cornstalks, the switchgrass and brome provided decent cover as he made his way nearer the two-story farmhouse.

It was white, with aluminum siding, and at some point in the not-so-distant past, the farmer who'd lived there had invested in one of the metal roofs that had been in vogue before the bombs. The sheet metal was an inoffensive hunter green and cut a stark contrast with the dimpled red barn roof, which had undergone no such renovation. The pair of farrowing houses, just as Levi had described, were arranged on the western portion of the property. Dez wondered how long the hogs that had lived within those white cinder block buildings had survived after the four winds, then banished the thought with a shiver.

Levi was waiting for him in a yellow folding chair in the side lawn. Dez was worried the boy would come running, enfold Dez in some gushy cinematic embrace. He considered drawing the crossbow just to disabuse Levi of the notion.

But the kid seemed to sense Dez's extraordinary weariness and settled for a grin and a companionable squeeze on the shoulder.

Dez asked where Michael and Iris were.

"Michael's asleep in the back bedroom," Levi answered. "Iris is cooking a wild turkey she shot."

Dez's mouth flooded with saliva. He hadn't recognized the sharp stomach pangs as hunger until now. He moved toward the front porch, Levi walking apace. "Any sign of Keaton's people?"

Levi shook his head. "We saw a Jeep go by this morning through the garage window in Buck Creek, but other than that, nothing."

Dez mounted the steps. He was too tired to shrug Levi off when the boy put a steadying hand on his back. "How was the garage?" Dez asked.

Levi chuckled. "Iris and Michael were pissed at me. Said it was the least comfortable place they'd ever tried to sleep."

As he neared the door, Dez glanced at him. "Did you sleep?"

Levi grinned. "I did. I don't think the others...." His grin faded. "You didn't find Tom?"

Dez fought off a wave of nausea. He told himself it wasn't guilt. "No," he said. "No sign of him."

If Levi had doubts about that, he didn't verbalize them.

"Hey, Dez?" Levi said.

Though bone-weary, Dez waited for Levi to speak.

"That doorman," Levi said.

"Lefebvre," Dez supplied.

"Him," Levi agreed. "Why'd he call you the Raven?"

"Maybe because I wear all black."

"Lots of things are all black."

"Lefebvre had an overactive imagination," Dez said. "Let's get inside."

But Levi made no move for the door.

Dez exhaled and studied the sky. "I used to teach the poem." He glanced at Levi. "You ever read it?"

"Sure," Levi said. "Poe's my favorite."

Dez closed his eyes and sought for a snatch of it, and despite his lassitude, despite the fact that he hadn't read it in years, the words came easily:

"Prophet!" said I, "thing of evil!—prophet still, if bird or devil!
Whether Tempter sent, or whether tempest tossed thee here ashore,
Desolate yet all undaunted, on this desert land enchanted—
On this home by Horror haunted – tell me truly, I implore—
Is there – is there balm in Gilead? – tell me – tell me, I implore!"
Quoth the Raven "Nevermore."

When Dez opened his eyes and looked at Levi, the kid was watching him with a look somewhere between fear and fascination.

"What?" Dez finally said.

"That's you," Levi said.

Dez frowned at him. "What the hell are you talking about?"

"'Desolate yet undaunted'," Levi said.

"Enough," Dez said, brushing past him. "I'm about to pass out."

They went in, and the scent of cooking meat nearly bowled Dez over. The farmhouse was furnished exactly the way he'd have imagined it: outdated furniture, oak trim, curios and knick-knacks on every shelf and table.

Dez followed the scent of cooking meat until he reached the kitchen, where Iris stood at the stove, her back to him. For a time, all Dez did was watch Iris's arms move – she'd donned a navy-blue sweatshirt – and inhale the maddening smell of frying turkey.

When Dez finally tottered into the kitchen, Iris glanced at him over her shoulder and said, "Don't get used to me cooking for you."

CHAPTER THIRTY-FIVE

Mending

Dez slept without dreams. When he awoke, he figured it was nearly dawn, or even the following evening, but Iris, kneeling at his bedside, said, "It's midnight."

Though it was dark in the bedroom – he was pretty sure he was upstairs, though he hardly remembered the climb up here after gorging himself with turkey – he could make out Iris's form well enough. Her arms were folded, her chin resting on her forearms, her face only a foot and a half from his. Self-conscious about his breath, he drew back a little, propped himself on his elbows, winced at the freshet of pain the movement brought on.

"I'll get a bath ready," she said.

Dez listened for a generator, heard nothing but the gentle sighing of the night breeze.

"I filled it up for myself earlier," she explained. "The stove's set up to run on a propane tank. We used it to heat water for both tubs, one downstairs, one up here."

Dez frowned at her.

"Michael's still asleep," she went on. "Levi took a bath downstairs. I carried water up here little by little in a bucket. I'll go heat some more to add to what's in the tub."

When Dez didn't speak, Iris smiled wryly. "You don't mind bathing after me, do you?"

"Uh-uh."

She patted his arm. "Rest a little more. It'll take several buckets to heat the tub."

Dez watched her go. She'd traded in her khaki pants and navy-blue sweatshirt for a light gray tank top that didn't quite reach the waistband of her gray athletic shorts. The effect was mind-blowing.

Dez slipped into a contented stasis. He felt slightly guilty watching Iris reappear with a fresh bucket every couple minutes, but the sound of her dumping the water into the tub was something he felt in his bones. Each time he heard the water sloshing, a wave of warm tingling steamrolled through him, and each time he watched Iris emerge from the bathroom with the empty bucket, he imagined she was communicating a message to him with her green eyes. It brought to mind that old Disney cartoon with Mickey and the deranged broomsticks, but he decided not to mention that to Iris.

At some point, she began to hum a soft, melancholy tune, and Dez experienced the oddest sensation. Like he was being drawn toward the sound, a rudderless barque sucked into a whirpool.

Iris came in, saw the look on his face, and stopped humming. She turned away quickly, her expression troubled.

What the hell? he thought.

She resumed filling the bathtub. After she'd emptied the bucket he didn't know how many times, she set it down outside the bathroom and moved over to where he lay.

"Come on," she said, and helped him out of bed.

On the way into the bathroom he couldn't help notice how the gray shorts hugged her rear end, how the slender shirt straps accentuated her unblemished skin. In a world where the majority of survivors looked haggard and far older than their actual age, Iris could have stepped right off a magazine cover. If there were still magazines.

There were candles burning on the sink, windowsill, and the edge of the clawfoot tub, the bathroom smelling like a combination of pine needles and cucumber melon.

"That jacket stank like a rotting carcass," she said. "I can still smell it on you."

"How do you know that's not my natural musk?"

"You didn't smell like that before. Here, the t-shirt first."

She helped him out of his t-shirt, but not without a great deal of discomfort. There were wounds on his shoulders and back of which he'd been unaware, but the scraping of Keaton's shirt over his skin enflamed them, recalling the harrowing night at the Four Winds.

"Brush your teeth," she said.

He found a toothbrush, dry but gently used, and a half-full tube of Crest. He brushed his teeth, taking his time about it. She'd even placed a glass of water on the sink edge, which he used to swish the paste out of his mouth.

"I count three spots that need stitches," she said, studying him.

They stood very close in the bathroom, which was relatively tight to begin with. Iris's skin seemed tawnier in the candlelight. She seemed shorter too, without her boots.

"The belt," she said, and he started to unbuckle it. Was she going to stay in the room while he bathed? The notion excited and alarmed him. He hadn't been naked with a woman – being semi-naked and strung up by chains didn't count, he decided – since Susan.

"Need help?" Iris asked.

Dez shook his head, realized he'd paused with a hand on his belt. He continued unclasping the buckle of Keaton's belt and unzipping Keaton's jeans.

Keaton was a good deal broader than Dez, and because of this the jeans slid down his legs on their own.

"Lean on the sink," Iris said, and bent to help him step out of the jeans. She stood erect, Keaton's jeans in her hands. "We don't need these anymore. The farmer who lived here was about your size."

The fact that she'd been searching for new clothes for him scarcely registered. Because the only thing on his mind was his impending nudity. And Iris.

"Something wrong?" Iris asked.

"You're staying?"

"That tub was a bitch to fill, and it's not getting any warmer. You stink, and you've got multiple cuts that need stitching. Now unless you're more limber than you're letting on, you need me in here to wash your wounds. So quit acting like a shy little boy."

Chastened, he peeled off his boxer briefs and turned toward the tub. He felt less self-conscious with his back to Iris, but he wondered what she'd thought of his private parts. Or if she'd even noticed them.

He eased down into the tub, which was fizzing, he realized, with some sort of powder Iris had shaken in. The water wasn't hot – he couldn't remember the last time he'd had a hot bath – but it was warm, and that alone sent pleasurable shivers scurrying up and down his spine.

Dez hissed as his injured butt cheek met water.

"Toughen up," she said, half-smiling.

"Says the woman without a bullet in her butt."

"It's a superficial wound," she said. "You got grazed pretty good, but there's no bullet in there. I could see that before you got into the tub."

Feeling a trifle foolish, Dez reached down, fingered the scratch on his buttock. Touching it made him wince, but upon further inspection, he decided she was right.

"The box said 'aroma therapy'," Iris explained, taking a seat on the toilet beside the tub. "It's supposed to be mint eucalyptus or something." She dipped a washcloth into the water, wrung it out. "I'm sure there's no medicinal value, but it felt good to pretend I was back in the old world again."

It did indeed feel good. Dez leaned back in the tub, but when his right shoulder met porcelain, he cringed.

"That's a bad one," she said. "Here." And she gently massaged the wound on his shoulder blade with the washcloth. She dipped it in the water, caressed the wound some more, and though it still hurt like a bitch, the fact that she might be preventing an infection went a long way toward helping him manage the pain.

"Lean forward," she directed. "There's one on your lower back I'm worried about."

He did as he was bidden, clasping his arms around his knees and peering at the tiled wall, the wallpapered section above that. Red apples with green stems and leaves, a background of checkered cream. The quintessential country bathroom.

"Damn," she said.

"What?"

"There's a good one right here."

He waited, felt a pinching sensation near his spine. He bit his tongue against the discomfort. "What are you doing to me?"

"You've got some fantastic blackheads."

He pulled away, glared back at her. "You're squeezing zits?"

She smiled unabashedly. "I've always been obsessed with them."

"Could we maybe focus on my injuries?"

"It's my fee for helping you. Now turn around."

Sighing, he did. She puttered around back there for a good three minutes, probing and pinching.

"Okay," she said. "That's all I can find. Let's wash out those wounds."

He shook his head, but he couldn't suppress a grin.

"Hold on." She stood, her body throwing shadows on the candlelit walls, then came back with something silver and shiny in one hand. Tweezers.

"There's something still in there," she said.

That sounds ominous, he thought. The tweezers prodded his skin, the object embedded in his lower back shifting, and though he tried not to seem weak, he couldn't help hissing and uttering a curse.

"I liked the zit-popping better," he said.

She ignored that. "I think it's...." A sharp pain. "Yep. It's a piece of glass. Hold on. I...there it comes."

She brought the bloody shard around for him to see. It was three quarters of an inch long, slightly curved. Blood dripped from it. The tweezers were smeared with his blood.

Dez looked away.

"Don't tell me you're squeamish," she said. He heard her drop the shard into a wastebasket and place the tweezers on the sink. "After what I watched you do last night? All the blood you spilled?"

He swallowed. "It's different when it's your own."

"Soap's over there," she said. "Shampoo too. Wash your hair."

He did, taking his time about it. When he'd finished lowering his head into the tub and rinsing out the shampoo, the water had cooled considerably. But it was still warmer than any he'd enjoyed since God knew when.

"Make sure to get your privates," she instructed.

He glanced up at her. "You mind?"

"For such a tough guy," she said, half-turning toward the door, "you're awfully delicate."

He washed his nether regions.

"Done?" she asked, fingers drumming on her elbows.

"It's a sizable job."

She rolled her eyes, but she was smiling.

"Can you hand me that towel?" he asked.

She slid a thick white towel off the metal towel rack. He stood to take it from her and only when the frigid air breathed over his privates did he realize he was semi-erect. Iris had her hands on his sides to help him up, but her eyes lowered, and he thought her skin reddened a little. With the candlelight, it was difficult to be sure.

She cleared her throat. "I laid out some clothes in there," she said, gesturing toward the bedroom.

"Might just sleep naked," he said.

"At least put underpants on," she said. "I need you to help me with something."

He paused, the towel cinched around his waist. "Help you with what?"

She waved a hand at him. "Oh, put on your underwear."

He grunted laughter. She remained in the bathroom while he dried off in the bedroom and slid on the Jockey shorts. They weren't boxer briefs, like he preferred, but they fit.

"What are you doing in there," Iris called from the bathroom, "admiring yourself in the mirror?"

Dez saw there was indeed an old-fashioned body-length mirror on a stand, and when he saw himself reflected there, he was pleasantly surprised. He needed to eat more, that much was plain. And with only one candle in here his reflection was slightly murky. Yet he could see how his muscles stood out, was stunned at the prominence of his abdominals. They'd been nonexistent before the bombs, but now, through the combination of deprivation and exercise, they stood out in knobby ripples.

"You *are* admiring yourself," Iris said from the doorway.

Dez couldn't suppress an embarrassed laugh. He followed her into the bathroom, where she surprised him by saying, "Let's get this over with," and sliding off her gray shorts.

The underwear beneath was magenta, low-rise, and skimpy in back, so that very little of her rear end was covered. Dez stood there, heart thumping. *Remember Susan*, he told himself.

She turned her back to him. "Do you see it?"

His mouth was open.

"Oh, for God's sakes," she muttered. "Sit on the toilet seat."

He did as he was told.

"Here," she said, pointing to a spot just under her right buttock, where the inner thigh began. "It needs to be sewn up. After you do mine, I'll get all yours. Hopefully, they'll be dry by then."

He nodded, attempted to don a professional demeanor, but it was difficult with Iris's glorious, half-naked buttocks a foot from his face.

He turned, retrieved the black thread and needle she'd prepared from the sink edge, then faced Iris again, this time doing his best to block out the fact that the low-rise underwear didn't conceal the cleft at the top of her buttocks, or the shadowy region between her legs that the semi-translucent underwear didn't totally obscure.

Dez brought the needle nearer the cut, which wasn't long but appeared pretty deep, and paused. "You sure you want me doing this? I typically use Crazy Glue when I get one."

"I've tried that," she said, showing him the side of her wrist. "It leaves too big a scar."

Shoddy stitches leave scars too, he thought.

"I've only done this once," he said, "and I wasn't very good—"

"Just sew," she said. "Didn't you ever take Home-Ec?"

"We didn't call it that, but yeah, I did." He reached up again, his hands trembling slightly. "Don't you want a shot of something? I'm sure they have liquor—"

"They don't. Levi and I checked."

"Maybe an ice cube to numb it?"

She glowered down at him.

"Right," he said. "Could you...I don't know, lean forward or something?"

"Like what, put my hands on my knees?"

The image made his head swim. "It's just...sort of an awkward spot. Difficult for me to reach."

She had her back turned, but he could hear the humor in her voice. "I'll bend over if you want."

He swallowed. "Okay."

She did, and though it made getting to the cut much easier, it stretched tight the magenta material, making it almost sheer against her rear end and her sex.

Dez's hands trembled, his throat burning with his need.

Focus, he told himself. *You're not a goddamned high schooler anymore. Focus.*

She twitched when the needle entered her skin, but the steel was slender enough to pass smoothly through the edges of the cut and form the first stitch. She'd tied the bottom of the eight-inch thread in a fat knot, so there was no question of pulling the thread too far. His fingers were still shaking slightly, but he threaded the needle through her skin again, this one better, a trifle shallower. Only once during the operation did he sink the needle too deep, but Iris only sucked in breath, her strong hamstrings flexing, and waited for him to finish. When he'd done, there were seven stitches, too close together, but otherwise a passable job. He snipped the string and, with a bit of fuss and cursing, finally managed to tie a knot at the end.

Iris went out and came back a few moments later. "Not bad," she said. She reached down, opened the cabinet beneath the sink, and came out with a first aid kit. "Now you."

Dez stood, noting as he did that she hadn't put her shorts back on.

Remember Susan! the voice in his head shouted.

"This is going to tug a little," she said, and without further delay she began to stitch up the wound in his lower back. She was done in less than a minute.

"Underwear down," she directed.

He slid the Jockey shorts down, blushed furiously while she stitched up his ass cheek.

"Now sit," she said. He did, wincing. She went to work on his shoulder blade. This one hurt a good deal more because there was no padding over the bone. He forced himself to remain still, knowing she'd tease him if he showed signs of discomfort.

"There," she said. "Keep them dry for a couple days."

"Shouldn't be too hard," he said, following her into the bedroom.

She turned to face him and crossed her arms.

"I can't sleep with you," Iris said.

He stood there, completely at a loss.

She watched him, her eyes frank, the pupils dilated from the lack of light.

"I can't have sex with you," she said.

Though his thoughts spun, he nodded. "That's understandable. We just met last night, after all." *Plus*, he mentally added, *I'm in love with someone else.*

Her lips pressed together, her expression pained. She looked like she was about to say something; then she turned and walked out.

Dez watched after her. He estimated it was well after one in the morning. He climbed into the bed, amazed at how good it felt. He thought of Iris's backside, her pubic hair beneath the gauzy magenta fabric, and the force of his arousal surprised him. He was even more surprised when sleep snowed him under.

CHAPTER THIRTY-SIX

Iris's Song

It was still dark and he was lying on his side when he felt the shape in bed behind him. Kneecaps nudged his hamstrings. What felt like knuckles nested against his spine.

"I hope that's you, Iris," he whispered.

"Couldn't sleep," she said.

He wanted to turn in bed and face her, but he didn't. Not yet.

"Are you afraid?" he asked.

A pause. "I'm always afraid."

He considered several responses. Finally he said, "Me too."

"When I told you I couldn't have sex with you—"

"It's okay," he said. "I wasn't offended."

She snorted. "I'm not worried about offending you."

He rolled over, and though the candles had winked out, there was a shaft of moonlight bisecting her face. He made out her brow, the lines there visible, but not deep. He saw how wide her eyes were, the way her lips remained slightly open, as though she was slightly amazed at what she saw.

He shifted onto his side. Much better. Their faces were ten inches apart. He was glad he'd brushed his teeth.

"What are you thinking about?" he asked.

He assumed she would make a smartass remark, blow holes in his ego, but her gaze never wavered.

"We can never make love," she said.

He thought of Susan, but when he did, it was with Iris's face.

"You're disappointed," she said.

He cleared his head. "It isn't that. It's Susan and..." He studied her expression. "Is it because of your husband?"

Did her eyes moisten a little? "Yes."

"You miss him," Dez said, "like I miss Susan."

She laughed, a brittle sound in the silent bedroom. "You're not getting it."

He frowned at her, waited.

"He was fine," she said. She gestured impatiently. "He was a husband. Decent. Steady." She sniffed. "But it wasn't like we were madly in love. Then again…" She drew in a ragged breath. "…he gave me Cassidy."

"So…you feel like sleeping with someone else is dishonoring—"

"Would you just shut up?"

Dez closed his mouth.

She seemed to relax, her head sinking into the pillow. "You remember what happened to Keaton," she said. "What he changed into?"

"The minotaur."

She closed her eyes, opened them. "Did you study that sort of thing?"

"What, mythology?"

When she didn't answer, he said, "Sure, some."

"Some of those Greek creatures were real." A shuddering breath. "Are real."

"I gathered that."

"Dez…."

"It's okay," he told her. Though he felt slightly treacherous lying here with her, both of them under the covers, both of them hardly dressed, there was no denying how wonderful it was, how intimate.

She appeared on the verge of tears.

"Don't worry," he told her. "I would never pressure you into—"

"I'm a siren."

He stared at her.

"Or I think I am."

He frowned. "How do you—"

"I was in the bathtub, singing a little. My husband wandered in with this dopey look on his face. I'd never seen him look like that. Like he was hypnotized. It creeped me out, and when I told him so, he blinked and looked around like he didn't know where he was." She wiped her nose. "Maybe I should have known then."

Dez stayed quiet, the dread evoked by her story slowly coiling around him.

"When the world was falling apart, I started having dreams," Iris said.

"Urges. I told myself they were just brought on by the terrible stories in the news, but there were aspects of the dreams that were so real. So *vivid*."

Her eyes were imploring. "I imagined I was on an island. There were other women there, but we didn't talk. We just sang. And we were *hungry*."

Dez listened, though he didn't want to hear the rest.

"That's how my husband died," she explained. "I was humming some melody, one I'd only heard in my dreams. The next thing I know, he's staring at me in that hypnotized way. We began to kiss, far more passionately than we ever had. I didn't know I'd changed until we were making love. I was on top of him, starting to climax, and...."

Dez's body had gone numb. Everything except the slam of his heart. He could feel that all right.

She swallowed, glanced up at the ceiling. "I didn't even realize what was happening until I'd torn his throat out. Even then it felt natural, like I had done it a million times before. It wasn't until I climbed off the bed and looked in the mirror and saw what I was...."

"Iris...."

She bared her teeth. "I'm a monster, Dez. I'm a fucking monster, just like Keaton. *Worse* than Keaton, worse than Tom Chaney."

He was incapable of speech.

"So you see?" she said, eyes imploring. "We can never be together. Not in that way."

Because he had absolutely no idea how to respond, he didn't respond at all. Just let her get it out. Don't hurt her by saying the wrong thing.

But evidently, she'd already said what she wanted. Was maybe waiting for him to speak.

"Okay," he said.

She narrowed her eyes at him.

"I get it," he said. "No sex." He shrugged. "I don't want to die any more than you do."

The glimmer of a smile on her lips?

He said, "There's no rule against us sharing a bed though."

Her expression darkened. "As long as you don't...."

"Try to fuck you?"

She swatted him, her mouth open in an incredulous grin. "*Dez*."

Through his laughter, he said, "Hit me if you want, but you're the one who's gonna have to stitch me up."

"What if I refuse?"

"I'll have Levi or Michael do it."

She grunted. "Michael's out cold. And Levi can't even tie his shoes, much less sew a wound."

Dez thought of how the kid had helped him in the Four Winds, how Levi had managed to stay alive this long on his own.

"Don't underestimate the kid," he said.

Iris didn't answer, but she wore a contented smile.

"You need to sleep," he told her.

"If I can."

"You have to," he said. "We have a long walk ahead of us tomorrow."

Her eyebrows rose.

"We're heading into vampire territory," he explained.

"Blood country," she corrected.

He hesitated. "You said most vampires are women."

"So?" she said. "Does that mean you won't be able to kill them?"

He shook his head. "We have to find Cassidy and Susan."

She searched his face, hope and doubt at war in her eyes.

"We'll find them," he said. "We'll find them and take them back."

A tear leaked from the corner of her right eye. "What if they're—"

"They're alive."

Her voice was scarcely a whisper. "You believe that?"

He returned her gaze. "I do."

Iris smiled then, a vulnerable, grateful smile, and not long after that she was asleep. Dez watched her a long time, wondered what the odds were of her daughter surviving a year with the vampires.

Slim. Less than slim.

Still…what choice did they have?

Dez closed his eyes and wondered how it would be in blood country.

He tried to sleep, but images of vampires kept intruding.

Even worse, memories of his little boy.

Dez tried to imagine Will as he'd be now, but found he was unable. To Dez he'd always be four years old. Four and full of wonder, full of laughter.

There were tears on his cheeks, but he made no move to wipe them away. He deserved the pain. He'd never forgive himself for failing to save his boy.

You can't change the past. You can only try to help Iris get her daughter back. You can save Cassidy, even if you couldn't save Will.

Dez closed his eyes and remembered his son.

When the first predawn glow began to creep over the countryside, Iris shuddered, murmured a few unintelligible sounds.

Dez reached out, touched her cheek. Told her it was okay, she was safe. Iris whispered the name of her daughter once, twice, and Dez told her Cassidy was safe. They'd find her soon.

God, he hoped he was right.

ACKNOWLEDGMENTS

Thanks to my pre-readers, Tim Slauter and Tod Clark, for their invaluable contributions. I owe an enormous debt to B.J. Austin, my rocket scientist friend who spent hours patiently explaining to me what could and could not be done with rockets, missiles, and all sorts of technology. If I got anything scientifically wrong in this book, blame me; anything right is totally attributable to B.J.

Thank you to editor Don D'Auria and publisher Nick Wells for believing in this book. Thank you also to Brian Keene for being the best big brother, mentor, and friend a person could have. Thanks to Josh Malerman, Caroline Kepnes, Jeff Strand, Kelli Owen, Becky Spratford, Bob Ford, Tim Waggoner, Kristopher Rufti, Ron Malfi, Sadie Hartmann, Paul Tremblay, Paul Goblirsch, Bryan Smith, and Mary SanGiovanni for their friendship. Thank you to my grandpa, Jack Janz, for spending time with me every weekend. Thank you to Ryan Lewis for being the greatest manager in the world. Thank you most of all to my wife, my son, and my two daughters. I love you and thank God for you every day. Being with you is the greatest blessing of my life.

FLAME TREE PRESS
FICTION WITHOUT FRONTIERS
Award-Winning Authors & Original Voices

Flame Tree Press is the trade fiction imprint of Flame Tree Publishing, focusing on excellent writing in horror and the supernatural, crime and mystery, science fiction and fantasy. Our aim is to explore beyond the boundaries of the everyday, with tales from both award-winning authors and original voices.

•

Other titles available by Jonathan Janz:
The Siren and the Specter
Wolf Land
The Sorrows
Savage Species
The Nightmare Girl
The Dark Game
House of Skin
Dust Devils
Castle of Sorrows
The Darkest Lullaby

Other horror and suspense titles available include:
Snowball by Gregory Bastianelli
The Hungry Moon by Ramsey Campbell
The Influence by Ramsey Campbell
The Wise Friend by Ramsey Campbell
The Garden of Bewitchment by Catherine Cavendish
The Devil's Equinox by John Everson
Sins of the Father by JG Faherty
One By One by D.W. Gillespie
Black Wings by Megan Hart
The Playing Card Killer by Russell James
Will Haunt You by Brian Kirk
We Are Monsters by Brian Kirk
Hearthstone Cottage by Frazer Lee
Those Who Came Before by J.H. Moncrieff
Slash by Hunter Shea
They Kill by Tim Waggoner
The Forever House by Tim Waggoner

•

Join our mailing list for free short stories, new release details, news about our authors and special promotions:

flametreepress.com